Rusted Rituals Retaliate

Roy Stephen Kunnel BEM

Contents

Acknowledgements

Humans survive this world of several uncertainties adopting the collective knowledge, developed across the world. Sharing the information empowers the current and future generations to be successful.

Written books are important to share knowledge, contributing to the quality of life in any part of the world. Appropriate language use is as important as the contents narrated in the books.

I sincerely appreciate the time and care devoted by the editorial board in reviewing the manuscript. Their meticulous attention to grammar, clarity, and overall readability has greatly enhanced the quality of the Book. The suggested improvement not only refined the language but also strengthened the flow and impact of the content.

Author

About the Author

Mr Roy Stephen Kunnel BEM, the author of the novel, is a leader and collaborator with numerous communities in Swindon, UK. Actively involved in the volunteer sector, in addition to full-time employment at UK Research and Innovation. The preferred activities include the management of community facilities, the leadership of community organisations, and the dissemination of information. He is particularly fond of initiating new cross-community initiatives and strengthening people relations.

By introducing new initiatives and empowering them to receive public funds and Gift Aids, he continues to fortify the communities and community organisations. He participates in challenge-oriented activities, having successfully completed the 'Three Peaks Challenge' in 2018 and the 'Swindon Half-Marathon' in 2019.

He spent five years in the Indian charity sector after serving in the Indian Air Force for nearly 17 years. In 2006, he relocated to the United Kingdom and has since maintained his engagement with both the migrant and host British communities. He spearheaded numerous community initiatives with the assistance of funding agencies, which fostered collaboration among individuals from a variety of backgrounds, thereby fostering acceptance and integration within the community.

He was awarded the British Empire Medal (BEM) in the 2017 Queen's Birthday List Honours and the Pride of Swindon Award in 2015 by the Swindon Borough Council. Additionally, he received numerous accolades from community organisations throughout the United Kingdom.

Previously published books:

1. Wonders of Community Inclusiveness – 2021 (English)

2. Collection of 21 stories -2021 (Malayalam)

3. Collection of 50 selected Articles -2021 (Malayalam)

4. Novel 'Apoorva Pathakal' – 2021 (Malayalam)

5. Novel 'Koodanayatha Kottan' – 2024 (Malayalam)

Foreword

This novel is entirely a work of fiction. The names, characters and incidents portrayed in it are the work of the author's imagination. Any resemblance to actual persons, living or dead, events or localities is entirely coincidental.

A multitude of internal and external forces dictate the course of contemporary human existence, many of which are beyond the control and influence of any individual. Intelligent humans develop routine activities to endure these forces, which are then repeated over time to form rituals. Following rituals, humans do experience miraculous powers, which offer them a surprising sense of peace and comfort in moments of tension, loneliness and sorrow.

Rituals have been an integral component of human culture throughout history. They are ingrained in the fabric of nearly every spiritual tradition worldwide, serving as conduits for the expression of beliefs, intentions, and experiences. A sacred space is established by the majority of the rituals, which enables individuals to engage profoundly with their spirituality.

Deep knowledge and devotion to spiritual forces with unlimited powers are necessary for the performance of rituals on behalf of others. The exploitation of people's beliefs for financial benefit is on the rise, and religious or spiritual practices have been abused for nefarious purposes.

Over time, both traditional and modern rituals that are misused become corroded and retaliate. The novel's characters illustrate their anguish and are the victims of rusted rituals, ultimately succumbing to its severe retributions.

Novelist

Chapter 1

Around the church, the world came to a halt and the surroundings wept. Through the empty skies, the Sun's beams dropped to the ground with ease. The wind stood still over the area, following the people's heartbreaking misery. Expressing their sorrow, resident pigeons on the church roof remained silent and other birds were unable to expand their wings. Soon, the presiding priest blessed the coffin, and the choir members sang the final hymn.

'May I leave this beautiful world to be with my lord in heaven?'

Many people silently walked out of the church to join the procession to the burial grounds while the hymn was played. A loud cry of sadness filled the church as a few of them raised the coffin, to start the procession:

'My God, how can you be so cruel? My beloved, you are leaving too soon.'

A few women assisted Mary to stay seated and restrained her from getting to the coffin.

All of them line up in a queue to join the deceased's eternal journey to the cemetery after the church's final hymn. Horrible clanks of chains pierced the air as the altar boy carrying the thurible emerged from the church first and flipped it in all ways. The fumes that rose from the incense burning inside the thurible headed directly for the heavens above. The aromatic smoke rises to the Almighty, purifying the church grounds and the mourners. The wooden cross, representing devotees' faith, sacrifice, and assurance of eternal life, is positioned in front. A number of altar boys holding signs of faith and resurrection trailed after them. The funeral procession started as the coffin passed through the huge church entrance, signalled by the ringing of an ancient, large, half-muffled church bell.

He felt like the world's most distressed man, carrying his own teenage daughter's coffin on his right shoulder. Chackochan walked alongside five others, being extremely cautious not to upset the coffin's symmetry. His adorable daughter was declared dead without a cause of death after three days of being unconscious. One of his many wonderful hopes has now been mercilessly stolen by the cruel world around. Standing on the right side with his cherished niece's mortal remains on his left shoulder was Chackochan's brother-in-law. Standing behind him with the coffin slung over his right shoulder was his maternal cousin. While two other family members stood behind his brother's side and the third person on his side was carrying the coffin, his boyhood friend. The lovely adolescent girl was adored by all pallbearers, who are now sorrowfully carrying her cold and still body.

Half-muffled church bells rang repeatedly to signal the start of the funeral procession heading to the cemetery. He had a few minutes left to spend with the human remains of his beloved daughter. In order to gain additional time and slow down the procession, Chackochan shortened the distance between his steps.

For over fourteen years, he laboured nonstop to help raise a small infant into a brilliant adolescent. She frequently inspired him to live and then to put in a lot of effort for the family. In actuality, her physique outgrew a handful of her companions, and she was unable to recognise the dangers in time. His expectations were high with her taking on home duties and looking after her younger siblings. All dreams dashed, with the remorseless doctor's decision to turn off her life support.

Soon, the half-muffled church bells echoed softly, while the intermittent single and double rings of the handheld bell resonated clearly. Chackochan's elder son grips the bell with its handle, skillfully shaking his wrists to ensure the clapper strikes the bell at the appropriate moment. He proceeded at a measured pace, allowing his younger brother to close the distance between them.

Residing together in a single room within their modest home, they demonstrated mutual care and maintained strong relationships. Despite his strong protective instincts towards his sister, he overlooked the clandestine connections and the impending malevolent forces. Although he is a teenager, he demonstrates sensibility and responsibility by taking ownership of several household tasks. Considering his age and stature, he comprehends his responsibilities within the family remarkably well, contributing to the generation of income for the entire household.

As he holds his brother's hand, Chackochan's younger son remains unaware of the reason behind their slow pace and the number of individuals trailing behind them. He continually scanned the area for recognisable individuals and felt uneasy in the presence of numerous unfamiliar people. He grasped his brother's hand firmly, ensuring they remained together and did not get lost in the crowd. Struggling to interpret the expressions on his brother's face, the younger sibling recognised that something was amiss between them. He looked around for his mother and her invisibility further compelled him to grasp his elder brother's hand firmly.

The son of his close friend led the procession, holding the wooden cross with both hands. He walked with a measured and deliberate pace. The intense heat did not deter him and he held the cross firm and raised it high. Although he was not pleased, his self-satisfied expression indicates that he does not perceive himself as a failure. He appeared significantly improved now compared to a few days ago, when he walked with a heavy heart. Accompanied his mother and provided support to his younger sister during the funeral procession of his beloved father.

The altar servers from the church, dressed in their white albs, formed a queue alongside his son. He has been acquainted with them for several years, and they admire him and his family. The thurible, incense, and holy water were carried by them for the priest to sanctify the burial ground. They participated in the procession not only to pay respects to his late daughter but also to offer support to their colleague and his son. The vicar was not particularly enthusiastic about their line-up but was unable to prevent it. Displaying respect for the deceased and offering support to the family was of utmost importance, surpassing outdated rituals.

His wife has remained by their daughter's hospital bedside for the past three days. She continued to call her, softly speaking in her ear, reminding her of her favourite foods, materials, and reciting some of her beloved songs. In her pursuit of a complete recovery, she assisted the medical team by providing personal care and administering medication. Unable to observe the medical team disconnecting the life support, she succumbed to despair. She was unconscious and admitted to the ward, while her daughter's deceased body was wheeled to the mortuary. Unable to stand or see her beloved daughter laid to rest, she remained seated in the church throughout the prayers. Her relatives are assisting her as she walks in the procession, bidding a final farewell to her vibrant daughter.

Her classmates and friends from school gathered with flowers to extend their farewell. In their school uniforms, many displayed tears while others mourned in silence. She was admired by all and was a favourite among many whom she knew personally. The students adhered to their teachers' guidance and adorned the approaching coffin with flowers. Many wished to see their friends' lifeless face one last time, and delays in hiring an ambulance deeply affected them. Departing from this beautiful planet without fully experiencing its natural and cultural aesthetic qualities exceeds their vivid imaginations.

Understanding his struggle, friends and villagers adjusted their pace to match his steps. Those present were committed to fully engaging in the funeral rituals, taking the time to support him in his time of sorrow. They are mourning alongside him, seeking understanding rather than posing questions. The villagers were not as informed as he and his family. Their desire was for the truths surrounding the untimely death of the teenager, which brought profound sorrow and anguish. The villagers, while closely connected, typically have limited knowledge of one another's personal lives. Few were aware of the unknown, yet for the time being, they chose to remain silent and hoped for the family's strength in coping with their loss.

Observing the setting sun, the parish priest hurriedly instructed one of the church trustees, 'Please expedite the process, we must complete the rite of committal before sunset.'

The trustee appeared uncertain, gazing at the priest in disbelief for a few moments. The trustee increased his pace to notify the boy, holding the cross at the front. Upon receiving the direction, the boy extended his spacing, prompting the attendees to accelerate their pace, which in turn required the pallbearers to widen their spacing.

Shortly, the procession arrived at the burial grounds, where the priest quickly commenced the rite of committal. The priest summoned the altar boy carrying the incense to approach, and he proceeded to add more to the smouldering thurible. The priest meticulously handled the thurible, moving his hands in a forward and backward motion while occasionally rotating it. Dark fumes were dispersed towards the grave to dispel the evil spirits. The priest then took the sprinkler filled with holy water and recited prayers to the holy father. He evenly distributed the holy water over the grave and made the sign of the Holy Cross to cleanse it of all evils. The priest gazed around for the coffin, which had not yet been positioned near the grave.

The priest requested to expedite the burial of the coffin prior to the sun setting below the horizon. Chackochan guided the other pallbearers to the centre of the Cemetery Chapel and placed the coffin on the floor. As he looked upon his daughter's face, he found himself overwhelmed by grief, exclaiming,

'I am deeply sorry, my dear daughter. I was unable to shield you from the evils of this world, but I will ensure they face the consequences.'

He then kissed her on the face and continued to weep. Those present exchanged glances, and one of the church trustees offered consolations, advising,

'We are here for you. Please adhere to the priest's guidance and proceed with the burial of your daughter.'

Chacko maintained his grip on the coffin as his wife was brought close to him. She cried out loud and grasped the coffin with all her strength.

Disregarding the subtle request, Chacko carefully wiped his daughter's serene face with a white towel. Upon seeing that the towel is marked with a cross, the trustee reiterated,

'That towel is designated solely for the final kiss.'

Chacko and his wife remained unresponsive, grieving as they held tightly to their daughter's coffin. The gentleman articulated,

'The white piece of cloth is reminiscent of the burial cloth of Jesus and should be regarded as sacred while awaiting the final resurrection.'

Chacko was filled with rage. 'Are you discussing the indifferent God who took my innocent daughter from me? Allow me to spend a bit more time with her.'

The gentleman responded with patience, saying, 'My dear, I understand your pain. The truth is that your daughter's spirit is watching over you and everyone gathered here, to bid farewell to her.'

Chacko looked around in disbelief as the nobleman elaborated, 'We believe that the spirit begins its eternal journey to join our holy father in heaven only after the mortal remains are buried in the earth.'

The priest, having lost his patience, approached and said, 'Please, someone assist this man. We must bury the dead before the sun disappears.'

The gentleman intervened once more and asked the priest to be patient, stating, 'Allow the grieving family to have their time.'

Attendees assembled were cognisant that the deceased were transported to the church directly from the mortuary. The family had limited time to be with the mortal remains of their beloved young girl. A few attempted to offer comfort, but Chacko persisted in holding the coffin and cried out loudly. The priest was visibly shaken and taken aback, as uncertainty permeated the surrounding environment.

With the handheld bell in hand, his son approached, gently touched his father's shoulder, and whispered in his ear,

'Pappa, don't worry, the devils have been dealt with decisively. Let her go now.'

Chacko was taken aback and stared in disbelief at his son's face. Chacko was uncertain if his son had surpassed him or if he had simply become too pragmatic. Observing his father's incredulous expression, he shifted his eyes to his friend, who offered a sceptical smile while maintaining a confident posture.

A tall and imposing figure approached, commanding attention as he instructed,

'Chacko, step aside, and allow the esteemed priest to perform his duties.'

He used both hands to attempt to pull Chacko away from the coffin. Chacko was disturbed and fiercely looked at the man's face, recognising him as his neighbour. Chacko promptly rose to respond, but his son held him back, saying,

'Pappa, let it go now.'

Another person came running and whispered something to his neighbours' ears. His neighbour halted instantly, directing a fierce stare at Chacko and at all others. The tall and imposing figure hurriedly turned back and departed the cemetery with the informer. A few others quickly followed him, and the priest looked around for answers.

In collaboration with the esteemed trustee and a select group, Chacko and his wife were liberated from their firm hold on the coffin. With the white Turin embroidered with a red cross draped over her face, Chacko's son bestowed a final kiss upon his beloved sister.

The church trustees promptly secured the lid and carried the coffin to the burial pit. The priest advised them to position the head towards the west, facilitating the ascent of the departed soul alongside the rising Lord from the east. The coffin was gently lowered into the grave as attendees respectfully showered incense and flower petals from above. As soon as the undertaker completed the burial, the heavens opened, releasing a torrential downpour.

Chapter 2

'Sunny, you'll be late again. Babumon will lead the procession with the Thurible.'

The low-pitched contralto voice said, 'Come on, get up, don't be a loser.'

Sunnymon Chacko rubbed his tired eyes and could barely see anything in the dark. Staring at the darkness, he felt the cold and sought the cotton sheet that had been shielding him earlier. When he felt for it, he knew that his younger brother Sunil had wrapped it around him. He is sound asleep, and the sheet is completely covering him from head to toe. It wasn't a neat and comfortable bed sheet; it was an old dhoti that his father used to wear around the house. The gloomy and chilly winter season will end soon, and he will take it back to use as his work dhoti. The corners of the hard mattress made of dry bamboo are falling apart, and Mom still blames him for it. Sunil is sound asleep on his wet half-pants, which were Sunny's a few years ago. When kids outgrow their own clothes, it's normal for them to get their older siblings' clothes.

'Sunny, Sunny,' a pleasant and musical voice said, 'don't forget to pick up the empty milk bottle.'

Then the voice raised concerns, 'Oh my God! The bottle cap is missing again.'

He slowly came back to his senses and woke up in the morning to reality. His half-opened eyes could see the dim light from the kerosene lamp in the kitchen. The light from the lamp keeps coming through the cracks and gaps in the wooden door that separates their chamber from the main room of their little house. The roof of the modest house, which has two rooms and a kitchen, is made of bamboo and is covered with sheets of dried coconut leaves. His mother has warned his Pappa several times in the previous few days that the dried coconut leaves are falling apart. These dried leaves make sheets that are connected to a bamboo canopy that needs to be changed every year. It won't keep them safe from the heavy rains that are likely to happen this time of year.

'Sunny, my dear, get up. If you don't, Mom will come over and wake me up too. Please go now.'

That was his older sister Celine, who is in ninth grade and is one year older than him. Celine is overweight and bigger than most kids her age, and her mother protects her from other kids who make fun of her.

'She has a unique health issue that she got from her grandmother.'

Sunny doesn't remember his grandmother, but he's heard a lot of fascinating stories about her. She adored his family and gave them a lot of money to build their two-bedroom house. She loved cute Celine and quickly gave her a set of gold earrings during her baptism.

Sadly, his grandmother died from a snake bite during her old age. A large king cobra struck her while she tried to get eggs from the chicken coop. People said that when the old lady came up to the coop extremely late in the evening, the snake tried to hide the egg with its big head. In the dimming light of evening, she may have spotted the white eggs from a distance but not the black snake. The black cobra might not have been seen within the little coop. No one knows why her favourite birds didn't raise an alarm. She didn't know it was there, so she tried to retrieve the egg through the small door to the coop. The cobra was angry and aggressive, didn't like that and savagely bit on the extended arm, injecting a lot of venom.

Celine is gorgeous and nice, and she takes good care of her younger siblings. Very similar to her grandmother, she is committed to supporting her offspring. While they were in primary school, Celine accompanied him and made sure that his free lunch, which was fried Upma prepared from American corn, was clear of mice and dead bugs. Even though dry upma produced from American maize isn't as popular now, it was quite healthy, and many underprivileged kids loved it back then. Teachers encouraged disadvantaged families to take advantage of this free meal because whole maize is high in a number of nutrients, such as fibre and antioxidants.

Both are now in high school, but Celine still thinks of Sunny as a child and sometimes offers to escort him home. Sunny would rather stay behind and enjoy football club sessions after school. His mother keeps telling him to come back shortly after school. She wants children to come home immediately after school to help her with chores around the house.

'Sunny, please go,' Celine begged again.

'Okay, shh... calm down, don't yell.' Don't wake Sunil Kuttan up, he's still sleeping.' He turned around and made sure his precious and lovely little brother was sound asleep.

'Good boy,' Celine said. 'I'll get you another lemon sweet.'

Not long ago, Celine was discreetly feeding them lemon candies, and Sunny wondered where she got them. Their mother doesn't give them pocket money very often, and there aren't any coins in their house that they can steal. Their father doesn't make much money at work; therefore, he has a hard time meeting their daily necessities.

Celine told them to keep it a secret from their parents, which made him even more worried.

His mother called again, 'Sunny, you're late.'

Sunny replied to his sister, 'I don't want your cheap sweet, but you have to clean Sunil. He's wet again, change his half pant and put the mattress outside to dry.'

The answer came late, but was quiet, 'Okay, don't worry, I'll take care of it.' Sunny knew she would do it without a bargain, but he preferred an assurance.

He stood up from the floor and immediately smacked his head on the bamboo rack where he and his sister stored their schoolbooks. The rack is formed of bamboo sticks that have been peeled and dried, and they are held together with a coir, which is a short, coarse fibre that comes from the outer shell of coconuts. Another set of worn-out coir is holding the rack up from the roof.

'Be careful, the rack will fall off,' his sister warned again.

The strong strands are now breaking in parts, as if they are bored of being tightly coiled together for long. When the bamboo rack was put together, it was sturdy and brown in colour. Over time, it turned red and now it is breaking down. His dad promised to replace it with a robust string that had been properly dried and aged.

Celine is more worried about her makeup, which has been more important to her lately. A little tin of Cuticura white talcum powder, a little box with black eye ink, and a broken mirror that she holds in her palm. Their mum bought the white talcum powder during the last church festival, which was over a year ago. Celine preserves it as a treasure and doesn't share it with people too often. Sunny doesn't like it because it makes him itch, but Celine smells good with it and is extremely cautious to ensure it lasts forever. Sunil wants it, but Celine keeps it for herself. He merely wants to smell the lid, which fascinates him, but Celine becomes mad. She tells him all the time to keep the lid covered so that the air doesn't get to it and it doesn't lose its aromatic smell.

Sunny never liked the black ink that was almost dry and smelt bad, but Celine likes to put it on the tips of her eyelids. After that, she puts some of that on her eyebrows to make them even darker. She uses the broken mirror to put it on very carefully. When she's happy with it, she clarifies with a big smile on her face,

'Sunny, look at me, is it okay?.'

She is so gorgeous, and her grin makes him happy, but he never wanted to admit how beautiful she is.

'Sunny, you're jealous. Look how fair and charming I am.'

He is really proud of how she looks. She is much lighter than he is, who is virtually dark-skinned. She is healthy and fat, whereas he is quite thin. She is smart and does well in school as well. She is glad to help him with some of the hard English terms and arithmetic problems.

He didn't feel the agony when his head hit the rack like he usually does, but his sister was worried and whispered to him.

'Sunny, does it hurt you?' she worriedly asked, especially in the morning when she had a lot of unpleasant things to do.

'No, it's fine.'

'How many times do I have to remind you to be careful next time?'

He didn't say anything and headed to the wooden door. The door opened, making a weird sound again. His mother yelled from the kitchen as she tried to start the fire with dried coconut leaves and small wooden logs.

'Oh my God, hurry up and get ready. You have to run now, or that Pillechan will be mad.'

It's still virtually pitch-black outdoors, and the mornings are getting considerably colder again. It's winter, and Christmas is coming up quickly, which is his favourite time of the year. Sunny went outside to go to the toilet and tried to listen to his favourite bird's chirping sound. The bird had light brown feathers, yellow beaks, yellow legs, and a yellow ring around its neck. He wanted to keep one as a pet within a grilled cage, but his mom hastily declined.

She sounded fair, 'God gave birds wings so they could fly around freely instead of being caged.'

He agreed with her argument, even though he knew it wasn't the genuine reason. She is busy and always needs help taking care of Sunil and her other household animals.

'Meow,' that was his beloved brown cat, whom he called 'glory,' attempting to get his attention. He gives her a pat to start her day, and then he turns around right away to look for his other pet, 'Kaiser.' The dog is chained to a pole and sleeping well, but Sunny knows that Kaiser is always on the lookout. A highly alert, intelligent dog has a short coat and a curly tail. Kaiser thinks independently and is well adapted to the living environment. He walked towards and touched his forehead. Tired of night watch, Kaiser kept his head down and pretended to be asleep, knowing that his master was happy with him. Sunny returned to Glory, who was still lying on the floor waiting for him to pay attention. Glory has brown and white fur and is a quick learner, happily plays with them and is friendly to Kaiser. Appreciating them in the early mornings would strengthen their link and improve their relationship.

'Don't mess with them, run now.'

Following that, he heard further instructions from his mother to put on a shirt since it was cold outside and otherwise, he would get sick.

He stepped back to the front porch, putting his foot firmly on the movable rock piece from the ground. The little rock is in the middle of the porch, which is raised higher than the ground, so that he and his brother may easily get to their house. Every week, they put cow manure from their neighbour's cowshed on the uneven and rough veranda floor to make it smoother. His mother makes a thin covering on every surface of their modest home by mixing cow dung with a little amount of loose soil. It keeps the house warm and free of little flies and mosquitoes, which would otherwise be a big problem for them. The fresh smell of the mixture is terrible and the scent goes away quickly when the combination dries.

He said that cow dung shouldn't be used and that alternative materials that are smooth and shining, like the floor of his school, should be used instead. People like the idea of cement floors that are bright and spotless and don't need much or any regular maintenance.

She advocated, 'We use cow dung because it is more of a herbal or natural medicine that keeps flies away and keeps us safe from getting sick.'

Cow dung is what is left over after cows eat leaves and plants every day. When a cow eats all of these plants, grass, and leaves, they boil in its stomach and then stick together, making healthy chemical bonds. Once it's dried up, they and the occasional guests can walk barefoot on the floor with ease. The natural herbal substances that get into people's bodies through their feet's pores are soothing.

He understood that his mother was very dedicated and worked hard to take care of the family. Managing the chores around the house is time-consuming and never-ending; it goes in a continual circle. She never complains and is happy to repeat the same thing over and over again. She puts her kids' needs ahead of her own and has a higher level of work ethic. She is strong and always completes the varied tasks and never complains.

'Sunny, I'm sick of you. I'm going to tell your pappa about this. You know he keeps that fresh coffee plant branch to punish you. Now, no more delays, go fast.'

His mother yelled again, and he couldn't hide because she is the boss of the house. Sunny can't recall what time of day it is when she sees her resting from her normal chores. She is busy all day taking care of him and his siblings, cooking for them, and taking care of the three goats. She has to create that sheet of rubber from the tree sap over the winter and summer, which his dad gets as a reward for working hard in the morning. Changes in farming culture make farmers with a lot of land prosperous. The new rubber plantations took the place of the old coconut and cassava farms. The rubber sap, which is used to make rubber sheets, is in higher demand and requires less work.

He remembers when one of his elementary school instructors asked about people's jobs and he was proud to speak up.

'My pappa is a rubber tapper.'

The teacher was extremely nice to tell the other kids that his papa has a good profession.

'Every job is important and deserves respect. Rubber tapping is not a silly job; it requires skill.' Then she went on to clarify by asking, 'What happens when you get hurt or feel pain?'

All of the kids were quiet so they could hear their teacher well.

'When we are hurt, we get weak,' she explained after a moment. 'When we are weak, we are less productive, taking care of our injury and worrying more until we are fully healed.' Similarly, the rubber tree produces its very rich sap when it isn't hurt throughout the sapping process. The tapper cuts off the proper quantity of bark with a sharp knife, going down to a depth of one-quarter inch (6.4 mm). This depth depends on the size of the rubber tree and does not injure the trunk or body of the tree.

After that, she used a piece of white chalk to sketch a picture of the rubber tree on the blackboard to explain it more.

'Look at this picture. The outer bark protects the rubber tree's main trunk. The experienced tapper chops the bark very carefully, without hurting the trunk. This is how the rubber tree makes white sap that contains the latex that people want. In Chemistry, which you will master in higher grades, Latex is a complicated molecule made up of proteins, alkaloids, starches, sugars, and other things that harden when they come into contact with air. This stretchy substance is what makes up all rubber items.

Kids were quiet for a while, but one of them had a question that was related. 'Teacher, what will happen if the rubber tree's trunk gets hurt?' The teacher didn't answer, instead she said, 'What will happen if you hurt yourself or by accident?' The youngster quickly said, 'I feel the pain.' The teacher asked, 'And what if you are bleeding?' The student couldn't answer right away, so the teacher said, 'When you bleed, you will lose strength, and if the bleeding isn't stopped or controlled right away, you will be unconscious.' The student didn't say anything, so she went on, 'If the trunk is penetrated during the tapping process, the rubber tree will also get weaker and won't be able to make the rubber sap anymore.'

'Teacher, how do you use this white sap to make big black rubber tyres?'

The teacher took a deep breath. 'It's a long process, as I said before. You will learn the chemical process and the engineering process that goes along with it in higher classes.'

Sunny came to his senses when he felt the coldness of the glass bottle on his right palm and then heard a kind voice. 'Put this shirt on and hurry up'

That was the second set of clothes he got. 'No, Mom, I need this for church, so I'll wear the old torn one.'

'You're already late. Take this milk to the coffee shop and then go to church.' She gently pushed him towards the stepping stones on the large stone wall in front of their house.

He didn't want to agree right away; he stood still for a moment before nodding.

'Okay, I'll go to church from there.'

Chapter 3

Chacko Punnoose is a daily wager, working as a seasonal farmer and general support worker. He lives with his wife, Mary (Mariyam), and three children in Kaineervila village, where people make a living from seasonal farming. In addition to rubber tapping, Chacko undertakes any form of manual work in his village. He does not demand a fixed wage and will gladly accept wages in cash or in kind. He quickly learnt to tap rubber trees when the majority of farmers converted their traditional grain farming to rubber. Rubber-producing trees, sometimes known as the 'rubber tree', generate significant income with comparatively less effort. The growing global demand for rubber, together with lower maintenance costs and higher returns, prompted many conventional growers to shift to rubber plantations. The rainy climate is favourable, and many people have transformed their coconut, arecanut, and tapioca farms into rubber plantations.

Benny Mathew, a local community activist and established farmer, is a childhood companion of Chacko who has a deep appreciation for the natural world. He opposed the destruction of naturally grown fruit trees in order to establish rubber plantations. Rubber trees are not conducive to animal life, resulting in an imbalance of the natural fauna. Consequently, natural diversity has been destroyed. Over time, the latest tall and diminutive mixed rubber trees could be outgrown by coconut trees; however, the arecanut and cashew trees were entirely eradicated. Many small and medium-sized rodents, including squirrels, as well as indigenous birds, have experienced a decline in their natural food sources. Many other social issues arose as a result of Benny's advocacy against the imbalance caused to nature's highly regarded biodiversity.

Chacko and his family of five resided in a modest home situated on a small plot of land that was generously donated by their neighbour, Mr Thomas Joseph, a high school teacher. From the same village, Mr Thomas belonged to a prosperous and affluent family. Through his marriage to Achamma, the only daughter, he acquired numerous acres of land from his father-in-law. Additionally, she served as a language teacher at the village primary school.

During the early years of Indian independence, Achamma's father, Mr Vareeth Mappila, was a merchant. Prior to independence, he was a spice trader engaged in wholesale transactions with English and Portuguese merchants. In addition, he was a local political leader who claimed to have been involved in the Indian independence movement alongside Mahatma Gandhi. He asserted that he had attended the Dandi March and Dandi Satyagraha, both non-violent demonstrations against the British salt monopoly. He was a hero to the villagers and was widely respected due to his financial power, which he used to switch sides with ease during the independence period.

Mr Vareeth Mappila was born into a business family and inherited much of his ruthless business character. Few villagers knew from their elders that Vareeth's grandparents had been involved in the slave trade. Numerous farm labourers disappeared while transporting goods to markets located some distance away, primarily to harbour ports. The products were sold to both internal and external traders, and the workers were compelled to carry them on their heads. For several days, employees had to traverse the wilderness and forests to transport the goods. Those sold as captives were either said to have been killed by wild animals or to have joined gangs of thieves. Enslaving the wives and children of absconding or missing labourers was an additional penalty. Their family members were forced to serve the master until the loss was fully recovered. His ancestors amassed immense wealth by enslaving their own relatives and selling labourers as slaves.

The small, inaccessible plot was initially earned by Chacko's father but later termed a donation from Vareeth Mappila in exchange for his exceptionally rigorous labour. Chacko's father was an exceptional farmer who possessed a natural aptitude for sowing rice seeds in the paddy fields. The villagers admired his remarkable ability, which saved money and effort in replanting rice seedlings. During the seeding season, his services were in high demand. His son Chacko emulated his approach, receiving payments for services in both currency and kind.

Vareeth Mappila was ruthless, amassing a substantial fortune by exploiting the labour of the underprivileged. He forced many to work additional hours for minimal wages, insufficient to cover daily sustenance. Vareeth was also highly influential and corrupt among the affluent. In exchange for donating a portion of land to establish a primary school in his village, he secured a teaching position for his only daughter, Achamma. Later it was discovered that the land had been unlawfully acquired using forged land revenue documents. However, he was able to obstruct subsequent investigations through his political influence and financial status.

Achamma, Vareeth's only daughter, was born several years after his marriage to Nytho, who had suffered numerous miscarriages. It was rumoured that Achamma was born still, but an experienced and skilful local midwife successfully revived her. Nytho was unable to sustain good health due to repeated miscarriages, and the infant was affected by her mother's declining health during pregnancy. The midwife's only option was to save either the mother or the infant. Villagers believed that Mr Vareeth chose to save the child, and Achamma's mother passed away.

Vareeth did not remarry but employed numerous servants to care for his daughter. His elder sister, Theruthi, was born with a disability and remained unmarried. Although her right arm was not fully developed, she was exceptionally kind and diligent. Since Vareeth's relationship with his wife had not been cordial, Theruthi often acted as a mediator, offering both emotional and physical support. She cared for Achamma as her own child, filling the void of a mother. They formed a strong bond, but it was short-lived; Theruthi died of malaria shortly after Achamma reached adolescence.

Achamma received her initial education in the Malayalam language and basic mathematics through a single-teacher system. The Kalari, which is highly regarded, represents both fundamental education and traditional martial arts training in the state. Educational Kalari is a single classroom designed for children with the ability to learn. Admission is granted to children of all ages and social backgrounds.

Pupils used pencils made of white graphite to write Malayalam words on a black graphite surface. Kalari was generally overseen by a single teacher, known as the Kalari-Ashan, though larger groups occasionally had more than one. Pupils typically attended from morning until noon before returning home for lunch.

Achamma attended Kalari for two to three years and then moved to an upper primary school in the nearest town, as her village lacked one. She was joined by a handful of other students, and together they walked nearly two hours to school. Occasionally, they travelled by bullock cart, usually used to transport vegetables and groceries from the town. Achamma successfully completed her eighth standard and was preparing to advance further when her aspirations were dashed by multiple natural calamities. The school was forced to close for an extended period after being struck by lightning and set on fire, necessitating reconstruction. This was followed by a malaria outbreak, which claimed many lives not only in their village but across much of the state.

She married Thomas Joseph, a teacher from the same high school she had attended, within a year of finishing her schooling. Mr Thomas and his family were from the same village but lived on the opposite side. Vareeth Mappila quickly approved the proposal, despite Thomas belonging to a large but less wealthy family. Vareeth stipulated that Thomas must live with them permanently, as Achamma was his only daughter. Thomas's family accepted the proposal, and they were married at St George Catholic Church. The marriage was blessed by a bishop and numerous priests, as one of Thomas's siblings was a priest.

Within a year of marriage, Achamma was appointed as a teacher at the newly established primary school in their village.

They had four children: two boys and two girls. Susanna, the eldest daughter, married and moved to Delhi with her husband, a central government employee. Cyril, their second child, enrolled in teacher training in another city. Initially, he had joined the seminary, but he was expelled after physically assaulting a senior cleric. Soman, the third child, joined the Indian army and was posted to the eastern regions of India. Soman prioritised sports over education. The youngest, a girl named Lovely, attended higher secondary school and commuted regularly with her father.

Cyril, the second child, was eight years younger than his elder sibling, while the others were born one to two years apart. Shortly after the birth of their eldest daughter, Mr Thomas was transferred to a school far from their village. Rumour had it that the transfer was orchestrated by his father-in-law after discovering Thomas's affair with another teacher from a different religion. Thomas was unable to return to his village until his father-in-law's sudden death from a severe cardiac arrest.

Some villagers believed that Vareeth discovered the illicit affair, leading to speculation that Thomas had eloped with his beloved when reassigned. Physically larger and stronger, Vareeth disciplined his son-in-law to uphold morality and Catholic principles of fidelity. Villagers also suspected that Mr Thomas had fathered two children from the affair and continued to support them financially.

Initially, Vareeth Mappila convinced his daughter to divorce Thomas. Achamma was unwilling, as her toddler daughter Susanna had contracted an unexpected ailment, which required over a year for complete recovery. By the time Vareeth regained his conscience, he had to attend to numerous other matters. Achamma, who was diagnosed with depression, stopped teaching at the school shortly after Susanna's recovery. Thomas's mother was exceedingly compassionate and made frequent visits to care for her, which helped her return to a more ordinary life.

Mr Thomas Joseph began visiting his parents and family within three or four years of separation. However, he was hesitant to meet Achamma and their daughter. Following a prolonged process of persuasion by his mother, Thomas eventually took the initiative to meet his wife and child. Achamma forgave him after six years of separation, on the condition that they all put the past behind them. By that time, Mr Thomas had already been transferred to another school located close to their village. Achamma's relatives guaranteed that Mr Thomas had no further involvement with his former admirer. The sudden demise of Vareeth Mappila presented Thomas with an opportunity to reunite with his family. Mr Thomas's relatives promptly intervened and acted as mediators to reconcile their differences. Achamma's sole condition was that he remain a devoted husband and provide for their children.

After a further two years, Mr Thomas was appointed head teacher of his former school, and the family was fully reunited. Their second son, Cyril, was born nine years after their initial separation.

Subsequently, they had two more children at regular intervals. After their elder daughter married and moved to Delhi with her husband, their youngest daughter, Lovely, was born. Susanna was initially reluctant to accept the truth, but within two years of her marriage, she gave birth to her first son, Abyson. Her mother, Achamma, gave her compassionate care throughout the pregnancy and provided essential support during childbirth, which took place in a hospital rather than at home. Abyson and his aunt, Lovely, were less than a year apart in age.

Through timely intervention by church authorities and with much persuasion from his wife, Thomas Joseph legally transferred a small plot of land to Chacko when he returned to live in Kaineervila. Mr Thomas also contributed some construction materials for a modest home for Chacko's family, which at the time consisted of his wife and two children. Achamma greatly valued and generously compensated Mary, Chacko's wife, for her work as a housemaid in their household. Chacko remained unwaveringly loyal to Thomas Joseph and was content with the compensation he received, both in currency and in kind. Mary later gave birth to their third child, Sunil, after a few years of living in the new home. Sunil bore a striking resemblance to their elder daughter, Celine, due to his fair complexion.

Chapter 4

The lighting was inadequate; however, Sunny was acquainted with and accustomed to the standard walking path. It was a daily activity for him to deliver a bottle of goat's milk to the tea shop in the village centre, and thereafter attend the early morning Holy Mass at St Stephen's Church. Mr Thomas had failed to provide satisfactory access to the primary road when the house was built on the donated land. Sunny and his family adhered to a specific route that was mutually agreed upon. The path encompassed a section of hilly, elevated terrain that acted as a barrier between the residences. The donated land was significantly lower than the adjacent plot, separated by a stone wall. Chackochan's family relied on steep stepping stones to ascend and descend to their home. Sunny could manage the path in a single stride, but his younger sibling, Sunil, required assistance to cross the narrow pedestrian route. The walking path to the main road passed through the gate of their neighbour's large house.

As he traversed the mansion's gate and approached the road, Mr Thomas Mathew called his name.

'Sunny, da Sunny, please retrieve my newspaper upon your return.'

Sunny was aware of the newspaper delivery routine, yet, in an effort to clarify, he responded with a query:

'Yes, it is not an issue. What happened to Kunjumon? Is he sick again?'

Mr Thomas Mathew replied, 'I am not sure. I haven't seen him since yesterday.'

Kunjumon was the regular newspaper boy, a few years older than Sunny. He usually delivered the papers on an old bicycle that had belonged to his father. Newspapers were distributed throughout the village during the early hours by both father and son, who shared the same bicycle. In addition, Raghavan Kaniyan, Kunjumon's father, operated a newsstand in the village centre that sold a variety of newspapers and popular weekly periodicals.

During the brief conversation, Sunny glanced at Mr Thomas Mathew's mansion. It was not uncommon for Lovely, the younger daughter, to be awake and engaged in her studies. He looked for her, as she was always kind towards him. Her room was located on the second floor, but this time it was not illuminated. He then realised that it was Saturday and that the schools were closed for the weekend. Yet it was also customary for her to attend Mass on Saturdays. She might already have gone to church or be getting ready.

Throughout this time, Sunny did not pause but continued walking, conscious of the limited time remaining to deliver the precious container of goat's milk. Beyond providing a source of income for his modest family, the milk was also essential to the teashop's operations. Its early morning sales depended upon that delivery. Aware of its importance to both himself and the shopkeeper, he hastened towards the village centre.

He soon arrived at the main road leading to the village, where the first rays of light pierced the lofty branches of the trees on either side. In comparison with their narrow footpath, the rough village road was considerably wider. At that time, the unlevelled road was a desolate expanse of land, characterised by gullies and boulders. He remained cautious to avoid slippery rocks and concealed ditches, which were hazardous. Sunny cherished this season, when the sun's rays were slow to reach the earth in the early morning. The air was cold, and the much-anticipated Christmas holiday was rapidly approaching. He delighted in the festive activities and customs of Christmas: Christmas Pappa, carol singing, the beating of drums, the hand tambourine, and the procession around the houses to proclaim the birth of the Saviour. He especially enjoyed strolling through the village at night, knowing that a few households were more generous in sharing cakes, snacks, and sweets.

Then he heard the first chime of the church bell, symbolising the opening of heaven and the voice of the Almighty. 'The church bell has the capacity to lessen the rain, and the high winds always cease to let the chimes travel far,' his mother's voice echoed in his ears.

The interval between the bell's chimes denoted whether it was the first, second, or third. Sunny had to be present in the church or in the small hall near the sanctum before the third chime. Otherwise, he would forfeit the honour of leading the procession as the Thurifer, a role he held in high regard.

After hearing faint chimes from a distance, he recognised the sound of Mr Thommy's bullock cart. People and goods were transported between the village and the nearest town by its regular service. Whether the cart was ahead of him or approaching from the opposite direction was unclear. Sunny relished the opportunity to walk alongside the bullocks, enjoying the tinkling of the bell affixed to the cartwheel. Hurrying forward in thought, he suddenly lost his balance on a slippery slope. At first he was relieved to discover that the bottle was unharmed, but that relief quickly gave way to pain as his right knuckles throbbed intensely.

'Ouch!' he exclaimed, feeling dampness on his right palm. Though the skin on his knuckles had split, he could not detect much blood. Quickly, he plucked tender leaves from a nearby bush, crushed them in his palm, and applied them to the wound. The plant, commonly referred to as 'communist green', grows naturally in wasteland areas. When the delicate stems and leaves are crushed, they produce a green juice that gives immediate relief to moderate skin rashes and helps stop bleeding.

Apprehensive about examining the wound too closely, Sunny closed his eyes as he applied the remedy. A slight burning sensation lasted only a few moments before the pain subsided. Feeling relief, he resumed walking with greater caution. Schoolyard falls during games often resulted in bruises and cuts, so he was no stranger to minor injuries.

'Sunny Kutta, you are not very late today.'

He had already arrived at the teashop when a sudden voice startled him from his thoughts. The shop's sole front room was engulfed in smoke from the adjacent kitchen's fireplace. Pillechan, the proprietor, was unusually calm that day. He acknowledged Sunny with a smile and repeated his customary request, even though delivering the milk was not Sunny's only purpose.

'Upon my return from church, I will collect the empty bottle.'

Sunny never took the empty bottle to church, even though the shortcut from the church to home made it easier. He claimed there was no safe place to keep it there. The real reason was that he felt embarrassed by the comments and jokes others made about him.

Before leaving, he noticed that the teashop and neighbourhood had fewer customers than usual, which was unusual for that hour. Normally, the place bustled with labourers commuting to other towns for work. Most would begin their day with a cup of tea or coffee from the shop. The masala coffee, prepared with local coffee granules, dried ginger, and jaggery, was especially popular among early-morning customers.

Coffee plants are not subject to the same level of maintenance as other crops, and only a small number of households in the village are involved in their cultivation. They are naturally grown and produce an abundance of beans, sufficient for most domestic needs. Many villages permit neighbours to collect surplus beans for their own consumption. Sunny personally prefers the juicy fruits that turn red when fully mature. It is crucial to harvest the beans at the right time to guarantee their quality, flavour, and longevity.

Soon after, he heard a faint noise from a considerable distance, the familiar bus service that transported passengers to the nearest settlement and on to the main city. The bus route was established to connect the primary commercial town with the local villages, enabling improved commercial services. The service commenced in his village and continued until late evening. The sound abruptly ceased, and, despite his curiosity, he disregarded it and walked on towards the church.

St Stephen's Church had a rich history of more than fifty years. At the centre of the predominantly Christian village, the imposing church was built on a slightly elevated site. There were three Hindu temples in the village, where various deities were venerated, and the community comprised both Christian and Hindu believers. The church tower was the tallest structure in the village, its summit adorned with a concrete cross. The building had several entrances on three of its sides, including two very large doors, known as the 'elephant doors', which contained small built-in doors. The annual church festival was the only occasion on which the massive doors were opened wide.

'Sunny, hurry, the vicar is on his way.'

Bobby, his companion, called from a distance. He was almost a year younger and in the same class. Always willing to spend time with Sunny, he accompanied him at school, during leisure, and in play.

Fr Luke Thenetth, the vicar, was an elderly priest who planned to retire from active parish duties. He was originally from their village, and diocesan officials had granted him permission to return to his home parish for a second time, allowing him to spend more time with close relatives.

Although he seldom chuckled, he maintained an exceptionally pleasant demeanour. He was highly regarded by parishioners for his punctuality and his consistent support of many impoverished families, regardless of religion. He primarily resided in the presbytery, located close to the church. He was assisted by a cook, Uthupp Chettan, an accomplished chef despite being unmarried. On occasion, Uthupp also helped with church activities when the regular *Kappyar* (acolyte) was unwell or absent.

Bobby paused briefly to let Sunny catch up. On entering the preparation chamber, they both knelt before the cross and purified themselves with holy water. Sunny gazed up at the crucifix, whose eyes seemed fixed upon him. Unable to hold the gaze for long, he turned away. He then noticed that no one else was in the preparation room and was about to mention it to his friend.

Bobby murmured, 'Be quiet, the vicar is on his way.'

Fr Luke entered, crossed himself with holy water, and sat on the cushioned chair reserved for him. Mr Kurian emerged from the sacristy and spoke quietly to the vicar, who nodded in agreement. The third bell rang loudly, signalling the commencement of the liturgy. Kurian then entered the preparation room, and the vicar proceeded to the sacristy.

Sunny glanced at Bobby, and they walked together to the sacristy. Mr Kurian assisted the vicar in donning the *Kottina*, a pale-yellow, long tunic-style garment. He then presented the *Urara*, a vestment worn around the neck, decorated with fine embroidery. The vicar fastened the *Zunara*, a strip of cloth resembling a belt, over the *Kottina*. Kurian also helped him secure the *Zande*, or cuffs, to his wrists. Finally, the *Paina*, the outermost vestment, was draped carefully over his shoulders. The vicar adjusted it securely and cleaned his glasses for a clear view.

Incense in the thurible was burned using dried coconut shells, which retained heat for an extended period, ensuring fragrant smoke throughout the Mass. Mr Uthupp usually prepared the partially charred shells each day using the fire from the presbytery.

Bobby picked up the *ding-ling*, a hand-bell with three chimes, and stood behind Sunny, who carried the thurible already emitting fragrant smoke. As Sunny lifted it, the vessel made a heavy clanking sound with each swing, echoing with every forward and backward motion.

Chapter 5

Sunny, along with his fellow altar servers, returned to the sacristy after Mass. The *Kappyar* was responsible for any additional special rituals, such as assisting with prayers for the deceased. Bobby reminded Sunny about their regular swimming practice at the riverside before they bid farewell.

'I am not sure, but I'll let you know.' Sunny paused and then asked again,

'Are the water currents too strong? Sunil might want to join.'

'That shouldn't be an issue, it's just the normal flow around this time of year.' Sunny replied,

'Okay, I'll make an attempt.'

Thereafter, he proceeded to the teashop to collect the empty milk bottle. As he crossed the church gate, his response was audible to those returning from the service. One of them cautioned,

'Be careful, there are strong undercurrents in the river's centre.'

They smiled at the warning and went on their way. The road leading to the village centre was unusually empty, and Sunny looked around for a reason. There was no one about other than the devotees returning home from church. At the teashop, he was surprised to hear:

'The bottle is not yet empty. Do you want to collect it tomorrow?' Pillechan asked gently.

'What happened?'

'You don't know? Today is *Hartal* across the town, oh no, across the state.'

'What's that?'

'The Communists are fighting for civil justice. Some of their comrades were brutally attacked by the police, and now they are seeking revenge by stalling public life. I have fewer customers than usual, and I'll be starving today.'

Sunny didn't understand much of the conversation but raised his concern.

'Mum won't be happy, but I'll collect it tomorrow.'

Before heading home, he paused for a moment and added,

'Oh no, Pappa will collect it later today.'

'Be careful on the road,' Pillechan reminded him from afar.

As usual, Sunny moved quickly, noticing the closed shops. He wondered about the *Hartal* that forced all shops, including Kunjumon's father's, to shut.

'Newspapers didn't get delivered today, and the usual bus service is also affected by the *Hartal*,' Pillechan had already anticipated Sunny's thoughts and cautioned him again.

'Perhaps not today, but you can collect both days' papers together tomorrow.'

Sunny nodded, grateful for Pillechan's foresight. The sun shone brightly, and he quickened his pace towards home.

Sunny was preoccupied with the day's plans as he walked alone. His priority was to meet his friend at the river to continue swimming practice. He was unbeatable, and Bobby always admired his ability to master the strongest currents. As it was difficult to get parental consent, Sunny sought a simple way to persuade his mother. Aware of his passion for swimming, she was concerned for his safety. Usually, the water flow was either too slow or nearly still at this time of year, suitable for children to learn. Then he remembered that Celine often washed clothes by the river at weekends. On one or two occasions he had gone with her, but she was too cautious, keeping to the shallow parts. She preferred him to practise in the plains, where it was safer.

Then he heard the cycle bell's *ding-dong* behind him. He turned and saw a cyclist in the distance, waving. A faint voice called his name.

'Sunny, da Sunny!' He recognised the voice, Kunjumon, the newspaper boy.

Sunny waited for him to catch up. It took a while, as the hill was steep. Kunjumon pushed the bike with effort, gasping when he finally reached him. After pausing to recover, he made a request.

'Will you kindly give this newspaper to your neighbour, Thomas Sir?'

Sunny agreed enthusiastically.

'Yes, he reminded me this morning and is waiting for it.'

Curious, Sunny asked,

'But hold on, Pillechan said it's *Hartal* and no buses are running today. How was it delivered?'

Kunjumon puffed up with pride.

'What do you know about us, Common Boy? We have the resources to finish our work.'

Sunny raised his eyebrows, unimpressed by the nasty tone.

'All right, then deliver it yourself with your superhuman abilities. I won't take it. Pedal yourself and fall before you get there.' Then, after a pause, he added,

'Loser! Keep smoking that rubbish in secret, and you won't have the strength to live.'

Kunjumon quickly changed his tone, sounding more pleading.

'Oh, Sunny, I was joking. Our newspapers were delivered by a special *Villies Jeep* service, and the Communists don't stop them. They spread their messages through newspapers, so they make sure these are delivered on time.'

Sunny was ready to leave, unable to fully understand the explanation.

Sensing his reluctance, Kunjumon begged,

'It'll be difficult for me if you don't deliver it, Sunny. Please forget it, we're friends.'

Sunny took the paper and walked on. A few paces later, Kunjumon called out with a strange question.

'Sunny, it's Saturday. Will Celine be joining you at the riverside?'

Sunny froze, unable to reply, and kept walking. He heard the cycle bell again a short while later but continued without stopping or turning. The odd question lingered in his mind. Why would a fool like

Kunjumon ask about his sister Celine? On weekends she often helped their mother by doing laundry at the river.

Although none of Sunny's friends or other villagers liked Kunjumon, everyone respected his father, Raghavan Kaniyan. Once a temple performer, Raghavan rarely performed now. His late wife, Panchami Kaniyatti, had been the village midwife and astrologer. In addition to their two daughters, Kunjumon was their youngest child. Having failed the fourth grade three times, with little formal schooling, he now worked in his father's shop. Because of their age difference and the fact he had never met them, Sunny knew little about Kunjumon's sisters. Since Kunjumon was not his friend, he wondered why the boy would enquire about his sister's routine.

Overwhelmed by thoughts, Sunny reached Mr Thomas's gate. He preferred not to go inside and tried to slip the newspaper through. But luck wasn't with him, his name was loudly called.

'Sunny, da Sunny, bring in the paper.'

He had no choice but to open the gate and walk towards the bungalow.

'It's *Hartal* today,' he said, hoping to keep the visit brief.

'I know.' Mr Thomas looked at him. 'How do you know?'

Sunny looked aside and answered honestly.

'There aren't any vehicles on the road, and Pillechan explained.'

Then came the request he dreaded.

'Sunny, it's market day. Could you get some fresh fish?' Mrs Achamma Thomas asked.

Luckily, Lovely quickly defended him.

'Mum, Sunny's just a kid. Why not ask someone else?'

'I can't find anyone. Sunny is grown up now, strong enough to carry fish from the market.' Achamma turned to her husband. 'Achaya, give him the money, he'll be quick.'

Mr Thomas knew it wasn't a request but an instruction. Mrs Achamma often addressed him as Achayan in a soft tone. He looked at Sunny, who had turned pale, and made up his mind.

'No. Today is *Hartal*, there won't be any market.'

Achamma objected, but Mr Thomas stood firm. Ignoring her arguments, Sunny felt relieved and rushed home.

His mother was waiting.

'Oh, thank God you're back. Are you all right? Pappa said you mustn't go out today.'

'Yes, Mam, it is *Hartal* today.'

'What's that?'

'I don't know, but Pillechan said it's by the Communists. They want the government to suffer by stopping people's movements and keeping them at home.'

'All right, don't worry. You're not going anywhere today. Do you want boiled cassava or *pazham kanji*? Don't know whether Celine left some or finished it all.'

Celine, feeding Sunil in the kitchen, replied,

'There's enough kanji for you.'

Sunny changed his clothes and sat in the kitchen for breakfast. Sunil smiled and hugged him.

'Where's Pappa? If it's *Hartal*, shouldn't he stay at home?'

Their mother answered,

'No, he's working. He isn't aware of the *Hartal* limits, and I have to go and help him.'

Sunny sat on the floor as Celine served kanji on a steel plate. Sunil approached at once, and Sunny asked, 'Do you want some?' Sunil giggled, and Sunny hand-fed him slowly.

Then his mother instructed,

'Take care of Sunil. Celine needs to feed the goats and clean the shed.'

Sunil leapt onto Sunny's lap as soon as Celine left the kitchen.

Celine was very attached to the family's two adult goats and two lambs. Normally she fed them in their shed, but on weekends she took them to graze in nearby bushes and fields. Mr Thomas and his family owned the land, but they did not mind as long as the goats were restrained with coir leads and not left to wander. By sunset the animals had plenty of grass to eat.

That day it took Celine longer than usual to return. She went straight to their small room and stayed there for a while before beginning to clean the goat pen. Its floor was made of wooden planks with mesh, allowing waste to fall through so the pen remained tidy. She swept the pen with an old broom to clear the debris.

Goat droppings were regularly removed from the bottom pit and taken to their neighbour's cocoa plantations. Lovely, the neighbour's daughter, often asked Sunny for some, as it was good for her cherished rose plants. She kept reminding him that the manure boosted fertility, strengthened the soil, and provided her garden plants with long-term nourishment. She occasionally offered flowers in return, but Sunny never found them particularly appealing or useful.

Sunny was still playing on their veranda with his younger brother, with a ball made from rubber sap. Chacko collected the long, sticky rubber sap from the trees every day before tapping the fresh bark and fashioned tiny balls out of it. By removing the inner bark before making new cuts, the trees protected themselves and healed their wounds. Rubber tappers kept some of the sap to supplement their income. Sunny's father allowed him to make small balls for them to play with at home.

Before lunch was served, Celine asked if they might wash clothes at the riverside. Although it was their usual weekend routine, because of the *Hartal* her mother was uncertain.

'Ask your pappa. It may not be safe there today, when there aren't many people around.'

Celine was not convinced.

'It is our personal need, and *Hartal* is for employees and other daily wagers.'

Mary wasn't sure and stayed silent, continuing with her housework.

When Sunny's pappa, Mr Chacko, returned for lunch, Sunil ran towards him calling 'Pappa!' and waiting for a hug. Chacko knelt before him and stroked his forehead lovingly.

'No, I can't hug you now, I'm a bit smelly. Sunny, take care of him.'

Sunny was just behind and picked Sunil up in his arms. He always longed to hug his father but never quite found the opportunity; his father worked hard seven days a week, leaving early in the morning and returning late at night.

Chacko quickly washed his hands and feet with water from the earthen pot and reminded his wife:

'Mary, keep this pot away when the children are playing around, they might accidentally break it.'

Mary, busy in the kitchen, immediately called Celine.

'Mole, please move the pot from the veranda.'

She paused a moment, then asked:

'Is it all right if Celine goes to the riverside? There are too many clothes to wash.'

Chacko didn't respond straight away but sat down in his usual place on the kitchen floor, ready for lunch. Another earthen pot, almost full of boiled rice, was placed in front of him with a steel plate. The steam rose hotly, and he looked up to request:

'Mary, get me the serving spoon.'

Mary looked around and found the coconut-shell spoon. She then placed a dish of diluted curd with a few chillies, followed by chargrilled dried fish, and remarked:

'Fresh fish wasn't delivered today because of the *Hartal*.'

Chacko made no comment and began eating. He knew his wife was caring and would always serve the best food she could find.

After finishing, he went back to the veranda and asked his wife to serve food to the children. They quickly disappeared into the kitchen. Sitting with his back to the wall, Chacko stretched his legs and lit a small handmade cigarette, a dried temburni leaf rolled and filled with tobacco. Locally called *beedi*, it was cheap and widely available in the market, often referred to as the poor man's cigar. Chacko smoked only one or two a day, and this after-lunch smoke was his favourite.

Soon, his snoring began, first irregular, then steady. Afternoon naps after early morning labour were common, and the family used that time to rest. While Celine went to fetch the goats from the field, Mary settled Sunil down for his siesta. Sunny sat beside his father, listening to the rhythm of his snores. Remembering his promise to his friend, he waited for the right moment to ask his father's permission. His mother noticed and gestured for him to keep quiet. He didn't want to disturb his father, but he longed to ask.

After a while, Sunny approached his mother, who was feeding the chickens. Pointing to a plump hen, she said with a smile:

'Sunny, that's your favourite. It's laying eggs now, we could hatch them, and before Christmas we'll have more chickens for ourselves.'

Sunny thought it the right moment.

'Mum, can I go to the riverside? My friend is coming.'

'Ask your pappa.'

'He's sleeping,' Sunny replied quickly.

By that time, Celine had returned with the goats, and Mary helped her tie them in the pen. Turning to her, she instructed:

'Celine, go to the riverside and get the clothes washed. Take Sunny with you.'

Sunny was thrilled, but Celine wasn't impressed. She looked at him and reminded their mother:

'He doesn't always listen, he'll just go swimming on his own.'

Mary cautioned him:

'Stay with your sister and help her with the washing.' She paused, then added firmly:

'Don't swim in the deep parts of the river.'

Chapter 6

Celine walked in front carrying the dirty clothing in a plastic bucket. Sunny followed with a bag containing a selection of his clothes. Celine warned him to be cautious of the river's strong current, which could be more powerful than usual. Sunny took Kaiser with him; Celine objected to taking the household dog. Sunny argued strongly, saying it would be a good occasion to give the dog a thorough bath. Celine consented on the condition that Kaiser remain tied to the lead and under control. Sunny knew it was challenging to discipline the dog, as it would immediately engage any other dog that crossed its path.

The riverside was a ten- to twelve-minute walk from their home. A convenient and safe spot for washing and bathing lay a further ten-minute walk away. The secure area, with its expansive sandbanks, was popular and generally busy. At weekends the place was frequently occupied by familiar faces and occasionally relatives.

There were lots of people enjoying a refreshing swim in the river or washing their clothes. The river's source is the Western Ghats, the mountain range that divides the east and west coastlines of the Indian southern peninsula. The water was nearly pristine for both human and agricultural use due to the river's consistent flow.

Celine chose a place where she could use a flat boulder that stood on top of several small stones and above the water level. Villagers commonly use these flat rocks to beat clothing and remove hard dirt. She began by applying a portion of soap to each piece of cloth. She then placed the garments in the container and stirred them to distribute the detergent evenly. After soaking all the clothing in the bucket, she removed each item and massaged it on the rock while rinsing out the dirty water. She checked each garment for discolouration and exerted her full force against the rock. At times, removing grime and hard stains was difficult and could damage clothes. They had no other alternative to get their used clothes washed and clean.

Sunny looked for his friend Bobby, who had promised to come but was not yet visible. Consequently, Sunny continued watching over his sister and the others. The majority were doing laundry, while a few were swimming. A small number of people had completed their baths and were now drying themselves on the sandbanks. Kaiser, the companion dog, feared flowing water and was fastened to a small tree. While waiting for his friend, Sunny used the time to bathe the dog. Kaiser was extremely reluctant as he was dragged to the sandbanks. Nevertheless, Celine intervened and pushed the dog towards the water. The dog did enjoy a brief period of play; soon the lead loosened and he promptly fled to the protection of the small tree.

She shouted at Sunny, who was bored and sitting on the bank, asking, 'Would you like to assist me or go swimming?' Sunny could not resist Celine's persistence this time.

He came over to help, removed the garments from the container and immersed them in the water. She handed him the cloth she had been beating against the rock. 'No, it hasn't been washed yet. Take these,' she said. Sunny began rinsing his father's shirt, spreading the cloth towards the water.

Celine continued to dip the clothing briefly in the water to rinse off any excess soap and then resumed beating them against the rock. Celine was highly proficient at washing. She repeatedly grabbed portions of a garment and slammed them against the stone, dislodging stubborn grime and soap. Before beating them, she stretched out a few items and then repeated the process.

To Sunny's relief, he heard his name called, it was his friend Bobby. 'Okay, your friend is here now. Don't go too deep; stay close to the shore,' Celine warned, generous and affectionate.

Bobby was quick to jump into the river with a white towel tied tightly around his waist. Sunny shouted and followed him. 'Wait, let me go first.'

They stayed together where the riverbed was firmer and the water reached waist height. Given the muddy and sandy conditions, the companions made sure their feet were planted firmly. They kept talking while showing off their swimming skills and testing their underwater endurance; Sunny was able to stay under longer, and Bobby accused him of counting slowly.

'Sunny, could you help me spread the clothes for drying?' Celine called from afar. Sunny had been expecting the request and Bobby was willing to help.

Celine made sure any remaining soap was gone by completing one last rinse. When they came near, Celine described the method for quickly drying the clothes. 'Spread each piece out, holding the four corners, and gently flap it over,' she instructed. When she showed them, Bobby remarked, 'I know this.'

Both were quick to spread clothes along the sandy riverbank. A few others followed the same procedure. Thereafter they resumed enjoying their swim. Celine cleaned and dried the bucket to take the dried clothes home after finishing the last items. She then joined them and they began swimming across the river. She warned them not to follow her as she wanted to show off her swimming skill.

Both boys watched in awe at her daring style and endurance as she swam across, using both arms and legs to propel herself. The water on the other side was colder and deeper. Numerous huge trees on that bank provided shade and helped keep the water cool.

As soon as Celine arrived at the opposite bank, they heard a whistle from the treetops. Glancing up, Celine began swimming back. Stunned, both boys glanced at each other. 'Who's hiding there?' they asked. They turned to see Celine straining to swim back. She had intended to take a long break before returning because she was tired from washing the clothes. Although it took her longer than before, she managed to cross the deeper section with the strength she had left.

'Someone was laughing at me from the top of the tree,' she said. Looking at that area, they saw the newspaper boy, Kunjumon, leap from a branch into the river and begin swimming towards them.

Sunny was furious as he recalled Kunjumon's earlier rambling. Bobby said, 'Don't bother him, he's a pervert,' and kept swimming. Distressed, Celine went to the shore and began putting on dry clothes.

With his long arms and slender frame, Kunjumon was a quick swimmer. Reaching them, he asked, 'How are you, Sunny? I arrived much earlier than you lot.'

Sunny was enraged and a little taken aback. He detested the sly smile on Kunjumon's face and could not appreciate his unexpected appearance; the boy's attitude plainly displayed an unpleasant intent. Sunny couldn't tell whether Kunjumon was showing off or making fun of him.

Sunny wasn't about to give up, but Bobby ignored Kunjumon and kept swimming in another direction.

'Are you serious? Why were you hiding in the tree and whistling at my sister? Are you trying to scare her?' Sunny demanded.

Maintaining his sardonic grin, Kunjumon evaded the question and dived into the water, vaguely attempting to blend in with Bobby. Then, out of nowhere, Kunjumon grabbed Sunny's feet beneath the water, hoisted him above the surface and tried to throw him. Sunny grabbed Kunjumon's long hair and pulled him down before he could toss him, catching Kunjumon off guard. Sunny was so angry that he shoved Kunjumon's head under the water while still holding his hair. Perceiving the gravity of the situation, Bobby yelled, 'Sunny, leave him alone, he will drown,' which drew the attention of other people bathing nearby. By the time Kunjumon freed himself and began swimming away, Celine had already rushed to the scene.

'What are you doing? I'll tell your dad about this, and he'll discipline you,' Celine said, trying to calm Sunny.

'Come on, man, he's silly and a coward; see, he runs away now. Let's finish our games,' Bobby said, trying to soothe Sunny as he didn't fully understand why Sunny had become so irate with Kunjumon.

Still furious, Sunny attempted to pursue Kunjumon, but Celine drew him back to the shore.

Bobby begged once more, 'Leave him, Sunny. Let's swim and enjoy.'

Sunny tried to break free of Celine's firm grip, but she held him close. Unable to get away, Sunny calmed down and did as she said. Even though Bobby wasn't impressed, he decided to call it off.

When Celine attempted to help him wipe the water from his head, he declined.

'Leave me alone, I can do it myself.'

Bobby picked up his clothes and left the scene without further upsetting them.

Celine quickly collected the mostly dry clothes, filled the bucket, and headed for their house. Sunny was upset that Kaiser had not stayed with him when he untied him.

'You couldn't take a proper bath,' he said, slapping the unresponsive dog. The poor dog quietly followed him.

Sunny replayed the entire incident in his mind as he followed Celine, and it was clear that Kunjumon wasn't getting any better. When he realised that Kunjumon had been waiting for Celine to swim across, his rage grew. Why had he whistled at her at all? He ought to have been more cautious in warning his sister. Kunjumon pretended to be a close friend even though he was not. *Is he a stalker?* Sunny asked himself.

'Why don't you walk faster?' Celine urged him.

Celine turned when she didn't hear his reply, glancing oddly at Sunny before ignoring him and walking more quickly. Their pet dog suddenly turned around, hesitated for a moment, and began to bark.

Sunny turned back to see why Celine had hurried. He noticed that someone else was following them, but the stranger quickly vanished behind the bushes.

Sunny voiced his doubts. 'Is someone following us?'

'I don't know,' Celine replied without looking back. 'Let's walk fast.'

Sunny looked back again, but no one was there. He turned to the agitated dog, waiting for orders, but chose to ignore him. Then he recalled that Celine had threatened to complain to Pappa, which would have had dire consequences.

'You don't have to tell Pappa everything. I don't like Kunjumon, and I'll discipline him if it happens again.'

'Hey, you're just a child, don't act like an adult. I'll report this for sure,' Celine warned.

Sunny remained silent and kept following her. He glanced back to ensure no one was pursuing them.

As they approached their house, Celine said, 'All right, I'm giving you another chance. Don't do this again. That filthy Kunjumon is much bigger than you.'

Sunny didn't reply, unsure he had caught the full warning. Their father wasn't home, and their mother was busy preparing dinner. Without making much noise, Celine began helping her mother in the kitchen after putting the clothes outside to dry.

Sunil played with a ball while he waited for Sunny to return. He asked their mother for more tea and biscuits, and Sunny gladly gave him his portion.

During the evening prayers, Celine read the Bible at an unusually high volume. Sunny, preoccupied with the events of the day, wasn't paying much attention.

'Sunny, be mindful during prayer time,' his mother reminded.

'Pappa isn't here yet,' Sunil commented, looking towards the entrance.

'Pappa will be late; he's helping someone with their wedding function tomorrow.'

'Are we attending the wedding?' Celine asked eagerly.

'No, Pappa is only assisting the chef. Now finish the prayers,' Mum replied.

They sat on the kitchen floor and ate dinner together. The meal included fried fish and boiled rice with curd curry. As usual, Sunil was lovingly hand-fed by their mother and siblings.

'Are we buying meat tomorrow? It's Sunday , I can get it from the butcher,' Sunny asked his mother.

Her reply was delayed. 'Ask your Pappa in the morning. Now it's time to sleep.'

Mary led them to their room with a kerosene lamp. She ensured their small space was secure and insect-free. Sunil and Sunny shared bedding on the floor, which she unfolded neatly. It was Celine's turn to sleep on the bed. Sunil begged to sleep with their mother again, but the request was refused.

Sunny hugged Sunil and whispered, 'Don't wet your half-pants again. Do you want to pee now?'

Sunil giggled and whispered, 'Not now, maybe later.'

After Mary removed the lamp, the room became completely dark. Sunil gave his brother a hug and firmly closed his eyes.

Sunny wanted to talk to his sister but wasn't sure how to begin. He was exhausted yet unable to sleep. Even though he didn't want to, he couldn't help but think about Kunjumon. Once, Kunjumon had tried to give him a magazine containing indecent pictures of men and women. He had claimed it was common for kids their age to read such periodicals. Although tempting, Sunny disliked Kunjumon's companionship and never trusted him.

Chapter 7

On Sunday morning, Mary continuously called Sunny and knocked on the wooden door of her children's room. Instead of waiting for Celine to remind him this time, Sunny got up on his own, feeling relieved, and turned to face his sleeping pets. His mother reminded him to return the empty steel carrier. The goat's milk had been poured into a pot, temporarily borrowed from their neighbour.

'Mum, why don't we buy one of these for ourselves?' Sunny asked after discovering how comfortable it was to carry around.

'It's from Delhi and expensive. Let's use only our own glass bottles,' came her prompt reply. She reminded him, 'Get the bottles from Pillechan and tell him that we won't give him milk again if he doesn't return them.'

Sunny knew that selling the milk was just as crucial to Pillechan as purchasing it. It was a reciprocal arrangement, essential to their survival.

'Mum, is Pappa not attending the early mass? Today is Sunday,' he asked, noticing his father was still asleep.

After a brief pause, his mother replied, 'Don't raise your voice, your pappa is upset; he came back very late.' She clarified further, 'He will attend the afternoon mass. I'll explain later. Now deliver the milk quickly.'

Sunny was puzzled, as there were only two Sunday holy masses. Children attended the late morning mass, which was followed by catechism classes, while the elderly and parents usually went to the early one.

With the dim light from their home, he climbed the stepping stones on the wall in front of their house. Crossing the neighbour's gate in silence, he tried not to look at their mansion. After passing quickly, he glanced back at the porch, scanning for activity or lights. To his surprise, the entire mansion was dark and still, which startled him.

The village roads in the early morning also seemed unusually quiet. Sunny waited to hear the chirping of morning birds and looked around for them. The road to the village centre was deserted, and the calmness was unsettling. He recalled his beloved schoolteacher's advice: morning light is not only vital for human health but also provides much-needed nutrients to the ecosystem and its inhabitants. It helps preserve human dominance over the planet. It is also essential for pleasure, as it improves cognitive function and aids concentration, crucial for learning, understanding, and responding appropriately to ensure a successful life.

The tea stall was open, and Pillechan was sitting on his cashier's chair instead of by the constantly boiling tea pot, unusual for him. Sunny felt uneasy, as none of the regular early morning customers were present. He wondered if this was another Hartal day, requiring people to remain indoors.

'Where are the customers, Pillechan Cheta? Am I too early?' he shouted.

Despite looking extremely exhausted, Pillechan rose from his chair and reached out with his right arm to take the milk pot. He hardly said anything before handing Sunny the empty pot. 'Is Pappa at home? He collected the other empty bottles.' Without waiting for an answer, Pillechan turned and went back to his seat.

After a moment of shock, Sunny looked around again and began to make his way back. For a time, he felt strange and wondered if he was the only person in the world. Then a large coucal bird landed on the path in front of him. The bird's broad brown wings spread out in the dawn light reassured him that he wasn't alone. As the crow pheasant symbolises hope, he briefly felt uplifted. He was startled when it uttered its characteristic call, a resonant 'coo-coo-coo.' His surroundings were suddenly filled with wonder and reverence as the beautiful sound reverberated.

Crossing by his neighbour's mansion again, Sunny recalled Pillechan's question about his father, which left him uneasy. He leapt across the stepping stones and hurried home. As he ran back, his mother warned, 'Go slow, you'll slip and injure yourself.'

Not paying attention, Sunny asked, 'Is Pappa still asleep? What's going on today? Will there be another Hartal?' His mother's pale face revealed her stress. Daily chores and endless housework had never been an issue before, but her sudden change in mood worried him. She was bent over, brushing their tiny front garden. Realising she must respond, she stood up and paused.

'Sunny, your friend Bobby lost his dear Pappa.' She waited to gauge his reaction.

Sunny was stunned. 'What? Bobby's Pappa died? Benny Uncle?' Mary stepped forward, held his hands, and embraced him firmly. Reading her eyes, Sunny felt the weight of the news, though he did not cry.

'The funeral will be at the church this afternoon. Your pappa came back from their house early this morning,' Mary added, sobbing and holding him close.

Sunny stretched his legs across the mud floor as he sat on the veranda. Mary brought him a glass of black coffee. 'We've run out of sugar, do you want a piece of jaggery?' she asked. He nodded, and she returned to the kitchen to fetch it.

Sunny turned to Kaiser, their pet dog, chained to a pillar supporting the roof. He recalled how Bobby had helped him bathe the dog. His thoughts drifted to Bobby's father, Benny Mathew Uncle, who always wore immaculately polished white clothing. He was exceedingly generous to the underprivileged and always carried a pen and black diary in his pocket.

'It's good with coffee, made from our own sugarcane,' Mary said, offering him a piece of jaggery. It reminded him of his maternal uncle, Joyachan, who often brought them bundles of jaggery. Joyachan kept good relations with the family and visited frequently, though his wife was reluctant to come because she disliked climbing the steep, single stepping stones in front. Mary seldom visited them either, as they lived some distance away.

Mary returned and suggested, 'Would you like to attend the children's mass and then the funeral mass?' Sunny was uncertain but eager to see Bobby. His mother added, 'The police are conducting further investigations and will release the body by lunchtime.' Once again, Sunny was puzzled as to why the police were involved, and he looked to his mother for clarification. Collecting the empty coffee glass, Mary said, 'Ask your pappa, he knows the details.'

Their pet cat approached, letting out a plaintive mew as if begging for affection, but Sunil wasn't interested. The cat circled him, trying to climb onto his knee. Sunny's mind, however, was preoccupied with Bobby and how he would endure his father's sudden departure to the heavens. As the cat purred, he stroked it absently while gazing at the solid stone wall surrounding their house.

'Remove that cat, it may have fleas,' Celine said disapprovingly. She was never fond of cats. Sunny refrained from answering, knowing cats were quite capable of protecting themselves from parasites. Slowly, he wrapped his hand around the cat and continued stroking it.

As soon as Celine reached the kitchen, Mary broke the news of Benny Uncle's untimely death. She was devastated and began to cry. Benny had paid them frequent visits and was more than just a friend to her father. He had drafted supporting documents and urged her father to seek financial assistance from the local authorities to rebuild their crumbling home. He was more than a companion, he spent time with her pappa in public settings and recognised him as a dedicated farmer rather than just a daily wager.

When Celine asked for more information, Mary reiterated that only their pappa was aware of the details. Mary said that she herself would not attend the church's Sunday morning service but would go to the funeral mass that afternoon. She instructed Celine to take her siblings to the customary late-morning mass before going to Benny Uncle's house to view his body and comfort his family. When the burial rites began at home, they would have a better opportunity to see the mortal remains up close. Since he was a well-liked community activist, a sizable crowd from the village and his associates from surrounding places was anticipated. She cautioned that younger children might struggle during the lengthy funeral procession leading to the church.

Sunny was silently mourning his friend's loss, and Mary raised her concern with Celine, who approached him and said, 'Why don't you see if Sunil is still asleep?' Sunny's eyes were teary and on the verge of breaking. He gazed at her and begged, 'Sister, please come with me to their house so I can see Bobby right now.' Celine felt sorry for Sunny when she saw him crying and knelt beside him. 'We could go with Pappa, but their home is far away,' she said. Mary overheard and repeated, 'You two visit them after the early holy mass.' After a brief pause, she added, 'You'll have Sunil with you when we go to the funeral mass, but I will take care of him for now.'

After a little while, Mary asked Celine to feed the goats. Then they heard their mother's name being called by their father. At the rear of the home, Mary was busy chopping wood for the kitchen fire. Once again, she requested that Celine get their pappa a glass of coffee. Celine got up immediately and made it.

Chacko came out to the veranda and sat in his usual place. Celine poured black coffee from the hot pot into a glass. Sitting close to Sunny, he asked Celine to fetch a fire stick from the kitchen to light his beedi. Normally he would light it directly from the kitchen fireplace, but he seemed unusually tired. Celine warned Sunny to stay away from the fire stick as she cautiously carried it over. The cat leapt off Sunny's lap and fled towards the back of the house when it saw the flames.

'Don't scare the poor pets, they can't speak like you,' Chackochan warned her.

Chacko explained, 'It is very unfortunate. The body will be brought home around lunchtime, and the Vicar insists it be buried this afternoon itself.' Sunny was filled with sorrow and could not respond. Chacko continued, 'Leelamma and Bobby are really upset because they don't have many relatives in our village.' He then proposed, 'Do you want to come with me? I'm going there soon.' Sunny was still hesitant to answer, so Celine suggested, 'I can take Sunny straight from church, otherwise I'll be walking alone.'

Mary supported Celine's suggestion and told Sunny to go to holy mass first and then honour Benny Uncle at his home. Chacko agreed quietly.

'I'll go with Pappa and come to church before the late-morning mass,' Sunny said, refusing to give in. 'I really want to see Bobby and tell him how sorry I am,' he added, glancing at Celine. Mary wasn't persuaded, but Celine was willing to agree because she knew how close the two boys were. From the kitchen, Mary reminded, 'Sunny, listen to your sister, she can't walk to church by herself.'

'Don't worry, I'll be fine, and Sunny will come to church anyway to accompany me,' Celine reassured her.

Mary remained silent and went about the determined task of cutting large hardwood logs into small pieces with an axe. To keep the fire in their oven alive, they needed small, dried, and split logs. On a strong brick platform, three parallel furnaces made of clay soil were set up. The other two also received heat from the central oven. The firewood was stored safely outside the kitchen, under an extended roof to keep it dry.

The kitchen had been purposefully built on the left side of their home, as suggested by Raghavan Kaniyan, an authority on the traditional astrologically based building theory known as *Vastu Shastra*. He maintained that the kitchen must be constructed in the proper spot, as it was the place where raw food was transformed into wholesome, balanced meals. He said, this, provided the family with the positive energy needed to work and survive. Thanks to the vitality of the food, the household would live longer, he believed. A wrongly positioned kitchen, however, could create negative energy and harm the family's health.

Benny Mathew had been sceptical of the scientific basis of *Vastu Shastra*, but he had not stopped Chacko from consulting Raghavan Kaniyan. He believed it advisable to position the kitchen on the east side, since the wind usually blew from west to east. With the wind blowing in the opposite direction, there was less risk of an uncontrolled fire spreading to the rest of the house. He was also a strong advocate of healthful living and the careful storing and processing of grains. He recommended eating freshly prepared food at all times and advised against consuming leftovers from the previous day.

While in the kitchen, Mary asked her husband whether he preferred the newly boiled tapioca for breakfast or *pazham kanji*. Chacko declined breakfast, saying he wasn't hungry. Mary insisted that he eat something, noticing the reason for his lack of appetite. He eventually agreed and walked towards their natural pig toilet to relieve himself.

The family's female pig was housed in a restricted space by the boundary wall. A small stairway had been built above the enclosure so family members could relieve themselves there. The pig eagerly ate the warm human droppings, which provided a quick and practical way of disposing of waste. Additionally, the pig was fed kitchen scraps and leftovers. Sometimes, especially when the pig was pregnant, Chacko brought home leftover vegetables from the market. The nutrient-rich pig droppings was used as fertilizer for their coconut and palm plantations. Each year, the pig produced around twelve to fourteen piglets, which were sold at market for extra income.

Celine had recently expressed her desire for a modern and hygienic lavatory facility. She preferred a modern bathroom like those of their wealthier neighbours and some of her schoolmates. Mary too recognised the importance of safe, sanitary toilets, particularly for women. However, they were constrained by their finances: they lacked the funds to build a modern facility, and would lose their low-cost pig farming, which otherwise provided additional income.

Sunny hurried to their room when he heard Sunil frantically calling for their mother. Celine followed, having been feeding the goats. Sunny found Sunil wet again when he tried to help him out of bed. Celine changed his trousers and gave him a wash outside the house. Sunil was sipping a glass of goat's milk when their pappa returned. Seeing him, Sunil rushed forward, only to be disappointed when Chacko refused to take his arm. Sunny sat beside him and helped him sip the milk. Chacko reminded Sunny to prepare himself, as they would soon be leaving for Benny's house.

Chapter 8

Sunny followed his pappa, who silently began walking towards Benny Mathew's home after carefully climbing over the stepping stones on the stone wall. Celine reminded Sunny to meet her near the granite cross in front of the church after mass.

Mar Thoma Sleeva, a substantial rock sculpture, stood in front of the church to symbolise the resurrection of Jesus Christ through the cross. The cross, also known as the Saint Thomas Cross, is traditionally devoid of the effigy of Jesus Christ, serving as a reminder to devotees that the cross is the path to eternity. St Thomas successfully converted many non-Christians during his missionary days, assuring them of eternal life as they bore their own crosses of uncertainty and hardship. The four edges of the cross are adorned with a floral design symbolising the fruition and vitality of the tree of life. The plain *Mar Thoma Cross*, lacking an effigy of Jesus, symbolises the empty tomb revealed on the third day after his death on the cross. The natural evil forces of death were defeated by Jesus during his earthly life, bearing witness to his promised resurrection.

Sunny's catechism teacher had taught him that human existence is like a flowing river: it does not always adhere to its own course but seeks alternative routes when confronted with barriers. It surpasses some obstacles and flows around others that cannot be overcome. Human life is not a straight line from birth to death. It is full of uncertainties and crossroads. It is the responsibility of each individual to choose their path. By making the right decisions, they can achieve the eternal life of love and peace promised by Jesus Christ.

The father and son quickly passed the gates of their neighbours, and Sunny, as usual, cautiously glanced towards the mansion. There was no one outside and nothing unusual. He then realised it was Sunday and that most of them would be attending the early morning mass at the church.

Chacko was unusually silent, walking briskly, ignoring his son's slower pace. Curious, Sunny asked, 'How did it happen? He was so young.'

Chacko abruptly halted and looked into his son's face. 'These are not matters to be discussed with children. He was not merely a friend to me, he was my brother. They inflicted terrible injuries upon him.'

Sunny froze, unable to respond immediately. He felt the depth of his father's agony and looked down, realising that his pappa was on the brink of emotional collapse.

Chacko quickly regained his composure and glanced around to see whether anyone was watching. He used the tip of his white dhoti to wipe away the tears that welled in his eyes. He was dressed in a white half-sleeved shirt and a neat, double-lined white loincloth around his waist. He owned only two pairs of respectable clothes, which he wore to church programmes and significant events.

'It's not for you to know everything now, but Benny Uncle was a good man,' he said slowly, taking a deep breath before turning back to his son. 'He may have died too soon, but in many ways he helped a lot of people in our village.'

He walked steadily towards his friend's house, holding his son's hand. Sunny silently followed, wondering why his close friend's father had died so suddenly. They walked the bumpy rural paths for nearly thirty minutes before the house came into view.

From a distance, Sunny noticed the peculiar silence enveloping the area. The sun's faint rays barely touched the eastern horizon as Sunday morning dawned. The blue skies looked barren without the soft presence of white clouds. The trees and the path stood still, as though the wind itself paused to mourn. A very active and vibrant man, who had cared for nature, was no longer there.

Sunny heard Leelamma Aunty, Benny Uncle's wife, sobbing loudly. It was clear that both his family and the very surroundings grieved his premature death.

This was the first time Sunny had ever visited his closest friend Bobby's house. It stood in a remote location on the slope of a small hill, at the outskirts of the village. Benny Mathew had been a farmer who owned a substantial coconut grove and many fruit-bearing trees across several acres of land. Sunny marvelled at the way the artificial man-made home blended with the natural environment to provide shelter. He noticed small cocoa trees growing between tall teakwood and cashew trees. The tranquillity of the place seemed to shape the behaviour of its inhabitants.

The stone steps to the house were formed from naturally placed small boulders. Stepping carefully, Sunny and his father walked to the front. For the convenience of visitors, a temporary fabric tent had been erected in the courtyard. Sunny eyed the middle of the roof with unease, seeing the white cloth laid out to mark where the coffin would soon rest.

The veranda was wide, with a few people seated on the hanging bed and nearby chairs. Chacko led Sunny to a side room. Inside, Leelamma and her children, Bobby and his younger sibling, just over two years old, were surrounded by a few women.

Bobby burst into tears upon seeing his grieving friend, and Leelamma sobbed uncontrollably. 'Bobby, my dear son, your friend is here, but your pappa is not here to greet him. My dear God, why have you done this to us?'

Sunny could no longer control himself. A rumbling rose from deep in his chest until it broke from his throat in loud sobs. For a moment he could not speak at all. Chacko tried to hold him, but he fled to his friend and grasped his hand. Seeing their sorrow, the women nearby were also unable to suppress their emotions. Around them, nature itself seemed to stand still as their cries of grief reverberated through the morning.

On a chair rested a framed black-and-white photograph of Benny Mathew. In front of it, on a small table, two candles burned alongside incense sticks releasing fragrant smoke, with fresh flowers laid beside them. The candles were lit in memory of the deceased; the incense sticks, to ease depression and comfort the bereaved. Before the picture, a few women and children recited prayers for the departed.

After allowing his son time with his friend and the grieving family, Chacko left the room. He sought someone to ask when the body would be brought and about the burial plans. He looked around before approaching three elderly men seated on a wooden cot in the patio. The headboard was beautifully curved, and the bed itself was crafted from mature teakwood. The seating area was woven with coir strings. On a steel plate lay smoking materials, locally rolled beedis, a cigarette packet, and several matchboxes. Another plate held solid white lime paste, dried tobacco, opened areca nuts, and fresh green betel leaves.

Many of them were chewing *paan*, the local betel quid made from slaked lime, a piece of areca nut, a betel leaf, and a little tobacco. Chewing betel quid, as it is commonly known, is more of a pastime than a habit for many. Each ingredient has its own colour, but once chewed together it turns a deep red. Nicotine, present in the mixture, can cause addiction and discolour the teeth and gums, often leaving a reddish-brown stain. Many consider it an art to prepare the perfect combination: the right amount of tobacco, a finely sliced piece of areca nut, and the correct application of lime on the leaf. Youngsters often acquire the habit of chewing betel quid or smoking tobacco by imitating their peers or family members.

Chacko respectfully declined when offered a beedi and instead asked for an update on the funeral plans. The three men exchanged glances before one muttered, 'Not very sure. The police must complete their investigation, and the doctors at the government hospital are finishing the post-mortem before handing over the body for burial in the cemetery.'

Turning to the others, the second man added, 'The vicar has requested that the police release the body at the earliest so the burial formalities can be completed today itself.'

The third said, 'His father's brother is at the hospital to expedite the procedures.'

Unfamiliar with such protocols, Chacko voiced his concern. 'What about the president of the co-operative bank? He was a very close associate.' After a pause, he added, 'The president of the panchayat was also his friend.' The three men looked blankly at him and did not answer.

When Chacko attempted to light a beedi, his matches failed. He accepted a light from one of the onlookers and drew deeply, exhaling smoke through his nostrils and mouth. Moments later he was overtaken by a harsh cough, as though the smoke was choking him.

'Chacko, you should see a doctor. There's a good one at the government hospital,' one of them suggested.

'It's fine , this doesn't help when I'm under stress,' Chacko replied, discarding the half-smoked beedi.

Another of the men remarked, 'Benny's relations with the panchayat president were strained. It seems he won't be of much help now.'

The second agreed, saying, 'They shared political views, but they despised each other.'

The third added, after a pause, 'Benny was good at heart. He always promoted peace in society. Indeed, he was a good man.'

They were interrupted by the sound of approaching footsteps. A church team had arrived carrying sacred items required for the burial rituals. A few men rushed down to help them carry the items up. The group was led by Uthup Chettan, the vicar's culinary assistant. Realising the body had not yet been brought home, he promptly returned to the church.

'Uthup Chettan is helpful,' one of the men noted. 'He'll ask the vicar to contact the hospital and speed up the release.'

Black coffee was served by the nearest neighbour to those gathered. Chacko took the opportunity to remind his son that he was due to meet his sister after the late morning mass. Sunny was meanwhile sitting beside Bobby on a bed in an adjoining room. Recognising the need for the boys to be together, Chacko decided to walk to church himself to meet his daughter.

As he descended the steps, the neighbour who had served the coffee walked with him and explained that he was preparing lunch for the family. Chacko, unable to speak, listened as the man continued:

'Benny was generous to us. It seems this tragic incident is linked to a conspiracy at the co-operative bank. Benny had accused the Secretary, Shashankan Nair, of financial irregularities.'

Chacko gave no reply. The neighbour pressed on. 'Benny was only a board member. He should have been made Secretary, if not for the interference of the panchayat president.'

Chacko, still silent, offered no comment as they reached a small junction where the neighbour went his separate way. The man invited Chacko to his home, but he declined and continued on towards the church.

Within an hour Chacko was back at Benny's house. A few people were waiting on the road, and the crowd in the courtyard had grown larger. By then, the late Sunday liturgy was almost over. Chacko told Celine to return home and look after Sunil, so that his wife would be free to attend the funeral mass later.

Leelamma, Benny's wife, refused to eat or drink until her husband's body was returned. On hearing of his sudden death the previous night, she had fainted. During which Chacko and a few friends visited them. When Chacko saw Bobby and his younger sister go hungry, he and Sunny had taken them to a neighbour's house for food. Chacko himself had declined to eat but made sure the children were fed. He thanked the neighbour for their kindness but offered no comment when the man began speaking about Benny's strained political relations.

By late morning, the family was still waiting. Before noon, Uthup Chettan returned and reassured everyone that the body was on its way. The medical procedures had been completed, and the body released. He and a few others began preparing the courtyard for the final prayers.

When the coffin was finally carried into the house by Benny's colleagues, Leelamma collapsed once more and it took time to revive her. The coffin was brought inside for the family to pay their respects.

A large scar ran across Benny's face, above his left eye, sewn neatly but still visible. Leelamma and Bobby sobbed uncontrollably, their cries piercing the silence. Chacko turned his face away, unable to look at the body of his closest friend.

After the vicar, Fr Luke Theneth, arrived with other church officials, the body was moved to the courtyard. Leelamma clung desperately to the coffin until she was gently pulled away. Friends and family came forward to pay their last respects.

As the final prayers at home were about to begin, Leelamma and her children were brought out to the courtyard. Overcome with grief, she cried loudly until the vicar himself grew impatient. Two reverend nuns were then asked to comfort her. Sitting quietly on either side of her, their gentle words and prayerful presence finally helped her calm down.

As more people arrived to pay their final respects, the vicar and his assistants began the prayers. During the service, the vicar delivered a longer sermon in which he praised Benny's love of the natural world and his generosity towards the underprivileged. He recalled how Benny had inspired many farmers in the village to adopt modern agricultural practices to improve grain production and feed more families. He concluded by declaring that Benny's premature passing was an irreplaceable loss to both his family and the villagers. He prayed for justice to be done to his soul and assured the family that the church would support them through these trying times. He further promised that those responsible for Benny's untimely death would face consequences.

It was difficult for the sisters to control Leelama as the coffin was taken from their home. As the funeral procession moved towards the church, nature itself seemed to grieve. Strong gusts of wind swept through the air. Sunny led the procession, swinging the smoking thurible, while Bobby rang the hand bell. When the first clear chime echoed, the sound waves struck against the still air, and the atmosphere darkened. Heavy black clouds gathered, blocking the light. Flashes of lightning tore across the sky, followed by peals of thunder, but no rain fell. A few in the crowd were afraid, but the vicar reassured them, and the procession continued.

Although an open jeep was provided to transport the body, Chacko and his friends insisted on carrying Benny's remains on their shoulders. As Leelama was unable to walk, family members helped her and her baby daughter into the jeep. With the vicar seated at the front, they reached the church before the procession. A small group of parishioners had been waiting to raise a significant issue about Benny's funeral. The group was led by Thomas Joseph, a schoolteacher and Chacko's neighbour. Because of his prominent standing in the community, the vicar could not prevent him from speaking. After a brief meeting at the presbytery, the vicar proceeded with the prayers in the church.

He instructed the large gathering to line both sides of the entrance to receive the coffin. Members of the local communist party placed a red shawl and red roses upon it. The coffin was then brought into the church for the bidding prayers. In his homily, the vicar reminded the congregation that entry into heaven requires participation in all the

Catholic sacraments. Through baptism, he said, the Trinity seal is placed upon the human body, transforming it into the temple of the Holy Spirit. Every Christian should honour their body in life, and the church should respect the bodies of the departed as well as their eternal resting places. The resurrection of the dead, he declared, was a hope unique to Christianity: at the Lord's return, the earthly body would be restored to the soul. The vicar prayed for pardon for those who had failed to receive the sacraments in time, asking God to forgive their sins and welcome them with grace.

After the church prayers, the coffin was carried to the cemetery. It was then that Thomas Joseph's group demanded that the body be buried outside the grounds, claiming Benny was a sinner and not a true Christian. They alleged that he had not been a church member, had neglected the weekly sacred mass, and had not confessed his sins before death. They argued that such a man could not be laid to rest among the faithful awaiting eternal peace.

Leelama, however, stood up for her husband. A regular member of the church, she defended him through tears: 'My husband was baptised and received the sacraments here. We were only married at another church because of my grandfather's request.' Her words were met with strong support from the crowd, many of whom demanded that Benny be granted a proper Christian burial.

The communist activists also backed her, maintaining neutrality but affirming that the family's wishes must be respected. They urged that Benny's remains be interred with full dignity. The debate grew heated, with arguments breaking out. A large number of mourners, however, remained silent, unwilling to raise their voices. Elders pleaded with the vicar to intervene, while Thomas Joseph's faction pressed him to enforce strict Catholic rules.

The vicar looked at the grieving family. 'It is nearly sunset, and the body must be buried before dark,' he reminded them. He stressed the importance of confession before death, calling it an essential sacrament. He explained that the Church, through the authority given by Christ, had the power to absolve sins. Unlike baptism, absolution was judicial in nature: sins were pardoned when believers confessed and received penance. Administered solely by a priest, this sacrament brought forgiveness only when sought with repentance and grace.

Turning to Leelama, he asked, 'When did your husband last receive the holy sacraments?' Leelama fell silent, her face stricken. Members of her support group urged the vicar not to humiliate a young widow in her grief, reminding him that she had two small children.

Finally, Leelama spoke through her tears. 'My husband was mentally and physically tormented from his childhood. His mother's last wish was that all of her family should rest together for eternity.' She pleaded with the vicar: 'You must honour her wish. My husband must be buried in the family vault, with full honours.'

The vicar paused before replying. 'Christians are promised eternal life, gained by following Jesus and receiving the holy sacraments,' he said. 'It is my duty to uphold the promises made to both the living and the dead, for all are children of God.'

At this, some members of the crowd began chanting, sensing that the vicar might deny Leelama's request. The opposition, led by Thomas Joseph, stood firm, insisting on the church's authority and doctrines.

The vicar proposed a solution, mindful of the fading light and the need for a mutually acceptable conclusion. 'The Church has the authority to reserve certain cases. Benny Mathew was born a Catholic and received his sacraments in childhood. His unexpected and tragic death could not have been foreseen. His mortal remains may therefore be interred in the paupers' graves, since his wife and children are devout Catholics.'

Leelama broke down once more on hearing this decision. Chacko leaned towards her and said gently, 'There is a conspiracy against Benny, still unfolding. Let us accept the vicar's suggestion for now, and later we will transfer his remains to the family vault. The paupers' graves are not truly segregated from the others.'

The vicar was highly respected, and the majority of the mourners agreed with his decision. His supporters persuaded Mr Thomas Joseph, though reluctantly, to accept the compromise. Amid the unrest, Chacko and a few of Benny's close associates carried the body to the cemetery, where it was laid to rest just before sunset.

Leelama's grief was uncontainable. Chacko consoled her with quiet determination: 'Justice will come in time. The natural world does not easily reconcile itself with humanity's rusted rituals.'

Chapter 9

Chacko suggested that his wife and son return home immediately following the burial. He and a few others expressed apprehensions about the prospect of excavating a new grave at the negotiated burial site during the altercation. To their astonishment, a member of the church committee directed the undertaker to excavate a grave in the paupers' grave area in advance. The anticipated delay was swiftly followed by a decision, as influential community officials objected to Benny's burial in their family vault. Chacko was aware that the experienced undertaker was more likely to follow the directives of the parish priest than any other individual. The vicar had raised the issue through the parish council much earlier, and soon the highly influential individuals began to make threats.

Chacko walked with Leelama and her children back to their house. The family was in great distress. The head of the family and primary breadwinner had died in a horrible way, and they could not bury him in the family vault. Chacko helped Bobby, and others helped Leelama and the child climb the rocky stairs. A kind neighbour cooked for everyone who returned from the funeral. An older woman and Chacko convinced Leelama to eat dinner so that she might have the strength to face the hard realities ahead. Soon, everyone returned home, and nature wept with torrential rain.

Chacko was confined for an hour before going home due to the intensity of the rainfall. Thick clouds covered the sky, making it difficult to see in the dark. The neighbours prepared live fire torches for those who intended to return. When dried and bundled coconut leaves are set alight, the flame lasts significantly longer and casts light over a greater distance. For frequent use, residents in isolated places keep multiple bundles of these natural torches on hand.

As Chacko walked towards his home in the darkness, he realised how the environment in the area had changed over the years. The natural surroundings were being replaced by an increasing number of concrete dwellings, limiting the survival of native species. Houses that were significantly larger than necessary for smaller families consumed much more built-up space. The road ahead was partially visible by the light that emanated from adjacent houses.

Chacko traversed the irregular country roads, which were once pristine wilderness but had since been transformed into rubber plantations and farmlands. The introduction of high-yield cereals had increased production to meet the demands of the growing population. However, the quality of the cereals was diminished as soil nutrients were depleted through excessive farming. The natural environment continued to deteriorate as humans sought to satisfy their current needs. The late Benny Mathew had been passionate about the environment and dedicated his life to safeguarding it for the benefit of future generations.

Chacko Punnoose's parents and Benny Mathew's parents were once neighbours, and their families had resided in the same area for generations. Punnoose Mathai, Chacko's father, was a dedicated cultivator skilled in growing a particular variety of black pepper. The environment in that region was optimal for cultivating high-quality black pepper, a commodity in high demand worldwide. He possessed the ability to create novel variants but did not own sufficient land to produce them on a large scale. During that period, farming was the primary source of income for numerous families.

The conversion of untamed areas into agricultural land was restricted. Some families relocated to the hilly regions of the Cardamom Highlands, part of the Western Ghats to the east. To cultivate the land, migrants were forced to contend with wild animals, particularly elephants. The area became less popular due to frequent attacks from wild boars, leopards, and tigers, which posed serious threats to migrant cultivators. Many families were attracted by the news of extensive unused land in the Malabar region. Compared to the Western Ghats, Malabar was less hilly and required less fear of wildlife.

Punnoose Mathai was among the many families who relocated to Malabar in the hope of acquiring more land with fewer investments. Punnoose and his entire family moved to Malabar after selling their property to Benny Mathew's parents. At the time of relocation, Chacko was five years old and had two elder sisters. Through hard work, the newly acquired land was successfully transformed into cultivable farmland. Punnoose cultivated a variety of spices, including his preferred black pepper plants. When the unfortunate pandemic struck, the family was just beginning to stabilise, with all members working diligently.

The conversion of forest land into farmland had reduced the availability of water in certain areas, creating stagnant pools that became breeding grounds for mosquitoes. Consequently, malaria spread rapidly among the population. Punnoose was the first to contract the infection and was confined to bed for several weeks. His wife isolated the children and meticulously cared for him upon recognising the perilous situation. Soon after Punnoose recovered from the illness, his wife contracted it. She was taken to a poorly equipped health centre and placed in isolation. Her condition deteriorated, progressed to a coma, and she never recovered due to the unavailability of effective medication and the absence of proper nursing care.

Punnoose's physical and emotional health were severely impaired by grief after his wife's death. He was unable to provide consistent care to the vegetation he cherished. The household income dwindled, and overall yields declined due to irregular pest control, lack of water, and insufficient fertiliser. He was compelled to divide his income-generating farmland among his children. Both daughters were married off with portions of land, and the income from their shares was forfeited.

Balancing income and expenditure became a challenge for the father-and-son duo. Debts to the bank and money owed to relatives accumulated over time. When Chacko reached maturity, his father was diagnosed with tuberculosis, further weakening his condition. Unable to afford the costs of medical treatment and attendant care, Chacko was forced to sell part of his land to finance the expenses. Punnoose, his compassionate father, passed away four years after being diagnosed with the terminal illness, as the available medication proved ineffective.

Chacko was tormented by the high costs of medical treatment and other household expenses. He made the difficult decision to sell the house and the remaining land to pay off his debts. Mary, his childhood friend, became the centre of his affection during these difficult times. Mary's parents disapproved of their relationship, particularly after he became poor. The influence of Chacko's sisters proved unsuccessful, and he and Mary made the painful decision to elope from Malabar and return to Kaineervila.

Chacko reflected on his hard past as he walked up to his neighbour's front gates. There were lights on and loud shouting and arguing. The light from the ignited wrapped coconut leaf torch was dimming as it got closer to the end. He threw the bundle up in the air a few times to get it to light up again. He needed enough lighting to see the way down the steps in front of his house. He saw a dim light from his house and summoned his wife. She opened the front door and let the lights shine on the stepping stones while she waited. She gave him a bath towel and a bar of soap and remarked, 'The water might be cold now, but I left the fire going.'

He walked to the back of the house and quickly showered in the open area. She served the boiled rice and fish curry and he appreciated her, 'Fish curry tastes good, did the kids eat well?'

She replied, 'There wasn't enough time to buy fresh fish, so I used the dried fish.' Then she added, 'Sunny is still upset,' which made him worry. She didn't anticipate a response, and Chacko quietly finished his dinner.

They both sleep on a modest bed made of wooden planks and a basic mat made of dried screw pine leaves. The mat is rough, yet it works as a small cushion between the body and the hard surface of the bed. People put these natural mats on wooden floors and use them on the rough floor to make it more comfortable. These mats are affordable, long-lasting, and comfortable to use all year long.

Mary's parents were relocated to Malabar, and they were raised in a location that was not their original home. Several migrants relocated to other areas due to the repetitive threats to their lives and their farmlands from wild animals and the absence of roads. Abraham Mathan, Mary's father, married and relocated from Wayanad to reside with his wife's family in a distinct region of Malabar. Varghese Mathan, Abraham's sibling, was a political activist who advocated for the rights of impoverished and homeless farm workers. He campaigned and led numerous agitations against influential landlords who harassed and tormented the poor. Abraham did not attend school during his childhood, while Varghese attended primary school. Varghese was fortunate to receive additional education at the secondary school. Following this, he participated in communist student movements and subsequently became a hard-core communist who advocated for the rights of impoverished people.

Abraham, Mary's father, attempted to discipline his brother and subsequently urged him to return to the traditional farmer's lifestyle. At some point, Varghese became weary of the internal politics and power struggle within his communist organisation and returned to his home to resume a normal existence. He was arrested for a crime for which he was not implicated or committed from his home. The police detained him for more than six months during the investigation. He was reunited with his companions from a different state while in police custody. It was then that he came to the realisation that the police inspector who is currently overseeing the investigation is preparing for revenge. The inspector is a close relative of a prominent landlord from their village, and they were collaborating to avenge previous atrocities against them.

The country's transition to independence resulted in the abolition of compulsory labour and the implementation of numerous measures to guarantee labour welfare, including equitable compensation. Enacting legislation that guarantees an appropriate wage for farm labourers and unskilled labourers. Affluent landlords within remote areas were unwilling to adopt new welfare measures. A landlord's son was assaulted several years ago for racially abusing a low-income labourer.

A few years later, the landlord's son committed suicide for an entirely different reason. The landlord attributed the incident to the previous assault and was determined to avenge. When Varghese and other prisoners were conveyed to the court, the inspector of police devised a plan to assassinate him. Their strategy failed, as the van that was transporting the captives was overturned prior to reaching the designated location. Until Varghese recovered from the injuries he sustained in the accident, he and three of the other inmates sought refuge in the forest and resided with impoverished adhivasis. There was unconfirmed information that he escaped to a nearby state and was slain in a police force encounter a few years later. He never returned home, and the property was inherited by Mary's father, Abraham, upon the death of her grandfather, Mathan.

Mary was the oldest of Abraham's six children. She had three younger sisters and two younger brothers. Abraham made the initiative to provide his kids with the best education possible, but Mary wasn't very good at it. She quit school early and assisted with chores around the house. She took care of the animals on the farm and was adept at milking cows and goats. She also had to take the milk to the co-op stores in their little town, and she became friends with Chacko. When they were young, they were drawn to each other, and as the years went by, their relationship grew deeper and more intimate. Her siblings got a better education and migrated to different regions of the country because she worked hard. Her father was equally well-liked in society and took part in activities that helped the community grow.

Abraham, too, wanted to help the needy, but he did it in a different way than his brother, who was rebellious. He cooperated with the police and was open to trying new things, which helped keep the calm in the area. He learnt from his brothers' rigid values and sought a democratic way to share responsibilities. He thought that sharing power was necessary to keep political stability, avoid violent confrontations, and stop the tyranny of the majority. He valued the influence of landlords and important community leaders and pushed for more people to get involved.

Abraham Mathan was successful with his very adaptable outlook on everyday life. A harmonious society, which may strive for unity within a divided society, was the foundation of his beliefs. He encouraged critical thinking in their sophisticated communication as well as acceptable and successful social communication. With his strong linguistic abilities, Abraham was able to interact well with his family and others around him. He was eager to find new farming techniques and quick to adopt more effective ones to boost revenue. He was well-liked since he was glad to share his established expertise with others.

Abraham Mathan devised an indigenous method to preserve paddy seeds year-round. The rice grains were previously loaned to impoverished and medium-level farmers by their landlords during the seed-sowing process. The rich landlords impose exorbitant prices on the rice grains due to their ability to store them for an extended period. Landlords enforce their ownership of over half of the harvest, leaving little for diligent producers. The landlords consistently demand their portion, regardless of the quantity of crops harvested, which forces farmers to pursue alternative methods. Landlords constructed large, robust timber boxes that were shielded from extreme heat, cold, and pests. Additionally, farmers who had sufficient land were having trouble effectively storing the crops for the upcoming years.

Abraham Mathan excavated a large, square-shaped pit in the ground and constructed a protective wall around it using mud bricks. Then, a second layer of protection was added by utilising desiccated paddy hay. Another basket was constructed from dried coconut leaves to ensure the rice seeds were stored securely. The ground storage facility, however, was not adequately protected from torrential rain and was also susceptible to pest infestations. The seedlings were damaged because of moisture accumulation and insufficient ventilation.

Next, he developed an alternative approach, to construct a cylindrical storage facility. Using charred mud bricks, he built a firm platform. Thereafter, using dried hay, several smaller rings were made and fixed on the platform, each reaching a height of approximately five feet. Again, green coconut fronds were used to construct a large basket that would fit within the rings. The paddy grains were promptly placed into the basket, and a canopy was constructed from dried paddy plants to safeguard the top. The new method proved more effective, and farmers from that area and neighbouring communities appreciated his efforts to create a secure and affordable storage facility.

Abraham's popularity among the farming community increased as a result of the sustainability and affordability of the new storage facility. Additionally, he played a crucial role in establishing a farmers' cooperative society. Through it, they were able to access a broader market and secure better prices for their produce. In the absence of improved storage facilities, numerous producers had previously suffered product losses.

However, access to multiple markets proved advantageous for many. He was elected to the municipal government at the community's request, thereby effectively representing them. His proposals to promote sustainable agricultural methods and provide assistance to farmers were widely welcomed. However, when he opposed corruption and policies that undermined public welfare, his standing within the governing community declined. His political leaders did not appreciate his campaign against corrupt government employees.

His crusade against the corrupt local government officers led to further complications, including the fabrication of fraudulent allegations against Abraham. Staff at the local land registry office lodged complaints that Abraham's father-in-law had previously encroached upon government land that must be returned. The government claimed ownership of a small portion of genuine land for which Abraham had been paying taxes. Although he possessed the necessary documentation to verify ownership, they insisted that the land he held fell under the jurisdiction of the forest department. The officers ignored Abraham's request to conduct a formal land survey to verify their claims and instead instructed him to vacate the disputed portion of land.

It took several years to resolve the lawsuit Abraham filed against the local government in the civil courts. During this time, local officials continued to torment him, despite his strong support from the community. Gradually, he withdrew from public life and became more involved in religious activities, weary of political repercussions and false accusations. He continued to advocate love and harmony within the community, but he could not reconcile himself to his elder daughter's affection for Chackochan.

Abraham was unable to accept the fact that his elder daughter had eloped, and he experienced severe mental trauma that partially paralysed him. Despite receiving treatment for an extended period, he never recovered and ultimately succumbed to medical complications.

Mary was treated with kindness by her mother, who provided both emotional and material support. She instructed her other children to stand by Mary whenever needed.

93

Chapter 10

For the inhabitants of this extraordinary world, each day is a new beginning. It is frequently another opportunity to recommence their daily routines and maintain their existence in this world. Each day commences with routine activities, followed by a return to their own lifestyle. The commoners, in contrast to the all-knowing, believe that the mighty sun orbits them, resulting in a precious day following an indolent night. On the opposite side of the globe, the moon rises as the sun descends.

With the exception of humans, none of the living organisms in this world of marvels are concerned about the laborious tasks that await them shortly after sunrise. Their routines are influenced by any modifications to their living environment, and for some, it signifies a new beginning. The routines of birds and small animals are influenced by changes in the atmosphere. They are able to locate an effortless supper due to the early sunlight brought by clear skies. Although cloudy skies are a nuisance for predators, they allow nightcrawlers more time to flee to safety. Habitat changes present opportunities for some, but challenges for others.

Mary rose before the sun appeared over the eastern horizon the next day, as she always did, and resumed her routine. She called Sunny's name over and over until he asked Sunil whether he was wet again. Celine reminded him a few times, and then he was ready to go to the town coffee shop with a bottle of goat's milk, as he always did. The sun's rays shone through the neighbours' cocoa plantations, and the sky was clear. Sunny had no trouble climbing the stepping stones to cross the stone wall in front of their house. Mary kept an eye on him until he crossed and disappeared to the other side.

Sunny walked past the neighbour's mansion and, to his relief, the gate was closed. The bungalow's narrow path gradually widened and joined the country road, which was, as usual, desolate at that hour. He noticed movement not far ahead as the light from the red eastern horizon illuminated the roadside wildflowers, allowing him to see clearly. He continued, taking a deep breath and keeping a vigilant watch for any sudden appearances. His prediction was accurate; he soon approached Lovely Thomas, the youngest daughter of the neighbour.

'Sunny, I have been waiting for you to turn up; I knew you would be on your way.'

She wore a headscarf, indicating she was en route to the church. He glanced at her; she was truly breathtaking, particularly with her veil. He continued walking towards her, and soon she began to walk closely alongside him.

The silence stretched between them for a moment before Lovely broke it. 'Do you happen to know how Bobby Mathew died?'

Sunny thought for a moment and replied with a question, 'I don't know.' He followed up, 'Did you happen to be there at the funeral yesterday?'

The answer was spontaneous: 'I'm not allowed to attend other people's funerals.' She then explained, 'Dad told everyone not to go, it would be too moving and emotional, especially for children and girls.'

He looked at her again, unsure of how to respond, and walked on in silence. Then she suddenly asked another question. 'How is Celine?'

Sunny immediately froze, stopped in the middle of the road, and looked at her before replying, 'She's fine, why do you ask?'

Lovely didn't stop or look at him but continued walking ahead, whispering, 'I was just curious. I haven't talked to her in a while.'

Then they heard the distant sound of a bell chiming. Lovely looked around, and Sunny assured her, 'That's the regular bullock cart that transports the village's necessities.'

He looked at her once more and raised his doubt, 'Why are you alone at this time?' He paused and elaborated, 'Typically, you are with your mother or brothers.'

She appeared somewhat uneasy, but responded confidently, 'I am an adult and capable of managing my own affairs.'

Sunny was certain those were not the genuine reasons, as her father was exceedingly protective, not only of her but of the entire family. Mr Thomas Joseph prohibited all members of his household from engaging in social activities with strangers, even those from their own village.

Lovely walked forward a few steps before turning around and placing her hands on his shoulders. 'Look, if you need anything, don't hesitate to ask me, I'm here to help you all,' she said firmly, staring down at him; she was much taller than he was.

Sunny sensed she wasn't sincere. Bewildered, he stared at her pale face. Her expressionless features suggested she was sad and deeply troubled by something she could not openly express.

Sunny was unsettled, not by her assurance, but by her manner and the way she stood above him. Feeling uneasy, he turned his head away, lowered his shoulder, and stepped back slightly. 'I'm fine. Don't touch me again,' he remarked, continuing to walk towards the town centre.

Lovely stood still for a while and called after him, 'Sunny, forget it, I just want to assure you that you don't need to hide anything from me.' She then followed him and, realising his discomfort, added softly, 'Sunny, please listen, don't tell anyone. It will harm everyone.' Sunny continued walking ahead without paying attention or turning back.

When they reached the side road that led to the church, Sunny was startled and chose not to look back to see whether Lovely was following him or heading to the church.

Soon, he reached the teashop.

'Thank God you're on time,' said Pillechan. 'Otherwise, I would have lost the customers who were waiting.'

Three stout men were sitting there, one with a long beard, and the other two with thick black moustaches. One of them stroked the tip of his beard and gazed ferociously at Sunny, while the other two watched. Sunny asked Pillechan to return the bottle as soon as possible.

Pillechan, more friendly than usual, said politely, 'Sunny, don't worry, sit down.'

Then he offered the delicacy, 'Have this neyyappam; it's fresh and very tasty.' Neyyappam is prepared with rice flour and a variety of other delectable spices, fried in coconut oil. The freshly made snack contained crisp fried coconut pieces that Sunny enjoyed chewing.

Pillechan swiftly prepared his special cardamom-rich coffee, added boiled goat's milk for his new customers, and reminded them, 'Pailey should be on the way, could be here anytime.'

One of the guests nodded, while the others sipped their coffee and enjoyed the freshly made neyyappam. Pillechan's wife typically prepared snacks at home for his early morning customers.

Sunny was acquainted with Pailey, who was also a close associate of the late Benny Mathew. He lived on the opposite side of the village, over the hilly area, and was widely known as 'Kunnumpurath Pailey' by the villagers. When the men noticed the boy was listening, one of them prompted Pillechan, who quietly handed him the emptied milk bottle.

Sunny soon crossed the road that led to the church. He reflected on his conversation with Lovely and her untimely assurances. His thoughts were disturbed by her repeated promises of unconditional support, anytime, to everyone. Her father was extremely protective of his family, constantly monitoring their routines and, when necessary, controlling their activities and attendance at public functions. It was peculiar to encounter Lovely in such an isolated location, and it was clear that she had purposefully waited for him at that unexpected hour.

The primary source of revenue for Sunny's family was the income generated from his father's work at their rubber plantations. Occasionally, his mother received some financial compensation for her domestic duties. At times, they also purchased goat's milk and eggs from their own home. Their interactions with their neighbours were cordial, but they were not regarded as equals.

On the way, Sunny passed the big mango tree, which, at that time of year, yielded delicious fruit. Around the tree, he looked for ripe and fallen mangoes. His brother, Sunil, would be thrilled to have one of those organic treats at any time of day. He was walking down the road when all of a sudden there was a rush of air, and he saw Kunnumpurath Pailey racing towards him. With a white towel in his right hand and barely a shred of trousers on, Pailey ran at full speed.

Sunny was terrified by the sight; he couldn't believe it. Pailey was almost flying, his legs barely touching the ground, his arms slicing through the air as if he were pushing it backwards. Sunny stopped in shock and hid behind the big mango tree. In an instant, a gust of disturbed wind followed as Pailey ran past. Watching him disappear towards the steep side of the village and vanish in seconds, Sunny trembled in fear as three strangers from the teashop came running after him. He dropped to the ground and closed his eyes in panic. As they passed the tree, he could hear their heavy breathing and the thud of their boots. They whispered hurriedly to one another as they ran.

Sunny waited for a while, listening to the strange sounds around him. After those tense seconds, the area grew quiet again. He took a deep breath and strained his ears; there were odd noises echoing faintly from both ends of the road. A strange, heavy silence lingered, the kind that settles after a storm. Then he acted swiftly, came out from his hiding place, and looked both ways. Seeing no one nearby, he began to run. He thought of Pailey's terrified sprint, how people in danger often find unnatural strength to escape. Mimicking Pailey's frantic run, Sunny flung his arms and legs as he dashed forward, too frightened to look back. He only stopped when he reached the stepping stones of the stone wall separating his home from the higher terrain above.

Chacko was drinking his usual black coffee when Sunny came bounding down the steps and nearly slipped.

'Sunny, be careful! What happened?'

Sunny almost fell on the porch and pleaded for water, which his mother quickly brought. Chacko helped him sit on the floor and drink slowly. After a moment, Sunny looked up at his father and said breathlessly, 'Three people were chasing Pailey Uncle, and he was running naked!'

Chacko looked shocked, then glanced at his wife and children, who were equally stunned. Sunny went on to explain what he had seen on his way home from the shop. He insisted, 'Nobody can outrun Pailey Uncle. He was flying, way ahead of the chasers. He must have escaped into the hill valley.'

Mary urged Chacko to be cautious, as he leaned back in his chair, which wobbled because of a loose leg.

Chacko stared at her and murmured, 'It's possible the police were pursuing Pailey. He may know something about Benny's unfortunate death.'

His wife abruptly intervened. 'Please refrain from discussing this matter at home. The children are sensitive.' She then turned to Sunny and said firmly, 'Now, forget about it and get ready for school.' As she walked towards the kitchen, she added, 'And don't mention this to anyone, especially your friends at school. You haven't seen anything, nor did anything happen.'

The family quickly resumed their daily routine. Their neighbour, Mr Thomas Joseph, appeared on the higher ground in front and called out, 'Chacko, what happened? You haven't tapped the rubber trees today. The bark will dry up, and the trees will stop producing latex sap.'

Chacko offered a polite apology. 'Sorry, sir, I was extremely tired and returned home late last night.'

It was clear that Mr Thomas was dissatisfied with the answer. To conceal his displeasure, he changed the subject. 'How are Leelamma and her children? Are you planning to visit them again today?'

Chacko replied promptly, 'Yes, we are visiting them today. I offered to take them to Benny's tomb for prayers.'

Thomas appeared uncertain, hesitated briefly, and then departed abruptly without another word.

Sunny had nearly finished his breakfast when Celine entered the kitchen. He noticed bruise marks just below her left ear. Frowning, he asked, 'What happened? Did you fall and get that bruise?'

Celine tried to ignore him and walked out, but Mary, having overheard, came in and examined her daughter's face closely.

'Mother, are you mad?' Celine protested. 'I told you, it happened when I was trying to stop Sunil from falling.' She turned to Sunny. 'I'm not in pain, it's healing already.'

Mary was unconvinced but decided to let it go and resumed her household chores.

Later, Mary agreed to go with Chacko to visit Leelama and her children to take them some food. However, Sunil felt unwell as they were getting ready, so Mary stayed behind to care for him. Celine and Sunny went to school, while Chacko set off on foot, carrying the food to Benny Mathew's house.

To save time, he took a shortcut through the wild paths, as he was already running late. On the way, he passed a small rubber-processing shed that had recently been built but was not yet in use. The plantation nearby was still too young to tap. It was nearly midday when he walked past the shed, and someone inside suddenly whispered his name. At first, he ignored it and kept walking, but then the voice called again, louder this time, followed by tapping on the door.

Chacko quickly turned back and saw that the door was bolted from the outside.

'Who are you? Why are you locked in?' he asked.

'Chacko, keep your voice down,' came the muffled reply.

Chacko froze for a moment, then composed himself and whispered back, 'What happened? Who locked you in?'

Chacko didn't hear anything from within, so he picked up a stone and began striking the lock. It wasn't strong and broke open after a few blows. The door swung open quickly, and Pailey rushed out to relieve himself. He had a white towel draped over his shoulders and was wearing striped knickers.

'Chacko dear, I'm very hungry,' Pailey begged. 'I haven't even had my morning coffee yet. They beat me up there, and now they're chasing me.'

Chacko couldn't believe what he was seeing. Whatever his son had witnessed that morning was true. He quickly handed the food to Pailey, who sat on the floor and ate ravenously. Pailey struggled to swallow the boiled rice with coconut chutney and looked around for water. Chacko gently rubbed his back and said, 'Slow down, take a deep breath, or you'll choke.'

After finishing the meal, Pailey became more alert and aware of the danger he was in. He pleaded for help, saying, 'Vasu cheated me.' He took a deep breath before continuing, 'He locked me up, and must have informed the police by now.'

Chacko looked blank, uncertain what to think, until Pailey explained.

Pailey had made his usual trip to the teashop for his morning coffee, unaware of the danger awaiting him there. The strangers were already present, though he couldn't tell if they had been expecting him. As soon as his coffee was served, one of them grabbed him and accused him of killing Benny Mathew. They demanded to know who his accomplices were and who else was involved. Without any further questioning, the three men began to beat him.

Pailey thought they were going to kill him, it was a surprise attack, but he managed to shove them away and flee for his life. On his way, he encountered Vasavan Kaniyan, who led him to the nearby machine shed. Fortunately, the three strangers couldn't outrun him. Vasu recognised them as plainclothes police officers who had been interrogating several villagers.

Still shocked, Chacko asked why Vasu had locked him inside. Pailey, unsure, replied, 'Vasu told me to hide somewhere in the shed and promised he'd bring me some clothes.'

After a moment's hesitation, Pailey again begged for help, and Chacko couldn't refuse. He asked, 'Do you have anything to do with Benny's murder?'

Looking pale and indignant, Pailey replied, 'Benny helped me many times, how could I ever think of harming him?'

Pailey's next revelation stunned Chacko. 'But I know it has something to do with the bank scams. There were strangers in the village the day before, or maybe even several days before, Benny's murder.'

Chacko remained silent, unable to find any reason to doubt him. Pailey asked for clothes and assistance to evade the police. Chacko led him to a large tree covered with enormous leaves and told him to hide there until he returned with clothing. Before leaving, Chacko made sure to use the same lock to secure the machine shed.

He hurried on, trying to make up for lost time, but by the time he reached Leelama's house, Benny's widow, she and her children had already gone with other relatives to pray at Benny's grave. When they returned, Chacko promised further help and support. Leelama seemed calmer and more composed, having regained her strength to face the challenges ahead.

She mentioned that there had been some strangers at the cemetery, observing others during the prayers. They hadn't spoken or asked questions. Chacko warned her to be cautious, explaining that the police had stepped up their investigations. However, he said nothing about Pailey or the pursuit.

After borrowing a half-sleeved shirt and one of Benny's dhotis, Chacko made his way back to the isolated machine room. He remained alert, constantly checking to ensure no one was following him. From a distance, he saw Vasu and three others standing in front of the shed, confirming his suspicion that Vasu was a traitor.

Chacko immediately hid behind the trees and watched carefully. He was certain they were searching the surrounding area for Pailey. It was possible they had already discovered that someone had helped him escape and might soon intensify their search. Realising that Pailey was naked and defenceless up in the treetop, Chacko's first instinct was to leave before anyone recognised him.

He waited patiently for them to move away before shifting to a better hiding spot. Convinced that the shed would remain under watch, he finally approached Pailey, handed him Benny's clothes, and asked whether he recognised the men who had been chasing him.

Pailey confirmed that they were indeed the same three strangers and assured Chacko that, even if caught, he would never reveal his name or the help he had received. After gratefully accepting a small amount of cash from Chacko, the two men went their separate ways.

Chapter 11

Chacko went to Mr Thomas Joseph's house next door to ask for help and advice. Once again, he took a longer route to avoid running into people and to cover his tracks. He was confident that the police would question him soon, and he needed to consult someone experienced. Pailey was now a suspect who had either escaped or run away from the police, and meeting or assisting him by accident could make matters worse for Chacko.

Pailey was physically fit, with shoulders broader and heavier than normal. He had a bald head and short hair on the sides. People were often intimidated by his appearance, though those who knew him agreed that he was harmless and rather timid. He was also an alcoholic who spent most of his money on drink and food. His mother had raised him after his father's death many years ago. He was the only son in the family. His marriage hadn't lasted long, as his wife had run away with a neighbour to another village for no clear reason. His mother passed away not long afterwards. Since then, Pailey had spent most of his time at the local toddy bar, helping the barman and getting free toddy in return. The bar owner maintained order largely thanks to Pailey's intimidating presence and willingness to assist.

Chacko was certain that Pailey was hiding from the police out of fear rather than guilt. The police might want to question him, and their methods were known to be intimidating to common people. They often used harsh tactics, so men like Pailey defended themselves by evading or fleeing from them. He had never been involved in a police investigation before. At times, he had argued with villagers over trivial matters, but there was never any indication of physical violence or threats. He spent most of his time in town or at the toddy bar rather than at home. He had been close to the late Benny Mathew, who had often provided him with money and support. Chacko was sure that any link between Pailey and the perpetrators of the murder was exceedingly unlikely.

In contrast, Vasavan Kaniyan, a social activist from their village, was associated with the political party that had once led the Indian independence movement. Vasu maintained relationships with most of the villagers owing to his popularity and familiarity. He might now use the situation to share what he knew, settle scores, or gain influence by assisting in the police investigation. In either case, it made Chacko more vulnerable, both to the police and to others involved. Without a doubt, Vasu was an opportunist who sought to capitalise on uncertainty, either to exact revenge or to seek personal benefit.

Vasu claimed that his political party was the only organisation capable of promoting development in all aspects of public life. He asserted that its policies benefited both the wealthy and the poor alike. He had once been elected as a ward councillor but was defeated by the late Benny Mathew in the most recent local elections. As Vasu was neither an experienced farmer nor a skilled labourer, he called himself a full-time social activist. His wife, Sumathi, worked as a domestic support worker at a nearby hospital, which served as their primary source of income. Vasu was president of the parent–teacher association at their local school, where his two young children studied.

He was also related to Raghavan Kaniyan, who held newspaper distribution rights, and had numerous relatives across the village.

It struck Chacko as strange that he had to wait so long after ringing the doorbell. Mr Thomas's wife, Achamma, opened the door, raised her eyes in question, and then Mr Thomas himself appeared. Achamma looked upset and quickly turned away. Locking the front door behind him, Thomas asked Chacko to sit down on the large porch. Chacko quickly noticed that Mr Thomas seemed deeply anxious and fearful of what might happen next. There was no doubt he was hiding something. Achamma's worried look and her swift retreat suggested unspoken tension between them.

Chacko explained his unexpected encounter with Pailey but deliberately kept his son's earlier experience a secret. He asked Mr Thomas for guidance. Mr Thomas, appearing somewhat relieved, hurried inside and returned with a glass of black coffee.

'Have this coffee, let me think for a moment,' he said.

Chacko waited quietly while sipping. Mr Thomas finally advised, 'From what I understand, the police are naturally focusing their investigation on potential suspects and will arrest the killers, it's a very serious murder case.' He turned towards the open door, which someone inside quickly closed, and continued, 'I suggest you cooperate with the police and answer only what they ask.'

After a pause, he warned, 'Don't mention your meeting with Pailey.'

Chacko hesitated. 'What if they ask about him?'

Thomas replied, 'Tell them you know him like anyone else in the village, but that you haven't seen him today. There's no need to mention your earlier encounter.'

Chacko found the advice practical and sincere. He stood up, thanked Mr Thomas for his timely counsel, and was about to leave when Mr Thomas spoke again.

'How is everyone at home? Let me know if you need anything.' He paused, then added, 'Wait, I'll get you some money. It could be useful for Leelamma as well.'

Chacko was astonished. Mr Thomas was usually cautious about giving money, though he was very generous to the church, where he served as head of the parish council. He slipped some notes into Chacko's hand and said, 'Please use it wisely, and tell me if you need anything else.'

Chacko couldn't refuse the kind offer; he needed money both for himself and to help Benny's family. Though he was too moved to express his gratitude fully, he smiled, thanked him again, and turned to leave. Mr Thomas stood on the porch, watching until Chacko passed through the large grilled gates of his mansion.

When Chacko reached home, Mary's brother, Joyachan, was waiting on the veranda. Mary was the first to ask about his whereabouts.

'Where did you go? Joyachan was about to leave.'

Joyachan quickly explained, 'I visited Leelamma after you left her house.'

His visit at that time once again caught Chacko off guard. He was aware that Joyachan's wife, Laly, was related to Leelamma. Chacko had been unable to inform them promptly about the horrific death.

Joyachan continued, 'Laly was distraught and wanted to accompany me, but she couldn't get leave from work.'

Laly, Joyachan's wife, was a primary school teacher at their village school. Mary served coffee to both men and suggested that Sunny might meet his friend Bobby after school. Then they heard a faint call from inside the house, and Mary rushed off, saying, 'Sunil's awake, he's not well and hasn't been sleeping properly.' The sound of crying stopped shortly afterwards.

Joyachan asked about the tragedy. 'How did this happen? That family has suffered so many heartbreaking incidents.'

Chacko was aware of the earlier tragedies that had taken place during his time in Malabar many years before. He tried to offer a few details.

'Benny had both social and political rivals. There were petty disagreements, but nothing life-threatening like this,' he said, pausing before continuing. 'He was a kind man, very supportive of many poor villagers.'

Joyachan asked about the earlier land boundary disputes involving Benny's parents and their neighbours. Since returning from Malabar, Chacko hadn't received any fresh information about those events.

'The prime accused, Preman Chettiar, committed suicide,' Chacko said. 'And his father, Sukumaran Chettiar, died of a mysterious illness.' He looked at Joyachan for more information.

Joyachan nodded. 'With the exception of Preman's wife and child, none of them survived. They moved to her parents' home.'

Chacko went on to describe what he knew of the incident. 'Sukumaran's daughter, Sumithra Chettiar, died in a fire along with Babychan Mathew. That tragedy was an eye-opener for Sukumaran, who later confessed to his own misdeeds against Benny's parents.'

He added, 'Benny once told me what little he knew, he was only a child then. The memory of his elder brother and the neighbour's daughter burning alive haunted him all his life.'

Joyachan sighed deeply. 'That horrible crime all started with a minor argument at the village toddy bar, where most farmers and daily-wage workers socialise.'

Before that, Kaineervila village had been a peaceful place where Christians and Hindus lived side by side in harmony. Both communities respected each other, and there had never been reports of one group trying to dominate the other.

Most Hindus followed a set of beliefs rooted in their ideology and identified themselves by their distinct castes, a system in which a person's family and birth star determined their place in society.

In Kaineervila, there were a few Nampoothiris, who had the right to lead worship at temples. Within the Hindu community, they were regarded as the most learned people; many were teachers or respected government employees. Most Hindus identified as Kshatriyas, warriors and merchants. Some belonged to the Nair community, which itself had several subgroups. Many labourers were Sudras, lower on the social ladder, while the Pulayans occupied the lowest rungs of the caste hierarchy and were found in both Hindu and Christian families.

The village of Kaineervila had long sustained a peaceful, self-reliant society. People lived simple, balanced lives, seeking fulfilment rather than wealth. They cooperated across faiths and classes, living with mutual respect and trust. Most were farmers, content with their way of life regardless of the duties associated with their caste. Only a few upper-caste Nampoothiris were strict vegetarians; the majority enjoyed a balanced diet that included vegetables, fish, and meat.

The villagers were fortunate to have abundant fresh water from the river and the several streams that flowed through their fields. The people of Kaineervila cherished the beauty of nature and lived healthy, tranquil lives.

The community celebrated both religious and social festivals together. The village had a Christian church and an old, grand temple dedicated to Lord Subramania Swami, as well as three smaller temples devoted to other deities.

It was commonly believed that Sri Subramania Swami regarded all women who visited his temple as his mother. The ten-day festival at the Swami temple attracted people from far and wide, and the final day, Arattu, was a spectacular event. Like many temples in the state, trained captive elephants were a central feature of the celebrations. A replica of the deity was placed upon a large golden howdah on the lead elephant's forehead. Skilled artisans crafted these ornate howdahs to fit each elephant's face and frame precisely.

The southern peninsula is a natural home for elephants, with its wetlands, forests, and grasslands. Most of them live healthy lives there. Many people wish to own elephants, as they can be used in numerous ways. Elephants kept in captivity are trained to move large pieces of wood so that they can be transported easily to sawmills. Most of these elephants are also paraded during temple festivals, while some are kept as trophies or symbols of pride. In the Hindu community, owning an elephant is a sign of wealth and authority. People in the village regard elephants as part of civilisation itself, as they play an important role in their celebrations. When elephants take part in major festivities, thousands of people gather to see them.

A large bull elephant from a nearby village was once brought in to move a wild jackfruit tree, unusually big, from Sukumaran Chettiar's land. The wild jackfruits from that tree were exceptionally tasty and popular among the neighbours, many of whom discouraged Sukumaran from cutting it down. However, Sukumaran was remodelling his house, and the head carpenter requested timber from a fully grown wild jackfruit tree. There were other suitable trees, but the carpenter insisted that wood from mature wild jackfruit trees would last much longer.

A skilled tree cutter felled the tree so that it would fall into a small creek rather than onto the nearby banana plantation. The stream's water was used for irrigation and served as the area's main source of fresh water. Cutting down the big tree impeded the natural flow of the stream and created a pond on the neighbouring land. Residents downstream began complaining about the water quality once the flow was disrupted.

Mathai Tharakan, father of the late Benny, owned a portion of the land where the tree had fallen. The boundary between the properties was disputed, and Mathai had acquired his share from Chacko's parents prior to their relocation to Malabar. Sukumaran assured Mathai that the enormous tree would be removed as soon as possible.

It took longer than expected to bring the elephant to move the fallen tree. During the delay, the pond grew larger, and a wide pool of water formed on Mathai's land. When the elephant finally arrived, there wasn't enough space for it to reach the tree. The elephant's regular mahout had been suspended for neglecting the animal and treating it harshly. The new mahout was unfamiliar with the elephant, which loved to bathe and play in cool river water.

The elephant soon approached the big fallen tree and stepped into the water. The mahout, seated on its back, tried hard to steer it towards the trunk. Frustrated that the animal wasn't obeying commands and kept walking deeper into the water, he used his bullhook, a sharp metal tool, to prod the edge of the elephant's ear. The elephant ignored the pain and continued towards the pool, its favourite place.

A crowd had gathered, and they began laughing at the mahout's inability to control the animal. This angered him further. He kept striking the elephant's ear until the metal hook became lodged beneath its tough skin, and he couldn't pull it free.

The elephant bellowed and shook violently in agony, trying to rid itself of the mahout. Each time the man tugged at the hook, it tore at the wound, causing greater pain. The elephant lifted its head and trunk, trumpeted repeatedly, and thrashed about. The onlookers, terrified by its cries and frantic movements, began screaming and running away. The noise and panic further agitated the elephant. At last, the mahout lost his grip on the bullhook, which remained stuck in the animal's ear. The elephant then quietened, the pain easing slightly, and moved to the centre of the pool. Still, it kept shaking its head and body to dislodge the mahout, who clung on for his life. He knew that if he fell, the elephant might kill him with its tusks or crush him beneath its heavy feet.

Once the elephant reached the middle of the pool, it began to calm down. The mahout remained on its back, and those watching were unsure how to help. Mathai Tharakan suggested tying a large rope to a nearby tree so that the mahout could reach it and climb off quickly. Someone warned that the elephant was faster than any man, and that even a short delay could be fatal.

They eventually tied a rope between two trees and ran a second rope across the middle for support. With the doubled ropes, it would be easier for the mahout to escape. After several attempts, he managed to grab hold of the rope. People on the far side shouted loudly to distract the elephant, and the mahout swung himself across as fast as he could. The angry elephant tried to chase him, but the crowd pulled him safely out of the water and out of reach.

The great animal could run fast on solid ground, but it was hampered by the muddy pool. It raised its head, pointed its tusks, and sprayed water from its trunk towards the bank in fury.

The people by the pool kept making loud howling noises, which eventually drove the elephant back into the water. It stayed there for a long time, comforted by the coolness of the pool. The new mahout refused to go near it again, choosing instead to control it from the shore. Those present decided to leave the animal there overnight, and the mahout reluctantly agreed.

Mathai Tharakan, however, was displeased with the prolonged delay and the mahout's inability to control the beast.

The next morning, a bundle of bananas lured the elephant to the shore. The hungry animal ran towards the food and out of the pool. The mahout quickly chained it up. Once it had eaten enough, he was able to handle and lead it to the fallen tree. The tree was enormous, and the elephant couldn't move it all at once. The tree cutters used their handsaws to chop it into halves. The elephant then dragged the logs along the wider road that ran through Mathew Tharakan's farm, damaging part of his boundary fence in the process. Sukumaran promised to repair it, and Mathew believed him. Once the tree was removed, the stream that had been blocked began to flow normally again, and the large pool disappeared.

Two days later, wild mushrooms sprouted on the patch of ground where the water had drained. Many people from the community came to pick them, as there were enough for everyone. A small group of customers who ate fried mushrooms with coconut toddy at the local toddy bar soon fell ill. Some vomited, while others suffered diarrhoea and had to be taken to hospital.

A week later, one of those who had fallen sick confronted Sukumaran Chettiar, accusing him of flooding the land deliberately. Their quarrel turned into a heated argument, drawing others into the dispute. Soon, a physical fight broke out, and Sukumaran was injured. Some claimed Sukumaran had ignored the disputed boundary out of fear of Mathew Tharakan. Sukumaran maintained that the land legally belonged to the former owner, who had sold it to Mathew Tharakan.

Then one of the men, drunk and agitated, accused him of being too soft because his daughter was having an affair with Baby Tharakan, Mathew's elder son.

Sukumaran knew the two young people were close friends, they had lived next door to each other and had been companions since childhood. His daughter swore their relationship was purely platonic and nothing more. Mathew Tharakan, too, did not wish their friendship to become too intimate and had warned his son accordingly.

One of the drunks claimed to have seen them together in town and insisted they were keeping the relationship secret. Another man supported the allegation, saying Sukumaran was being too lenient and not upholding the standards of his own community. The accusations struck Sukumaran deeply, wounding his pride.

Sukumaran's son, Preman, was a quiet young man who rarely spoke and devoted himself to tending the family farm. Panchami Kaniyatti, the village midwife, claimed that Preman had been stillborn, and that she had brought him back to life. Some villagers blamed Panchami, saying it was her fault because she had prevented Preman's mother, Radhamma, from going to hospital when she needed to. They also blamed Sukumaran, who had been a drunkard at the time of his son's birth.

Sukumaran had been asleep when Preman was born, and a neighbour had called Panchami to assist with the delivery. For several years, Preman was unable to speak and only began talking at the age of five. He started school when he was eight but left after being mocked by other children, who called him dumb and deaf. Sukumaran taught him farming skills, and over time Preman became a capable and diligent cultivator.

By the time Preman was in his late teens, Sukumaran's second daughter, Sumithra, was born. She was bright and beautiful, completing her intermediate studies and teacher training on time. She was considering job offers from nearby schools when tragedy struck.

Chapter 12

The family sought advice and remedial therapy from Panchami Kaniyatti when the parents noticed that Preman was becoming less verbal. She was known for her ability to perform black magic and witchcraft to alleviate the effects of curses on individuals. She consented to conduct a pooja to appease their family divinity, whom their forebears had once worshipped. Once their family deity was satisfied, she reiterated that an additional pooja must be performed to appease the deity of wisdom. She clarified that the Goddess Saraswati, also known as Vak Devi, bestows the ability to speak upon her devotees. Additionally, she recommended that Preman and his parents engage in a variety of rituals and prayers to eliminate the demons challenging their financial prosperity.

Panchami suggested a three-stage prayer process that encompassed numerous rituals, beginning with prayers to appease their family deity, Chamundi, one of the manifestations of Mahakali. The fierce goddess defeated and killed the demons Chanda and Munda. Following that, special prayers and rituals were to be performed to appease Goddess Saraswati. Finally, the family members were to resume prayers to Lord Maha Vishnu to safeguard them from malevolent eyes. She advised that all family members prepare themselves to gain the most from the rituals. She stressed that only those devotees who maintained a pure body and mind would receive blessings from the gods. Radhamma's menstrual cycle was verified to agree on the dates for the chain of rituals. The goddesses would bless only those devotees maintaining both physical and mental purity ten days prior to the rituals.

Panchami Kaniyatti drafted directives for the family for the following seven days. She primarily recommended that all maintain tranquility and consume only plant-based food at home. All males were required to take a cold-water shower before sunrise each morning and offer prayers at the village temple. Each morning and evening, the lamp with seven threads had to be illuminated, beginning with one thread on the first day and continuing until all seven threads were lit on the seventh day. They were to recite from holy literature and conduct consistent morning and evening prayers at home. They should raise a rooster that was fully mature and had a variety of colours for sacrifice. The rooster had to be provided with timely feeds to maintain its vigour and kept in isolation for the next seven days. The sacrificial rooster had to be maintained in a virgin and robust state to produce pure and viscous sacrificial blood. The family deity could only be pleased with pure blood, and following the instructions was everyone's responsibility.

Sukumaran Chettiar obtained all the readily available materials for the rituals from the nearby town. Panchami agreed to provide a few of the peculiar items that were not easily available on the market. She visited them three days after they began the prescribed spiritual journey. This was to verify that the family adhered to the instructions and to assess the sacrificial rooster's condition. She inspected the four corners of the home, listened to the surrounding nature, and stared at the opposite house. Then she issued a warning:

'Your neighbours are malevolent; they intend to destroy your house through natural disasters such as lightning and fire.'

She pointed to neighbour's kitchen chimney and stated, 'They deliberately constructed it higher than the top of your house.'

Thereafter, Panchami rushed hysterically into the house and asked Sukumaran to promptly close the front door. She performed an internal inquiry and detected odours emanating from the ceilings and corners of the house. She continued to warn them with confidence, 'I can sense evil. Have you recently received cooked food from strangers?'

Radha thought for a moment before replying, 'Yes, the neighbours brought rice pancakes and duck roast curry on Easter Day.'

Panchami thought for a moment and asked, 'Did you return the vessels empty?'

Radha responded promptly, 'Yes, it was exceedingly delicious. We consumed it and promptly returned the empty vessels.'

Panchami looked at Radha and confirmed, 'Look, my instincts are always spot-on. You are a naïve woman, and your neighbours performed black magic on you using that food. You should have returned the vessels with something inside, and the evil omen would have gone back to them.'

She then turned to Sukumaran and reassured him, 'Do not be frightened. I am here now. Strictly follow my instructions, and I will redirect the evil spirit to their home.'

Panchami sat on a chair and requested a white sheet of paper and a pencil, which Radha promptly fetched. Panchami drew a depiction of Bhadrakali on the sheet and positioned it in the centre of their veranda. She then explained, 'In order to fortify the protective layer surrounding the house, the *kalam* must be significantly larger than I had anticipated, and the rituals must be more profound and powerful.'

Subsequently, she drew on the four corners of the page and glanced at them. 'I can complete this task alone; however, the results will be delayed. To achieve rapid and efficient results, I must invite an accomplice.'

Panchami continued, 'You have a multitude of problems here. Firstly, your family deity's power has diminished, and secondly, you invited a bad omen by accepting the food without reciprocating.' She paused briefly before continuing, 'The family deity can regain power and return to your home if the bad omen willingly departs. To achieve this, we must fulfil the demands of the bad omen.'

Panchami demanded advance fees for the rituals as both remained silent at her propositions. She justified her demand to buy more expensive materials and to make advance payments to her accomplice ensuring his availability. Sukumaran paid the sum right away without hesitation and begged her to get rid of the bad omen at the earliest.

Panchami continued to warn, 'The bad omen is very aggressive and is currently controlling Preman's tongue. If we don't get rid of it soon, it will attack other members.' She looked into their eyes and warned, 'One of you will become mute.'

Folding both hands, she stood still and prayed in front of a picture of their family's god on the wall. She pulled out a box of sticky ash from her purse. It was made from a mix of sandalwood and charcoal ash. She closed her eyes and prayed while holding the box close to her left chest with her right hand. After that, she opened the box, pulled out the sticky ash with her right-hand forefinger, and applied it to their foreheads, drawing a thick band. She cautioned, 'Don't take this off until tomorrow morning.'

She walked out but returned and warned again, 'If the blessed ash makes you feel itchy or uncomfortable, it's the bad omen trying to get you to wipe it off. Don't fall for its temptations.'

She firmly stated, 'When I walk out the front door, don't call me back. I won't come back.' Then she stormed out of the house, spat loudly facing their neighbours' house, and briskly walked towards the shining sun.

Fear surrounded them, and they developed a hatred for their wicked neighbour, who had virtually poisoned their food to destroy them. To survive, they strictly followed the instructions and stayed indoors for the subsequent days. They did not speak to their neighbours and kept their plans for the chain of rituals to themselves.

On the fifth day, Panchami came back to inspect the surroundings again. Dissatisfied, she warned them, 'Unfortunately, nothing has changed. It seems that the bad omen is stronger than before, and I can feel it.' To demonstrate what the terrible omen could do, she asked Radhamma to half-boil an egg from their own house. She sat firmly on the floor in front of their family deity's picture, placing her left foot flat on the ground and her right foot facing upwards.

She prayed with her palms together until the half-boiled egg was handed to her on a steel plate. She asked for two new leaves from the same Chinese hibiscus flower bud and a bunch of flame-of-the-woods flowers. Most homes had these flowers in their garden, so it was easy to get them. Panchami arranged the flowers around the boiled egg and prayed for a few more minutes. She took the boiled egg and, using her left-hand thumbnail, broke open the eggshell. The eggshell cracked, and a faint blue colour spread over the yolk inside. She showed them the spreading blue colour, then closed the shell and put the egg back on the plate. She asked them to close their eyes and pray with full devotion to get rid of the bad omen, stating, 'It's much stronger than I thought.'

Meanwhile, she removed the blue chalk piece hidden beneath her thumbnails. Looking at her blinded captives, she stated, 'If the bad omen is not chased out during the first attempt, these procedures will have to be repeated in three months' time.' She turned to face the enthralled husband and wife, who were prepared to obey her. Panchami made decisions based on her ability to read their minds.

'Musicians are now required to appease the Gandharvas. They will recite hymns, and the poignant bhajans will evoke intense devotion, which will also appease your family deity.' She then gave supportive directions, saying, 'It is worthwhile to spend a little more on skilled musicians because the sounds of musical instruments please the gods.

The bad omen will be easily pushed away as the gods become more powerful, and they will be afraid to return anytime soon.'

Sukumaran Chettiar and his wife Radhamma readily accepted the extra costs to make it the most blessed of rituals. They invited family members from distant places to partake in the rituals and to receive blessings. An arch was erected in front of the house and embellished with green leaves from coconut trees. The path leading from the front to their porch was decorated with flowers. On either side of the porch, two fully grown banana plants, complete with their stems, were placed. On either side of the path, within a foot of each other, oiled live lamps were set up. There were forty-one oil lamps in all, with the largest, a seven-tiered lamp, positioned at the front of the house.

Three hours before the ceremony began, Panchami Kaniyatti's assistant arrived and prepared the floor for *Kalamezhuthu*. Panchami's warning forced Sukumaran to stay with the assistant, meeting all his demands: 'The entire *kalam* rituals could be ruined by a single error.' The floral painting had to begin shortly before dusk and be finished by midnight, when the ceremonies were over. The floor was prepared by the assistant using a mixture of cow dung and rice powder. Following the instructions, Sukumaran collected the dung, which had to be the first dropping of a virgin cow for the day.

Earlier, he had been warned that the whole process of making the *kalam* could take two to five hours. From east to west, the assistant drew a straight line and, using white rice powder, outlined the image. After that, he painted the entire image by hand and waited for Panchami to arrive before finishing the eyes. The assistant reasoned that when the deity's eyes were painted open, the *kalam* would come to life.

The assistant used five colours (*panchavarnam*) to symbolise *Panch Bhoota*, the five elements of nature: mighty Earth, abundant Air, limitless Sky, soothing Water, and cleansing Fire. Yellow represented Earth, green represented Air, white for Water, black symbolised the Sky, and red represented Fire. The assistant enthusiastically detailed the process of preparing each colour. To achieve a white colour, white rice powder was used. Yellow was produced by powdered turmeric, black by charcoal or charred rice husk, and green by the leaves of the Gulmohar tree. The assistant stated that using natural materials gave the *kalam* a strong, fragrant scent that heightened its devotional ambience. Sukumaran supplied fresh flowers and petals upon request, which the assistant displayed in various places to add fragrance and create a three-dimensional effect.

Subsequently, the assistant constructed a sacred fireplace situated beneath the painting. Using red mud bricks, he built a square-shaped fireplace and coated it with a mixture of rice powder and cow dung. Freshly cut and dried fire logs were placed, and ghee made from cow's milk was poured over them to ensure they were well coated. Thereafter, he placed materials to initiate the fire and sustain high flames in the fireplace. The oil lamp would be lit to initiate the fire. A sufficient quantity of ghee, cow's milk, curd, sugar, saffron, grains, coconut, perfumed water, incense, seeds, petals, and herbs was made available. He explained to Sukumaran that the lead performer would pour offerings and libations into the fire while hymns were sung to the sounds of *Svaha*.

To meet the needs of the devotees through the rituals, the assistant painted the goddess Bhadrakali with an angry expression to scare and eliminate the evil omen. He prepared a twenty-foot *kalam* that was proportional to the size of the home. Sukumaran and his family resided in a large, traditional house. Sukumaran extended an invitation to the entire neighbourhood to observe and participate in the rituals. As the *kalam* neared completion, women began to sing evening hymns to honour and appease the gods. A group of performers, including traditional vocalists and drummers, arrived with Panchami Kaniyatti. The drummers and vocalists entered the premises while she was still at the entrance and immediately began playing the ritual songs. Then the assistant finished the eyes of Bhadrakali, and Panchami entered the *kalam*, followed by the praises and chanting of devotees, resulting in a princely procession.

Panchami Kaniyatti was curvy and had ample features. She wore a white blouse without lining and a thin white saree, which clearly revealed her large and striking body features. Her hair, long and black, was folded and pinned on top of her head in a pyramid shape, with the tip of the hair dangling in a ponytail. The fierceness of her appearance was accentuated by the thick black eyeliner that extended beyond her eyelids. She applied a thick swathe of *tilak* to her forehead, composed of ash, sandalwood, vermilion, and turmeric. Prominently visible was a large, rounded crimson dot situated between her eyebrows. The reddish hue of her lips came from chewing *pan masala*, and her lips were unusually large. A long red flower garland was draped around her neck, extending to the lower abdomen, well below her prominent navel.

The belly button disappeared into the soft, fleshy lower abdomen, set deep within the navel area. She wore two chains of large *rudraksha* beads beneath the floral garland. The light-brown nipples and her large breasts were evident beneath the white transparent blouse. The rhythm of her stamping caused them to tremble with excitement as she walked with a straight back. Small yellow and red flowers were attached to the pyramid-shaped tresses. Mehndi was applied to her palms and feet, and a tiny floral band was affixed to both wrists. Her right wrist was encircled by a chain of miniature *rudraksha* beads. She approached the *Kalamezhuthu* while wearing anklets and a thick waist belt adorned with numerous small bells that jingled in unison.

Panchami maintained an apprehensive expression and refrained from making eye contact with others until she reached the base of the Bhadrakali painting. The area was filled with fumes from sandal candles, and numerous oil lanterns were lit. She stood with her feet together, folded her hands, closed her eyes, raised her head, and began to pray. Next, she extended her right arm and extracted a substantial quantity of *Kalabham*, which was composed of sandalwood paste, aromatic ingredients, and *Kasthuri*. She applied the paste to her forehead, arms, and other parts of her body. The performance of traditional vocalists, drummers, and flute players intensified.

The onlookers were deeply affected by the rising pitch of the music, and many began to dance and fold their hands in devotion.

Panchami gazed at the painting's eyes as the rituals captivated the entire congregation. Shortly thereafter, her eyes widened and expanded, and her cheekbones began to tremble. The tremor gradually spread to other parts of her body, and she began to move her legs forward and backward.

She was immediately presented with a small oil lamp by her assistant to ignite the sacrificial fire. Panchami began to move around the fire pit while holding the lamp in her right hand, taking care not to step on the Bhadrakali painting on the floor. She completed seven circuits around the fire pit, and her assistant nodded. She then sat down on a *peedam* beside the pit and gradually lit the logs, igniting the rituals. In an instant, a large fireball and black vapours emerged, causing the devotees nearby to panic and retreat to a safe distance. As the initial burst of fire subsided, she picked up a small bell in her left hand and, using her right hand, added more ghee to the fire pit. She continued to ring the bell with her left hand while adding sacrificial materials to the fire with her right. Her assistant chanted in unison and presented her with additional offerings one by one.

With a fierce stare at Sukumaran, she ordered that young Preman sit right next to the sacrificial fire pit. The boy was hiding behind his mother, unable to speak and terrified by Panchami's frightening appearance. He was hesitant to come forward, and Sukumaran forced him to obey. The boy's faith was shaken by fear, and he broke down in tears. Radhamma came forward to offer her support, but the assistant requested that she maintain a sufficient distance.

Upon the assistant's signal to advance the rituals to the second stage, the main celebrant, Panchami, rose and began to move back and forth in rhythm with the music and songs. The pitch of the music rose, and the singers and instrumentalists stood up. Panchami then began to stamp her feet heavily on the ground and roll her neck from side to side. The singers started to circle around her, and the devotees all stood and began clapping in time with the music. Panchami soon began to dance frenetically, and the assistant realised that she had transformed into an oracle, a conduit between the divine and the devotees.

The assistant approached Panchami when the first howling sound was heard. He raised a sickle-shaped bronze sword adorned with bells and a red scarf to aid its handling. The sword was held by the assistant in front of the sacrificial fire for a while before Panchami grasped its handle. Then she began to move around the fire, raising the sword above her head. The vocalists and musicians were encouraged to increase the pitch of their music and sound. The assistant stood behind Panchami while she faced the Bhadrakali painting. Panchami continued to dance, taking care not to step on the painting. Whenever she attempted to strike the back of the sword against her forehead, the assistant positioned a hard cloth between them to cushion the blow.

When she again attempted to harm herself with the sword, the third assistant ordered the sacrificial rooster to be brought in, and the dancing continued. The rooster was brought from the cage, and Sukumaran held it in both palms. Panchami performed a three-step dance around Sukumaran before touching his forehead and bestowing a blessing upon him. She then chanted loudly, 'Devi, you are the supreme power. You secure the world and all its inhabitants. You control all three worlds, the earth, the heavens above, and the hell beneath.'

Subsequently, she looked at her assistant, who took the rooster from Sukumaran and placed it on a platform above the sacrificial fire. Panchami continued to scream and began to run around the painting. After completing three rounds, she chanted, 'Devi, accept this sacrifice and relieve the bad omen from this house.'

She then used the sword to cut off the rooster's head. The surrounding area filled with dense smoke and a burning odour as the rooster's body oozed blood into the sacrificial fire.

Preman, the young child, collapsed to the ground unconscious upon witnessing the headless carcass of the trembling rooster. Panchami danced in a trance, her dishevelled tresses accentuated by rapid movements as she brandished the bloodstained sword. The blood on her face, like that of a wounded but victorious warrior, was reminiscent of the vermilion paste on her forehead, now saturated with perspiration and dripping down her cheeks. She continued to dance around the sacrificial fireplace, emitting war cries in celebration of her triumph over evil. She ordered the malevolent omen to refrain from entering the home, employing a variety of profane language.

Subsequently, she consumed the blood of the rooster from the sword. She raised the sword towards the painting and chanted in gratitude to the deity, 'Devi, you are the strongest of all, the protector of the poor and helpless. Please remove the bad omen from this boy.'

Then, for a brief period, her entire body trembled. Towards the conclusion, she once more caressed the bloodstains and placed them on Preman's lips. The unconscious boy was unable to taste or respond. Then she handed over the sword to her assistant, who took it to each devotee to taste the bloodstains. Some of them tasted it, while others joined their hands and rendered a respectful gesture to be blessed.

The sword was returned to the sacred spot by the assistant, who also informed the vocalists that the ritual was now entering its final phase. The painting was surrounded by the singers and musicians, and a few women joined them to complete the circle. They initiated a distinct melody and background rhythm, moving sideways and occasionally forward and backward. They clapped their hands in appreciation for the removal of the malevolent omen from the residence and for allowing the lad to speak.

When the songs and music reached their zenith, Panchami leapt into the centre of the circle and resumed her frantic dance. A small number of the dancing devotees who were making their way around the *kalam* began to collapse one by one and were subsequently dragged out. Panchami began to erase the painting from the feet to the head after a few minutes of dancing. She then fainted and collapsed onto the *kalam*. The assistant promptly took her into the house with the support of other devotees.

The main celebrant, Panchami, collapsed shortly after the painting was erased, and the entire ritual concluded. *Prasadam*, composed of cooked rice, desiccated coconut, and jaggery with spices, was distributed to the attendees. Special refreshments were provided to the singers and instrumentalists in addition to the *prasadam*. After waiting for Panchami to recover for an hour, they departed the place altogether. On his way out, Panchami's assistant urged Sukumaran to allow the fire to burn out completely and to bury the rooster's carcass in the ground, precisely beneath the sacrificial fire pit. He emphasised that the carcass of the sacrificial animal should not be exposed to sunlight the following day. Panchami consented to evaluate the boy's condition in one week.

There was no evidence to suggest that the ritual was effective in curing young Preman. In the aftermath of the incident, he developed a fear of Panchami and distanced himself from her. The ritual *Kalamezhuthu* and Panchami Kaniyatti were highly praised by Sukumaran, who believed that they had been extremely beneficial for Preman. Sukumaran asserted that Preman began speaking after the rituals, a claim that neither the villagers nor their acquaintances bothered to verify.

Chapter 13

Sumithra was born at a time when the family was on the brink of losing hope for another child. Both parents dedicated their time and energy to assisting Preman in his speech development and in obtaining a more comprehensive education. Following several years of homeschooling, he enrolled in the village primary school but was unable to endure the peer abuse. During that period, Sukumaran developed discomfort in his backbone, which necessitated over a year of conventional Ayurvedic therapies for relief. Preman was unable to continue his studies as he missed classes regularly. Eventually, he assumed responsibility for the family's agriculture and achieved instant success. Sukumaran was granted the opportunity to receive better treatment once the family attained financial stability. Subsequently, he experienced an improvement in his health and resumed his routine.

Panchami Kaniyatti frequently advised Sukumaran to remain patient and to maintain faith in order to conceive a second child. Radhamma was not persuaded by her recommendation to perform the rituals multiple times again to appease their family deity. The promised results had not been achieved despite the costly rituals performed to cure Preman's speech. Preman was unable to communicate effectively and continued to stammer, leading to his school dropout. The family faced a financial crisis that made conducting another ritual of this nature impossible. Preman was not in favour of another ritual with many attendees due to his introverted nature. Sukumaran was beginning to lose faith when Radhamma's fertility declined over the years, and to their surprise, she became pregnant as she approached menopause.

Preman was overjoyed and urged his mother to prioritise her health, considering the potential arrival of a sibling. In addition to his farming obligations, he voluntarily assisted his mother with domestic chores in anticipation of having a healthy baby. He ensured that his mother received medical advice that was both timely and efficient, rather than relying on conventional maternity care. Panchami Kaniyatti was enraged when Preman forbade his parents from obtaining assistance and guidance from her. While Preman was absent, Panchami conducted a physical examination of Radhamma. Sukumaran was delighted when Panchami foretold that the baby would be a male, and he pledged to conduct an additional ceremony. She reassured Sukumaran that Radhamma was in good health and no longer required any additional medical assistance. Once again, she took a stroll around the house to verify that no negative omens were present and that Radhamma was in excellent health to deliver a healthy boy at home.

Radhamma was not ready to accept Panchami's good wishes immediately, so she continued going to the hospital for evaluation by skilled doctors. Sukumaran chose the customary path and ignored Radhamma's wishes to be admitted to hospital near the delivery date. When Radhamma did not feel any pain at the expected moment, she rushed to the local hospital, where the physicians helped her deliver a healthy baby girl. Sukumaran acted as though he were happy, but Radhamma and Preman were genuinely delighted to have a girl child.

The family returned home a few days after Radhamma and the baby were deemed healthy.

A few days later, Panchami came to see them with the newborn girl's astrological chart, showing the position of the *Navagrahas* at the time of her birth. The mother planet, Earth, like other planets, transitions from one zodiac sign to another. The *Janma Nakshatra* is determined by the Moon's position at the time of birth. Panchami determined the precise time of delivery and declared that Sumithra was the *Magam Piranna Manka* of the family, and her star was *Magam*.

She anticipated that Sumithra's existence would result in increased wealth and prosperity for the family. She firmly stated, 'She will be recognised as a leader by the community and receive the appropriate level of support.'

She then explained, '*Magam* is the tenth *Nakshatra* on the zodiac belt, and Ketu is its ruler. It is responsible for spirituality and brings prosperity to the devotee's family.' It bestows prosperity, health, and fortune upon the family to which Sumithra belongs.

Panchami was not entirely optimistic and cautioned, 'It is probable that Ketu will remain in Sumithra's life.' She then elaborated, saying, 'For Ketu, darkness is the light. Sumithra will not be fixated on any particular subject in this lifetime, as she has already encountered every possible situation in her previous lives. As Ketu imparts spiritual tendencies and non-attachment to worldly desires and ambitions, she must be sustained in her motivation throughout her life.'

Panchami warned them, 'Children born under *Magam Nakshathram* are likely to be very adamant and may be demanding. They have a propensity to disregard obstacles and objections from others and work quietly towards their own objectives.'

The warnings were not accepted by any member of the family, who were delighted that their daughter was born with the uncommon *Magam Nakshatra*. The family anticipated a multitude of blessings, including prosperity and happiness, and were proud of their potential to impress the community.

Sumithra was blessed with an abundance of love and affection from her parents and brother, which she cherished. She perceived her desires as her inherent entitlement, and they were fulfilled without her awareness of their necessity. There were few individuals with whom she could engage in deep conversation, despite her intelligence and strong logical reasoning abilities. Sumithra was enrolled in a local single-teacher school at the age of four to acquire the skills of reading and writing. The teacher was astounded by her rapid learning pace and commended her demeanour towards her peers. She quickly established friendships with them and began to spend more time in their company. She was willing to assist her peers and share her food with them. She had several female companions at primary school but experienced feelings of loneliness at home. She was prohibited from visiting her neighbours' houses due to her family's lack of cordial relations with them.

Sumithra was physically larger than other children of her age and was strikingly beautiful. She developed a preference for others to acknowledge her physical attractiveness. She felt confident and validated when others paid attention to her, which made her happier. She soon developed a fervour for being the centre of attention, which she found both enjoyable and thrilling. She was admired by numerous boys and girls during her primary school years, soon became an adolescent and she was more interested in admiration than in attention. Attaining teenagerhood, her body features changed rapidly due to hormonal shifts. She distinguished herself from the crowd because of her increased height, weight, and body shape, a fair-complexioned girl with dark blue eyes and a curved figure characterised by a noticeable waist and hips. Her long, curly black hair was thickened by the consistent use of coconut oil, enhancing the charm and pleasantness of her visage.

Preman was disturbed by the young woman's breathtaking appearance and her maturation, and he subsequently distanced himself from her. Sumithra pursued active relationships with other individuals due to the decreased interaction between the siblings. The numerous restrictions and overprotectiveness of her parents caused her to feel uneasy. She sought liberation and desired challenging activities.

Sumithra was strictly prohibited from going into the river for any reason, in accordance with Panchami's previous recommendation to implement safety protocols. In contrast, Preman was an accomplished swimmer and frequently relished the opportunity to take a complete dip. Sumithra was often invited by her peers to join them and enjoy the river's natural flow. They repeatedly emphasised that a dip in fresh water alleviates physical and mental tension. They continued to captivate her with descriptions of the river's natural, refreshing environment, ideal for bathing and washing clothes. Dirt, sweat, and dead skin cells could be effectively removed from the body by the flowing water, resulting in a sense of rejuvenation and cleanliness.

Unable to defy her parents, Sumithra awaited the appropriate moment to escape to the riverside. She discreetly followed Preman to the riverbanks on a tranquil afternoon while both her parents were away. The river was accessible via a narrow and uneven path that was scarcely navigable. She was extremely cautious, ensuring that she did not attract attention and kept a sufficient distance from others. The villagers were fortunate to have a gentle and leisurely current flowing through the slow-moving river. Preman proceeded directly to the broadest section, a popular spot for villagers to bathe and wash their clothes. When Sumithra first saw the natural flow of water, she was captivated by its majesty and apprehensive about its deep blue shade. She initially considered returning home but was uncertain about when the next opportunity might arise.

Sumithra chose an isolated location on the riverbank where the water appeared calm and undisturbed to avoid the attention of others. She trod cautiously on the slippery bank, which was covered in mud and grit. Feeling the uneven sand beneath her feet, she stepped quickly onto a rock that was unsteady. Losing her balance, she plunged backwards into the water with a low thud. She promptly regained consciousness and stood up, but her movements were impaired due to the low water levels. Consumed by fear and anxiety, she attempted to escape from the unfamiliar water. The predicament worsened as she repeatedly tried to move her legs on the granular mix of sand and clay beneath the surface. She was unable to free her limb, and fear compelled her to jump up with all her strength, causing her to fall back into the water and lose consciousness.

Her consciousness returned with the gentle pressure applied to her right chest, sending electric waves through her body. Her heartbeat was restricted by lack of oxygen, and her congested lungs could not retain any air. Then, the unpleasant flavour of salt and sweat penetrated her mouth, causing her to exhale more air. Her body was not yet ready to absorb oxygen and expelled it, along with a small amount of water. She again detected the salt and perspiration on her lips, though it took longer this time. Her lungs expelled more water, and on the third occasion, they absorbed oxygen and released additional water through her mouth. She gradually regained consciousness, spitting out more water as the pressure on her chest increased.

As she lay on the sand dune at the riverbank, staring upward at the blue sky, she recalled the peculiar taste on her lips. Once again, she sensed the specific saline flavour of another person's mouth as she folded her lips inward and brushed them with her tongue. She forcibly closed her eyes as she gazed at the radiant blue eyes of a young man with curly dark hair and a faint line of moustache standing beside her. She then attempted to recall the previous few moments during which she had lost consciousness. Frantically, she looked around for others.

A bold and reassuring voice said, 'Don't worry, there is no one else nearby and no one saw you fall into the river.' She was unable to respond, but again heard the soft, reassuring voice: 'You're fine now.

Would you like me to help you sit?' He extended his right arm, securely holding her as he helped her sit on the sand dune.

Within moments, she sat upright and withdrew her hand from him, saying, 'Please don't touch me.' Then she glanced at his face and pleaded, 'Please don't tell anyone, my mother will beat me to death.'

He looked into her eyes and assured, 'You've said that, and I'll keep this between us forever.'

Sumithra quickly checked her clothing, which was completely soaked. The young man offered his dry towel, which she promptly took. She stood, dried her long hair, and rubbed her head to shake off the water droplets. The young man continued to admire her beauty before saying, 'I'll help you take a shortcut to your home. Please follow me this way.'

She followed him without hesitation and carefully ascended a steep, muddy slope until they reached another narrow path. He pointed to a wall of shrubs and said, 'Cross the opening in the wall, and you'll reach your neighbour's premises. From there, you can follow the same route you took behind Preman to reach your home.'

Sumithra rushed home without looking back, anticipating the arrival of her brother and parents. She quickly crossed the wall gap and found the pathway that led home. As soon as she changed out of her wet clothes, she began to shiver and immediately sought refuge on the bed.

Radhamma awoke her from a deep sleep with a steaming cup of masala coffee, a natural botanical beverage that alleviates fever and cold symptoms, a piping hot cup of black coffee seasoned with dried ginger, pulverised black pepper, cumin, and holy basil.

'My dear, this hot beverage is the most effective and rapid remedy for your raised temperature.'

She arose and looked around the room, asking, 'Where is my brother, Preman?'

Her father replied, 'He is about to leave to get your medication from the doctor.' He touched her forehead and expressed relief. 'It's not that bad; masala coffee is the best medicine for a speedy recovery.'

She stared at her mother and asked, 'Have you added any jaggery to the drink? Otherwise, it would be too tart for me to drink.' Radhamma glanced at her husband, who offered additional assurance.

'Sumithra, have faith, the medicine will be more effective without the sweetener.'

Her brother Preman entered the room, saying, 'I got some jaggery.' He continued, taking small packets of Ayurvedic medication from a cotton bag.

'The vaidyar advised that the medicine should be taken only if the *chukku coffee* is not effective.'

Radhamma was furious with Preman, questioning why she had been left alone for such a long period. She was concerned that Sumithra might have been frightened being alone at home. Preman remained silent, as though acknowledging his fault. He then looked at his parents and left the room without responding. Sukumaran attempted to ease the situation by asserting, 'Preman is a responsible brother who consistently provides for his sister.' He then placed his hands on Sumithra's forehead and reassured her, 'It's possible that you're suffering from a common cold. Eat a healthy diet and rest, you should be fine by tomorrow morning.'

With some difficulty, Radhamma assisted Sumithra to sit on the bed and placed the masala coffee cup near her lips.

As soon as her parents left the room, Sumithra tried to recall her experiences at the riverside. The peculiar taste on her lips returned as she remembered the moments after regaining consciousness. A sensation of nausea rose from her lower abdomen and remained lodged in her throat. She immediately used her hands to cover her mouth. When she touched her lips, a pleasant aroma lingered on her fingertips, transmitting sensations to her brain. The natural biological impulse generated by her brain neurons spread through every inch of her body. The peculiar taste on her lips gradually dissipated, giving way to a vague sense of pleasure.

The activation of her dormant mirror-neural system resulted in a delighted expression on her face. Her immature mind filled with tingles as she yearned for an undefined sense of belonging. The adolescent crush was detected by a maturing yet inexperienced body. Her young body lost control and curled together as the peculiar taste transformed into a lingering sweetness. Her hormones were triggered by a sudden emotional upheaval in her brain, initiating her menstrual cycle significantly earlier than usual. She cried out in agony as the sudden flow of menstrual blood and tissue passed from her uterus through the small cervical opening.

She screamed aloud, 'Mother, help me!'

Radhamma was relieved and comforted her, saying, 'Thank God, your symptoms were due to your menstrual cycle. Please rest and refrain from entering the kitchen for the next three days.' She reflected on the unusual and early onset of the situation as she handed her daughter a fresh set of white linen clothing. She paused briefly and reassured her, 'Do not worry, these occurrences are not unusual.'

Sumithra was aware that she would be isolated for the next three days in accordance with their traditions. The blood loss on the first day weakened her, though she typically regained her strength by the second day. Nevertheless, she was required to adhere strictly to the isolation, which she had always despised. Sumithra harboured a deep-seated aversion to the prevailing belief that menstruation was associated with impurity and uncleanliness. Additionally, she was prohibited from attending school, which meant missing time with her dear friends.

She reasoned with her mother, explaining that the scientific cause of menstruation was ovulation followed by a failed opportunity to conceive. The human body was preparing for the next cycle by discarding unused cells through haemorrhage from the endometrial vessels. Although Radhamma understood the phenomenon, she was reluctant to disregard centuries-old customs and beliefs. She was, however, generous in ensuring her daughter was well cared for and provided with her preferred, highly nutritious food.

The acute lower abdominal pain, combined with concern over the isolation period, caused her to fall into a deep sleep. After experiencing an unexpectedly pleasant dream, she awoke well before sunrise. She found herself floating through thin air, surrounded by drifting white clouds, dressed in a long white cloth. A young man on a white horse was far ahead of her. She kept calling out to him, but the young man remained unresponsive and continued to ride. She then felt heat building on her back and was compelled to look behind as the source of the warmth began to burn her. At that moment, she realised she was not chasing the young man but fleeing from a massive fireball. She was consumed in flames and lost sight of the rider as the heat became unbearable. She screamed aloud as the fireball engulfed her and her flowing white cloth.

No one could hear her cries, trapped as they were in her throat. Struggling to rise from the bed, she coughed and massaged her throat gently. She tried to recall the beautiful dream but could not remember much beyond pursuing a young man on a horse.

Sumithra, now in her mid-teens, was experiencing physiological and psychological changes as she reflected on her accidental encounter. The emotional turmoil brought on by the unfamiliar individual sent a jolt down her spine, forcing her to recline on the bed. She closed her eyes tightly, replaying and reliving the intimate moments, smiling faintly as she lay on her side. Sumithra longed to return to her beautiful dream, to ride alongside the young man on the horse and traverse together the boundless expanses of the world.

Chapter 14

Sumithra enrolled in the pre-degree course at her new college; soon, she achieved exceptional grades in Year 10. Her parents reluctantly permitted her to reside at the new college's women's hostel. They agreed to stay away in the absence of reliable public transport for her daily commute from their home. The hostel was a highly secure environment for female students, and it was managed by Christian missionary sisters. In alignment with her peers, she donned a long blouse that encompassed both her upper and lower abdomen, along with a long skirt. On the first day, she strolled alone because her roommate at the hostel was scheduled to attend the afternoon session. Standing pupils, who were on the lookout for newcomers, valued her bold demeanour and upright walking style. Their verbal comments, which expressed their admiration for her personality and their willingness to accompany her, were intriguing, and she deliberately disregarded them with a smile.

As part of their induction, the new students assembled at the college auditorium for prayers and introductions. Christian prayers were recited, as most students affiliated with that religion. She watched the entire ceremony with fascination. The college principal and the student union representatives from the previous year personally introduced themselves and extended a formal welcome. The principal, a Catholic priest, conveyed the importance of preserving a healthy learning environment. He reminded newcomers to prioritise the requirements of other students and preserve the peaceful atmosphere within the campus. Outside the auditorium, a group of students were chanting in protest towards the college authorities. They demanded the immediate reinstatement of a small number of suspended students who had damaged college furniture during a student protest. The prayers and introductions were conducted as scheduled, and the principal disregarded their requests.

In her classroom, there were approximately forty students, with over half of them being female. Sumithra's exceptional charisma and stunning appearance immediately garnered the admiration of both male and female students. Realising that she was one of the taller students, she voluntarily sat in the last rows. She soon engaged in a conversation with the student who was seated next to her. Suddenly, a young man in a white shirt and white dhoti entered the classroom and stepped on to the dais, which was designated for teacher use. A few male students entered the classroom a few seconds before his arrival and occupied the vacant seats. The young man promptly ascended the dais and used a duster to clear the blackboard. The newcomers rose and extended their respect and wished, which compelled all new students to stand in respect of their new teacher on the dais. The young man, who was quite attractive, addressed the class, 'Good morning, my dear students.'

All students reciprocated his greeting, 'Good morning, Sir.'

He looked at the surroundings and said, 'Excellent, would you all please take your seats.'

He then looked directly into Sumithra's eyes for a moment and elevated his right arm, stating, 'You are all exceedingly obedient and have the right to acquire knowledge.'

He paused briefly and glanced outside before continuing, 'I am your class in-charge and also the social lead; you may consult me for any social or emotional requirements.'

One of the new students, who had entered the classroom prior to the teacher, reminded him, 'Sir, you forgot to take the mandatory oath.'

The teacher on the dais once more glanced outside and turned to the students, saying, 'Thank you, my boy, you are exceptionally intelligent and have a promising future.'

He requested that all students rise, and they promptly did so. The teacher then raised his right arm and directed the students to 'raise your right arm and repeat after me.'

Although a few students were hesitant to comply with the instructions, they were compelled to do so as the newcomers immediately followed. 'All my countrymen are my brothers and sisters, and I will prioritise the needs of my country over my personal well-being.'

After that, he asked all of them to remain seated, and they promptly followed the instructions. Then one of the male newcomers raised a question: 'Sir, how can I marry them if all of them are my sisters? My parents will not permit me to marry my sister, and I am in dire need of having children.'

All the other students started laughing, and the teacher asked them to keep silent. Afterwards, he responded, 'You have made a valid point; however, you have the option to remain unmarried for the remainder of your life.'

The teacher paused briefly before continuing, 'You could dedicate your manhood to God and become a priest.'

Once more, the students roared with laughter. The newcomer was adamant about not giving up, and he followed up with another inquiry: 'Was that the reason you left the seminary, or did they expel you?'

This time, the students laughed uncontrollably and stared at the instructor for an explanation.

Another young male entered the classroom through the door on the opposite side before the teacher could respond. The young man on the dais abruptly exited upon seeing the newcomer. All students who had entered the classroom before him immediately followed and exited the room without making any further comments. The attractive young man glanced at Sumithra's eyes once more before exiting the room, and she immediately recognised that he was both special and familiar to her.

The new entrant sat on the chair at the dais and opened a pocket diary to record the students' attendance. The students subsequently realised that the young man they had experienced earlier was not the genuine teacher, and that they had been subjected to ragging by their senior peers. Although it was not humiliating, they acquired a new lesson: it is not advisable to instantaneously trust strangers. Most of the students found the experience to be enjoyable, and the actual teacher, who was also quite youthful, chose not to pose questions.

Calling out their roll numbers, the new teacher started to mark everyone's attendance. Sumithra was unable to respond to her registration number as she was attempting to recollect her memories of the young man. The new teacher then elevated his voice and reminded her, 'Sumithra Chettiar, daydreaming will not assist you in passing the annual examinations. Please be vigilant.'

Upon hearing her name, she rose from her seat, and a few of the students began to chuckle once more. She was instantly embarrassed and sat back on the bench without responding to the teacher.

She used the break time to establish relationships with her peers and discovered that barely any of them resided at the hostel, as they all commuted daily. The pre-degree courses were being administered by the college in two sessions, and Sumithra's morning session concluded prior to lunch. She searched for the young man during the break time, but she failed in her search. She was taken aback when she noticed him conversing with others from afar on her way back to the hostel. The young man swiftly approached her upon recognising her, but she attempted to evade him by extending her strolling distance. He approached and called out her name, 'Sumithra, it's me, your neighbour.'

She was once again taken aback by the young man's recognition of her name and was puzzled as to how he had known. His reminder of them being neighbours caused her to halt and face him. He was taller than her and had a well-built frame. He peered into her eyes once more and said, 'I am Baby Tharakan, your neighbour.'

She was unable to respond, but she recognised that he was a person she knew. She attempted to respond to his introduction with a smile, and he proceeded to state, 'We are neighbours, but we have not been formally introduced.'

Sumithra saw that there were a few students passing by who were paying attention to them. She desired to depart; however, he persisted with his introduction, stating, 'I pursued my bachelor's degree at the seminary after matriculation.'

Sumithra responded with a smile and then began to walk towards the hostel. He briefly paused before swiftly approaching her. 'We are aware that our parents are not friendly, but we are neighbours, and we now live in a faraway place, far from our village and our parents' rivalry.'

Sumithra was unable to recall him, had no memory of him, and continued to regard him as a stranger. She was unable to respond appropriately and looked down. Sumithra began to walk towards the hostel as he soon disengaged from her path. Then, from behind, he reminded her, 'You may recall your fall into the river; I have not disclosed it to anyone else.'

It was a surprise and she was stunned for a brief period. She had kept the incident from everyone, but she had been secretly searching for her rescuer and aspired to come across him at any given moment. He was standing there, beaming at her, when she looked back.

Sumithra was astonished at his assertions and stared at him. Now, her divine rescuer stood before her, after more than two years. Suddenly, her mouth became parched, rendering her incapable of uttering a single word. Throughout the years, she discreetly pursued him, beaming with a smile; he was now standing before her. His companions were waiting for him as he turned back and disappeared towards the college boundaries.

Sumithra was momentarily taken aback, regained consciousness and walked calmly towards the hostel. She desired to boost the blissful pleasure, seeking someone to share the moments of excitement with. Her heart was pounding, and she was eager to prolong the amusement. She hurried into her room, only to find her roommate had left for an afternoon session. She promptly replenished herself and walked to the dining room for lunch. The serving lady was courteous and swiftly introduced herself; Sumithra limited her friendliness with a smile. Even though the lunch was not as delicious as had been promised, her elevated mood prevented her from making complaints. Her vision was obscured by the extraordinary and intense memories, rendering everything edible and delightful.

She hurried back to her room and lay on the bed, feeling a pleasurable sensation as the odd taste of sweat returned to her lips. A single cell's flash signal of comfort quickly spread throughout her body, and she enjoyed the fascinating bursts of excitement. She quickly shifted to a sideways position and coiled her body into a semicircle. In her veins, the unexplainable comfort and the positive emotion created a potent chemical cocktail. Then it happened again: the extra energy developed from the positive sensation was released by her internal organs as blood and dead cells, which were expelled through the little frontal aperture at the base of her upper body.

The tension that resulted from the unexpected events of the first day was soon replaced by enjoyable experiences. She was able to sleep soundly as a result of the physical and mental calm that her body's reaction mechanism provided.

Roommate Mercy Joseph did not disturb her with her own first-day experience at the college, as she recognised the physical anguish associated with the monthly cycle. Mercy was the youngest daughter of a prosperous and affluent family, and she had four other siblings. Mercy selected political science as her primary subject for future law studies. Her eldest sibling, who was a criminal lawyer at the state high courts, served as motivation for her. Her other two siblings were highly educated and held positions in the government that were of significant influence. Her immediate sibling was providing support to their father in the operation of the family business.

Sumithra's roommate was taken aback when she awoke early the following day to find that she was experiencing both physical and emotional strength. Mercy recognised her uniqueness and admired her capacity to endure physical discomfort. Mercy was eager to know more about Sumithra, but she was prepared to wait for the perfect opportunity.

They shared breakfast in the dining area and conversed with a small number of other students, some of whom were new and others were long-time residents. Mercy escorted Sumithra to a different room and introduced her distant cousin, despite her attempts to return to their room promptly. Stella Johnson was currently in her final year of college and was preparing for the competitive medical entrance examinations. Stella was compassionate and admired Sumithra's physical appearance and height. She encouraged her to join the college basketball team.

Sumithra highlighted her wide and attractive eyes by carefully applying her preferred eyeliner to both eyebrows and the margins of her eyelids. She was well dressed and meticulously applied facial makeup to resemble a lush look. She wore the best outfit, which consisted of a long skirt and a blouse with vibrant blue floral prints. She left the hostel slightly earlier to allow for the necessary time to meet the young man and other individuals along the way. She recognised that she was unable to recall his name as she reflected on him. It required some time for her to regain her memory and attempt to enunciate the word accurately. She then reminded herself that despite his youthful appearance, he might be older than she was, and she must respect him. She decided to address him as 'Baby Chettan' rather than simply calling him by his first name.

She joined another group of students as they walked towards the college, avoiding eye contact with bystanders while discreetly searching for Baby. She acknowledged the introductions of others, but she was longing to see Baby. She was unable to locate him on that day and for the subsequent two days. On the fourth day, he was waiting for her near the steps leading to the college building. Sumithra's eyes were wide open, and she was so delighted that she forgot her previous vow to refrain from staring at him quickly. She instantly approached him and asked, 'I have not seen you in many days; where did you disappear without warning?'

He looked into her eyes and responded, 'You are truly remarkable, and I had been watching you from afar.'

She was delighted with his reply, but she glanced down and sought a sincere response, 'Why did you decide to show up at this time?'

He walked towards her and murmured, 'I will answer your question later. Would you like to meet at the restaurant during the break?'

She noticed his expression, interpreting his sincere invitation and keen interest. She looked at him and walked away. His patience and attractive eyes pursued her, anticipating a prompt response. She glanced back and smiled at him once more before walking to the classroom.

Sumithra was excited to know more about her life saviour during their initial date. In a private corner of the college cafeteria, Baby Tharakan narrated his life story, looking into her radiant eyes. He was born in their village and finished his education in a village that was far off. His mother was bedridden for several years because of complications during his early birth, and her twin sister provided him with a loving upbringing. He attended a boarding school for his higher secondary education and subsequently enrolled in the seminary to dedicate his life to Christian missionary work.

He visited numerous regions in northern India as part of his training and lived with the most impoverished tribal communities. There, he came to the realisation that it was more important to advocate for improved governance at the grassroots level than to spread good news to serve the invisible God. After six years of training, he left the seminary and enrolled in a college to earn a bachelor's degree in political science. His father was dissatisfied with the decision and advised him to pursue a master's degree to establish a professional career.

Sumithra was once again taken aback when Baby expressed his admiration for her from when they were kids. Although he had followed her from childhood days, he was unable to approach her due to her limited movements outside home. He spent many of his holidays in his aunt's village and surreptitiously followed Sumithra whenever he visited his home. Sumithra was delighted to find out that Baby had attended the village temple festival a few times and had been following her. Baby was in admiration of the magnificent dress and the way she fastened the flowers to her tresses. On numerous occasions, Baby attempted to approach her, but their families' troubled relationship forbade him. On one of those days, he observed her walking alone to the riverbank, where he rescued her from the shallow waters. He attempted to introduce himself to Sumithra on the riverbank, but she was too frightened, and he realised that it was not the appropriate time.

Baby added that Preman, Sumithra's older sibling, was cordial with him, whereas their interactions were limited. Sumithra then came to the realisation that her sibling was not particularly interested in engaging in discussions regarding their family's land disputes and rather maintained a neutral stance. Baby acknowledged that he was at odds with his father regarding the ongoing land dispute with Sumithra's family. He urged other family members to resolve the matter rather than continue to be eternal adversaries. Sumithra was cognisant of certain disputes among their neighbours, and she was not permitted to provide commentary or participate in any discussions. For unexplained reasons, her parents prevented her from interacting with neighbours. They both vowed to disregard the family dispute and continue to be close friends, as well as neighbours.

Sumithra was a good articulator and could tell anything impressively to any kind of audience. While Sumithra was mainly interested in environmental protection, a few political student activists urged her to join their groups. One of the political student organisations persuaded Baby to represent them in the next college union elections after realising his strong relations with Sumithra. With the help of Sumithra, who consented on the condition that he look after her priorities of environmental protection, Baby won the election.

The main factor in Baby Tharakan's election victory was his self-assured personality, but his opponents also relied on Sumithra's backing, garnering most of the female support. Rumours that both were in love and shortly to be married were gradually propagated by the rival group. One of the opposing gang members was apprehended while attempting to hang a wall poster featuring their names on a kissing pair. Their arguments escalated into a fistfight, which quickly swept throughout the college campus as opposing students engaged in combat from both sides.

The college authorities' timely intervention was successful, and their suggestion to maintain peace was accepted. Both parties agreed to an immediate ceasefire. The political leadership outside the college aided with compelling guidance, resulting in the final restoration of peace. Following that, Sumithra and her colleagues from the forestry group emphasised the necessity of maintaining a clean environment at the college. Baby Tharakan, in collaboration with his peers, organised an action day to clean the college and eliminate all hate hoardings and wall writings both inside and outside the campus. They were able to recommence their studies shortly after a peaceful educational environment was restored. Baby and Sumithra frequently convened at various locations, strengthening their friendship.

Sumithra was elected to the executive committee of the forestry club, which was dedicated to advancing the relevance and significance of natural forests and the rights of their inhabitants. The forestry club initiated campaigns to combat the encroachment of farmers on forest land and urged the government to remove them and protect wild animals. The practice of poaching wild elephants for their tusks and killing wild animals for their flesh was prevalent among the population residing in the vicinity of these forests.

The political masters of Baby Tharakan did not appreciate the campaigns, as their broader supporters were members of the migrant farming community. The encroachment of farmland grew worse with the lack of strict regulation and the numerous uncertainties that were created by the weak and corrupt government machinery. Baby requested more time to manage the protesters, as the campaigns were conducted on a national scale. The academic teaching was disrupted for more than a month by the campaigns, and the students were forcibly prevented from participating in any additional demonstrations.

A few months later, the forestry club organised a three-day educational leisure getaway to Moonnar, a renowned hill station that is surrounded by a vast forest and a variety of wild animals. Additionally, the region is distinguished by its expansive lakes and towering mountains. Forest hiking is a preferred activity among visitors, as it is guided and supported by local Adivasis. The college student union provided support for the tour; Baby, along with a few of his companions, joined the forestry club members.

The group, which consisted of forty students and teachers, travelled by coach and was fortunate enough to spot a herd of elephants crossing their path. They relished the breathtaking scenery along the way. The group derived pleasure from the unaltered natural environment. The coach arrived at their destination at a late hour, having traversed the meandering roads with numerous hairpin turns and tall trees on either side. The group relished their evening, which was complemented by delectable local cuisine and a roaring bonfire.

The team members participated in the scheduled forest trekking on the second day, which was accompanied by expert forest guards. They observed rare birds and listened to their melodious songs. Some of the birds were chirping, while others were either whistling or humming. A group of monkeys with lion tails followed them for a short distance before parting ways when the team was reluctant to share fruits and food. The guides who accompanied them forbade them from sharing any form of food with wild animals.

They arrived at one of the many Adivasi Kudi after trekking for over four hours through the perilous highlands. There were over one hundred Adivasis residing in impoverished conditions, lacking essential amenities. Most of the dwellings were partially decaying, constructed from mud and featuring thatched roofs. They engaged in conversation with tribal members and participated in a meal that had been specially prepared for them. The boiled jackfruit and uncommon wild honey were shared over banana leaves, much to the enjoyment of the students. While many of them were resting, the skies darkened with thick black clouds, followed by heavy rainfall.

The Adivasi ladies were conversing with Baby and Sumithra, as well as their close friends, when the unexpected rain poured down. Despite the Adivasis' suggestion to seek refuge in their confined area, Baby adored the refreshing sensation of the torrential rain. Sumithra joined him in the open space; soon the heavy rain's intensity reduced. They both enjoyed the refreshing waters and proceeded to walk towards the tree line.

Soon enough, they heard a ferocious roar and noticed a solitary wild tusker attempting to remove the remaining thatching from the dwellings. Sumithra cried out loud and fled to the opposite side to maintain a secure distance from the elephant, and in protection Baby followed her. During the commotion they were both separated from the group and sought refuge in a nearby cave as the rain intensified.

Baby put his hand around Sumithra's waist just as she was nearly to pass out from fear. She soon sought refuge on him, and Baby drew her close to him, holding her for a while. After realising the awkward situation, she objected, saying, 'No, stay away from me.'

Baby muttered as he drew nearer, 'I love you, Sumithra.'

After noticing his genuine expression, she turned to face him and said, 'No, we are just friends; we are not meant to be lovers.'

'You are mine forever, and I can't imagine my life without you,' he said as he drew her closer to him.

She peered into his eyes once again as those words struck a chord with her. After a period of silence, she added, 'We are different; we don't follow similar life paths.' She went on, 'My parents won't agree, and I don't want to disobey them.'

He again drew her to him and reassured her, 'Once we have finished our courses, we can elope and find a suitable place to spend the rest of our lives in peace.'

There was a brief period of silence between them. Baby gave her a moment to contemplate before he drew her in and reassured her again, 'We can relocate to Delhi, and I have friends there to provide support.'

He then gently kissed her forehead. The lightning of love that enveloped her was accompanied by the heavy thunder that echoed outside the cave. She gradually turned her face towards him, and they exchanged glances. They were unaware of the water droplets that were raining on them; water seeped through the small openings above their heads.

The two bodies gradually drew closer, and Baby tightly held her to him. Sumithra experienced the comforting warmth emanating from his chest, and they were deeply connected. She raised her lips towards him, and the heavens burst forth through her lower parts. She immediately sat on the floor and wept loudly as dead cells and thick blood forced out through the tiny opening.

Chapter 15

Before Joyachan could continue to share his further knowledge on late Benny Mathew's family, Mary's voice was heard from the kitchen, asking, 'Do you require an additional cup of coffee?'

Chacko promptly replied, 'I require an additional cup.'

Mary immediately instructed her daughter, 'Celine, mole, boil some more water for coffee.'

Celine was not immediately impressed, as she was feeding the goats outside the home. She hurried towards the kitchen and almost collided with Sunny, who was on his way out. Celine became enraged and pushed Sunny to the side, shouting, 'Why can't you be more careful, you moron?'

Sunny was about to strike back when he regained balance and spotted far-off movements. He sprinted to the far end of their courtyard and looked around but was unable to find anything. At once, he heard his mother's voice: 'Sunny, have you lost something? What are you looking at?'

He returned to the goats' pen and looked out for Celine, who was already preparing coffee. Sunny then stared at his mother, but he was unable to provide an explanation and casually glanced around. He was uncertain, but he once more looked at the goats and began to stroke them.

Joyachan took the steel tumbler containing the coffee from Celine, stating, 'I personally prefer very hot coffee.'

He asked about her studies after taking a sip of coffee. Celine smiled and returned to the kitchen. Chacko responded, 'She is not as bright as Sunny, who is very sharp.' He paused briefly before continuing, 'Sunny will be a matter of pride for me; he will secure a well-paid position, and we will be just fine.'

Celine was unappreciative of the comments and felt bad. She opened the book on her return to her small room, and the lemon sweet that was concealed fell to the floor. She immediately returned to the book's outer cover, and a refreshing smile returned to her.

'That was the agreement between Baby and Sumithra,' Joyachan explained, and Chacko eagerly listened to him. Chacko lit another beedi and handed it to Joyachan, who declined and continued to sip the hot coffee. After a brief pause, Chacko asked, 'Sumithra was trained as a teacher and was preparing to join the village primary school.'

To that Joyachan replied, 'That's right. The year Baby completed the degree course at the college, Sumithra too completed her pre-degree course.' He paused to drink coffee and continued, 'She had plans to enrol at the same college for a degree course, but her father insisted she become a teacher and admitted her for Teacher Training Course at a different town.'

On request, Joyachan explained when both decided to deepen their relationship and become life partners rather than friends.

The lone tusker was chased by the Adivasis, who were fully equipped to survive in the wild. Among wild elephants, lone tuskers are the most aggressive. They become outcasts when excluded from their herd for various reasons, including losing battles against other dominant males. When they are unable to be accepted into other herds or fail to establish their own herds, they become increasingly enraged and attack any animal, including humans. The attack on that day was unexpected, whereas the Adivasis effectively resisted. The tusker was remarkably cunning and waited for the right opportunity of heavy rain and pitch darkness. The experienced jungle people courageously retaliated and chased the lone tusker to protect themselves and their guests.

Despite the frantic and spooky moments, Baby held Sumithra safely until they reached a secure cave that was not far from the Adivasi makeshifts. Sumithra was enjoying the care and protection of Baby during those uncertain and frightening moments. The natural monthly menstruation was causing her agony, but Baby held her comfortably. Sumithra realised that it was more convenient to remain in close reach of him as their relationship evolved. The committed Adivasis spotted them as they were basking in the showers of the heavens.

The students' group was promptly reunited, and the solitary tusker was chased back to the forest. Women and a small number of male students were frightened and demanded a quick return to their secure campsite. Acknowledging the fact that it was already late and returning during the night would attract more dangers, the group decided to spend the night with the Adivasis. The forest guards and the Adivasi elders agreed to guard them during the night. The group departed for the campsite in the early morning after spending a sleepless, long night.

A new era of life began for them, as their lives as butterflies were transformed by increased love hormones. Their initial attraction evolved into a romantic relationship as they entrusted one another, shared experiences, and provided support during difficult times. Their intimacy transitioned from infatuation to a more enduring connection, which bonded them and induced feelings of euphoria. The intensity of their feelings towards each other increased as a result of the consistent discharge of happy chemicals into their brains. They began to spend more time together during their college days, which extended to the weekends. The rumours of their covert marriage became a hot topic, and the news of their belonging spread like wildfire. The college principal advised them to take more caution and refrain from engaging in public. He was certain that a healthy relationship would either transition into everlasting love or end for good reasons after the initial passion and obsession subsided.

Joyachan was interfered with by Chacko's question, 'Did they elope to Delhi?' Realising Joyachan was disrupted, Chacko clarified, 'At least that is what I have heard from other sources.'

Joyachan exhaled deeply and looked at the stone wall in front of Chacko's home that obstructed their view beyond it, and replied, 'Life is akin to the wall that stands in front of you; it obstructs the reality beyond the wall and compels us to make numerous assumptions that are not always accurate.'

In pursuit of employment opportunities, Baby relocated to Delhi shortly after receiving his degree. Initially he was offered a teaching position at a private school and had other plans to live together. Later working for a multinational company, he spent a year in Delhi and was visiting his parents when the unfortunate incidents happened.

Chacko reiterated his reservations, 'You are implying that they did not travel to Delhi together?'

Joyachan patiently replied, 'It is likely that they had the plans, which was not their fate.'

Chacko stared at him, and Joyachan further narrated, 'Their story is incomplete without mentioning Purushothaman Vanniyan, the village collector, or *Pravarthiyar*, who possessed power and authority comparable to that of the current village officer.'

Acknowledging Chacko's keen interest to learn more about the role of the Pravarthiyar, Joyachan explained, 'In those days, the Pravarthiyar had unquestionable authority over land disputes, and their decisions on both government and private lands, including any type of properties, were considered final.' Inhaling a big breath, he reasoned, 'Purushothaman had an eye on Sumithra, and to favourably resolve their land dispute with Baby's family, he demanded that Sumithra should marry him.'

Chacko was taken aback at this time but remained a quiet listener.

Despite his appealing appearance and well-built physique, Purushothaman Vanniyan was a womaniser. He was previously married and had a daughter from that union. His wife's suicide was an enigmatic event that persisted in perpetuity. His substantial influence at both the political and bureaucratic levels led to the stalling of additional investigations. He engaged in illicit relationships with numerous women, and thus Sumithra's mother declined his proposal. Sumithra's parents considered the proposition due to the apprehension of possible elopement along with rumours of her affair with Baby Tharakan. Purushothaman gained the complete backing of their religious authority and a small number of community leaders, who exerted pressure on Sumithra's family.

Purushothaman devised a strategy to secure the parents' complete trust to satisfy his profound affection for the remarkable young woman. He obtained a formal complaint from Sukumaran Chettiar, who claimed that his neighbour, Mathew Tharakan, had forcibly built a boundary wall and encroached on his property, furthermore requesting that the legal official re-survey the land and formally establish his claims. In response to the legal notice from Purushothaman, Mathew Tharakan submitted his original title documents, claiming the land belonged to him.

Purushothaman collaborated with another colleague to conduct a re-survey of the disputed land. Purushothaman and his colleague intentionally employed inaccurate calculations and reached a conclusion that favoured Sukumaran's assertions. He ordered Mathew to promptly tear down the section of the boundary wall, thereby granting Sukumaran access to his legal land. Mathew requested additional time to complete a re-survey, but Purushothaman categorically rejected his request. Mathew obtained a legal decree from the court to preserve the status quo until an additional re-survey of the land was completed.

Mathew Tharakan was ready to follow the official verdict without knowing what it really meant and to forget the long-running disagreement with his neighbour. One day, his pride was questioned during a casual talk at the village toddy bar. Kuttappan, a coconut tree climber by profession, labelled him a coward and said he was a dumbass who couldn't read between the lines. In an inebriated condition, Kuttappan commented, 'Mathew mappila might be a rich and powerful person in this village, but he is dumb and can't see how Sukumaran is cheating.'

Kuttappan made the allegations in the absence of Mathew Tharakan and his accomplices. A few people advised Kuttappan to raise the accusation in front of Mathew. Another drunk person challenged Kuttappan to disclose his source of information. He accepted the challenge and stated, 'The new pravarthiyar is a womaniser; he secretly visits all the homes where men are weak, and his next target is Sukumaran's daughter.'

Another inebriated person said, 'Sukumaran's daughter is very smart and not an easy target. Mathew Mappila's older son Baby will marry her.' Everyone who was inebriated was quiet for a moment after hearing the statement. Many thought the stunning news was completely out of the blue.

The accusation was so serious that one of the drunkards yelled, 'You are a fool and a drunkard; don't make false accusations and ruin the lives of educated young people.'

Kuttappan affirmed his findings and stated, 'Don't underestimate them; there are things that the poor villagers can't even imagine.'

When everyone turned to Kuttappan to back up his statements, he firmly said, 'Many of you don't know that they both went to the same college. Baby is going to Delhi to look for work.' Then he glanced around and said, 'He will be back soon, and when he is, they will run away together.'

One of the older people said, 'Kuttappa, don't make assumptions. You will resent them, and their future will be ruined.'

This time, Kuttappan was quite angry. 'You old fool, what do you know about the new generation?' When no one responded, he stated, 'They are very smart and don't care about their religion, customs, or practices. They are in love, and I have more proof.'

Mathew Tharakan arrived at the toddy bar to enjoy his customary beverage; everyone else looked at him and kept quiet. Mathew began to drink his customary toddy, and one of them asked him, 'Mathew mappile, is it correct that you are relinquishing your claim to the ancestral land in order to make peace with Sukumaran?' Mathew stared at him but did not instantly respond. He then began to enjoy his favourite boiled tapioca and fish curry.

After a brief period, another individual commented, 'He is silent, which implies that it is true.'

Kuttappan was quick to comment, 'Now you are aware that what I said was right.'

Mathew stared at Kuttappan with interest and wondered, 'What did you say about me?' Then Mathew said, 'Who are you to make comments on me? I can do anything I want.' None of them responded.

Mathew continued to enjoy his drink and munchies when an elderly man commented, 'Proud Mappila children don't marry Ezhava children, particularly when there is an ongoing dispute between them.' Mathew was extremely disturbed this time and rose from his seat in a fit of rage, asking, 'What are you talking about?'

Mathew's anger was so intense that the elderly person was scared and refrained from responding. Mathew looked around and restated his question, 'I am unable to fully understand your topic and concerns; could someone specify?'

At that moment, another elder clarified the previous discussions: 'Kuttappan states that you agreed to the re-survey and you are prepared to accept the arrogant pravarthiyar's scrupulous decisions.'

Mathew was enraged and asserted, 'It is my land, and I have the authority to do whatever I wish. I may even donate it to anyone.'

Kuttappan abruptly rose from his seat and yelled, 'Now you all know that Mathew is a coward; otherwise, who would consent to the decision of that womaniser?'

This time, Mathew lost control, leapt and slapped Kuttappan on the face, making him fall to the ground. Kuttappan was short and lean, while Mathew was well-built with a robust physique. The proprietor of the toddy shop intervened and stood himself between the two, imploring Mathew to disregard Kuttappan's blabbering, as if they were illogical.

Kuttappan promptly rose from the floor and regained his footing to confront Mathew. Quickly, the inebriated villagers restrained them from attacking each other.

Elders attempted to make things better. 'We're not here to fight; we're here to drink and spend time together.' Then one of them cautioned Kuttappan, 'Don't make false claims and mind your own business.'

This made Kuttappan even angrier. 'I've told you what I heard, and it's up to Mathew Mappila to say if it's true.' He paused for a moment and then said, 'If it's not wrong, why did he slap me?'

One of the older people stood beside Mathew cautioned Kuttappan, 'You don't have the right to call someone a coward.'

Another elder urged Mathew to explain: 'Kuttappan says that Pravarthiyar is cheating you by lying about the survey reports and favouring Sukumaran.'

Someone else added, 'Pravarthiyar is eyeing his daughter.'

Mathew looked around as though he didn't understand any of them. 'What is going on here? Why are you talking about me and the survey reports?'

Kuttappan then said, 'Now he is acting very innocent; he doesn't understand any of us.' After that, he looked around and said, 'You will feel the pain when your son Baby elopes with Sukumaran's daughter.'

At that point, one of the men restraining Kuttappan got very angry, freed him and warned 'You rat, don't ever wish bad things on other people.' As soon as Kuttappan faced him, Mathew booted him in the stomach with his right leg. Kuttappan couldn't take the hard kick and collapsed to the floor with both his hands on his stomach.

The toddy shop owner shouted, 'Oh God, you've killed him! I can't let this happen in my shop!'

Mathew's fury grew. 'Let the idiot die; it's good for others.'

One of them poured water on Kuttappan's face, and he moved his arms and legs. The elders were relieved and said, 'Thank God, he is alive.'

Someone else commented, 'Otherwise, Mathew Mappila could have gone to jail.'

Mathew replied, 'I don't care about it; I've been to worse jails in my life.'

After a while, the toddy shop owner and a few others helped Kuttappan get up from the floor. They gave him more water to drink and helped him sit down on the bench. He was still mad at Mathew Tharakan and said that he didn't get what he really wanted. He thought that when he provided facts, people would notice and thank him. He wanted to warn Mathew Tharakan, not condemn him for not taking the threat seriously.

The elders tried once again to step in. They took Mathew outside the bar, told him what Kuttappan had said, and shared their worries. 'The new Pravarthiyar is a sly fox who is trying to get ahead of everyone else and is cheating you and others.'

Mathew Tharakan calmly listened and explained why he wanted to go along with the illegal decision. 'I didn't want to accept his decision, but my sick wife and kids insisted that we work things out with the neighbours.'

The working class in the village drank socially and were smart enough to stay together. Most of them were friends, and others were part of the extended family. They all knew that Mathew's wife was not doing well. They quickly chose to back Mathew Tharakan and dispute the new Pravarthiyar's decision.

For the hard-working farmers, drinking toddy was a way to taste its sourness and get drunk right away. The drink, which is made by natural fermentation, helps them feel less weary after a long day of hard work. The effect lasts for a few hours, depending on how much they drink.

Mathew returned with the older people and asked Kuttappan for details. At first, Kuttappan didn't want to speak, but an appeal from the social drinkers changed his mind. 'Pravarthiyar is selfish and stupid; he needs to be punished.'

He looked at Mathew and said, 'Sumithra is a treasure. She doesn't think harmful thoughts about other people, and she would be a good match for a good man.' He looked around and said, 'Purushothaman is trying to steal her.'

He looked around again and told them, 'You all know he is evil and cruel. He killed his first wife, so he shouldn't get another chance to kill another woman, especially one from our village.'

None of them responded, and Kuttappan made a statement that shocked Mathew Tharakan: 'Sumithra is educated and smart; she is a good match for Baby.'

Mathew Tharakan briefly appeared stunned before he abruptly exclaimed, 'Are you referring to my son, Baby? How can you establish a connection with him, given that he is employed in Delhi?'

Kuttappan dismissed the matter by stating, 'It is peculiar that you are not informed of their relationship. They were classmates at the college, and their relationship is well-known to all, including the college principal.'

One of the elders intervened before Mathew could respond: 'Kuttappan, let's refrain from discussing Baby; let his family make the decision. Do you have any additional information on Purushothaman?' The elder then sought the opinions of others, but none responded.

While Mathew Tharakan maintained his silence, Kuttappan declared, 'Sukumaran is aware of their relationship, which is one of the reasons he consented to the unity of Sumithra and Purushothaman.'

Kuttappan, noticing Mathew Tharakan's quiescence, stated, 'I understand that Baby intends to take Sumithra to Delhi, pretending better employment scope.'

Mathew raised his voice. 'You rat, refrain from debating my family matter any further. I can discipline my children, and they will stick to my instructions.'

Kuttappan was adamant about not ceding what he believed. 'You are not required to hold me accountable for your ignorance. Consider it a timely reminder from my part.' He looked at the other drinkers. 'It may be too late at this point; their relationship is strong.'

He paused for a moment and commented, 'Sukumaran is on the brink of placing his daughter under house arrest, and he may soon forcibly marry her to Purushothaman.'

Another elderly individual once again reminded them, 'No-one has the authority to interfere in Sukumaran's personal affairs or question his decision regarding their family relations.'

Mathew rose from his seat and walked towards the exit door. Other elders followed him and expressed their apprehension regarding the unjust ruling on Mathew's disputed land, asserting, 'Ignore Kuttappan; he is a dumb ass who bluffs and talks nonsense. You should not ignore the need to deal with the Pravarthiyar.'

Mathew Tharakan returned to the toddy bar and spoke from his heart. 'I deny the accusations against my son. He is an adult and has the capacity to make his own decisions.'

Looking at everyone, he firmly stated, 'If it is contrary to my will and my culture, he is an outsider.' Then he turned to Kuttappan and said, 'You are an opportunist. If your accusations are true, I will ensure that the idiot Pravarthiyar is dealt with.'

Another elder advised Mathew Tharakan to exercise prudence, as Purushothaman Pravarthiyar possessed judicial authority. Another elder commented, 'In order to conquer a thorn, it is necessary to choose a thorn that is sharper.'

The elder responded to a clarification by stating, 'If the Pravarthiyar has judicial authority, Mathew Tharakan needs to use more powerful and influential methods.'

Mathew Tharakan responded with patience and firmness, stating, 'I am mindful of his power and authority, but I was unaware of his corrupt behaviour. I can effectively deal with rogue personalities.'

Feeling satisfied with his surgically precise decision, most social drinkers reiterated their strong backing by tapping on the wooden desks. Mathew Tharakan was verbally reassured by one of the elders: 'Bonded together, we are much stronger than any judicial or political authority. If injustice happens to Mathew today, it could happen to any of us. We must resist and defeat evil for the benefit of all.'

With that assurance, Mathew thankfully looked at everyone and walked out of the toddy shop.

Chapter 16

Chacko deeply inhaled the remains of the nicotine-flavoured smoke arising from a portion of the burnt-out beedi. He quickly threw away the lit bud when the heat scorched the thin layer of skin on his fingertip. The beedi smoke had made his lips and the tips of his fore and middle fingers black. He looked towards the stone wall in front and randomly told his wife, who was busy in the kitchen, 'You know Joyachan's likes, add more spices and finally pour some coconut milk on the fish curry to make it taste better.'

Mary quickly responded, 'Yes, the spices are not too strong and they smell great. I'm sure Joyachan will love it.'

Joyachan stayed quiet since he trusted Mary's great cuisine and knew she would take his tastes into account. She always used extracts from roasted tamarinds to add more flavour, which made the fish curry spicier. Chacko was happy with his wife's response; he walked to the farthest corner of his land and discharged himself. A long, pleasant sigh of satisfaction was heard as soon as his full bladder was empty.

Chacko went back to his spot on the porch and tried to explain himself by saying, 'Relieving in the open keeps the dangerous reptiles away.'

Joyachan grinned and said, 'That's not very correct. Try putting ammonia-soaked rags around the areas where you see any dangerous species and they won't come back.'

Chacko knew Joyachan was smarter and readily agreed with his correction. 'Our ancestors used that trick; the modern world has better resources.'

The villagers' extreme assumptions were proven wrong by the barbaric events that followed, as Pravarthiyar Purushothaman was far more evil than they had imagined. Mathew Tharakan obtained an injunction order, which temporarily but immediately halted Pravarthiyar's efforts to impress Sukumaran. His plan to propose to Sumithra with significant benefit to her father failed. He noticed the villagers now had a greater appreciation for Mathew's courage and were realising that there was a superior judicial mechanism that surpassed Pravarthiyar's illogical orders. This information was novel to the villagers, as it indicated that his decisions could be called into doubt at any moment. Purushothaman was disappointed by the loss of his power and authority to Mathew, and he vowed to take revenge and reclaim his lost prestige.

In those days, the barter system was practised by the villagers, exchanging their home-grown products and commodities. Numerous villages were self-sufficient, fulfilling their fundamental requirements for food and clothing. Farmers and weavers were present in all villages, and they provided mutual support. During the weekly and monthly markets, additional goods or rare domestic and cosmetic items were brought in from faraway places and exchanged. The monthly markets were significantly larger, drawing a diverse array of merchants from distant locations. These routine markets also provided villagers with the chance to reconnect and strengthen their relations. Occasionally, they were used to resolve varied disputes through physical challenges and negotiations, generally to settle a score.

Pravarthiyar Purushothaman and an accomplice from the local police force devised a plan to confront Mathew Tharakan during the monthly market. They intended to cause both physical and mental anguish by insulting and defaming Mathew Tharakan in public.

The market was also referred to as *Mattachantha*, where individuals exchanged their home-grown products for other items. In exchange for the space they occupied, sellers and trading vendors paid a fixed amount of rent, known as *Thara Vadaka*, in currency. Rent was typically collected by an authorised agent or representative of the Pravarthiyar's office. Much to the surprise of many, Pravarthiyar Purushothaman arrived at the market that day to oversee the rent collections.

Mathew Tharakan brought in a few piglets for sale on that day, in addition to his customary commodities of black pepper and spices. One of his employees was selling them when the tax collector approached him for the rent. The seller requested more time to pay, as he was expecting a customer's payment in currency. Piglets were mostly bought by poor farmers in exchange for their goods rather than for coins.

The tax representative demanded the rent be paid in advance, or the space would be vacated. The worker begged, 'Sir, we are at the beginning of our business. We were only able to sell one of them in exchange for a bag of pepper. I will pay you as soon as a coin is received.' He pointed to the small bag in his vicinity and reminded him, 'This is standard practice, and we are not strangers.'

The employee glanced at Mathew Tharakan, who was enjoying a cup of tea, and firmly reiterated, 'This is our customary location, for which we consistently pay rent.'

The tax collector was enraged by the claimants' assertion of their rights to the permanent spots. He raised his voice, 'None of you in this market have permanent space allocations; the first person to occupy an ideal or their favourite space will do so.'

Mathew's worker was defended by another vendor, who stated, 'That is not the practice; we have been occupying this location for generations and have the right to it.'

Before the tax collector could respond, another vendor reminded him, 'The market is becoming increasingly crowded, please leave and allow everyone to carry out their business.'

The tax collector was furious and ignored warnings from others. He pushed Mathew's worker away and shouted, 'You scoundrel, how dare you not follow my instructions? I am the one who sets the rules here. I will expel you from this market.'

The young man was unable to resist the force of the thrust and inevitably fell to the ground. He cried aloud in agony as he struck his head on the hard earth.

The old rag basket that the piglets were safe in came loose during the chaos, and several of them got away in various directions. When Mathew heard his worker's scream, he ran to the scene and grabbed one of the runaway piglets. He put it back in the basket and asked why they were fighting.

He urged the tax collector to leave and come back later to collect the rent when he realised that the tax collector had made the situation difficult. The tax collector looked around and yelled, 'You have to pay now or get out of the way so others can use it.'

Mathew's worker suffered injury, with small bruises on his chin, but he got over the shock and punched the tax collector in the face, saying, 'How dare you push me?'

The tax collector was ready for the action and swiftly ducked away. Mathew held his worker back before the tax collector could hit him.

Pravarthiyar Purushothaman suddenly appeared out of nowhere and grabbed Mathew by the neck. 'You son of a bitch, how dare you not follow my orders?'

Mathew and everyone else who was there were shocked when Pravarthiar Purushothaman showed up out of nowhere. Even though Mathew knew right away that something wasn't right, he couldn't help but respond and protect himself. Mathew was powerful enough to grab Purushothaman's hands and break free of his grip on his neck. Mathew pushed Purushothaman away with both hands and freed himself. Purushothaman fell to the ground, and his aide helped him get back up.

The bruises on Purushothaman's cheek progressively grew bigger, and the red dots at the fractures swelled into bubbles. His anger made his blood pressure go up, and more blood surged through the ruptures.

Soon, several red bubbles fell to the ground. They both stood up to Mathew and stared at each other for a time. Mathew was keeping himself and his worker safe from more harm.

Suddenly the young worker jumped up, flew through the air, and kicked the tax man in the chest. Immediately, Mathew stepped in and urged him to restrain himself. 'This is a public space and not an opportunity to score points against others.' The young man was unable to be tamed due to his anger. The tax collector was inadvertently knocked to the ground by the force of the kick.

Purushothaman's anger intensified, and he turned to the young man, saying, 'You pig, how dare you touch my man.'

Mathew swiftly stood between them, and a few other bystanders came forward to restrain them from further physical assault. Another senior vendor requested that they maintain peace: 'This is not the time to engage in conflict; any disputes can be resolved at a later time.'

A few other individuals also expressed the necessity of operating the market, stating, 'You are causing a challenge for both vendors and customers, as there are numerous perishable items.'

Pravarthiar Purushothaman was unwilling to restrain himself; however, his tax collector was having trouble breathing. He was then advised by the elderly to 'take him to the doctor and we will discuss the dispute later.'

He looked around once more and assured himself, 'I am responsible for paying the thara vadaka even if Mathew is unwilling.'

Mathew was on the brink of responding when the elder requested that he remain silent, stating, 'Let the business be conducted.' Then, noticing the individuals who had gathered, he said, 'Now, everyone, disperse and attend to your own affairs.' He patted Mathew's shoulder and reassured him, 'It is essential that we resolve the issues, sustain the market, and complete the business.'

A member of the audience offered the tax collector a glass of water, and a few individuals assisted Purushothaman in moving him to a more comfortable place. Purushothaman realised that Mathew had a greater number of supporters at the market. He gave a severe warning to Mathew prior to his leaving: 'You will be held accountable for this, and I will ensure that you endure a significant amount of pain.'

Mathew was on the brink of responding, but the people gathered urged him to remain silent and reassured him, 'Barking dogs seldom bite.'

Mathew Tharakan and many others who witnessed the unprovoked assaults were unaware that Purushothaman's threats were serious. The village was left in tears by the horrific and brutal incidents that ensued.

Mathew Tharakan adopted many steps to prevent further disputes with Purushothaman while acknowledging the cautionary advice of his relatives and friends. To mitigate the risks associated with isolation, he avoided being lonely and ensured the company of others while walking through the village or to nearby places. Additionally, he discouraged his family members from travelling at night, even to locations that were well known to them. He advised them to take caution and prioritise their safety.

The precautions Mathew took weren't enough to protect him and his family and were the victims of an unanticipated turn of events.

Joyachan's words were frail as he continued, 'Our elders mentioned that the majority of serious crimes, including murders, are planned and executed during the night, particularly during the early hours. These periods are optimal because their targets are less resistant. Most of the victims are either recuperating or fatigued from their long days of labour, which results in a decrease in their level of resistance.'

In support, Joyachan detailed an example from their fundamental belief. The Jews were influenced by Roman culture and divided the night into four watches. They deployed powerful soldiers for the early night and named it the first watch. Chacko provided additional clarifications: 'Jesus was apprehended by Roman soldiers in the early morning hours at Gethsemane, while he was praying and his disciples were resting.'

Joyachan regarded Chacko's appropriate example and stated, 'The Jews primarily executed their plans to arrest and sentence a noble man during the night in order to prevent large public gatherings.'

Chacko promptly responded, 'Precisely to prevent the involvement of many of the supporters and beneficiaries of Jesus' kindness and noble acts.'

Joyachan paused before continuing, 'Mathew Tharakan was unable to resist, nor was there anyone to protect the family. The most gruesome murders in the history of their village occurred during the morning hours.' Chacko was unable to respond, and neither of them realised that Mary and their children were discreetly listening to them.

In those days, it was uncommon to receive an injection order against the Pravarthiyar's ruling. Many experts subsequently asserted that it was the first of its kind. The judicial system had a defined hierarchy. Although Pravarthiyar could present his argument against the injunction, he was unwilling to do so. Rather, he attempted to enforce his previous directive by physically removing the land-border barrier that had been erected by Mathew Tharakan.

Unfortunately, the day was unlucky for Mathew Tharakan's family. The day was a Friday, and the villagers found out that the Pravarthiyar's police associate had deliberately selected that day. The moment Joyachan realised Chacko wasn't following, he clarified, 'The village was supervised by a head constable and two constables, who manned a police outpost.'

Chacko stared at Joyachan's eyes in disbelief. 'On Friday mornings, the head constable delegates his responsibilities to his deputies and travels to his home, which was located farther away. He returns only on the following Monday morning.'

Joyachan elaborated after a brief period, 'The head constable anticipates working the entire Friday; however, he typically does not. Instead, he will travel early to his home to reach before sunset. His superiors at the nearby main police station have authorised these local arrangements, despite the fact that they are against the rules. The villagers were relatively law-abiding and maintained harmony among themselves.'

He briefly paused before continuing, 'Until that day.'

The person who suffered the most was Baby Tharakan, who unexpectedly visited home from his workplace in Delhi. He reached home with a well-defined strategy, which was disclosed only after the traumatic event.

The day before the incident, Baby Tharakan arrived home in a quiet way and remained indoors, as is normal. His parents did not anticipate his arrival until Christmas, which was still two months away. He reasoned that his workplace was closed for a week during the Diwali festivals, and visiting them would be the most effective manner of utilising that time. The family relished the dinner that evening, and Mathew reminded him to visit his auntie before returning to Delhi.

In the mid-morning hours of that day, Mathew's wife heard loud noises and shouting from the boundary side between them and Sukumaran's land. She notified Mathew, who promptly reached the spot and was appalled to see Sukumaran destroying the wooden fence. Pravarthiyar Purushothaman was shouting and issuing orders, while his associate was assisting Sukumaran in removing the solid wooden fences.

Sukumaran was pushed to the other side by Mathew, who had come sprinting. 'How dare you touch my fence on my land!'

The police constable was swift to respond, slapping Mathew on the face and saying, 'You son of a bitch, how dare you disobey the official orders.'

The blow to the face was severe, causing Mathew to fall to the ground. However, he promptly regained his strength and responded, 'You have no right to get involved in this matter.'

Concurrently, surpassing the severity of the physical assault he suffered, Mathew delivered a powerful kick to the police constable's abdomen. The constable screamed in agony, 'You scumbag, you've killed me!'

He plummeted to the ground while holding his palms on his stomach. The constable was in severe agony, nearly collapsing, and was screaming.

Although both of his accomplices fell to the ground, Purushothaman remained unharmed. He confronted Mathew and challenged, 'You are an idiot, you are unable to evade me. I have more effective methods of dealing with you.'

Mathew courageously confronted him with a warning, 'The higher court has frozen your orders, and you are now violating the court order yourself.'

Purushothaman was hurriedly approaching Mathew and failed to notice the uneven ground. He tripped over a pebble and fell to the ground, suffering a severe facial injury. Mathew struck Purushothaman on the back before he could rise. Purushothaman's wrath multiplied, and he abruptly turned around and exerted a significant amount of force on Mathew. Baby Tharakan held Mathew in his arms before Mathew fell to the ground.

'Dad, what is going on here?' The questions were repeated to others. 'Who are you all, and how dare you remove the fences?' he asked as he nervously looked around.

Sukumaran responded promptly, 'You coward, you were hiding yourself within the house and devising a plan to marry my adored daughter. I would kill you before that.' All present were taken aback by the news, and they began to stare at one another.

Mathew was equally shocked and could not believe what he had heard. He looked at his son incredulously and said, 'What is happening? You returned earlier than Christmas, with this plan?'

Baby looked at the surroundings before turning his attention to Sukumaran's house. He then murmured to Mathew, 'Dad, I can explain it later, let us stop this madness for a few inches of land.'

Mathew's fury intensified, and he declared, 'This land belongs to my parents, and I am not willing to give it up to cowards like you.' He then stared at Purushothaman, who appeared puzzled. 'You are not a match for me, and I will teach you a lesson.'

He picked up a wooden plank from the ground and was about to strike Purushothaman's head with it. Baby promptly objected and pleaded, 'Dad, I am begging you once more to end this madness. He will die, and you will be detained as a murderer.'

Mathew was furious. 'You are not worthy to protect your own land, leave me now.' Unable to respond to his dad, Baby turned to his home, where his mother and younger brother stood helpless.

Mathew became irritated and repeated the question, pointing towards Sukumaran's house: 'Are you with me or part of that family? Please clarify what I am hearing.' Baby could not respond and continued to hold his father more tightly.

Purushothaman promptly got up from the ground and pushed the father–son pair before Baby could respond. Baby stood firm and successfully resisted it before retaliating with a kick. Purushothaman was unable to withstand the impact, tripped, and collapsed to the ground.

By the time Purushothaman's police accomplice recovered from the agony and yelled, 'Sir, are you fine?' he failed to get an immediate response and looked around the area. He turned to Mathew and Baby and warned, 'You are resisting the law and attacking officials, for which you will be punished.'

Following this, Purushothaman gave him further instructions: 'Fetch the cans, you should teach them a lesson.'

Sukumaran appeared bewildered, as he was unaware of his accomplice's impending actions. He had initially suggested that the fences be removed quietly, a proposal that Purushothaman declined. It was now evident that they had different plans, as they intended to avenge rather than enforce his own legal decision.

Sukumaran attempted to help Purushothaman get up from the ground by extending his arm. Purushothaman responded by shouting, 'I will not tolerate anyone who has ever attempted to deceive me. You have promised me your daughter in marriage, but you are hiding their intentions to elope.'

Sukumaran was unable to respond. He stared at Baby before turning to his home, which was a bit far. Pointing to Mathew, Sukumaran reiterated to Purushothaman, 'This idiot will not be my daughter's father-in-law for as long as I live.'

Mathew was unable to maintain his composure and yelled at his own son, 'You are now defaming me. How could you ever consider marrying the daughter of this dog?'

Baby was unable to respond immediately and turned his attention to Sukumaran's home, where he noticed Preman trying to restrain Sumithra.

Following that, he noticed Preman screaming at a person who was approaching from another direction. In the distance, Baby noticed Purushothaman's police accomplice, who was carrying two cans and running towards them.

Preman quickly confined Sumithra in the home and chased the accomplice, who had already been ahead of him. Baby only had a brief period to realise the imminent danger. He immediately notified Mathew, 'Dad, get out of here, he must be bringing something to burn the fence.'

The silence persisted for a few more seconds before Mathew prepared to confront the accomplice. The constable who was carrying the cans reached near to them.

In between them, Sukumaran stood and warned, 'This is my property, and you are not allowed here.'

Seeing his accomplice near, Purushothaman abruptly got up from the ground and threatened Sukumaran, 'You deceive me and I will also kill you,' and then kicked him in the back. Sukumaran was unable to hold onto his footing and plummeted to the ground.

Baby immediately reacted, and using both his hands he raised Purushothaman from the ground and hurled him towards his accomplice.

Purushothaman and his accomplice were unable to withstand the sudden and rapid action. Unable to protect themselves, both plummeted to the ground. The area was filled with the foul odour of kerosene, as the viscous liquid oozed out of one of the cans. Preman appeared at this moment and supported Sukumaran in getting up from the ground.

Mathew was immediately requested by Sukumaran to evacuate the area, as the Pravarthiyar was notoriously obstinate and had threatened to take revenge by killing him. Subsequently, Sukumaran saw Sumithra sprinting towards them, while his wife Radhamma followed her, repeatedly asking her to return home. Sukumaran turned to his son and said, 'Prema, please control Sumithra and send them home.'

Instead, Preman begged him, 'Father, please leave them alone. Sumithra and Baby are in love, allow them to live their lives together.' Sukumaran stared at Mathew, who was looking at Sumithra, who was fast approaching them.

Pravarthiyar Purushothaman stood from the ground and looked at all. He then seized a full can, opened the lid, and hurled the liquid at Mathew, shouting, 'You son of a bitch, you will die now.' Baby leapt and positioned himself between Mathew and Purushothaman prior to Sumithra's swift approach. Baby took in most of the liquid, while Mathew received only a few drips.

Sukumaran raised the alarm, warning everyone, 'Get out of the area, the policeman will start a fire.' Upon hearing the alarm, Preman leapt towards the constable but wasn't quick enough. The lighted matchstick was hurled towards Mathew, but it struck Baby Tharakan.

For a moment the environment stood still, but then Baby's dhoti caught fire, and Mathew quickly tore it away. But it was too late— Baby's shirt was on fire. Mathew shouted at him, 'Baby, my son, roll over!'

Baby didn't feel the heat, but he saw the angel running towards him. Sumithra stood in front of Baby, looked into his eyes, and then hugged his burning body. The fire grew larger, as Sumithra was wearing a silk saree. For a few seconds, both of them stood still, then slumped to the ground. They couldn't roll over anymore, but they held on to each other until their bodies, which were almost burned, stopped moving.

Preman flung the blazing dhoti at the policeman, who was also wet with kerosene, and in no time he was on fire. The flaming cop tried to sprint to the other side of the fence, but he fell before reaching it. The smell of burning human flesh surrounded the area.

Both families ran towards them, and soon several neighbours arrived to help. Sukumaran couldn't control his grief and rage; he grabbed a big piece of wood and hit Purushothaman on the head. Radhamma fell to the ground unconscious, and Mathew's wife screamed and passed out.

Chapter 17

Chacko, along with others who covertly listened, was horrified and remained breathless for the next few minutes. He once again stared at the substantial stone wall that towered above his head, thereby limiting his views beyond that point. It continued to serve as a deterrent to the rest of the world until he was able to get past it. The survival of Chacko and his family is contingent upon their ability to traverse that substantial wall on a daily basis. His capacity to ascend to higher levels provides people like him with the opportunity to engage with the world, as well as to resolve many ambiguities. Every day, he stares at the wall in front of him, and the effort necessary to ascend it serves as a source of discouragement. The courage to transcend the lifetime barrier of his existence is derived from his love for his family. He is driven to ascend each stepping stone in front of him by his determination to maintain the fireplace's flame and to provide for his children.

The tranquil moment between Joyachan and Chacko was abruptly interrupted by a booming sob, which was followed by profound weeping from inside. Celine was unable to suppress her emotions and burst into tears. Between the kitchen and the inner room, Mary swiftly walked through the doorless corridor. She hugged her daughter tightly to her chest, wrapping both of her arms around her. 'Don't worry, sweetheart, life is always unpredictable and difficult.'

Celine struggled to maintain her composure and breathed heavily. Mary acknowledged her distress and offered her a glass of water, advising her, 'Come on, child, drink this water and relax.' She then turned to Sunny, who was on the brink of sobbing. He turned away from her when the tears in his eyes burst, as they were filled with grief. He moved to his place within the house; consequently, Mary recognised that her son's capabilities exceeded her expectations.

Mary served the lunch to her husband and to her brother on the veranda due to the insufficient space and lighting in the kitchen. Joyachan invited the children to join them, but Mary was more empathetic, stating, 'Do not be concerned, they require time to recover, and I will provide them with food at a later time.'

The youngest son, Sunil, appeared with a smile, and Joyachan promptly took him onto his lap. Joyachan fed him a handful of rice and appreciated his pleasantness. 'He will be stronger than your other children.'

Mary took Sunil from his comfortable place and advised her brother, 'Ignore him and enjoy your favourite rice and fish curry. He is naughty and I will feed him.' Celine swiftly recovered and quickly served drinking water for all.

After they finished their lunch, Mary requested Joyachan to take a nap, but he refused, saying, 'I have to get home before it's dark, I need to catch the earliest bus from the town.'

Chacko urged him, 'Spend the night here, my children will be happy.' Looking at his young children watching them from the veranda, Chacko insisted, 'You can leave early morning.'

Joyachan walked towards the stone wall in front and Chacko joined him, offering a lighted beedi. Joyachan accepted, took a puff, and commented, 'Not very good, but okay.'

Chacko followed up with another question to clear his doubts: 'Why did Preman commit suicide? Was he depressed over the horrifying deaths?'

To be sure no one was listening, Joyachan ensured they were away from the children and explained.

Pravarthiyar Purushothaman recovered from severe head and body injuries within three months. He turned against Sukumaran after realising that he had been nearly killed by him. He filed formal complaints with the police, alleging that officials were intentionally injured and that the judiciary was misled.

Earlier, the head constable of the police outpost was exceedingly considerate of both families. Mathew Tharakan was still recuperating from burn injuries, and they had lost their beloved children. He was unable to disregard the fact that a police constable was killed during the unwarranted incident.

The police initially filed a case against Purushothaman and the deceased officer for the use of a hazardous substance against innocent people. The investigation was subsequently advanced by the police as accidental rather than intentional death, thereby shielding both families from additional criminal proceedings.

Purushothaman deployed his personal influence at the highest possible level when he realised that his complaint was being disregarded. The police investigation determined that the deceased officer was carrying the flammable liquid, which resulted in Purushothaman's complaints against Mathew being dismissed. According to the initial findings, the constable carried the liquid in accordance with Purushothaman's directives, rendering him the primary suspect in the incident.

The accusations against Purushothaman were disregarded by the higher police officials, who conducted special investigations and considered him a victim of violence. Purushothaman claimed that both Sukumaran and Mathew would be prosecuted. A new case was registered against Sukumaran, and Mathew was considered a victim of violence.

Sukumaran and Preman were subsequently apprehended by the police on charges of assault that resulted in the murder of a police officer. It was alleged that the police spared Mathew due to their concern for the general public's outrage, harbouring both sympathy and support for him.

The special investigation team subjected both the father and son to brutal torture at the main police station, where they were taken for further interrogation. In those days, police officers were notorious for deploying the fear factor to terrorise the general populace. They regularly used foul language to incite fear through threats and abuses. They deployed obscene language on the suspects and their relatives, which was a form of mental torture that could result in lifelong mental distress.

The use of foul language by police personnel was intended to create fear in the suspects, compelling them to either confess the truth or accept the charges against them. The suspects were subsequently subjected to physical abuse using a variety of wooden rods and canes, and at times iron rods were used to inflict the most severe agony. It was common for suspects to be subjected to brutal custodial violence, and both the father and son were subjected to inhumane torture.

Police brutality was met with absolute censorship, to which the media yielded without much resistance.

While Sukumaran narrated the truth, the police accused him of bringing kerosene to the crime scene. They made him sign a declaration to that effect, but both father and son refused. Due to his advanced age, Sukumaran was unable to endure the beatings from the iron rod and repeatedly passed out. Preman, his son, was stronger, which infuriated the police officers, who then subjected him to the most brutal forms of torture.

Preman was devastated to see his sister and her lover perish tragically in a fire. He blamed Pravarthiyar Purushothaman for the premature deaths. Preman repeatedly declared that he was determined to avenge the death of his devoted sister and continued to confront the cops who were torturing him. When the cops saw Preman refusing to comply with their demands, they unleashed all of their violence.

They started using more harsh methods once the standard verbal and physical abuse, deprivation of food and drink, and torture failed. They used sharp instruments to cause deep incisions on their bodies, and then they applied chilli powder to create a burning sensation. They removed the entire nail from the toes and placed paper pegs beneath the fingernails. For a week, the special police team subjected them both to various forms of torture.

While his son Preman was stubborn, Sukumaran was on the verge of losing it. Sukumaran was brutally abused and humiliated in front of Preman by the police squad to get him to agree to their demands. They threatened to imprison them for the rest of their lives if they didn't drop the accusations against Purushothaman.

The police team threatened the father and son with severe repercussions if they did not consent, leaving them naked and famished for an entire night. The following day, they separated them and tormented them individually. Unable to sustain the cruel torture, Sukumaran accepted that the whole incident was designed by him.

Preman refused to comply with their demands, and they persisted in torturing him inhumanely. He begged for a glass of water, but they compelled him to drink his own urine. Subsequently, they implemented the most notorious torture techniques, descending a heavy iron pole onto his thighs. They compelled him to lie down on a wooden bench, initially in an upside-down position, and then rolled a massive iron rod from his waist to his toes.

His forearms were securely fastened to the legs of the bench in a backwards pattern. The iron rod was rolled down by two police torturers, who stood on either side of the bench and applied their entire body weight to the rods. The vital blood vessels between the bones were crushed when the epidermis was pressed against them. The abrupt release of adrenaline resulted in dizziness, and Preman immediately lost consciousness when the free-flowing blood was constrained.

The iron rod was repeatedly rolled over the same skin, causing additional injury and causing the area to burst, resulting in internal bleeding. The iron rod rolled over the kneecaps, producing the sound of 'bone breaking.' He was unable to produce any sound with the rug covering his mouth. Many times, his body trembled in agony when the iron rod reached the sole of his toe. He repeatedly choked while trying to take a breath, as his mouth filled with saliva. Every time he exhaled, his eyes bulged with tears.

The cruel police team repeatedly rolled the iron rod over his naked and unresponsive legs, repeating the process from waist level to the bottom. In a matter of seconds, his testicles were fractured, and blood splattered onto the floor.

One of them kicked him when he became unresponsive to the harsh torture, causing his unconscious body to fall to the hard floor. 'Senseless swine, unwilling to co-operate, doesn't fear the mighty police force, lost the right to live,' they grumbled, spitting on his body.

'You are stupid, do you want to listen to us?' they asked, as one of them took the rug out of his mouth. 'The hog is hard to break, let's leave him here.'

Preman was gasping for air as his chest failed to respond. Without noticing that he was internally bleeding as well as externally, they walked out of the torture chamber, leaving his still body on the floor.

Both tormentors returned after an hour and proceeded to boot him once more. 'You son of a b*tch, are you actually dead?'

The eyes and mouth of Preman were open, and his rigid body did not move. One of the torturers raised the alarm while inspecting his body, stating, 'He has no pulse, he may be dead. What should we do?' They sprayed water on his face and gradually trickled it through his still-open mouth. Water rushed through the sides as the mouth became overfilled.

'Wake up, you stupid, you brought this on yourself,' shouted one of the torturers as he raised his stiff head. They made numerous attempts to revive him, but they soon realised that it was no longer feasible, and his body became increasingly rigid.

They both began a discussion and sought the advice of their other colleague, who then came and conducted an examination of the body. They quickly fastened the body to one of the beams on the room ceiling using a thick coir rope. He stated that 'hanging marks are required to prove that he committed suicide in response to the tragic death of his sister.'

The police team promptly took Sukumaran to a government hospital, as he was unconscious in another room. The doctor was pressured to disregard the torture marks and ordered to issue a health certificate. Then the police asked him to leave the station while they conducted additional enquiries.

Sukumaran was unwilling to leave the station without his son. The police responded by stating, 'We have already released him on conditional bail, and he left the station for home.' Then they cautioned him, 'You are both required to report to the station on a daily basis for additional questioning.' Subsequently, they exchanged glances, and one of them reminded, 'Every morning, before 10:00 a.m.'

Sukumaran was unable to walk, so the police arranged for another villager to assist him in getting home.

After reaching home, Sukumaran found his son Preman was missing and went back to the police station with his family and neighbours. They rejected the police claims of his release the previous day. They threatened to attack the station unless they met him immediately. The small group gradually grew in numbers and shouted slogans against police abuse and called for his immediate release.

Local social leaders' intervention wasn't helpful either, and the angry mob threatened to attack the police. Following the summoning of additional police officers, the gathering was shortly dispersed using their heavy canes.

Preman's body was found hanging from a tree branch near his house when the residents began searching through the area.

The villagers initially protested police brutality and refused to remove the body from the tree until a special inquiry was ordered. Villagers were forcibly dispersed as the police promptly brought additional personnel. The court accepted the police version regarding the wounds on his body, and the post-mortem confirmed that his death was caused by hanging.

Preman attempted to evade police custody and collapsed during the pursuit to be recaptured. The police investigation concluded that the cruel torture murder of an innocent individual was a suicide.

Sukumaran and his relatives were aware of Preman's death while in police custody, and they hung his corpse in close vicinity to their home. The police's findings of suicide and sorrow in response to his sister's gruesome death were upheld by the court. Sukumaran submitted an appeal against the verdict; however, it was either ignored or rejected.

Sukumaran suffered health problems within one year of the incident. He was diagnosed with tuberculosis, which was likely the result of severe police torture. The coughing was intolerable, and his sputum soon contained blood strands. The late Preman's wife and child were relocated to her home, which was located outside the village, due to concerns regarding tuberculosis infection. Radhamma, his wife, cared for him for nearly six months while he was bedridden. Within six months, Sukumaran passed away, and Preman's wife and child returned to Radhamma's home.

Mathew also experienced multiple health complications because of the injuries. Within a year of the incident, he passed away naturally, and the villagers suspected that his death was the result of profound mourning. He was open to accepting Sumithra as his daughter-in-law, despite his external protests to his late son's affairs.

The two families never entered or used the disputed land for any purpose after the incident. The villagers believed that the innocent souls of the loving couple, Baby and Sumithra, continued to wander the area as a result of their untimely deaths. A couple of villagers claimed to have spotted them strolling together during full moon nights, which resulted in the area being forbidden for several years.

Chacko was enthusiastic about finding Pravarthiyar Purushothaman, and Joyachan shared the information he had gathered from elsewhere. Purushothaman was transferred to a different village after entirely recovering from the incident within six months. He was a natural womaniser, which contributed to his tragic and puzzling death. It was not determined whether the death was accidental or the result of killing. His body was recovered from an abandoned well in a remote location, where it was nearly decomposed.

He developed another illicit relationship with a wealthy widow in a different village where he was stationed. Other than her married son, no one objected or made complaints when he visited her regularly at night. The widow had strained relationships with her son, who resided with his wife and children in an entirely different town. The widow was in excellent health and possessed considerable wealth. She frequently provided cash loans to rural residents, who repaid the money with interest. She provided gold loans and financial assistance to impoverished rural residents.

Purushothaman was an opportunist who exploited her intimate relationship for financial gain. He devised strategies to defraud her by providing her with fake gold accessories to secure a substantial loan. It seems that the widow possessed an uncommon level of intelligence to identify the counterfeit gold. She soon realised his intentions, and it is possible that she ended the relationship. No one noticed that Purushothaman had been missing for more than a month.

The village shepherds, who were in search of their missing goats, reported a foul odour emanating from the abandoned well. The overgrown plants obstructed their view from above, preventing them from obtaining a clear view of the well. At first, the news was disregarded by most people; later, a small number eventually decided to investigate and pulled out Purushothaman's nearly decomposed body.

The police conducted their initial enquiries, and their enthusiasm diminished when none of his relatives actively pursued the cause of his death. The police concluded the investigation after several months, confirming that the death was accidental.

In those days, it was an uncommon and rare incident in any place within the villagers' reach. As is usual, time served as an effective medicine, and the survivors resumed their lives. In addition to their immediate family members, the villagers also forgot and continued with their routines.

Even though it was a significant loss for Benny, who was extremely young at the time, he confronted numerous challenges. Benny succeeded in finishing his high school education and, in the same spirit as his father, emerged as a respected member of the community. Benny's mother was a strong-willed individual who, despite her difficult medical conditions and significant loss, took the saddle and worked tirelessly to raise him. Her father and siblings provided her with assistance during that period. They collaborated to effectively oversee the family farming ventures.

Joyachan checked the ticking dial on his watch and noted that he had enough time to catch the next bus. He then turned to Chacko and said, 'Perhaps you will be able to establish a connection to the entire narrative once you know about Panchami Kaniyatti's fate, who foretold a long and prosperous life for Sumithra.'

He continued, 'Panchami also met a horrific death, which could have been accidental, during the follow-up Kali Pooja held after Sukumaran's death.'

As he looked back to the house, where Mary and their children were waiting on the veranda, Chacko was speechless. 'After all of these tragic incidents, I cannot believe that another ritual was conducted.' Out of curiosity, Chacko asked, 'Was it to change the family's bad luck and bring back their lost glory?'

This time, Joyachan wasn't sure 'whether she died accidentally, or someone played rogue, or the possibility that her dear deity wasn't pleased with her rituals or intentions.' He corrected himself, 'People's perceptions of the invisible God vary, but improper worship practices lead to adverse and severe consequences.' Looking up at the heavens, he commented again, 'Beyond imaginations of many.'

Although the appearance of Gods and Goddesses varies, many devotees believe that all Gods are manifestations of a single ultimate divinity, the most divine or the one with supreme power, who controls the entire Universe. They can be reached through prayers to any form of God, much like nurturing the root of a tree nourishes all its branches. The mantra, 'I bow to all Devatas, in various forms', is chanted by most devotees when confronted with uncertainty surrounding the scope of the power of many Gods.

Chacko was amused, stating, 'It is effortless for devotees to avoid provoking their ignorance.' Joyachan smiled and continued.

Maha Kali is considered one of the most ferocious deities, as evidenced by her appearance and beliefs. Addressing her as 'Mother' with the intention of causing injury to others could result in negative consequences and devastation. Many were unable to dismiss the likelihood of Panchami Kaniyatti's gruesome death.

Villagers were dissatisfied with Panchami Kaniyatti's exploitation of both believers and non-believers. Devotees refer to Maha Kali as Mother Kali, as she is a loving and protective mother who watches over her followers. However, it is rare for a few to recognise that Maha Kali disciplines her devotees in the same manner as a mother corrects her children.

The suggested rituals were also conducted by Sukumaran's family in response to the promised peace and prosperity. Villagers were demoralised by the tragic deaths of the family members, some of which were particularly distressing. Some of the villagers continued to believe that Radhamma was either incensed or delusional due to the fraudulent assurances. She avenged Panchami's failed and deceptive promises while performing rituals to Maha Kali.

Maha Kali devotees maintain that frightening visages are genuine and convey numerous implications. The Goddess bestows blessings upon those who possess purity and noble intentions, but she also condemns those who approach her casually and with malicious intentions.

A significant number of focused rituals were devised to eliminate their rivals, in contrast to the earlier rituals that were intended to provide protection and blessings. The villagers were uncertain as to whether Panchami Kaniyatti orchestrated the entire incident or whether Radhamma devised alternative strategies to exact revenge. The rituals were performed in private, and none of the villagers, including the neighbours, were present to witness the horrific death. Neighbours raced to their home in the middle of the night, detecting the aroma of burnt flesh in the smoke and fire. Panchami Kaniyatti's charred remains were found in the embers, much to the neighbours' astonishment.

The villagers accused Panchami Kaniyatti of abusing the sacred practice of firewalking, which is conducted exclusively under the rigorous supervision of skilled Tantrics. Few attempted to defend Panchami, as she may have tried to prove her innocence through the fire walk, and she was also faulted for conducting the event in private.

In the house, the villagers found Radhamma unconscious, and they were compelled to force open the locked door, which was suspicious. Both the police and the villagers were unconvinced by her subsequent assertion that Panchami had forcibly locked her prior to the rituals. Radhamma's statement was more convincing than the gruesome death of Panchami. The police and the villagers were sympathetic to Radhamma, who was perceived as defenceless and isolated.

Panchami Kaniyatti proposed corrective and more intense rituals, which were carried out without Radhamma's full consent. Panchami abstained from her customary accomplices and performed the rituals on her own when Radhamma declined to bear the costs. Radhamma, as is customary, assisted in the preparation of the sacred fire pit and its surrounding decorations. However, she was unaware of the planned fire walk over an ember.

Radhamma was compelled to sit near the holy fire pit and, upon request, to add oil to the fire. During the ritual, Panchami assumed a ferocious appearance and initiated a ritualistic performance in close proximity to the holy fire.

In a swift move, she grabbed Radhamma by the hair and thrust her face towards the sacred fire multiple times. Panchami chanted loudly and repeatedly; Radhamma tried to escape from Panchami's tight grip when the sword was shown against her head. Radhamma screamed and raced to the house, but Panchami chased her down. Panchami was considerably stronger and chanted repeatedly as she dragged Radhamma to the fire.

Radhamma had given up any hope of getting away, and for a split second, Panchami froze and started to shiver as if someone else was holding her back. Radhamma took advantage of the chance to get away and locked the front door to her home from the inside. She saw Panchami making the ember ready through the window by spreading the burned pieces of wood from the holy fire.

Radhamma passed out immediately after she saw Panchami Kaniyatti step over the ember and cry loudly as she was totally on fire, like a human torch.

Chapter 18

The following day, Chacko resumed his daily routine and walked to his neighbour's rubber plantation in the early morning to make the incisions on the bark. Through the protruding stepping stones, he ascended the stone wall. The initial refreshment of the day, black coffee sweetened with jaggery, provides the body with the necessary nutrients to prepare for the demanding tasks ahead. A strapped torch on the head allows for the necessary freedom to use both hands to rapidly sieve the hard bark of each tree.

The four-acre property is naturally landscaped and features a variety of elevations, as well as approximately one thousand rubber trees. Wild bean plants facilitate the production of more latex by promoting higher humidity and mild temperatures. Chacko has set up a routine path that allows him to swiftly and conveniently tap all trees, as he is well versed in the land's topography. He ensures that the trees are not damaged by his expert hands and that all of them are effectively bled within a three- to four-hour timeframe. Early morning, before sunrise, is the optimal time for the trees to rapidly discharge the milky fluid. The plants produce a significant quantity of latex and reduced coagulation prior to the day's temperature increase.

His sleep was disrupted last night, and he suffered from vivid and dreadful dreams that persisted throughout the night. He felt sorrowful sentiments regarding his deceased friend and his family. Numerous adversities had befallen them over the course of various years. Mary, who was also unable to sleep, offered him a glass of water in the middle of the night. He made some peculiar noises and was sweating, which disrupted her sleep.

When he nearly fell, reality jolted him back to his senses as he stumbled and narrowly averted the fall by maintaining a firm hold on a nearby tree. Joyachan, who was in a hurry to catch the last bus, was in his thoughts as he adjusted the blinking headlamp. He would later return with his wife to visit the family of the late Benny Mathew.

Chacko required additional time to complete his daily responsibilities due to his insomnia and his erratic thoughts. Mary came to help him when he returned to collect latex from the trees he had tapped earlier. Together, they finished the collection and carried the latex to the rubber machine room for further processing. Thereafter Mary returned home.

Chacko initiated the process of combining latex with acid to produce rubber sheeting. As he completed his morning routine, Chacko noticed Soman, his neighbour's third and youngest son, approaching from a distance. Chacko was surprised to see him at that time of the year, as he typically visited during festivals or special family celebrations.

Soman is proud to be a member of the elite Defence Services and is taller than his siblings. He also has an athletic build. His mother is fond of him due to his physical resemblance to her father, the renowned Vareeth Mappila. Soman is a quiet person who is highly action-oriented, in contrast to the other soldiers in the village who are overly self-centred. Chacko then recalled that Soman's most recent visit was during the harvest season, which signified the conclusion of the rainy season.

His family's favourite holiday was Christmas, but he preferred to celebrate Onam. He chose to participate in the village sports games that were part of the Onam celebrations, despite his mother's request to take part in the Christmas festivities. He was an outstanding goalkeeper due to his long limbs and actively engaged in tug-of-war and kabaddi games.

His loud and irritating voice interrupted Chacko's thoughts while he was mixing the latex. 'Hey, Chacko mate, you finished early, man.' Chacko was conscious that he was referring to the standard latex blending process. Before Chacko could respond, Soman complimented him, 'You are a dedicated and decent guy.'

Chacko was once again taken aback; he was not accustomed to expressing or receiving gratitude. He greeted Soman with a smile and asked, 'When did you get here? Haven't seen you anytime earlier.'

Soman greeted Chacko with a cordial gesture, extended his hand, and tapped him on the shoulder. He then said, 'You are perpetually preoccupied, take some time to enjoy your life.'

Chacko was indifferent, but he did not discourage him. 'My family will starve to death if I do not work every day.' Given the circumstances, it was not anticipated that a response would be forthcoming. Chacko comprehended Soman's silence and responded with courtesy, 'Your arrival at an unusual time is surprising.'

Soman was moved, smiled, and responded, 'I anticipated that you would bring this up, so I brought it for you.' Subsequently, Soman presented him with a bottle of rum that bore a distinctive, ornate label that read (For military consumption only).

Chacko extended his arms to receive the entire bottle, expressed gratitude, and smiled naturally. Soman was hesitant to give in, saying, 'This is only for strong-willed soldiers. However, you are special today. Let's have a drink together first, and then you can take home the entire bottle.'

Chacko is a day labourer who takes great pride in maintaining his financial stability. He retracted his extended arms, saying, 'Don't worry, I will visit the toddy bar later tonight to enjoy my customary drinks.'

Soman looked over the area. 'Chacko Chettan, retain your cool and refrain from being overly dismissive of yourself. Let's work together.'

The offer was tempting for Chacko, but he refrained after noticing Mary's lack of appreciation for him. He declined the offer, stating, 'Soman, not at this time, it is only the morning hours, and I have plenty of essential work to complete.'

Chacko resumed his routine by turning away and disregarding his presence. Soman was adamant about not giving up. 'Nothing is more important than our moments of pleasure. Come on, Chacko Chettan, please spare some time for me.'

Chacko noticed that the meeting, which appeared to be informal, was not merely friendly. He then contemplated their relationship, which was never friendly. Soman was significantly younger than him, and there was no necessity for him to establish a connection with Chacko, as they shared no sort of commonality.

Chacko spotted Soman's father, Thomas Joseph, coming from a distance. Chacko advised him, 'Your father is approaching, he may wish to discuss something else with me. You could leave now.'

Soman commented as he looked in that direction, 'He is of no use, do not be concerned, I will deal with him at a later time.' In that instant, Chacko recognised that Soman was inebriated and not in his right mindset.

Soman then posed the peculiar inquiry: 'Are you visiting the family of the late Benny? He was a kind man,' he looked again at his approaching father and admitted, 'but I was unable to attend his funeral.'

Chacko stared at him and said, 'Do not be concerned, we were friends, and I am required to care for his family.'

Thomas Joseph was irritated by the time he reached them and warned Soman, 'I advised you not to leave the house.'

Thomas corrected himself upon noticing Chacko. 'It is not a suitable time to wander around, there are dangerous reptiles, and you are unfamiliar with the area.'

Staring at them, Soman did not respond immediately and was not readily agreeing. Thomas grew upset and raised his voice, stating, 'Soman, please leave now and remain indoors. I will address your concerns upon my return.'

This time, Soman became frustrated and raised his voice against his father, 'I am aware of my actions, I am no longer a child, and you should not be disciplining me constantly.'

Thomas Joseph maintained his composure, his hands shaking with fury. Soman's anger caused him to glance away, and he then turned to Chacko as if he intended to tell him something. Soman stared into his father's eyes once more and walked away towards their mansion.

Thomas Joseph watched him as he walked towards their home. He needed a few additional moments to regain his composure before he remarked, 'Silly man, don't bother him, he returned home last night.' Awaiting Chacko's response, he continued, 'He is in good health and is simply enjoying his time.'

Thomas Joseph looked around and then tallied the aluminium containers that were placed on the floor with a latex mix. 'What is happening now? The number is lower than usual, I anticipated a higher production rate, especially since one day was lost.'

Chacko hesitated to respond, subsequently tallied the basins, and replied, 'It is Christmas time, the temperature is dropping in the early morning, and the trees are taking a long time to produce enough latex.'

Thomas Joseph was more compassionate. 'It is acceptable, you should ensure that you do not miss any days from now on.' He paused and stressed, 'Latex is a valuable resource, harvest the trees daily.'

He looked at the machine room and the plantations in the distance, remarking, 'The precious trees are not in good health, the climate is changing.'

Thomas Joseph contemplated for a moment and was reminded of his previous commitment. 'Please inform me if you require any support.' After a brief delay, he reminded again, 'In addition, disregard Soman, he continues to behave like a child.'

Thomas Joseph reminded once more before heading home, 'Give that money to Leelamma, please, and don't be afraid to ask for more if you need it.'

Chacko hurried to complete the mixing procedure without replying. He saw the bottle of rum in a corner, ignored it, and hurriedly mixed the latex in the basins with an iron rod. Chacko was certain that Soman would return for the rum and decided not to touch it.

He once more contemplated the recent reminders of Thomas Joseph as he walked back home. Benny Mathew, who passed away, was not related to them nor was he cordial with them. Suddenly, they were becoming quite inquisitive about him, his widow and their children. He then came to the realisation that individuals are not always the same; their attitudes and behaviours towards others can change over time and in response to varying circumstances.

Mary promptly served him his preferred boiled tapioca with hot spicy chutney and hot coffee, as she was anticipating his arrival. Finishing breakfast, he sat in his usual place, reclining against the mud wall of the kitchen, with a lighted beedi on the corner of the veranda.

Typically, at that hour he was fatigued by physical labour, but the circumstances were different that day. He was repeatedly aggravated by the recollection of Soman's visit. He experienced an unusual sensation, as if there was something amiss with him. Soman had never been cordial towards him, and he had previously treated him as a destitute labourer who was entirely dependent on the generosity of his wealthy father.

Chacko was on the brink of passing out when an individual touched him. Benny Mathew, his late friend, reminded him of Thomas Joseph's spoilt child, Soman Thomas.

Soman was unusually tall for a child his age and was in good health. He was perceived as a youth with less mental development by his peers, which resulted in a decrease in his social acceptance within the group. It was posited that his peculiar behaviour was the result of his parents' negligence and their peculiar, strained relationships.

Throughout his primary education, he experienced behavioural issues. Soon after his junior sibling was born, his demeanour improved. He acquired the ability to be patient with other children and was subsequently welcomed into the circle of a new friend.

His acquaintances and family were not taken aback by his failure to pass the final examinations. However, he astonished his peers by successfully completing the examinations on his second attempt. He was subsequently enlisted in the Indian Army because of his active sports participation, which earned him merits.

Furthermore, Soman was able to circumvent police custody and additional criminal proceedings because of the opportune intervention of late Benny Mathew. Soman was accused of selling illegal drugs to young school children after being caught red-handed. Soman was able to overcome his substance addiction through hospitalised rehabilitation treatment.

He was an asset to the Army for six years, and he was once again hospitalised for alcohol addiction treatment.

During his three-month medical leave, Soman spent a greater amount of time with Benny, who was a social activist at the time. Through his association with Benny, he was able to surmount the stigma and trauma that are commonly associated with rehabilitation. Soman shared a few of his exhilarating experiences while serving in the north-eastern states, the border region of India, and China during that time. He could have advanced his career by pursuing life-changing experiences, rather than becoming an alcoholic.

Soman was accepted into the infantry battalion and subsequently received training to become an armoured tank driver. He was delighted with the position, as it offered him the opportunity to pursue his aspirations for adventure. He was dispatched to the India–Pakistan frontier following his initial training, which had resulted in his becoming a disciplined soldier. He was able to endure the harsh conditions at the frontier posts. He demonstrated his exceptional mental strength by enduring the severe solitary conditions. He successfully commanded single-man security posts for weeks, despite the limited food supply. An early promotion was given in recognition of his dedication and diligence in safeguarding the borders during severe weather conditions.

He was sent to the armoured battalion for additional training after effectively fulfilling his security commitments in the perilous border regions. His confidence and courage were bolstered by the rigorous training he received on the complete management of artillery tank operations. In addition to acquiring a deeper understanding of the various weapons systems and ammunition employed, he also acquired the ability to operate vehicles. His initial assignment was to serve as the ammunition loader, as is customary within the armoured battalion.

Soman Thomas was responsible for ensuring that the tank's weapons were supplied with the necessary and appropriate ammunition. During maintenance periods, he served as the gunner's and driver's assistant. During fire-practice exercises and actual operations, he was responsible for loading the appropriate round as designated by the tank commander. Should the tank be equipped with a loader's machine gun, he would retract the external security opening. Additionally, the tank commander had the option to assign him to other responsibilities, such as adversary-verification searches and forward search.

To acquire a comprehensive understanding of the procedures of an armoured tank, he was also deployed to inspect and maintain communication equipment, as well as to switch nets. Within a brief period, Soman emerged as an all-rounder by effectively capitalising on the opportunity. He favoured the tank-driver position, as it afforded him the opportunity to negotiate challenging and unfamiliar terrain while operating a majestic vehicle. He was anticipating an opportunity to showcase his capabilities and value in a highly demanding circumstance.

An experienced officer typically commands armoured vehicles. The commander is accountable for the tank, the crew, and all ancillary equipment. The commander issues orders to the gunner, who is responsible for the management of the weapons, including the execution of precise firing. The tank engine is maintained by the tank driver in accordance with the commander's directives. The driver must operate the tank safely and position it appropriately to allow the turret to fire at enemy targets. The tank's loader is responsible for the timely loading of ammunition and the execution of any other tasks as directed by the other personnel.

The tank commander orders the fire command by designating the individual to fire during actual combat. The commander provides a description of the target type, the type of round, and an estimated range and direction. The gunner will corroborate the target, which they have both verified, and will then fire precisely at it. The effective destruction of hostile targets is guaranteed by adhering to the orders and coordinated actions of the relevant personnel.

The driver is subject to the tank commander's orders, with a certain amount of discretionary authority to ensure the safety of movements. The driver is accountable for evaluating the terrain, selecting the appropriate route, and circumventing insurmountable obstacles. Ensuring that the tank maintains the appropriate posture during discharge is crucial for achieving accuracy. The commander consults with the driver to direct all tactical manoeuvres of the vehicle during combat operations. During an emergency, all tank personnel provide mutual support, irrespective of their individual responsibilities. After careful consideration of their skills and expertise during numerous training sessions, specific role assignments are made.

Armoured vehicles necessitate numerous hours of cleaning and maintenance, contingent upon the size and type of weapons used. Three to five hours of cleaning at the base, where the tank is securely parked, are required for the actual operation of a tank for an hour. Even though designated personnel are responsible for the maintenance of specific areas, all team members collaborate to ensure that the machine is maintained to the highest operational standards. These are essential for the successful operation of the tank and the effective pursuit of the primary objective of preventing the enemy's advances.

Naik Soman became an armoured tank driver after a year of dedicated labour at the entry-level position of loader. He was instructed on outdated and exceedingly heavy British battle tanks that were transferred to the Indian Army after independence. India acquired superior-performing T-54 tanks from Russia in response to technological advancements that enhanced both defensive and offensive capabilities. In a dependable design, these tanks were equipped with substantial armament and armour protection. In addition to being smaller, these tanks were more manageable and lighter than other designs available in other parts of the world.

The tank was mechanically straightforward and durable, providing personnel with a sense of security and dependability. The minimum four-member crews were adequately safeguarded against all older weapons and penetrating projectiles.

During that period, the Indian Army personnel were highly motivated by the acquisition of these more secure and efficient tanks. The T-54, a 40-ton battle tank that was significantly lighter, was mounted with two 7.62 mm machine guns, one in the turret and the other in the superstructure. The turret at the loader's superstructure was equipped with a third machine gun. The armoured battalion of Naik Soman Thomas received three of the recently dispatched T-54 tanks from Russia.

The initial stock of these items was not entirely new; they had previously been used by the Russian military but were subsequently refurbished prior to delivery. Soman and several of his colleagues received timely training on the refurbished machines.

Once fought together for an independent country against uninvited occupiers for a long time, they quickly became enemies after being divided into two countries. The formation of two countries was the result of an accepted but unagreed partition line, which was determined by the religious dominance of the majority. Pakistan is predominantly Muslim, while Hindustan is predominantly Hindu. The princely state of Jammu and Kashmir was granted the option to select between the two nations. Initially, the Maharaja of Kashmir pursued independence, asserting that Kashmir had been neglected and subjugated for centuries by conquering empires.

The two countries' claim on them compelled the Hindu Maharaja to join India in exchange for assistance against the invading Pakistani herdsmen. Pakistan acceded to a portion of Kashmir, despite the Indian armed forces' effective resistance to the invasion. The two-year-long conflict between them was provisionally resolved through mediation by the United Nations, which accepted the line of actual control at the time.

Until Indian independence from British rule, India and China maintained cordial relations throughout history. Following that, conflicts ensued as a result of the absence of clearly defined borders. The British had virtually drawn a line separating the two countries before declaring India independent. The Chinese disputed the 'McMahon Line', which was named after Sir Henry McMahon, while India acknowledged it as the official border.

The line on the maps extends from the eastern border of Bhutan, following the crest of the Himalayas, until it reaches the significant meander in the Brahmaputra River, where it emerges from its Tibetan course and flows into the Assam Valley.

The inhabitants of the frontier villages coexisted in harmony, fostering positive relationships and cooperation. India renamed the entire region the Northeast Frontier Tract and implemented administrative systems several years after achieving independence. China claimed it as their own and designated it a part of South Tibet in the absence of a clearly defined physical border. Armed guardians were deployed by both nations to safeguard their respective territories.

Chinese guards regularly engaged in armed confrontations with Indians, as they encroached on Indian land in the absence of distinct markings and fences. Major gunfights resulted from certain physical altercations between the soldiers of both sides, causing severe injuries and fatalities. Individual incidents were resolved, and peace was preserved through the regular meetings of guard commanders from both sides. Despite the absence of a clearly defined frontier, the border guards' disagreements persisted. During this period, both nations enhanced their national military capabilities and intensified their border patrols.

The bilateral relations between the two countries were weakened by the Chinese government's decision to annex Tibet. The Indian government alleged it was against the interest of the Tibetan people and granted asylum to Tibetan religious leaders. The troops defending their border were influenced by the unpopular decisions made against each other, as they challenged one another.

In 1962, the two nations engaged in a full-scale conflict because of the escalating number of border violations. With effective intervention by international agencies, the Chinese military was compelled to discontinue their aggression and return the captured areas. Both nations reverted to their pre-war governance structures.

The Chinese once more endeavoured to breach the line of control during the Indians' second conflict with their counterparts on the opposing side. The land soldiers responded to Chinese encroachments, while the Indians employed all three of their forces against their arch-rival. The Indian soldiers, who were once again brave, successfully engaged in combat with both nations and emerged triumphant on both fronts.

Initially, Chinese forces were hesitant to return the encroached land, but international pressure and consistent negotiations compelled them to return to their original positions. During this period, the

Indian government made the decision to acquire additional war apparatus from Russia, which included the T-54 tanks. Naik Soman Thomas was one of the skilled drivers who operated the new and robust war engine of the time.

The Chinese believed that the annexation of Tibet was incomplete without the Tawang Tract, which corresponds to the Tawang and West Kameng districts within the disputed area with India. The Tawang Tract is situated between the Assam plains and the Tibetan plateau, providing a natural pathway for effortless crossing of the current border. In the centre of the Tawang Tract, Se La is one of the high mountain ranges, and Tawang is the brief route between India and Tibet.

The Tawang monastery, the winter residence of the Tibetan administration, is located to the north of Se La. The sixth Dalai Lama, who was born in Tawang during the 17th century, is the paramount leader of Tibet. The Chinese leadership is disturbed by the fact that the current and 14th Dalai Lama have sought refuge and are currently residing in India. Tibet's completion, in their view, will be achieved upon the restoration of their holistic authority and the unification of the Tawang Tract to its previous status.

Chinese military aggression in 1962 was well organised, with the goal of unifying the Tawang Tract. Until that time, the border patrols of both nations exchanged greetings and maintained cordial relationships. The surprise assault resulted in the deaths of 17 Indian soldiers and the capture of 13 others, as the Indian authorities were unable to recognise the true intention behind the attack.

The Chinese occupied the historical Tawang monastery in two days with an easy walk across the frontier. The Chinese were unable to advance further due to the swift reinforcement on the Indian side, but they were able to achieve their primary objective. The Chinese reverted to their previous stance again with international mediation and acknowledged it as the true line of control.

Chapter 19

Naik Soman Thomas and his T54 tank colleagues were posted to the battalion at Guwahati, located in the north-eastern region of India. For a training exercise, they were directed to take up a position at Rangapara, a tribal region traditionally accessible by both train and road from Guwahati. These multi-force exercises assess the real-time war readiness of defence personnel. Ultimately, the objective is to assess the team's ability to protect the country by evaluating their proficiency in weapon usage, self-aid, and buddy care in a challenging environment. They enhance their abilities and prepare themselves for military operations in hazardous conditions and explosives containment through consistent exercise. These exercises are routine and assess soldiers' ability to endure and operate in a combat environment, as well as to effectively complete wartime missions.

Soman had previously participated in numerous combat exercises of a similar nature. In contrast, this was the most thrilling experience since it was the first one since joining the tank battalion. The critical role of tank driver was significantly more difficult due to the opportunity to deliver and support agile war-winning capabilities more effectively. On a Monday evening, he and his teammates embarked on an overnight journey to Rangapara by loading their new T54 tank onto the open goods train at Guwahati Central Station. Along with him, Second Lieutenant Rawat Singh, who was also new to tank operations and the battalion, served as the tank's commander. Havildar Surya Sekhara Reddy, the gunner, was acquainted with the frontier regions and had prior tank experience. Sepoy Saman Biswas, who was new to tank operations, was the loader and had a few years of battalion experience.

Both Army and Indian Air Force personnel, along with the Border Security Force, participated in the combined exercise. In addition to practising joint operations, the exercise aimed to improve border security and provide a prompt response to border breaches. Originally scheduled for nine days, it was extended by an additional six days to obtain experience in real-time war-like situations. The train carrying Naik Soman Thomas and the other tank men arrived at Rangapara railway station at midnight the following day. Their tanks' transfer to big tractors was delayed at the station due to inadequate lighting. When Soman swiftly moved the tanks from the train carriage, cautiously crossing the sturdy loading ramps, the tank commander was impressed by his driving abilities. Their other armoured comrades were halfway to their destination when they finally hit the road towards Tawang.

Initially, loose metal roads were constructed to convey defence vehicles, which transported both personnel and equipment to the border. The majority of the regions were barren, and the army convoy met a limited number of horse and bullock carriages in certain locations. The forest area through which the road was constructed was primarily desolate, and only a handful of half-naked villagers waved at them. Later, they realised that the impoverished villagers were not truly waving but rather pleading for food. The tanks were disembarked from the tractors halfway through their journey due to the insufficient width of the valley roads, which were characterised by numerous hairpin turns. The convoy of three tanks was led by Naik Soman Thomas, who expertly navigated the hard surface to reach the outskirts of Tawang monastery. The convoy of army personnel and their equipment travelled the challenging mountain terrain for nearly two days before reaching their destination.

The intent of the exercise in Tawang was also to evaluate new war equipment and to persuade the Chinese that the Indian military is adequately equipped to protect its territory. An unambiguous warning was being sent: any attempt to replicate the encroachments of 1962 would be met with severe consequences. The operational readiness of the Assam Regiment's specially trained mountain warfare personnel was demonstrated through their active participation, showcasing their capacity to launch instantaneous counterattacks and deploy heavy weapons at high altitudes for both defensive and offensive actions.

The exercise was attended by over 2,000 military personnel from various defence forces. The initial six days were meant to adapt the personnel to the challenging mountain terrain at high altitude. Subsequently, firing practices, fist fights, and mock combat exercises were conducted. Breathlessness was experienced by Soman and a significant number of personnel who were not exposed to high altitudes. To enhance their performance, they were instructed to become familiar with the limited oxygen conditions. Personnel who ascend from low ground levels are subjected to hypoxic stress, which induces a sequence of alterations in their bodily tissues. To become accustomed to low oxygen levels, daily ascending exercises were carried out at elevated altitudes with diminished physical activity. In addition to limiting alcohol and tobacco use, Soman was able to maintain improved health by pursuing an active lifestyle and consuming a high-protein diet.

To help the tank crew regularly clean the machinery, more soldiers were assigned. For a short period, Soman and his crew performed the routine daily maintenance. Most of their time was spent participating in drills and engaging in physical activities to stay healthy and familiarise themselves with the challenging terrain. Each set of participating soldiers visited the actual Line of Control after being split into multiple groups. Their numbers, discipline, strength, and war-machine capabilities astounded the Chinese soldiers who watched from a higher altitude. On both stationary and moving targets, Soman and his group routinely rehearsed fire drills. A few tents at the campsite were demolished by strong winds and heavy rain, resulting in two days of preparation being lost. Until ideal weather conditions returned, soldiers were instructed to limit their outdoor activities and remain active indoors.

Unanticipated severe weather resulted in landslides throughout the campsite, and a small boulder collided with a securely parked tank, causing damage to its top door. Crew members made immediate repairs and declared it operational, thereby meeting the wartime readiness criteria. The ground was wet, and the crew determined that heavy tank movements should be restricted until the ground was dry and suitable. Exercises that involved tanks and artillery guns were postponed, and exercises to combat direct fire and to burst enemy bunkers were resumed. Simulated exercises were conducted to evaluate the ability of individuals and teams to handle emergency situations.

A team of 12 members, including Soman and his tank crew companions, were deployed to practise bunker bursting. Participants were divided into two teams: one team was responsible for defending their shelter, while the other was tasked with bursting it. Two officers were armed with pistols, five carried the most recent self-loading Ishapore rifles, three carried traditional bolt-action rifles, and two carried ammunition and medical cases. The initial directive was to breach a solitary bunker that was manned and located over a steep cliff, far above ground level.

The crew carefully advanced towards their target as soon as they spotted the first signs of light on the eastern horizon. There were big trees and plants on the rocky mountain area. Walking through the bushes in a disciplined way was quite hard, and the team was having trouble staying together. Even experienced team leaders had difficulty finding landmarks and could not locate their target position. Leaders advised them to stay calm and not get distracted while walking over the wet and muddy stones. Everyone stayed alert and looked around to see if they could spot any movement and pinpoint their target. Members struggled with the weight of their backpacks as they were carrying hefty firearms and extra ammunition. The backpack also contained food, medicine, and other survival gadgets of various sizes.

Not long after that, the team members identified their target and followed the stated instructions to check and see how well they could retaliate. The crew came under fire from another location while they were planning their actions from a defensive position. The commander called out 'Dash' right away, ordering the team to get down. Everyone in the team fell to the ground, secured themselves, and then came together to look at the rival lines.

After that, the commander declared, 'Observe,' and the team looked for enemy positions. They found the second enemy station, which abruptly started firing at them.

The team immediately split into two groups after realising they had to attack two enemy targets. They looked around for more enemy bunkers before continuing. Following verification, the team members were instructed to find the target and shoot at it under the directive 'Fire at will.' After a while, the commander gave the orders, 'Prepare to advance,' followed by 'Advance.' The second squad supplied much-needed cover fire as the first team advanced to attack the bunker at a considerable distance. As soon as the observers confirmed the opposing targets' strengths and shooting power, the plan was to strike both bunkers at once. Additionally, observers were expected to report on enemy bunker support personnel stationed in the vicinity and any other obstacles to their attack.

Naik Soman Thomas was tasked with providing cover fire as his teammates launched an assault on the bunkers. He was also tasked with keeping an eye on the enemy's locations and waiting for the approaching team to give him tactical hand signals. As the enemy bunkers were situated on the hills, he was positioned at ground level and diligently observed actions above his level. Soman precisely followed the instructions he had received during training. With his elbows well under his body and his knees spread wide, he maintained a shooting position that was both accurate and efficient. He kept a tight eye on the targets while elevating his body above the ground. Soman breathed normally until he was ready to hold his breath, squeeze the trigger, and strike the target. Additionally, he was prepared to return to the more efficient kneeling firing posture when engaging moving targets.

Observers were cautiously positioned behind Soman and evaluated the flanks of the enemy bunker. They also sought a breaching point for the attacking team. It is crucial for the attack team to rapidly overpower the enemy by identifying a potential breaching point. Upon agreement of a breach area, they promptly assessed and cleared any potential mines that may have been present along their route. The handheld mine detector instrument, which is predominantly used to detect iron metals beneath the ground, was operated by the squad leader. They wore headphones that were connected to the cable linking the control box, which was worn over the standard soldier headgear. Areas that detected faded signals were also clearly indicated, as disregarding them could result in serious consequences, such as the loss of life.

The process of clearing minefields was extremely slow and terrifying during that era. Many of the alarms were false, as the detector was designed to emit a bleep sound immediately upon detecting a strong magnetic field. The beeping sound produced by a mine detector indicates the presence of ferrous metal components beneath the ground, necessitating further investigation. The initial tasks for advancing teams were to clearly designate the area and surroundings for the following mine-clearing team and to avoid those areas. Hours were required for mine clearers to excavate the precise location and identify the genuine threat. When an actual mine was identified, they required additional time to defuse and evacuate the area. The mine-clearing team was required to wear anti-blast goggles and heavy boots, which were not entirely protective without the full-proof whole-body protective clothing. The inability of both nations to deploy mines in a widespread manner was a source of relief for all those involved. Rather than confronting a genuine threat, the exercise consisted of routine practice in checking the ground for mines.

The original strategy was for attacking a single target in two phases. After identifying another enemy location, the commander decided to strike both bunkers in a single phase. One team member searched the nearby bunker, while Soman opted for the farthest bunker. Changing the attack plans, the commander then instructed the second squad to catch up and join the attack on the bunker that was the furthest away. To support the approaching attack team with fire, the plans were modified to place the second squad at a right angle.

Instead of forcing the rival to flee, the team's goal was to demolish the bunker and kill or capture the enemy alive. Soman was conscious that he needed to differentiate between his own advancing attack party and remained alert to identify enemy targets. The environment surrounding that area abruptly became gloomy, and the rising sunshine from the east was soon obscured by thick, heavy clouds. The advancing party carried out the direct attack as soon as the commander gave the order to 'attack.' Disguised behind the safety of their bunker, soldiers quickly advanced to assault their enemy in a direct physical attack, after removing their bayonet covers.

In response to the assault, four soldiers who were concealed behind the bunker emerged. Soman fired the rubber bullet at one of them with precision, resulting in a direct strike to the forehead. The attacking party engaged enemy members in a bayonet battle before he could aim at another target. Soman altered his objective and concentrated on the second bunker. He observed two targets that were moving towards the first bunker. Soman promptly redirected his attention to the moving target and fired once more. This time, he failed to hit them and was immediately met with retaliatory fire from the second bunker. Then he heard the rotor blades of the approaching helicopter above and turned his eyes towards the sky. It took an additional few minutes for a dark-grey flying machine to approach through the high-rising mountains. The helicopter was a Russian-made Mi-4 transport helicopter that had recently been introduced. This multi-purpose flying machine, operated by Air Force pilots, was introduced into the army exercise, thereby enhancing the combat efficacy of the combined military.

The chopper pilot contacted the platoon commander, who informed him where the enemy bunker was located. The chopper then fired rubber bullets that hit the target directly. Continuous gunfire from the sky almost destroyed the second bunker. Soman was shocked for a while, as he was not made aware of helicopter involvement and watched the exciting events from the ground. Hitting the enemy at heights that are hard to reach alters the equation for winning and might easily defeat them. Soman was enthralled by the action in the limitless skies and forgot for a moment that he was supposed to be giving cover fire. In those split seconds, the two enemy soldiers got close to the first bunker, where they helped their colleagues fight off the attack. The second sniper behind Soman was less distracted by the chopper and shot one of the attackers. The remaining opponent's support helped them resist the attack, which led to a prolonged bayonet fight.

Soldiers deploy the bayonet for a variety of purposes, in addition to attacking their adversaries. They use the bayonet's designated cover during the practice process. The purpose of practising bayonet fighting is to personally feel the enemy and experience aggressive physical combat. It serves as both an offensive weapon and a survival tool in the environment. The cutting edge always remains sharp, and the curved rear part is left hard to reduce its rib-parting ability. The blade's recesses function as blood channels, minimising the vacuum effect and facilitating a clean withdrawal from the body. The blade's ribbed section is intended for rope chopping. There is a notch at the forward end that is designed for use with the scabbard. The bayonet can be deployed as a fighting weapon in the event of a rifle malfunction or a depletion of ammunition, as the handle is designed to provide a secure grip.

The entire exercise took nearly two hours to complete, which was half an hour longer than the original timeframe. The exercise debriefs outlined the chronology of events and identified several flaws, including Soman's momentary distraction. The participation of the Air

Force helicopter was not known to a significant number of the team members. The initial bunker was captured by the assaulting team as a result of the timely firing from the skies. The debrief indicated that the attacking team performed marginally better than the defending team, as they successfully captured both bunkers. Naik Soman Thomas, along with numerous others, was criticised for the delay in firing at the defending team and was instructed to maintain vigilance. Soman and five other individuals were ordered to enhance their firearms abilities to improve their wartime efficiency.

For the next two days, exercises were put on hold until the weather in that area improved. Soman and his tank squad, along with a few others, stayed focused on taking care of their tanks. Most of the participants had a keen interest in viewing the actual border, which was still 'out of bounds' for them. They were restricted to the campsite, which was five kilometres away from the actual Line of Control. Civilians are not allowed to enter military areas or their boundaries. Military personnel are only allowed to visit specific sites to keep them secure and lower the risk of disclosures. Essentially, there are just a few places that are officially off-limits to military personnel. Military police patrol 'out of bounds' areas continuously and sometimes arrest personnel who are seen wandering there.

In general, the consumption of alcohol and tobacco is prohibited during exercise. A small number of individuals, such as Naik Soman Thomas, discreetly carried them for personal use. The unexpected prolongation of the exercise resulted in a depletion of their supplies, prompting a few of them to look out for local alcohol. Locally produced alcohol was available in nearby villages, despite the extreme isolation of border regions. Alcohol is produced by the tribal communities in that region through the fermentation of rice or millets with locally sourced ingredients. The claim made by Sepoy Saman Biswas, a member of their team, that locally brewed 'Madua' generates instant alcoholic effects was intriguing. Saman volunteered to explore the villages and was proficient in the local language. Soman readily agreed to accompany him, and others approved of their expedition and agreed to provide cover in their absence.

Armed guards protected the area surrounding the temporary campsite, which was not gated. Saman Biswas and Soman Thomas sneaked out without the guards noticing. After walking through the unfamiliar woodlands, both reached a nearby village which was out of bounds for military personnel. Despite being a native speaker, Saman Biswas had limited comprehension of the Bodo language, which is extensively spoken in that area. He was taken aback by the speech of the elderly villager they met first. As soon as he realised they were soldiers, the villager welcomed them with open arms. The villagers respect Indian soldiers who defend them from Chinese invaders, and the elderly villager took them to his wooden-plank house. They climbed the wooden steps to enter the single-room wooden house, which was elevated above ground level.

Smoke emanating from the wood stove heated the solitary room located on the upper level. The elderly villager sat on a thoughtfully placed rag on the floor and invited them to join him. Soman noticed the young woman seated in the corner, whom the villager introduced as 'my daughter-in-law; my son should be returning from the fields at any moment.' An elderly woman entered the room and extended a warm welcome. She brought the boiling kettle and poured a dark liquid into three earthen cups. The tea was made from handpicked tea leaves, with one tender leaf paired with two mature leaves, and it was incredibly delicious. The room was filled with a mesmerising aroma from the hot kettle, and both immediately expressed their gratitude, began to drink from the cups, and commented, 'It is indeed rejuvenating.'

The young woman in the corner kept her silence and appeared unbothered by the uninvited visitors. Soman peered at Saman Biswas, who then turned to the elderly man and said, 'We must return immediately. Are you able to get some Madua of superior quality for us?' The elderly man looked at his wife, who was returning towards them after replacing the teapot at the fireplace. Realising their need, the woman turned towards the young girl and whispered in their language. The young girl appeared perplexed and promptly left the room. The aged lady interrupted the silence between them by asking, 'Are you from Bengal?' Before they could respond, she further added, 'Or India?' Soman suppressed his imploring smile and looked at Saman, who responded, 'I am from Bengal.' Before she could pose further questions, they noticed an individual ascending the stairs.

The daughter-in-law hurried into the room after opening the door and then turned to glance back. She was on the verge of falling to the floor while holding an enormous earthenware vessel. Following her were four individuals, who barged into the room. The elderly man promptly rose from the floor and confronted them. The elderly woman stepped forward to provide protection for Soman and Saman Biswas. They continued to argue until the elderly man responded calmly to all their questions. He then turned to both of them and said something, which Saman Biswas clarified to Soman as, 'He wants us to leave this place immediately.' Soman stared at the elderly man, as he was unable to comprehend the circumstances. Without wasting any time, Saman Biswas rushed through the door, which was obstructed by the intruders.

There was no other choice for Soman but to follow Saman Biswas. The leader of the intruder squad nodded, and his colleagues permitted them to leave. The young woman followed them as they descended the stairs and handed over the earthenware vessel she was holding. Saman Biswas was only able to comprehend a portion of what she said. He whispered to Soman, 'Let's leave this place quickly; they hate Bengalis and are dangerous.'

Though unsure, Soman Thomas moved quickly to follow Saman Biswas, who was practically sprinting in the direction of their campsite. They quickly became lost in the wilderness due to the lack of moonlight. Their survival instincts told them not to panic but to keep moving, even though it was completely dark around them. As their blinded eyes could not perceive the typical crisp, fluid images, their brains were unable to process the surrounding structures. Before the sharp wooden arrow with a metal tip penetrated his left elbow, Saman Biswas was firmly grasping the clay vessel. Feeling helpless, Saman let out a loud cry of agony before losing control and collapsing to the ground. The clay vessel shattered, thick liquid alcohol leaked onto the ground, and a pungent, earthy stench filled the air. For a brief moment, Soman was unable to respond, but he quickly recovered and dropped to the ground for protection. Saman Biswas suppressed the pain and remained silent after realising that there was a greater risk to their lives from the piercing noises cruising through the air above them.

Chapter 20

'Saman, are you able to hear me? Please get up and drink this hot and relaxing drink.' Naik Soman Thomas continued to call Saman as he cautiously opened his eyes. Saman Biswas looked uncertain about the object in front of him. His questions were met with a blank stare, and he was unable to respond.

He then heard the words, 'Thank God, you are now awake. How are you feeling?' Saman Biswas extended his right arm towards his left forearm without altering his posture.

Soman Thomas reassured him, 'You are now in good health. The wooden arrow was removed, and you lost a minimal amount of blood.'

Another colleague at the bedside commented, 'The morphine injection was strong, but it is beneficial for a rapid recovery and healing.'

Saman Biswas did not respond, prompting Soman to express his apprehensions: 'Is he still in pain or not making a full recovery? Let's transfer him to the hospital.'

The temporary medical treatment room was surrounded by other team members, and someone shouted, 'The camp medical assistant is on his way. Please clear the area and provide him with sufficient space.'

The wound was not deep, and there was no sign of infection. Two of them examined Saman's vital signs and declared that he was in good health. The assurances were helpful to Saman Biswas, and Soman Thomas expressed gratitude, stating, 'Thank God, you are back and fighting.'

The medical team instructed all those present to leave the room. 'Allow him to rest for an additional day; he should be fine.'

Soman Thomas was hesitant to leave, and the medical team forced him out. He intended to ensure that Saman Biswas received regular support and medical care.

Havildar Surya Sekhara Reddy, the deputy commander of their tank team, was awaiting him outside. 'Naik Soman Thomas, the incident is serious and has been reported to higher-ups. You are required to provide a factual account of how you and your partner ended up in Chinese Border Patrol custody.'

Soman did not respond to the orders, and Surya provided more details. 'You are required to remain in Military Police custody; however, the regulations have been relaxed in light of the fact that you are currently engaged in an active operation.'

Surya again reminded him that the statement must be submitted by 12:00 p.m., which is the end of the day's lunchtime. Afterwards, Havildar Surya Sekhara Reddy returned to his office.

Upon returning to the tent, Soman attempted to remember the ordeal that had occurred the previous evening. Escaping from the tribal villagers was mere luck. Saman Biswas was unconscious, and Soman was able to pull him to safety beneath a densely foliaged bush until the assailants ceased chasing them. Soman waited until Saman Biswas regained consciousness before making an escape plan. The wooden arrow had not penetrated the shoulder very deeply, and Soman was able to extract it readily.

Saman could walk back to the camp after Soman promptly bound the wound with his shirt, preventing further bleeding. Dodging the eyes of the savage villagers, Soman escorted him towards the camp. They proceeded towards a dim light that they could see from a considerable distance. As they approached the light, they saw it was surrounded by a small number of armed soldiers.

The Chinese soldiers interrogated them but were unable to obtain much information. They did not hesitate to provide medical assistance to the injured Saman Biswas and questioned the uninjured Soman Thomas. The Chinese were unable to identify them in their civilian clothing. When both realised that they were in the custody of an enemy country, they kept silent.

Then a gust of wind swept towards them, and before the Chinese could react, a tide of Indian soldiers overpowered them. The Chinese soldiers quickly surrendered and released both without much resistance. Havildar Surya Sekhara Reddy subsequently confirmed that the village elder had informed them of the attack and the potential detention by the Chinese border force. It appears that the elderly person from the village followed them to guarantee their protection and safe passage through the ill-defined border.

The disciplinary procedure was more mentally torturous than the physical ordeal they had endured the day before. They were charged with indiscipline for entering 'out of bounds' areas, possibly within Chinese territory. The two soldiers maintained their narrative of ignorance, claiming they became lost in the wilderness during an evening walk around the camp boundaries. With their luck, the village elder did not disclose their initial objective of obtaining local alcohol.

Charges of gross misbehaviour were brought before the disciplinary board. The act of attempting to cross an international border is regarded as treasonous for defence personnel. The disciplinary board was unable to find any immediate evidence against them and subsequently decided to postpone the proceedings until the ongoing exercises were completed. As neither of them sustained any significant injuries and the Chinese did not file formal complaints or charges, they were permitted to participate in the remaining exercises.

The following day, Sepoy Saman Biswas recovered from his injury and rejoined the team to assist in operating their battle tank. The weather in the region improved as anticipated, and the exercise recommenced.

The battle tank was ultimately granted authorisation to participate in the exercise three weeks after their arrival. The tank operating team was instructed on their responsibilities, which included providing cover fire for the advancing infantry and firing shots at enemy fortifications that were strategically positioned. Lieutenant Rawat Singh, the Tank Commander, was relatively youthful in comparison to other team members. Havildar Surya Sekhara Reddy, in conjunction with his team, evaluated the terrain to ensure safe operations. Upon attaining complete satisfaction with the weather and terrain, the team declared their readiness to evaluate their combat skills.

The exercise commenced with the sound of a long siren that reverberated throughout the surrounding mountain range.

Subsequently, the company commander issued march-ahead commands. At the appropriate moment, Naik Soman Thomas ignited the tank engine and awaited orders to advance as the infantry marched to their attacking positions.

The entire battalion was suddenly under attack from the skies above, with heavily roaring sounds of jet engines. The advancing attacking party was destroyed when two MiG-21 fighter aircraft from the nearby Air Force base at Tezpur bombarded their battalion. The army battalion was appalled by the extraordinary performance of the powerful and formidable flying machines. The primary target was considerably outperformed by the MiG-21, which was agile at high altitudes with rapid acceleration and supersonic speeds.

The first day's drill of the final phase was immediately halted, as their tank was unable to adequately respond to the unexpected attack from the skies. They failed to protect themselves and the battalion against the MiG-21's high-speed hit-and-run strategy. The participation of the Air Force fighters was planned, but their attack was not expected on the first day. The exercise squad failed to defend themselves, but the participants were thrilled with India's newly acquired air superiority.

Returning to the campsite without engaging in any action on the first day was heartbreaking for many. The debriefing expressed concerns about their war readiness, concluding that they needed to be better prepared to face surprise attacks and challenges.

The recently acquired Mikoyan-Gurevich 21s were designed for mid-air warfare rather than interfering with the ground assault squad.

Modified versions of these aircraft were used in the exercise, and they were fitted with heat-sensing anti-tank missiles. Brilliant pilots accurately shot rubber bullets at the tank, demonstrating their fighting expertise and superiority. The first day of training was deemed very successful at the higher levels, as it achieved the objectives of a surprise attack. The tank team was not criticised for failing to effectively defend against the flying machines.

Further instructions were given to the tank unit, and training was conducted to avert aerial attacks. Over the next two days, the tank team underwent extensive training to assess and respond to aerial threats. On the third day, an exercise was conducted, and the tank crew was able to avoid frontal assaults but fell victim to persistent attacks. The crew considered additional lessons learnt from their ongoing experience and developed a strategy for dealing with the repeated aerial strikes.

The tank's main gun was clearly unable to fire straight at the assaulting jets due to the lack of aerial alignment. They also intended to place a machine gun on top of the tank, which could potentially target approaching airborne machinery, including jets. Soon, the team realised that the tanks were on the losing end unless they were fitted with anti-aircraft missiles. All moving forces, including tanks and mechanised infantry, require short-range air defences, a last line of defence usually consisting of guns or short-range missiles capable of targeting low-flying aircraft, jets, and helicopters. Accepting their inability to properly protect against air strikes, the crew continued to participate in the exercise.

Another air attack was practised two days before the exercise was supposed to end. Two MiG-21s emerged in the skies two hours after daybreak, while the morning mist quickly drifted from the mountain tops. The roar of their engines could be heard far ahead, alerting the tank team to defend themselves. The simulation was designed to train all participating tanks in how to avoid aerial attacks, conceal themselves securely, and, if possible, retaliate. MiG-21 fighters were fitted with extra fuel tanks to extend their flight time. Instead of a whole battalion, three platoons were assigned to go ahead of the tanks in an offensive formation. All three tanks were positioned in a row, with one of them carrying an anti-aircraft gun. Naik Soman Thomas and his teammates manned the middle tank.

As the first MiG-21 approached, the tanks on both sides parted ways, and the tank driver, Soman, fearlessly confronted the attack. The first fighter jet aimed its gun at the tank on the left but flew past without firing. The following jet attacked the centre tank, and Naik Soman used the pedals to brake and turn right. The deployed anti-aircraft guns fired continually at the jet without striking it. The jet delivered a bomb that fell short of the tank, and the tank squad successfully avoided the initial attack.

MiG-21s are extremely fast fighter jets that could outperform contemporary fighter aircraft of the time. Due to their agility, these war machines are well-known aerial dogfighters. They are capable of effectively pursuing aerial intruders and may quickly deploy to track and chase them. The tremendous speeds of these machines make it difficult to aim precisely at ground targets.

Several crucial dials in a small cockpit and limited frontal vision further restrict their effectiveness during ground attacks. The uneven topography of the mountain region complicates their visibility of ground targets. The aircrafts' radars had a limited range of 20 kilometres, and their lock-on range was reduced to 10 kilometres. These high-speed flying devices have a disadvantage in mountainous terrain, as pilots are more likely to lose orientation. Attacking ground troops with these high-speed planes was not always effective, offering the defensive tank operators an advantage.

The exceptionally manoeuvrable and speedy MiG-21s, equipped with a large cylinder and jet engine, quickly returned to practise their ground attack. Soman repositioned his tank to the side, while another tank resumed the central position, allowing the mounted gunner an unobstructed view of the incoming jets. The first jet was positioned in a straight line from the approach, ready to fire directly. Considering their objective, the tank drivers withdrew from the line of approach to prevent a direct impact. Realising the tactical move, the first jet rose up and flew well above them. The second jet approached from a different angle, striking the middle tank directly. The fighter jets won after switching from straight-line to cross-angle fire techniques.

MiG-21 fighter jets were unable to return for a third practice run due to their short aerial endurance, therefore the brigade continued to conduct regular drills for the remainder of the day. The tank commander commended Naik Soman Thomas's tank-driving ability. Evading an aerial strike is critical, as it shields the team and prepares the tank's armour for retaliation. The evaluation of the day's exercise indicated that the tank team's performance met the acceptable requirements.

Army brigade soldiers and border forces were scheduled to participate in an exercise on the final day. Drills were planned to attack enemy lines and free captive Border Security personnel. The goal was also to attack and reclaim land occupied by the opposition team. The practice comprised both attacking and defensive targets, as well as casualty evacuation drills.

All three tanks drew up behind the platoons, loaded with live ammunition for more gun practice. It was an all-out war mission, and tank driver Naik Soman Thomas relied on his commander, Lieutenant Rawat Singh, for safety. He had a physical vision of only five to six feet ahead and was primarily reliant on the tank commander for instructions and guidance. During genuine conflict, the two periscope eyes mounted on the top are frequently obstructed by the cannon.

All four tank members were connected by a radio system within the armoured vehicle's thick iron composite walls. Standard checks on their communication network were carried out to ensure that commands and responses were clearly heard and followed. The tank commander requested they get ready for the drill: 'Crew report.'

Soman responded, 'Driver ready.'

Commander Lieutenant Rawat Singh guided both the driver and the gunner. Havildar Surya Sekhara Reddy responded, 'Gunner ready, sabot indexed,' while Sepoy Saman Biswas, who had recovered from his earlier injury, shouted loudly and clearly, 'Loader ready, sabot loaded.'

They then checked the brigade-level communications. Tank Commander Rawat Singh responded to the operational readiness with, 'Steady and ready.' After a moment of stillness, the operations commander declared that the drill had begun. When Soman heard the command, he checked all the dials and prepared the tank to roll. After a few nervous moments, the tank crew received orders to drive forward and fire at the target at once.

Rawat Singh instructed the driver, 'Move out, keep straight.' Soman moved the tank forward into the open, clearing their lined-up position.

Soman turned the tank leftward and continued to drive after receiving the next instruction from the tank commander: 'Turn to ten o'clock.'

Moving forward, when the target was visible, the commander ordered, 'All right, twelve o'clock, and then swing over to one o'clock.' Soman moved the tank to the appropriate firing position and abruptly stopped when instructed. He straightened the revolving turret that held the primary firing cannon. As soon as the commander passed the target spot, the gunner raised his tank gun and pointed it at the target.

The tank commander instructed, 'Ready to fire,' and the loader armed the main gun and confirmed, 'Up.' The commander ordered again, 'Driver up.' Soman ensured that the tank was stable and ready to endure the gun's recoil.

The tank commander ordered, 'Fire.' The gunner instantly responded, 'On the fire,' and pulled the trigger. A huge boom followed as a hefty bullet burst through the barrel towards the target. The boom and a foul-smelling grey haze filled the tank, forcing Soman to cough repeatedly. The commander released the latch above, allowing fresh air to enter, and requested the status: 'Report.'

The gunner confirmed, 'Gun clear,' and the loader said, 'Ready,' whereas Soman's response was delayed, and he shouted, 'Steady.'

Soman was having trouble, and his body longed for additional exposure to fresh air. He resisted the urge to clear his airways and drank a mouthful of water. The inward rush of cold water blocked his air passage, causing him to lose consciousness for a short time. He regained full consciousness by spitting the water out.

The tank commander reiterated his question, 'Report,' after being dissatisfied with the earlier response. Soman then immediately reported, 'Steady, Sir,' almost shouting.

The gunner glanced at him to verify his condition. Next, the commander issued the order for the subsequent round of fire. The tank effectively fired nine rounds and then retracted, allowing other tanks to charge at the target.

The crew assessed the operational status of the tanks upon their return to their previous position. The commander appreciated their precise marksmanship and advised them to remain vigilant until they received additional instructions. Soman was experiencing unusual discomfort in both of his shoulders, and his stomach began to grumble. He suppressed his agony and reassured himself that he would remain strong and healthy to demonstrate his worthiness. He then recalled the small packet he had received from the village elder, which read, 'Spread a small portion on the tongue and you will instantly be recharged to perform better.'

Soman looked around and briefly observed his colleagues, who were busy monitoring their respective areas. Sitting in proximity, Gunner Reddy whispered over his shoulder, 'How are you doing? Are there any problems?' Soman turned to him and hesitantly responded, 'Good, I am awaiting the next move.'

Following that, they heard a large bang, followed by the sound of numerous gunshots. Reddy stated, 'Retaliation has commenced; we may need to move forward in a short while.'

Soman promptly opened the concealed pouch in his trouser pocket as everyone awaited the subsequent command. He applied the gelatinous substance to his tongue with his forefinger and then closed his eyes.

The jelly, with its savoury flavour, gradually dissolved in his mouth, generating electric currents that travelled through his nerves and immediately reached the brainstem. In pursuit of happiness and enjoyment, Soman's brain promptly responded to the jelly's surge in neurotransmitters. He was taken to a state of euphoria by the presence of dopamine in the substance. Soman's exhilaration was sudden and intense, and he reached into his concealed pocket to obtain more. At that moment, the tank commander issued the command, 'Driver up.'

His response was delayed by only a fraction of a second due to his excitement. Surya Sekhara Reddy, the deputy commander and his immediate superior, sat next to him and smacked him on the shoulder, reminding him, 'Wake up now.'

Soman was suffering from an unnaturally elevated sense of pride. He was on the brink of retaliating, and during that moment, the tank commander ordered, 'Driver, move out, straight ahead.' Soman jerked the tank forward as the excitement returned. His tank companions were thrown off balance by the abrupt change in acceleration.

The tank commander raised his voice, warning, 'Be cautious and reduce your speed.' The tank engine experienced a sudden change in acceleration, which caused it to stall. Soman promptly reignited the engine before his companions could comment further. Several peculiar noises emanated from various locations, including the turret; however, all of them soon diminished, and the tank moved.

As the jelly substance in his mouth fully dissolved, Soman's nerves were gradually overtaken by its effects. The usual recycling of neurotransmitters in his brain was disrupted. The unnatural and excessive neurotransmitter release from the gelatinous substance gradually seized control of his internal communication pathways. The prefrontal cortex was affected by the substance, limiting its ability to think, plan, and solve problems. Due to diminished impulse control, Soman became more inclined to make his own decisions rather than comply with directives from his tank commander and fellow soldiers.

The tank commander instructed the tank to advance and shift to the two o'clock position. Soldier Soman, unaware of his topographic disorientation, proceeded to the opposite side. Cognitive impairment resulting from the dissolution of the substance in his pharynx led to hallucinations. He steered the tank left as he advanced. The protruding tank gun appeared to him as a towering mountain in front of them due to his declining vision and cloudy eyes.

The commander ordered, 'Fire at the target,' seconds before Soman realised his mistake. The gunner fired, and the loader promptly executed the order. The commander immediately examined the target and exclaimed, 'Driver, return.' The shot had already been fired. The tank was to be halted promptly to prevent additional damage.

When Soman, who was hallucinating, reached for the controls, his limbs were unable to lift the lever due to a sudden loss of strength. The shell fired from the tank narrowly missed the nearby tank and ultimately landed in an open area. The turret of the adjacent tank was damaged by the impact of Soman's moving tank.

Gunner Surya Sekhara Reddy struck him on the shoulder and yelled, 'Are you insane? Stop the tank now!' The other tank was being pushed sideways by his moving tank. Surya Sekhara Reddy quickly pulled the lever, causing the tank to stall its engine and abruptly halt.

Soman was unresponsive to orders and questions from his tank companions and appeared to be in a state of apathy. The exercise proceeded without the tanks, as both were damaged. Soman was transferred to the sick lines and remained incapacitated for the remainder of the day. The medical team succeeded in recovering the concealed small packet from his pocket, which was promptly identified as uncommon wild honey. Sepoy Saman Biswas, his tank companion, admitted to the events of the previous night and the potential gift he received from the village elder. The villagers refer to wild honey as 'mad honey,' and they believe that consuming modest quantities increases their level of intoxication.

Wild honey, produced by wild bees that collect nectar from specific rhododendron flowers, is harvested by villagers who reside in high mountains. Villagers ingest small portions to enhance their vitality and prolong sexual orgasm. It is an effective medication for individuals with hypertension. Consuming the appropriate quantity may result in beneficial effects, but regular use can lead to addiction. Individuals who consume small quantities frequently experience a warm sensation in their bodies, as well as feelings of relaxation and joy.

Mild hallucinations may be experienced by certain amateurs, causing individuals to feel as though they are experiencing unusual sensations or visions. Nausea, vomiting, disorientation, and a decrease in heart rate are symptoms of consuming slightly more than the recommended amount.

Naik Soman Thomas was placed under medical care for the remainder of the exercise period. The tanks were repaired and returned to the army base in Guwahati. He was charged with indiscipline and substance abuse. The army court sentenced him to six weeks in prison and recommended addiction therapy. He was also demoted from the Naik rank to the Sepoy level. After completing his de-addiction treatment, he was sent home on medical leave.

Chapter 21

Chacko swiftly reached the main road after crossing the stone wall in front of his house and heading towards his friend, the late Benny Mathew's, home. He kept his head down as he walked past his neighbour Thomas Joseph's mansion and was relieved to see that the front gate was locked. Chacko was used to deserted roads and uneven pathways, but that day he wanted to meet others, so he looked around. He was quickly visiting his friend's home to check on their well-being and to hand over the money his neighbour had donated.

Then he planned to visit the village toddy bar for a quick drink, a bottle of fresh coconut toddy and deep-fried pork belly. Fresh and less-fermented toddy from an earthen pot is very refreshing. Chacko prefers a full pot with bubbles floating on top, and its wonderful smell goes straight to the head. A brain that has been supercooled sends out impulses that chill the whole body, relaxing the muscles. When the body relaxes, the soul ignores the daily challenges and struggles of everyday life.

Chacko walked the village's most remote paths, captivated by a quiet world of flourishing thoughts. He barely heard his name being called from nowhere: 'Chacko, mate, look at me.'

The repeated summons grew louder, compelling him to return gradually to reality. He paused in disbelief, attempted to listen, and then abruptly scanned the overgrown bushes. Again the voice called, and this time he heard clearly, 'Chacko, it's me, Pailey.'

Chacko was taken aback by the name and searched the area until he heard further directions: 'Climb the steps behind you, it is safer here.'

Chacko followed the instructions without delay and approached him through the overgrown wild foliage. Pailey looked at him quickly and nearly cried, 'You have not brought any food, I had only a jackfruit and am still hungry.' Chacko looked at the ground, which was littered with leftover jackfruit seeds and green and yellow shells.

Chacko stared at the poor man, who couldn't live a day without enough food. 'Pailey, you are a fugitive. If the police catch you, they will torture you to death.'

Pailey was in bad shape and about to lose all courage. 'I am happy to be arrested, but I can't go another day without food.'

Chacko couldn't believe what he was hearing.

Pailey stood firm. 'It's better to be beaten up than to die of hunger, at least they'll feed me.'

Chacko looked around again to make sure that no one was nearby and that they were safe. Pailey told him, 'These are no-man's lands; no one ever goes out into these wilds.' Pailey stood his ground like a lone warrior in his lonely kingdom. Chacko sat on the ground and asked him to sit next to him, but Pailey begged, 'Please, I'm hungry and I'll do anything to get food.'

Chacko behaved like an elder brother and said, 'Listen, don't get caught, the police will beat you to death.'

Pailey couldn't respond, and Chacko reminded him, 'The police want to find someone to blame for Benny's murder instead of catching the real murderers.'

Chacko patted his shoulder and said, 'I will get you some food, but I have to go back home.' Looking into his eyes, he assured him, 'Stay here and I'll be back before it gets too dark.'

As Chacko was about to get up, Pailey grabbed his hands and begged, 'Please, spare some time for me.'

Chacko was uncertain how to respond when Pailey added, 'Could you please fetch me a bottle of toddy?'

Chacko was once again taken aback, but Pailey pleaded, 'I have not slept in two days; perhaps I will be able to take a nap before I am caught in a police trap.'

Chacko was deeply uncertain. He had never purchased a bottle of toddy to take away or deliver to someone else. He also did not wish to discourage Pailey, so he responded, 'I cannot guarantee that the owner will permit me to take the bottle out of the shop.'

Pailey did not respond but reached into his inner pocket and extracted a few coins. He then offered them: 'Please take this; I may not have another chance in life.'

Chacko could not guarantee anything and replied, 'You should keep the change, it may be necessary at this time.' Looking at the exhausted man, he assured him, 'I cannot guarantee, but I will try.'

Pailey held Chacko's hand just as he was getting up to leave. 'I might know who is behind the plot against Benny.'

Chacko was surprised and looked at him seriously.

'It might not be true,' Pailey continued, 'but it might have something to do with the scam that Benny unearthed at the Kaineervila Co-operative Bank.'

Chacko considered it for a moment and warned, 'Pailey, gossip and rumours will only bring you more trouble.'

Pailey remained silent, but Chacko elaborated, 'Spreading rumours could lead the investigation towards the wrong people and hide the truth.'

Chacko thought Pailey was being foolish, but Pailey stood up and firmly stated, 'Chacko, I'm not kidding. There is something that no one has seen, or maybe they are hiding it.'

Chacko was astonished by the change in his voice and face. He asked, 'Are you sure you know something?'

Pailey looked away from Chacko and said, 'There were around five or six strangers in the village for several days, and they were gone soon after Benny was murdered.'

Chacko was shocked and moved closer. Pailey provided further details: 'Four of them came first, and one or two joined the day before the murder.'

There was a short pause, and Chacko was unsure what to ask next. Realising his confusion, Pailey added, 'Either they stayed with Divakara Kaimal or with Shashankan Nair.'

Chacko clarified, 'Divakaran, the ration shop owner?'

Pailey affirmed, 'Yes, and Shashankan Nair, the Co-operative Bank Manager.'

Chacko couldn't believe it and asked, 'How do you know? They might be related to them or just visiting.'

Pailey was upset this time. 'What do you think of me? I am not stupid.'

Then he clarified, 'Yes, I am acting like an idiot, but why should I not? I am an orphan and don't have any close relations in this village or in this world.'

He began to sob. 'I didn't know they had this plan; otherwise I would have protected my brother Benny… or I would have warned him.'

Chacko gradually recognised that Pailey was now revealing the truth rather than fabricating storylines out of fear and anxiety. Benny Mathew was assumed to have been murdered by a villager, but the perpetrator had yet to be found. Chacko had never heard of a killer from outside the village or of a paid killer. Pailey's voice broke as he sobbed and sat on the ground. Holding his hands, Chacko sat beside him and asked, 'Can you identify them if you see them again?'

Pailey cried, covered his face with both hands, and then shouted, 'I am sure that whore Vidya Devi is involved, she had an affair with the Bank Manager.'

Chacko was again alarmed. 'You mean the same Vidya, the former Farmers' Co-operative Bank secretary and current Panchayat member?'

Pailey glanced up, enraged. 'Yes, and her husband Madhubabu, the ruling political party's Branch Secretary, who brought the murderers from far away.'

Chacko refused to believe him and simply looked at him.

Pailey continued, 'Chacko, you are a noble person, supporting your poor family, whereas people around you are very cruel and soulless. They make plans to harm and at times even kill others.'

After a brief pause, Pailey stood up and declared, 'I will avenge Benny. I will kill both Madhubabu and his whore wife Vidya Devi.'

Chacko was once again appalled by the villagers' perception that Pailey was merely a fool or a moron. Everyone in the village was discreetly watched and monitored by him. It was in his nature to maintain a low profile and avoid public attention, as he was aware of his own social status. Chacko knew he was less influential than Pailey, but he also understood the resources at his disposal.

Chacko proposed that they pursue support and guidance. 'Pailey, the police are conducting a thorough search of the entire village for you. It is not the appropriate time to seek revenge or expose yourself to them.'

Pailey was enraged. 'Chacko, I am aware of my options. My priority now is to eat. Would you be able to fetch some food for me?'

Chacko realised that he could not control Pailey and needed to seek assistance elsewhere. 'Pailey, I will bring food for you. Please wait here until I return.'

Pailey thought for a moment, realising he had no choice, and urged, 'Hurry, I am starving.'

Chacko hastily began to walk, hesitated briefly, then turned to him and said, 'I will consult Thomas Joseph sir; he will devise a solution.'

Pailey erupted in rage, shouting, 'You naïve ass! He is the most venomous snake in this village. Do NOT approach him, he is part of the nexus and is likely the primary perpetrator.'

Chacko was stunned by the accusations. 'Do not speak a word against him. He is consistently supportive.'

Pailey then asked, 'Did you inform him of our previous meeting?'

Chacko was truthful. 'Yes, he advised me to keep away from you.'

Chacko rebuked him again: 'Wait, he did not enquire about your location specifically.'

Pailey grew furious. 'Chacko, you poor man. Mr Thomas is not publicly recognised for his nefarious activities, but he is highly influential and has vested interests far beyond the village.'

Chacko was taken aback once more. 'No, I can't believe it. He is mostly either at home or at school.'

Pailey expressed compassion. 'Mr Thomas makes monthly visits to the state capital to meet his political masters. He is the next political candidate from our area.'

Chacko was unable to comprehend the situation and stared at Pailey.

Pailey continued, 'Chacko, you poor fellow. Thomas has grand plans far beyond our awareness and capacity.' Looking around, he added, 'He maintains cordial relationships with all influential individuals in the village, despite facing numerous challenges at home and school.' After a pause, he said, 'He is trying to be popular, to involve himself in all of the village's significant events.'

Pailey came closer and whispered, 'It is possible that he was aware of Benny's murder. However, he may not have been involved.'

Chacko was stunned and stared at Pailey in shock. He wasn't ready to accept the accusations made against Thomas Joseph, his mentor and neighbour. Thomas had been kind to him and his family, even donating land and materials to build their home.

Pailey advised again, 'Chacko, don't go to him. Get me some food now, and I'll explain.'

Unsure of what he had just heard, Chacko was unable to reply and turned to leave.

Behind him, Pailey shouted again, 'Get some fried pork belly as well, and make sure no one follows you!'

Chacko walked quickly in the direction of the late Benny Mathew's house. Pailey yelled from afar, still warning, 'Don't go to Thomas, he will trick and cheat you!'

Chacko arrived just as Leelamma, Benny's wife, was cleaning the cowshed. She noticed him coming up the steps from a distance and asked her child to greet him.

Bobby was ready as soon as Chacko reached the house. 'Mum is feeding the cow, she'll be here soon. How is Sunny?' Bobby didn't wait for a response. 'Don't bother, I'll meet him at school.'

Chacko stayed quiet, reflecting on how children endure the hardest times of their lives.

Then Leelamma came over and said, 'Chacko, the cowshed is a mess. Let me wash my hands and I'll be back soon.' She quickly went to the back of the house.

Chacko stared after her, wondering how she seemed so quick to recover from the greatest loss of her life.

Leelamma returned shortly afterwards, holding a glass of black coffee. She said, 'I must visit the bank soon, there is a fixed deposit that must be transferred to the current account.'

Uncertain of her intent, Chacko refrained from responding.

Leelamma continued, 'Why don't you join me whenever you have the time?'

Chacko replied quickly, 'Tomorrow is a bank holiday, and the day after tomorrow should be fine.'

Leelamma nodded, and Chacko suggested, 'I will meet you in front of the Co-operative Bank in the town.'

Leelamma promptly corrected him: 'Not there, at the State Bank.'

Chacko stared at her in disbelief.

She clarified, 'Soon after his relationship with the managing team at the Co-operative Bank turned complicated, Benny transferred some money to the State Bank.'

Chacko drank the coffee and stared up at her again.

Leelamma explained, 'It all began with the transfer of money from the Co-op Bank to the State Bank. He knew they were mishandling the deposits and manipulating the loans.'

Chacko couldn't say anything and waited for Leelamma to reveal more. She looked up at him for an answer and then looked away, mumbling, 'It's not easy to understand all these shady deals.'

Bobby's voice was heard from inside: 'Mum, the baby is awake and crying.'

Leelamma turned to Chacko and asked, 'Do you need anything else?'

Chacko suddenly remembered why he was there and extended the envelope containing the money. Leelamma looked at it and said, 'I'm fine for now. If I need it, I'll take it later.' When he told her where it came from, her face turned scarlet. She contained her anger and said, 'I can't take the money at all. That man is cruel, please give it back to him.'

At that moment, the child's cry grew louder. As she walked inside, she reminded him, 'Visiting the bank is important. I need to withdraw the money in person.'

Chacko immediately left her house, thinking about her stubbornness as he hurried along. He proceeded to the village's toddy bar as planned. He followed a deserted route to reach the toddy shop swiftly and quietly, though it was considerably crowded. He immediately approached the barman. 'I require two bottles to take home, I have guests.'

Without waiting for a response, he went to the snacks counter and placed his order: 'Two plates of tapioca curry and deep-fried pork belly.' He reminded the staff, 'Please pack the food quickly.'

A familiar barman enquired, 'Is it for you or someone else?'

Another farmer seated nearby commented, 'Why do you ask such trivial questions? Chacko is not a stranger.'

He turned to Chacko and warned, 'A few strangers were here, not necessarily in search of you, but they asked questions about Kunnumpurath Pailey.'

Another inebriated man recalled, 'They did enquire about you,' and after a brief pause added, 'Someone mentioned you as a close associate of Pailey.'

Silence prevailed as others stared at him, hoping for more information. He shrugged in confusion. 'I am unsure. Chacko has nothing to do with Kunnumpurath Pailey.'

Chacko swiftly paid for the food and drinks without replying. He took the usual route home to avoid further questions. People had become more sceptical of him after things he had not foreseen, so he had to be careful. He looked out for strangers more often than usual. He came across a few familiar villagers who stared at him for no clear reason.

After some time, he heard a cycle bell ring and someone shouting his name: 'Chacko, wait for me!'

Raghavan Kaniyan's bike brakes were weak, and he struggled to stop, dragging both feet on the ground. He was breathing heavily and admitted he was having trouble cycling. 'Riding my bike uphill is getting really hard for me.' He took another long breath and commented, 'You're a tough guy, you walk faster than most people.'

Still panting, he wiped the sweat off his forehead with a long white towel. 'See, I wasn't kidding, it's really hard.'

Raghavan was shirtless, wearing only a coloured dothi around his waist, revealing his bare feet and thin figure. His bicycle's front carrier held bundles of newspapers and weekly publications. He served as the distribution agent for many outlets and supplied them to village shops. He was not a political activist; he maintained cordial relationships with everyone and supported communist movements. He knew almost all the villagers and was familiar with their daily lives, political issues, and social matters.

Chacko stared at him, anticipating a question about his friend's murder, but Raghavan asked something else instead. 'I've heard that Thomas Mash's soldier son returned a few days back. Have you seen him?'

Chacko was taken aback and turned to gauge his interest. As Raghavan waited patiently, Chacko briefly mentioned the casual encounter. A moment later he clarified, 'He seldom speaks to me and is not a friend of mine.'

Raghavan was not persuaded. 'You're their neighbour, and he returned from the border recently. There is something fishy about his quick arrival.'

Chacko remained silent and kept walking. Raghavan watched him leave, then called out, 'Please keep this between us, I have no interest in him.'

Chacko did not respond or turn back.

Raghavan cycled after him again, stopping abruptly beside him to warn, 'Chacko, you may not be aware, the police may come after you.'

Chacko was unsurprised this time. Calmly he asked, 'Why should they come after me?' He paused before adding, 'I'm either at work tapping the rubber trees or at home. They can meet me anytime.'

Raghavan was astonished by his nonchalance. 'I'm just warning you, but don't worry, we can help you… well, if needed.'

Chacko gazed at him silently and continued walking.

Raghavan shouted from behind, 'Don't expect Thomas Mash to help you this time, it's far beyond his reach!'

Chacko did not answer or turn back. Raghavan looked around to ensure no one else had overheard, then turned his cycle around and returned to his deliveries.

Chacko walked ahead, made sure he wasn't being followed, then rapidly crossed the deserted woodland, sprinting towards Pailey's hideout. Along the way, he thought about how several of his village friends had warned him to be cautious of his neighbour and employer, Thomas Joseph.

To Chacko, Thomas was more than a neighbour and employer, he provided guidance and support. His children, however, treated Chacko not as their father's loyal helper but as a servant who relied on their generosity. Chacko and his wife carefully managed their relationship with the family, always avoiding a breach of trust.

Hungry and impatient, Pailey kept watch to ensure no one followed Chacko to the hideout. He swallowed the entire bottle of toddy in one go and began devouring the food.

Chacko warned him, 'Be careful, pork fry contains bone pieces which could stick in your throat, and right now we cannot get you any medical help.'

Pailey was like a bull at that moment, rushing through his meal without listening. He swallowed faster than he ate. He emptied the second bottle slightly slower than the first and savoured the final piece of fried pork. Then he bent his torso and released the trapped air from his stomach with a long burp.

He was satisfied with the food and drink and thanked Chacko for returning quickly.

Chacko shared the concerns expressed by Raghavan, the newspaper agent. Pailey became irritated, stating, 'Listen, Chacko, he is another scorpion that spits a full load of venom.' Pailey's revelations multiplied Chacko's surprises, causing him to react slowly. The number of individuals in the village who are included in Pailey's 'excellent list' was very limited.

Pailey's neurons were soon overwhelmed by the toddy toxins, causing him to collapse to the ground. It was a sluggish process for his starving body to produce the necessary fuel and building blocks to withstand the toxins. He was on the brink of losing consciousness when Chacko reminded him, 'I am leaving, those police personnel may be searching for me, although they may not be able to descend the steep stairs in front of my house.'

Pailey abruptly rose from the ground and yelled, 'I must immediately locate Madhubabu and his whore wife, Vidya Devi!' Chacko had heard the same names earlier; Pailey's repeated insistence served as confirmation of his fixation on finding them.

Chacko was mindful that Pailey was extremely vulnerable in that condition and that leaving him would cause more harm than protection. Chacko could not find an immediate solution, and Pailey tried to get up again, saying, 'Chacko, please, we must meet them before it is too late.' His tone was more pleading than the authoritarian style of a drunkard.

Chacko was reminded of a Sunday sermon that said, *In wine there is truth.'* Pailey was only slightly inebriated, which caused a disinhibition of thoughts as he tried to consider the intricacies of various matters. Without a doubt, his entire life was a shambles that could not be reversed at this point. He was trying to make sense of his future moves.

Having lost significant clarity about the situation, part of his working mind focused solely on revenge, his top priority. His sense of clairvoyance was more perception than reality; he preferred to survive rather than pursue possibilities or confront daily problems.

Chacko was entirely different. A few people relied on him to survive the world's uncertainties. But he had chosen Pailey, despite everything, to help him find answers and unravel the riddles surrounding his friend's untimely murder.

Chapter 22

Pailey was stronger than his opponent, Madhubabu, who had practised Kalari in his youth. Pailey held him under his right arm and used his left arm to forcefully seal his mouth, preventing him from crying out. He clutched Madhubabu tightly until he became unconscious, then carefully lowered him to the floor. Pailey tied Madhubabu's hands behind his back with a piece of coir found under the bed and shoved a cloth towel into his mouth. He then tried to staunch the blood from his nose with a white linen cloth found in the room.

Pailey was in pain and briefly lost consciousness, but he regained enough strength to fight Madhubabu. He kicked him furiously each time he used the towel to wipe the blood from his own face. Then he looked at Chacko, who lay unconscious on the bed. Chacko had been unable to escape the rapid direct kick that struck his neck, causing him to choke and rendering him unconscious. Pailey couldn't protect poor Chacko, but he fought back and defeated Madhubabu.

A few hours earlier, Pailey had insisted that Chacko accompany him once he regained full consciousness from the toddy toxins. Chacko wasn't prepared, but he conceded to Pailey's reasoning. Any further delay could result in him being taken into police detention, and certain underlying truths might remain concealed indefinitely.

They waited until dark and once again walked the untamed village paths to reach Madhubabu's house. The house was in a remote area, enclosed by a fence that separated it from the adjacent fields. Pailey knew the farmlands well, having previously worked there with his mother. He crossed the barbed fencing by climbing a tree, and they both waited for the household to rest and for the lights to be switched off.

Although they expected both husband and wife to be present, only Madhubabu was found. Pailey entered the house through the rear door, and Chacko followed him. To their surprise, Madhubabu was awake and immediately confronted them with full force upon sensing their intrusion.

Pailey sprinkled some water on Chacko's face to restore his consciousness. It took several minutes and repeated prompts for him to open his eyes. Terrified, he stared at Pailey in disbelief. Seeing Madhubabu unconscious on the floor, he cried out, 'Did you already kill him?'

Pailey did not respond immediately. Instead, he held the kerosene lamp close to Madhubabu's face, checked, and confirmed, 'Not yet, we need answers from him.' He handed a cup of water to Chacko and cautioned, 'He is much stronger and cunning, keep a safe distance.' Chacko looked around and moved to a corner of the room to stay safe.

Using both hands, Pailey lifted Madhubabu and seated him on a chair. During this, Madhubabu regained some consciousness and attempted to defend himself. He was quickly subdued by Pailey's threat: 'You know both of us, now cooperate and tell us who murdered Benny.'

Pailey removed the cloth from his mouth and asked, 'Where is your wife? She may know more than you.'

Madhubabu became arrogant and shouted, 'Pailey, you scumbag! How dare you tie me? Untie me immediately and leave my house!'

Pailey grew incensed and struck him across the face, shouting, 'I have dealt with worse than you. Don't force me to kill you to get the truth.' Losing patience, he screamed, 'You son of a b*tch! You killed him, and now you're trying to frame me!' He kicked him in the stomach. Bound to the chair, Madhubabu fell with it to the floor and cried, 'Pailey, I have committed no offence, please don't hit me again!'

Pailey lifted him in the chair and repositioned him in the middle of the room.

Looking at Pailey, Madhubabu begged, 'You don't have to hit me again. Benny was a good man, and we were good friends.'

Pailey was unimpressed. 'You are lying. How did the hired killers enter the village without your knowledge and approval?'

Madhubabu remained silent with his head down.

Pailey threatened him again: 'You don't have much time, your silence means you are part of it.'

Madhubabu began shaking violently and fell with the chair again. Pailey grew worried and stared at Chacko, who approached to examine him. 'He is having a panic attack. Find a piece of iron, maybe a door key.'

Chacko quickly untied his hands and placed an iron key in them. Madhubabu's shaking subsided after a few minutes and he fell unconscious.

Chacko assured Pailey, 'When he wakes up, he needs something hot, perhaps a cup of coffee.'

While Pailey guarded him, Chacko went to the kitchen to make coffee for all of them. Madhubabu was very weak after the panic attack, and he readily drank the coffee. He stared at them and muttered, 'Yes… I agreed to threaten Benny, but I never imagined they would kill him.'

Pailey was enraged. 'He was a good man who helped many people in our village.' After a pause he added, 'He had a young family, and now you have orphaned them.'

Pailey was about to strike him again when Chacko held him back. 'Give him some time, he will tell us the truth.'

Madhubabu finished the rest of the coffee and described the events leading up to Benny's murder.

In his youth, Shashankan Nair had been employed as a temporary collection agent at the newly established Cooperative Bank in Kaineervila. He was from a fishermen community in the southern coastal region and had a very impoverished upbringing. However, he was talented and educated. The temporary position was offered to him on the recommendation of a regional political party secretary.

Cooperative banks were established by farmers to support their own produce rather than manage broader finances. They were the formalised version of earlier barter practices among farmers, who exchanged their goods for the goods of others. Commodities served as compensation for landless labourers. Later, coins and cash were introduced to balance the reward system, leading to the formation of cooperative bodies.

Farmers' cooperative banks were initially created to establish a self-supporting alliance. The financial management responsibilities of office bearers were voluntarily carried out by member-producers. As membership grew, the responsibilities increased. When it became clear that farmers could not fulfil dual roles, paid staff were recruited to manage organisational duties.

Additional staff were hired to run the bank's operations, and elected executives devised policies. Services were eventually extended to the public to expand the bank's reach. However, once non-farmers became members, disagreements arose. To address this, farmers' cooperative banks were transformed into much larger public cooperative banks.

Shashankan Nair, who was known as Sasi, was initially responsible for visiting the homes of members and collecting their daily savings on a consistent basis. Farmers' banks were established to leverage the savings of their members for the benefit of both themselves and others. The income saved by farmers, typically regarded as inactive or 'dead' money, was to be converted into income for themselves and others. Savers received interest on their deposits, while others capitalised on the same deposits as loans with significantly lower interest rates. Initially, these banks encouraged collective purchasing, selling, and other agricultural practices among their members. As time progressed, many cooperatives expanded into financial services, providing loans to individuals in need, in addition to serving their members.

Sasi soon became a well-known figure in the village, as he walked its streets daily to collect the savings of fellow members. His punctuality and honesty were met with gratitude and encouragement. He promoted saving habits, routinely updated their bank deposit books, and provided receipts for everyday collections. Over time, a small number of members became overly dependent on him and allowed him to retain their deposit documents for extended periods.

He participated actively in village leisure activities, befriended many, and spent evenings with the young people. He was also a well-known figure at the neighbourhood library. His diligent efforts enabled him to secure a permanent position at the bank. This facilitated his later appointment as treasurer when the new bank was established.

Rumours circulated about his illicit relationships with several women from the village. His romantic involvement with the daughter of the then Panchayat President, someone from a different faith, was particularly noteworthy. Their relationship ended and was soon forgotten, as she eventually married and moved away. Later, Sasi married a woman from his hometown and had two children, but he once again became involved in an illicit relationship.

Shashankan Nair was regarded by the villagers as a person of high intellect and skill. Many were aware of his earlier financial manipulations, while others believed they were merely unsubstantiated allegations. Either he successfully persuaded the bank trustees to appoint him, or someone within the ruling political party exerted influence on his behalf. The board conveniently overlooked his prior misdeeds and focused on his financial management skills. It is true that he assumed power and authority quickly, and most people eventually became admirers rather than critics.

He was meticulous in his dealings with bank members during his early years, but he also manipulated a few elderly non-members. The bank did not maintain a consistent record of the daily collections he took from them. He conspired with a small number of private financiers in the village to offer loans at higher interest rates. His daily routines included lending money to impoverished fish merchants and other small-scale entrepreneurs. He offered small loans without guarantees, highly attractive to impoverished villagers who were otherwise unable to finance their daily activities. He was also careful in selecting borrowers, ensuring he chose only those from whom repayment with interest could be readily recovered.

He was once chained to a post and beaten for assaulting a young woman from Velon Kudi, part of the Viswakarma community. Velons are inherently competent people from the lowest level of the religious caste hierarchy. Most are multi-skilled craftspeople who make their living from easily available natural resources. Many men and women are experienced potters who work with clayey soil. Their pots are used for storage, while their utensils serve for cooking and eating. The Vishwakarma community traces its origins to Prajapati, the first potter created by Vishwakarma himself, and pottery is a vital part of their identity and heritage.

In addition to ceramics, they run home-based enterprises to support themselves. Sasi had given Gopan a small loan to make pappadams. Traditionally, Gopan's family made pappadams, which were quite popular in the village. They produced small and large circular pappadams and sold them throughout the area. Small pappadams, thin and crispy flatbreads made from lentil flour, are fried in boiling oil or grilled over a live flame before eating. Large pappadams are thicker and are sold to coffee shops as crispy snacks.

Gopan was the eldest, and his two younger sisters assisted him in the family business. They often sold pappadams outside the village as well. Their father had died many years earlier, and their mother suffered from asthma, so they could not attend school and remained illiterate. They lived in a one-room temporary house and prepared the pappadams outside their modest home.

As usual, Sasi provided money to buy raw materials, which he collected with interest the next day. But Gopan was unable to return the money because it had gone missing from their home. He had borrowed several times before and had always repaid quickly with the agreed interest. Gopan's elder sister's fiancé had stolen the money and later claimed he had received it legitimately as part of the pending dowry.

Consanguineous marriages were common at the time, and Hindus encouraged first-cousin marriages to preserve ancestral wealth and property. Gopan's elder sister was the family's designated fiancée for his uncle's son, as is customary in such marriages. Despite their lower caste status, they followed Hindu traditions, and siblings' offspring could legally marry. Typically, the older son enjoyed these rights, while younger siblings sought partners elsewhere.

Gopan had a savings account at the bank and was eligible for a loan. When the stolen money was not returned, he requested a loan to repay the debt, but for unknown reasons the loan was not approved. He explained his situation to Sasi and asked for more time, but the request was denied.

Gopan threatened to reveal Sasi's financial misappropriations, and Sasi reacted aggressively, assaulting him and threatening him with severe consequences. He gave Gopan an ultimatum: repay the money with interest the next day.

Unfortunately, the following day, Gopan's elder sister was found dead near the riverbed. Initially, her family and relatives assumed it was suicide, but the post-mortem confirmed it was murder by strangulation. Her fiancé was first arrested and tortured by police, but he was later released. His parents and two acquaintances confirmed his presence elsewhere at the time of the murder. Police could not identify the murderer, and villagers became furious over perceived police incompetence. Political groups marched to the police station, and police responded with caning after stones were thrown at vehicles.

Under pressure, police apprehended Shashankan Nair for questioning. They determined that Sasi had not been at home that night but found no evidence linking him to the murder. Sasi was detained for two days before being released on conditional bail, requiring him to remain in the village until investigations were complete. He was allowed to work, but his reputation suffered, and he vowed to prove his innocence.

Gopan lived with his family on the outskirts of the village, very close to the river. There were other families from the same community living in the area. Most of them were poor, while others earned a better income from regular professions. They were neither farmers nor bank members. A few of them, like Gopan, had savings accounts but made inconsistent deposits. Sasi rarely entered this area, but he remained friendly with a few of the fewer account holders.

A week after Sasi was released from police detention, Gopan visited him to return the borrowed money, promising to repay the interest later. 'I lost my loving sister and the business; now it is difficult to manage life.'

Sasi accepted the money and expressed sorrow. 'It was a very unfortunate death.' He quickly added a clarification regarding his non-involvement: 'I didn't know him nor had any relation with your sister. Maybe I met her a couple of times, but nothing beyond that.'

Gopan did not respond, so Sasi asked, 'Do you suspect anyone else?'

Gopan hesitated. 'She was about to marry… and the police are still investigating.'

Gopan stood up to leave, and Sasi reiterated the enquiry: 'Did she have another affair?'

Gopan paused before responding, 'Two years ago she was working as a housemaid in another village and returned soon after she reached marriageable age. She was never known to have had an affair.'

Sasi enquired further, 'Are you certain she was satisfied with the current proposal?'

Gopan didn't react, so Sasi pressed again, 'Or did she have an affair with someone else in your neighbourhood?'

Gopan paused a moment. 'I haven't heard anything, and no one has mentioned anything.'

Sasi asked no further questions. Gopan walked away but later returned to apologise. 'I haven't mentioned your name to the police, it could be someone else.'

Sasi did not respond, so Gopan added, 'I will return your money as soon as I get a job.'

Sasi stared at him, handed the loaned money back, and advised, 'Restart your business and repay me every day with interest.'

Gopan refused, but Sasi insisted and asked, 'Has anyone recently moved to your neighbourhood?'

Gopan paused before replying, 'Not recently… but there was a man living with his in-laws. He is very friendly and helpful.'

Sasi wasn't sure and said casually, 'People differ, and things aren't always straightforward. Anyway, let the police sort it out, it is not my job.'

Gopan resumed walking, and Sasi reminded him, 'As usual, return the money daily, with interest.'

On the way back, Gopan was reminded of Sasi's remark about his neighbour. He attempted to recall someone who might have killed his sister or led to her murder. He was walking along the narrow roads when he reached the small canal that connected the larger paddy field to the village. A single coconut tree trunk had been set across the canal, enabling people to cross. The outer layer of the trunk was worn, making villagers wary of using it.

Gopan checked its firmness and found the old trunk unstable and fragile. He looked for something to steady it before crossing. He brought a few medium-sized stones and stacked them on both sides to make the trunk more stable.

He stepped carefully onto the bridge, but as he reached the opposite side, he slipped and plunged into the water. The canal wasn't deep, and with water just above knee level, he stood up quickly. He was soaked, and before he could regain his footing, the tree trunk collapsed onto his shoulders. He was almost knocked unconscious and fell again into the water.

He felt intense pain near his left ear, where the tree trunk had struck and nearly torn the skin. He fell face down into the canal, and before losing consciousness completely, he noticed the water around him turning red. He was bleeding from a nasty cut above his left ear when he sensed someone nearby.

He attempted to push aside the tree trunk, but it was too heavy. He pushed again and realised there was downward pressure from above.

Gopan nearly lost consciousness, but he regained enough strength to push the trunk upwards. The person pressing it down abruptly lost balance and fell backwards. Gopan raised his head above the surface and exhaled deeply. Fresh air filled his lungs, strengthening his body as his heart pumped life-saving oxygen through him.

He shifted the tree trunk towards the opposite bank of the canal, not realising another individual was being crushed beneath it.

It took him several seconds to fully regain awareness, during which time his opponent lost precious moments that might have saved his life. He looked carefully at the person, who was losing movement beneath the heavy trunk. Gopan shouted, 'Sibu Annan!' upon recognising him.

Gopan tried to lift the trunk so the man could escape. He removed the trunk and carried the body to the shore with difficulty, crying out for help. He attempted to rouse him, but Sibu Annan lay motionless.

There was no one around, so he jumped up and yelled loudly to attract attention. After several attempts, he heard fast footsteps approaching. An elderly man examined the still body and declared him dead.

Gopan was stunned for several minutes before he realised the consequences. People surrounding him looked for answers. He said, 'I heard a loud noise and saw him under the broken bridge.' Taking a deep breath, he continued, 'I tried to save him, but I think I was too late.'

Another man looked at the fallen trunk and said, 'Yes, it was very old and damaged. The poor man should have been more careful.'

Someone else added, 'Gopan, it's your neighbour Sibu.'

Gopan nodded, cried, and replied, 'I tried to help him.'

Gopan and his acquaintances referred to him as Sibu Annan, although his actual name was Sidharth Raman. He was a Tamil-speaking Brahmin from southern Tamil Nadu who had eloped with a woman of a lower caste. His parents rejected the marriage and revoked his authority to conduct poojas at temples, a profession he had inherited from his family. His wife's parents provided accommodation, and he was undergoing carpentry training under their guidance.

However, although they had been married for more than two years, they did not have children. Their marriage encountered complications within a few months due to their disparate lifestyles. Sibu was dissatisfied with the restricted space in the house and lacked the skills needed to learn carpentry. He consistently requested improved hygiene and tasty vegetarian food, which his in-laws were unable to provide. Ragini, his wife, expressed frustration with his frequent sexual desires and doubted his fertility.

The police determined his death to be accidental and expressed gratitude for Gopan's prompt actions in attempting to rescue him. Sibu's parents were notified of his tragic passing, but they declined to receive his mortal remains. His body was cremated at the public cremation site, where another Brahmin conducted the final rites on behalf of his parents. They also prohibited his wife Ragini and her parents from participating in the final rites.

Immediately following his death, Gopan felt uneasy about Ragini and her parents' behaviour. He believed they had not mourned his loss sufficiently and that they resumed their normal routines within just a few days.

Gopan was unsure whether Sibu had fallen into the canal by accident or intentionally. Gopan himself had slipped and tumbled into the canal, unaware of the tree trunk toppling over him. He had repaired the single wooden-plank bridge before stepping on it and had not seen Sibu nearby. It remained unclear whether Sibu had leapt into the canal to rescue him or had attempted to unbalance him. Gopan was unsure whether Sibu, or someone else, had pressed the tree trunk down on him, or whether the weight of the trunk alone had caused the pressure. He knew the true cause would remain a mystery. Fear of the consequences prevented him from sharing his suspicions with anyone.

The circumstances surrounding Gopan's sister's death and the identity of her true killer were never investigated further. Soon after Sidharth Raman died, Gopan lost the motivation to continue pursuing the case. His sorrow after accidentally killing Sibu Annan lingered, haunting him for days. Along with his family, the villagers quickly forgot the tragic events, until Sibu's wife Ragini made some shocking revelations much later.

Chapter 23

Shashankan Nair's promotion to a prominent position at the cooperative bank offered him further prospects for corruption. Many others were aware of his earlier problematic behaviour, but these were not officially recorded, and no disciplinary action was taken. It's possible that there was insufficient evidence to charge him, or that someone at a higher level protected him. He performed brilliantly in the early months before resuming his unethical behaviour. He would delay approved loan payments to consumers, claiming a shortage of cash, and would occasionally prevent cheque collections. Cash was only released after receiving some sort of favour from the customers. Initially, he was not involved in the loan approval process, but with time, he gained control of it.

Sasi would take both cash and in-kind gifts from prospective clients. He would accept something as simple as a complimentary bottle of milk from customers in need of favours. Clients obtained temporary loans from banks in exchange for their expensive jewels as security. He violated the bank's agreed-upon restrictions of limited sums against certain gold weights and authorised extra money when bribed. He often bought raw ingredients for daily use from needy farmers at a lower price than the market. He approved more than the eligible amount of cash loans against their savings deposits to cover his daily expenses. He approved a larger loan against less gold for a restaurant owner. His dining credit account at a tiny restaurant was waived in exchange for the owner's favours. Over time, all small merchants declined to do business with him. Either he refused to pay for the commodities and services received, or he demanded a significant cost reduction.

Using the vulnerabilities of the bank's board members, he claimed undue favours, thereby bolstering his dubious activities. He exploited their most profound human vulnerabilities and circumvented rational thought to access their emotional responses. He initially targeted a bank board member after coercing the victims to make impetuous decisions. Subsequently, they disseminated the methodology to entice others and lure them into their mode of operation, encouraging them to pursue regular favours and sharing a portion of the bribed money with them. He began with a small number of them, subsequently expanding to most of the board members. The majority of board members had a limited number of, or multiple, vested interests that necessitated the assistance of their colleagues. Few were concerned about immediate retribution or potential negative repercussions, and as a result, they refrained from reporting irregularities. Sasi achieved complete control over the bank's operations within a year and subsequently increased financial malpractices.

Shashankan Nair used a honeytrap to deceive a modest board member. Shobha Ranjan, a village whore, was hired by him to establish illicit relationships with the board member. It was unclear whether Sasi introduced the sexually promiscuous Shobha to the member or capitalised on their existing illicit relationship. He promised her a large loan amount to repair her broken house. In exchange, he requested concrete evidence of her sexual relationship with the board member.

Shobha, a divorced woman, was employed as a housemaid and resided with her three children shortly after her husband eloped with another woman. Her efforts to establish independence and provide for her children were unsuccessful when she was falsely accused of theft. Even though the police were not involved, the information disseminated like wildfire, and as a result, no one employed her. Her attempts as an impermanent labourer in the construction sector were also unsuccessful. Surviving necessitated exceedingly rigorous labour and inadequate compensation. She attempted alternative occupations, but they were unsuccessful as well, as she was unable to work for extended periods due to her deteriorating physical health.

She was compelled to seek a temporary loan from an old man and was unable to make timely payments. When she couldn't repay the money, he forced her into bed with him. He repeated it several times until he was tired of her and wrote off her debt. She understood that sharing a bed with others was a quick way to make money. She then offered herself to several others to survive in the materialistic world. She quickly established herself as the village whore, catering to men's insatiable sexual desires.

Villagers allege that Shobha uses black magic to lure wealthy and affluent men from anywhere. She is associated with a witch-crafter from a different village who is dedicated to the worship of malevolent spirits. During black-moon nights, when the forces of evil are at their most powerful, he enacts rituals. Kuttichathan, his deity, is fond of raw flesh and homemade spirits. In exchange, he requests favours to inflict harm or misfortune on his adversaries and specific targets. The fruits, drinks, and raw flesh that are offered to the malevolent deity are believed to be endowed with malevolent powers. The witch-crafter acquires these powers by consuming the remaining spirit and raw flesh that were offered to the deity. The remaining fruits and blossoms, which are said to possess magical powers, are distributed to other devotees. It is alleged that Shobha wears those used flowers while entertaining her customers, thereby captivating them and prompting frequent visits. She administers the sedated fruits to her affluent and prominent clients, who thereafter become her sexual slaves for life.

Shobha was strategically deployed by Shashankan Nair to intimidate one of the board members, a tactic that was kept confidential for a brief period. The bank accrued liability because of Shobha's loan secured by her meagre property. Shobha was unaware of the debts until she received an eviction notice from the bank. She asserted that she had repaid the loan amount and had previously requested that Sasi return the land documents. This infuriated her, as she was unaware that there was an additional loan against the property. Shobha publicly accused Sasi of deceiving her and utilising her to exert influence over the bank's board members. Sasi denied the accusations and retaliated stating Shobha failed to return public funds. Shobha's accusations were disregarded by bank customers and the public, who endorsed Sasi's assertions.

Ragini, the wife of Sidharth Raman, who met an untimely death in the canal, accused Shashankan Nair of orchestrating her husband's murder. This turned the tables on him. Ragini and her parents were alarmed by the fact that their dog had been killed by their irritated neighbour. The dog continued to wail at night since Sibu's untimely accidental death. Following Sibu's death and cremation, numerous canines in the neighbourhood emulated the unusual howling. The neighbour alleged that their dog had become insane and was inciting other canines. People were frightened by the frequent howling in their vicinity, which disrupted their sleep. The insensible wailing of a dog is believed to attract malevolent spirits, and many individuals were nervous about their safety.

Ragini claimed that her late husband, Sidharth Raman, was a womaniser who had illicit relationships with other women, including Gopan's late sister. She was killed while eloping with Sibu, and Ragini claims Sasi was involved. Few people knew anything about her husband, Sidharth Raman, who was a lazy and arrogant person. Sibu suffered from infertility and tried to hide it by blaming Ragini for her inability to conceive children. He first spoke to Sasi about getting business loans from the bank. Sasi consented to sanction the loans against Ragini's parents' property. Her parents declined since they knew he was lazy and incapable of running a business. Upset by their decision, Sibu Annan threatened to divorce her and remarry a wealthy girl.

Ragini further accused Shashankan Nair of scamming and falsifying documents to approve loans for her late husband. Sasi went to their house at night and took her father's thumb impressions on loan documents. His parents and brother were sedated with alcohol before attempting to obtain thumbprints. She foiled the plot that night and destroyed the legal documents. They both beat her cruelly, and when their neighbours heard her cry, they rescued her. When both resisted, the neighbours beat them and tied them to a pole. The next day, they were released with a warning not to enter their neighbourhood. Her relationship with her spouse had broken down, but her parents were helping to resolve issues. After Sibu tried to cheat them, Ragini's parents rejected him, not considering his apologies. When his efforts failed, Sibu planned to elope with Gopan's sister, and she suspects Sasi had more dubious plans for them.

After Sidharth Raman's body was cremated, his parents informed them of his drowning accident. They suggested Ragini's parents perform after-death rituals as he was a Brahmin. They explained the need and importance, but Ragini's parents ignored their advice because they were not devout followers. They rejected the suggested rituals, which are archaic and do not, in their view, benefit the afterlife of a lethargic individual.

According to Hindu mythology, a man's soul enters the heavens immediately after death. There, it has the option to meet Yama, the deity of death, to discuss his earthly activities. Yama will assess his daily actions and misdeeds and render a verdict required to earn moksha, the ultimate goal of life. Then Yama's men accompany the soul back to its home on earth. The soul will endeavour to re-establish communication with its relatives. It will quickly understand that none of them are listening to him, and he is unable to hear their talk. When mortal remains are cremated, it wants to return to them and cries out in despair. The soul loses both worldly and celestial connections as its body transforms into a handful of ash. The head takes longer to turn to ash, and the soul cries louder, but no one in the world or the heavens hears it.

Yama's soldiers return to take the spirit, which has lost its bodily form. The soldiers cannot drag the soul unless it assumes a shadowy form of its original bodily shape. When close relatives carry out death rituals for thirteen days in a row, the soul takes on this shadowy bodily form. Everyday traditions include creating rice balls and feeding them to crows in the open. Crows are thought to be guided by the deceased's soul to consume them. During these days, the shadowy human body is gradually restored, and on the thirteenth day, Yama's troops arrive to chain the soul. Depending on the verdict, the troops follow various harsh paths to punish or reward the soul. Soldiers bind enormous chains around its limbs and body and drag it all the way to heaven.

The duration of the voyage is contingent upon Yama's verdict, which takes into account their quality of life and good deeds during their lifetime. Yama's soldiers are unable to drag the soul unless it assumes a shadowy human form. Unless the human soul attains this shadowy form, it is caught between its home and its ultimate voyage. Sidharth Raman's soul has not attained the shadowy form because none of his relatives conducted the rituals. Dogs possess supernatural vision, which enables them to perceive and experience the anguish of these entrapped spirits. The relatives are encouraged to perform the rituals and release the soul for its final journey to the heavens by the dogs, who serve as their messengers.

Shashankan Nair's family defended him, claiming they were away at a temple celebration on the night of the tragic incidents. Gopan's parents and neighbours refused to comment on Ragini's allegations. Being a believer himself, Sasi instantly contacted Sidharth Raman's family to intervene and assist the soul in beginning its final voyage. As the stewards of the beliefs, they performed the necessary rites, allowing Yama's troops to chain the soul. Shashankan Nair survived another scandal, but his reputation suffered. Several Board members took further measures but were unable to adequately oppose his misconduct.

Shashankan Nair continued to defraud the co-operative bank until Benny Mathew was elected to its executive body. Benny was aware of his fraudulent activities because of many customer complaints. He was mindful of Sasi's influence on the management team and gathered evidence over the subsequent six months before compiling a report against him. Benny demanded that he be dismissed immediately and prosecuted for financial fraud.

Benny Mathew uncovered Shashankan Nair's previous life prior to his move to Kaineervila. He was a member of a group of influential young men who sexually assaulted and murdered a gifted adolescent girl. The police deliberately accused her father of sexually harassing the child, and the entire family committed suicide. The incident was extremely cruel and severely disrupted the fundamental foundation of trust between children and their parents. Benny Mathew also established Sasi's illegal relationships with the ruling political party. With the assistance of a crime reporter, he acquired additional evidence regarding Sasi's involvement. The initial police investigation accused the gang of murder, but this was overturned due to their influence at higher levels. The entire initial police squad was replaced by corrupt officials who manipulated the investigations and established that the whole incident was a family suicide. They concluded that the adolescent was pregnant by her father, and the entire family committed suicide to prevent public defamation.

Sreekala Vaidyanathan, a ninth-grade student, was raped and murdered by the gang. She was her parents' eldest child, with two younger siblings, a sister and a brother. Her parents were both live theatre artists from different religions. They fell in love while performing with the same stage troupe, which their parents disapproved of. They were residing in a rented house in the seaside village where Shashankan Nair lived. Sreekala did not excel in school but was far more attractive than her siblings. She inherited her parents' artistic talents and was an exceptional Mohiniyattam performer. She started dancing at a young age, and her teacher admired her delicate footwork and flowing body movements.

She also stated that her delicate facial gestures resembled the original Mohini, the female incarnation of Lord Vishnu Devan. Mohini is not an element of Lord Vishnu's Dashavatara, but rather a prominent female avatar of Vishnu. She was instrumental in churning the ocean and collecting Amrit, the elixir of immortality. Mohini deceived the Asuras with her beauty and seductive nature and presented Amrit to the Devas, assuring their immortality. Mohiniyattam represents Lord Vishnu in a female role, enticing the Asuras and stealing Amrit from them. Despite it being deceptively obtained, consuming Amrit strengthened the Devas, enabling them to defeat the otherwise formidable Asuras.

Sreekala Vaidyanathan embodied the mythical Mohini in both her appearance and her frenetic movements; however, she was ill-fated. During her early adolescent years, she had many admirers and was careful in her interactions with them. She was steadfast in her dedication to pursuing a career in dance and continued to follow her parents' guidance and instructions. She received many awards for her solo and group dance performances at the school and district levels. Several cast and crew professionals watched her performance at the state-level competitions and recommended that she pursue a career in the film industry.

There was a period when the visual and special effects of fast-moving motion pictures were more popular than the limited drama stages. Most drama artists aspired to be depicted on expansive white screens. The process of real-time onstage storytelling is more labour-intensive and demanding. Actors are idolised by the audience due to the perfect presentation of broader narratives in films. Many of the traditional drama groups that were disorganised were losing popularity to more vibrant movie screens. Sreekala's parents were thrilled that their daughter might be granted the opportunity she had long desired. They urged her to accept the most advantageous offer to become an instant celebrity, thereby attaining fame at a young age.

Shashankan Nair, along with two other young men, knocked on their door one day and introduced themselves as film producers. Sreekala's mother extended a warm welcome to them. The family was invited to an audition for a new film at a hotel in the area by the group. They indicated that Sreekala would be granted a significant role, contingent upon her abilities. Insisting that they accompany them immediately, young Sasi stated, 'The film director is extremely popular, and it is very difficult to get an appointment.'

Upon noticing that Sreekala had gone to school, they mutually consented to meet that evening. They reminded her, 'I am your neighbour, and the director is waiting on my request. A role in his film would be the most advantageous for Sreekala's future in the film industry.'

Sreekala's father returned home after they left and was not inclined to believe their claims. He expressed concern: 'She is inexperienced and young, and she is unable to manage the stress associated with acting and studies.'

Her mother was more optimistic: 'She is my daughter and will handle any challenging situation.'

They argued and were unable to reach a consensus. Both parents presented the benefits and drawbacks to Sreekala, who ultimately chose to support her father. 'Mohiniyattam is my passion, but it is more significant to complete matriculation.'

She then turned to her mother and said, 'I am eager to secure a job; a consistent income would ensure my future.'

Her mother's response was heartbreaking: 'You are not good in your studies; your siblings are intelligent and require support.'

Her father was frustrated: 'Stop talking nonsense. Sree is more intelligent than you. With a little more effort, she will excel in her studies.'

The next morning, Sasi and his friends reached their house in a white Ambassador car, saying, 'If we leave now, I can promise you all will return home in the evening.'

Before her mother could react, her father replied and raised questions: 'Where are we going? Are we going to the hotel or the studio?'

Since they had anticipated an easy agreement, Sasi and his companions were taken aback by the cross-examination. They considered it and responded, 'If you are busy, you do not need to come. Mum could accompany Sree, and both of them could return by the evening.'

Her father became irritated and asked them to leave. 'We need more time to decide, and her exams are quickly approaching.'

They stared at the mother, who quietly asked them to leave for now.

Her mother was adamant and had alternative plans. A week later, she requested that they come back while her father was performing on stage. Although Sreekala was reluctant to consent, her mother kept insisting, 'It will only be for a few hours, and you will be back home before your father and siblings return from school.'

Sreekala, a teenager, was unable to resist her mother, and that was the last time they were seen together at their home.

Her father returned home very late that evening and found that Sreekala's two siblings were alone in the house. One of the neighbours had helped the children inside and stated that Sreekala and her mother were seen departing the house in a white Ambassador car with strangers. The following morning, her father formally filed a missing person complaint at the nearest police station. The police collected the information and assured him they would locate them at the earliest.

The following day, Sreekala's siblings failed to report to school, and a friend of theirs expressed concerns to their parents. The neighbours came in search of the family and were unable to open the front door. They were horrified by the tragic scenes that they saw through a sliding window and promptly informed the police.

The police personnel were terrified by the scenes inside the home as they forced open the front door. The room was found to be emitting a foul odour. Using both ends of a single coir rope, the husband and wife were hanging from the ceiling. Sreekala was found dead on the bed, while her two siblings were discovered dead on the floor. The police promptly cordoned off the area and concluded their initial investigations. The family's suicide was announced to the public and to news agencies, stating that underlying causes were being investigated. The primary evidence was the house, which was locked from inside and did not exhibit any indications of intrusion. The police version was tentatively accepted by the neighbours and relatives until the autopsy reports were made public later that month.

Sreekala and her siblings died after consuming liquid poison, which was unusual for children their age. There was evidence of forced drinking on them. Sreekala was violently raped by multiple people some hours before her death. Her mother died a day before her and was sexually assaulted. Her father was hanged after death, and his body had several physical torture marks.

Police were unable to confirm the reports and remained tight-lipped after previously ruling out the presence of a third person inside the home. Police attempted to re-investigate using detection dogs, which was not possible since the crime scenes had been disrupted.

Investigations remained in limbo, with no breakthrough. Their neighbours and the public formed an action group, demanding that the matter be handed over to a competent police investigation team. The police formed a new task team, and the final reports were submitted within three months. They accused the father of sexually abusing his girls, and the mother took revenge by poisoning them. They were unable to verify the findings, including if the mother died earlier than the others, while sticking to their story.

It was only much later that it was disclosed that the initial police investigations had accurately identified the actual killers and their motivations. The request to arrest and prosecute Shashankan Nair and two of his friends, who are accused of killing the family, was declined by politicians and senior officers. The investigation team pursued the white Ambassador car's trace, which was exceedingly uncommon during that period. The crime was associated with a high-profile politician who was the legal owner of the vehicle. One of the defendants was the son of another prominent politician. Subsequently, the entire investigation was orchestrated to implicate the father in the rape and murder of his daughter and family.

The trio brought Sreekala and her mother to a hotel room on the day of the crime. They separated the mother and daughter for auditions, which were being conducted in another room. Several males raped Sreekala, who was served with drugged drinks. Her mother shouted and raised alarms when Sreekala was not returned until the evening. She lost consciousness when some of them assaulted her and struck her on the head. It was alleged that a couple of prominent politicians sexually assaulted both the mother and daughter while they were unconscious. Subsequently, when the pressure became excessive and the mother threatened to contact police, the entire family was murdered. Police investigations were subsequently orchestrated to portray the father as the perpetrator, and the actual murderers escaped without being prosecuted.

Chapter 24

Pailey, losing interest in Madubabu's tale, angrily yelled, 'What does it have to do with Benny's barbaric killing?'

He approached Madubabu and threatened him. Chacko was quick to intercede. 'Let him speak, there appears to be a connection with Sasi's criminal build-up.'

Pointing at Madubabu, Chacko advised Pailey, 'We need to know the truth, and he can lead us to the real killers.'

Madubabu remained silent and looked away, and Chacko admonished him, 'Do not make up stories to protect that pig. His days are already numbered; before that, tell us the truth.'

Chacko handed over the earthen pot filled with water at Madubabu's request, and he drank from it immediately.

Pailey couldn't contain his anger, snatched the pot, and threw it to the floor. With a bang, pieces of the earthen pot lay scattered across the room.

Madubabu was horrified and responded, 'All of this information was once a secret. Revealing it to the public made Benny Mathew the enemy.'

Turning towards them, he confessed, 'More than half of the bank's assets were siphoned off through unsecured loans to ineligible individuals.'

They glanced at each other, unable to understand. Seeing this, Madubabu clarified, 'Benny Mathew went to Sasi's village and collected evidence from his neighbours and from a confidential source, probably one of the honest policemen.'

Benny Mathew was astonished by Sasi's wealth and business empire. One of the finest mansions in the village was his family home. The fishing industry in the region was under the control of his close relatives, who owned numerous fishing boats. Sasi was the proprietor of many commercial buildings in the village and the adjacent municipality. His neighbours were unaware of his financial sources and confirmed that he had become wealthy overnight.

They were under the impression that he was employed in a wealthy Gulf country and owned an energy business exporting oil to impoverished nations. Sasi's visits to the village were restricted to once a year or during special family celebrations and temple festivals. To impress the villagers, he made generous donations, and in return, he was honoured at public assemblies. Many of the villagers were indebted to his brother's private bank. Their focus was on middle-class families, providing them with modest loans with a minimum guarantee. Poor consumers were subjected to exorbitant interest rates. Their daily savings were taken away by the bank's ruthless collection agents, who also routinely recovered the loan amount and interest.

Shashankan Nair exploited the cooperative banking sector's vulnerabilities to defraud investors, consumers and members. Most investors were deceived by their own greed for additional revenue. Their private bank offered significantly higher interest rates than the nationalised banks, which followed market trends. Numerous educated and influential individuals were lured by their dubious promises.

Madubabu recounted the tale of Unni Master, a former teacher who surrendered his family's property and all his retirement benefits.

Unnithan Kartha was widely appreciated for his vast knowledge and his dedication to promoting education among the illiterate. He worked as a teacher at the village primary school, and most of the people from the village had been his students. He was respected across society. He was persuaded to deposit his retirement benefits in return for higher interest rates. He quickly consented, since he wanted to safeguard the future of his disabled daughter.

He had three children, a boy and two daughters. Both daughters were attractive, and one of them was mute. Better interest rates than other institutions would keep her financial situation stable. He justified his action, claiming that the bank adhered to the principles of state cooperative banks. He was naïve to the fact that the bank was private and that all its operations were run by a handful of family members.

The bank sent regular interest payments to another savings account held in his name. Unni Master could withdraw the money he needed from his savings account regularly. The bank had secretly made him a member, limiting his power to withdraw fixed deposits. He was one of many secret members who had legal voting rights but was never informed of it.

He went to the bank to retrieve his fixed deposit when his disabled daughter's marriage was arranged. The bank then told him that he was a regular member and that members' fixed deposits could not be withdrawn before the agreed-upon time. He took out a loan for half of the fixed deposit amount, and the bank charged him a higher interest rate on the loan.

Unni Master filed a complaint against the bank with the police when he realised the bank was defrauding him and other depositors. The bank, along with the police, persuaded him to withdraw the complaint by offering a job for his son. Unni Master did not recognise that this was yet another scheme to defraud him.

His son was appointed as a field collection agent and was secretly assigned as supervisor to numerous other collection agents. He supervised nine agents and oversaw their daily cash collections. Physically, all collection agents deposited their daily cash into the bank. The bank, however, kept documents stating that the supervisor received the daily deposits from the agents. The supervisor's next responsibility was to deposit the collections of all agents who reported to him.

Four months into the job, the bank accused him of forgery and of deceiving the bank, the collection agents, and the customers. They claimed he had failed to deposit the funds collected by the other agents. The management demanded a substantial deposit by the next evening or he would face police charges. Other collection agents stood up to the bank, accusing him of taking money and defrauding customers. He had no choice but to ask his father to provide the needed amount.

Unni Master had no choice but to solicit another loan when he realised his son was trapped and needed to avoid prosecution. After trying unsuccessfully elsewhere, he returned to the same bank, where the managers demanded his land documents as collateral. A large plot of land and the family home were both registered under a single document.

He submitted the sole paper as a guarantee for the loan, not recognising their true intentions. He was able to deposit the initial monthly instalments but failed to make subsequent payments. Interest on missed instalments was added to the principal loan amount. To pay off the loan, he attempted to sell a portion of his property. The bank owners refused to return the original documents until the full loan amount was settled.

Finally, the bank controlled by Shashankan Nair's family annexed their entire property as a means of recovering an unpaid loan. The bank covertly carried out the public bidding process and sold the property to recover the loan amount. Unni Master and the villagers were informed only once the registration process was completed. Sasi's family purchased the home at a significantly lower price than market rates. A few bank employees and members of the public protested the unfair process and sought justice for Unni Master and his family. The bank's management committee remained quiet, and people's objections eventually dissipated. The village's long-time favourite, Unnithan Master, was saddened and found dead in his own home. On the day of their eviction, he committed suicide with poison. Later, his children received a portion of the bank deposits and moved away from the village. As time passed, the villagers forgot about the incident and returned to their normal lives.

Crooks, commanded by Shashankan Nair's family, recognised that annexing land was the easiest way to increase profits. Land transactions, both selling and buying through bank loans became more common. Bank members advocated a variety of loan strategies, such as house renovations and new business operations. The few who failed to repay the committed monthly instalments were then targeted, as were those who lost their investments in new businesses. The bank's management provided more loans to repay the earlier sums, increasing the interest rates. Customers were locked in a python-like grasp, with no choice except to forfeit their land to avoid eviction and prosecution.

Madubabu also explained how Shashankan Nair and his close family members made millions by creating fraudulent accounts. He obtained closed account holders' identity documents, claiming to validate their previous loans and complete an audit trail. He then modified the documents and falsified their signatures to grant them secondary loans. He regularly misled the bank's loan approval committee by concealing applicants' previous histories. He then created cash withdrawal records for applicants and moved the funds to his family bank. A few members of the bank's governing council were bribed to keep the secret, along with other unfair advantages. Benny Mathew traced the manipulations and published proof against Sasi and a few other management team members.

They planned to build their own shipyard in the seaside town and export fish to foreign markets. Initially, they utilised their private bank to fund small and medium-sized fishing vessels owned by others, leaving the owners broke. They then used their bank's henchmen to forcefully annex their boats to the bank. The bank handled fishing boat operations, forcing the true owners to work for the bank. Shashankan Nair's organisation quickly established itself as a mafia, claiming complete control of the town. They received adequate support from the ruling political party, as their leaders were bribed in various ways.

A conflict arose between Shashankan Nair's company and another fish-exporting business group from a nearby town. Andrew Gomez led the Nulayan group, a reputable organisation with a global name for its fish products. Dileep Nair, Sasi's brother, covertly entered their group while posing as an employee to obtain information about their clients. His goal was to acquire their global supplier information. Dileep started as an assistant on one of their medium-sized fishing boats and, in nine months' time, was assigned to a larger boat.

To fish successfully in the erratic deep seas, one must be bold and skilled in the face of strong storms and enormous waves. Fishermen needed both experience and talent to operate their boats during their weeks-long fishing trips. The Srank, Paraman, who commanded the nine-member crew, took the vessel to better fishing spots before many other vessels arrived. He could drive through large waves owing to his competitive navigation skills. Srank Paraman reminded the team, emphasising the need for timing, 'As usual, we aim to reach early, fill our storages with high-value fish, and then return ahead of others.'

The less-seasoned Dileep raised a question: 'Do we need to return before others?'

Silly questions didn't sit well with Srank Paraman. 'Just follow the instructions.'

He then issued an advance notice to all onboard: 'Ice storage will only last for a week. The boat needs to return before our lifebread catches start to decompose.'

He directed his second-in-command, Cherian Thomas, to verify that all necessary items for sea survival were in order prior to proceeding to his helm chamber. The boat was equipped with basic fishing nets and rods to ensure it could endure extended periods at sea. Just before entering the cabin, Srank reiterated, 'We will return in a week, even if we do not catch enough.'

Crew members were encouraged to fully dedicate themselves and contribute to their primary objective of capturing more fish. Their income was contingent upon the aggregate value of the fish they caught. Before the expedition commenced, the deck master, Cherian, reminded the crew that the boat owner would be requesting fifty per cent of the income, with twenty per cent going towards total expenses.

Another assistant wasn't happy. 'The owner is unjust, he should be claiming only thirty per cent.'

Cherian was incensed. 'Those who do not concur may depart at this time. Otherwise, keep in mind that your collective income is only thirty per cent.'

Realising their limitations, none of them asked further questions. Cherian turned his focus towards the boundless sea ahead and prayed, 'May the mother of the mighty sea protect us. We shall not take more than is necessary for our survival.'

The boat embarked on its epic voyage in search of sustenance amid clear skies and tranquil waters. They sailed throughout the day and night to reach the very edge of the national sea border, just before the sailing path for international ships. They maintained a safe distance from other fishing vessels and pursued an abundance of fish. On the second day, the temperature was extremely high, and the Srank instructed all of them to wear protective clothing to prevent sunburn.

When Dileep was about to remove the skin of a plankton from his personal bag, the deck master yelled at him, 'Don't peel the skin, throw it into the sea now.'

Dileep stared at them until one of the workers grabbed it and hurled it into the sea. Coming near him, Cherian warned, 'Are you naïve? Bringing a banana or plankton aboard is a curse. The sea goddess would cast a spell on you.'

Dileep continued to wonder, and one of his colleagues suggested, 'You must now catch a shellfish, and your curse will be lifted.'

Another added, 'Empty the shell and place some sand on it when we return to shore.'

Dileep lifted his eyebrows, and another clarified, 'You are a child of the sea. Sand in a seashell symbolises the joyful unfolding of time.'

Cherian cautioned, 'Do not bring fruits. If they are essential to your health, bring fully ripe pineapple instead.'

Dileep was uncertain but refrained from contradicting their rusty rituals and beliefs.

The cook prepared a fish curry and boiled rice after they caught a large fish using a fishing rod. The following day was uneventful, and by the evening, dense clouds had gathered over them. During the night, dangerous conditions prevailed with violent gusts and showers. The boat and its crew were at risk due to the increasing intensity and height of the waves. Srank Paraman was able to navigate the life-threatening turbulent weather with ease, owing to his experience and skills.

The following day was also cloudy, with intermittent rain. The deck master, Cherian, advised, 'We will wait until the weather clears.'

Other workers, including newcomer Dileep, were not convinced; out of fear, they refrained from asking questions. The workers looked at other vessels laying out their nets in an attempt to increase their chances of success. Srank Paraman defended his decisions: 'I possess a greater degree of expertise and am aware of the optimal moment for fish to emerge.'

He reassured his subordinates, 'Do not lose your energy, which is essential for securing a significant quantity at the right time.'

They were assured of improved fishing the following day, as the boat remained stationary throughout the day. The boat's engines began running during the night, while Dileep and the workers were sound asleep. The sound was sufficiently loud to prompt Dileep to rise, and to his surprise, he found himself confined to their cabin. The boat sailed further until it met with a substantial object shortly thereafter. He watched the transactions from a large cargo ship through a peering hole. The fish store was securely loaded with several large packets that came in from the cargo ship. The large ship sailed away within an hour.

The following day, Dileep raised questions and was warned to mind his role. Deck master Cherian clarified the situation: 'We were in need of drinking water, and the ship crew were generous enough to share a few packets of water.'

Upon realising that Dileep was dissatisfied with the response, Cherian advised, 'Mind your business, or we will not allow you to board this vessel again.'

Subsequently, he cautioned, 'None of the boats will employ you, and your family will perish from starvation.'

The boat crew were ordered to set the net the following day, despite the gloomy weather. They repeated their actions to amass a random catch, as there were insufficient fish to pull the net. Despite the meagre quantity, the deck master and Srank appeared to be more content. In pursuit of an abundance of fish, they navigated the waters at random. They suggested that the crew actively seek large fish on the final day at sea and reminded them of their share. They vowed to return by evening, even though the store was only half-full. The workers' pleas to remain for an additional day to fill up the stores were ignored by the Srank and the deck master.

They returned to the shore much earlier than anticipated, and Srank directed all workers to disembark and return to their homes. They were assured that they would receive their share of the haul later that evening. Dileep returned to the boat, pretending to retrieve his forgotten dress, and saw strangers unloading large boxes that had been moved from the ship. The transactions were supervised by Srank and the deck master, who once again warned Dileep against disclosing anything to others. Shashankan Nair and his relatives were promptly informed by Dileep.

The boxes were later found to contain illicit drugs, which were sold in other parts of the country. As instructed, Dileep continued to work on the boat and was able to ascertain the drug-trafficking routine. The anti-drug department was informed, and the subsequent delivery was intercepted. The deck master and Srank were apprehended for drug trafficking, and their vessels were confiscated. The police had been unaware of the trafficking taking place on fishermen's vessels and promptly responded by apprehending the criminals.

Additionally, the investigation resulted in numerous searches of the warehouse of the Nulayan Group and other relevant locations. The investigation team disrupted the supply chain, resulting in the confiscation of a substantial quantity of illegal narcotics. The illicit market was suspended, but international suppliers and dealers were not detained. Andrew Gomez, the owner of the group, was sentenced to a long prison term that exceeded the anticipated duration. Shashankan Nair's group promptly assumed control of their fish export business and the international drug trafficking operation.

Madubabu concluded that 'Shashankan Nair built an empire by deploying the funds that were withdrawn from our village cooperative bank.'

Benny presented the evidence to the governing board, demanding that Sasi be promptly removed from service and that the stolen money be recovered. Madubabu was having trouble speaking from a seated position. Chacko comprehended the rationale and looked at Pailey to be mindful. Pailey, who had no personal or public obligations, swore to avenge the unlawful killing of Benny Mathew. Pailey was not an extremist or a sadist for believing that individuals could murder others to conceal their crimes and avoid prosecution. Benny was one of the individuals for whom Pailey felt affection, despite his rough appearance.

Pailey found a long rod and began beating Madubabu, yelling, 'You scoundrel, you know all this and conspired with that stupid man to kill a nobleman!'

Madubabu begged, 'Please don't kill me, I have a family that depends on me.'

Pailey was about to strike him again when Chacko restrained him. Another scream from Pailey: 'Tell me, where is Sasi? I will send him to hell tonight. He doesn't deserve to live for a moment more!'

Pailey was stronger than Chacko, so he easily broke free and hit Madubabu in the face. Madubabu collapsed to the ground, nearly unconscious, clutching his hands together and pleading for mercy: 'Don't hit me again, I'll tell you.'

Madubabu took a deep breath. 'He was gone and is now back in the village, hiding at the forest border, near the old Vada Yakshi temple.'

Holding his neck with both hands and choking him, Pailey yelled again, 'You son of a bitch, you'd better tell the truth. No one will want to go there, it's a cursed place!'

Madubabu cried, 'Leave me alone, I'm telling the truth. He's hiding there, maybe with the killers.'

Chacko stepped in: 'You said before that the killers got away from the village.'

Pailey held his throat again, and Madhu said, 'At least two of them are with him.'

Pailey looked at Chacko and then at Madhu. 'Are you sure the killers are here? I'll kill them all.'

Madubabu's body shook, his veins gasping for air, and Pailey finally let go of his throat. Madubabu needed a few moments to recover, then said, 'The bank management is guarding them. You should get more people.'

Before Chacko could restrain him, Pailey struck Madubabu again and shouted, 'You are unfamiliar with me you haven't seen my angry face!'

He then pulled Chacko towards him and hurried out, unaware that Madubabu had fallen to the ground and was struggling to breathe. Chacko attempted to return, but Pailey reminded him, 'We should capture those criminals before they escape from that hideout.'

Pailey shut the door, but Chacko forbade him from locking it from the outside, as his wife Vidya Devi might return. Pityingly, Pailey looked at Chacko, who was unable to discern his facial features in the darkness. Pailey said, 'Chacko, you lead an exemplary life, while the villagers are aware that she is a whore.'

As he turned away from him, Pailey continued, 'I am confident that we will come across her at some point tonight.'

Moving forward, he advised, 'You will then understand the extent of her devotion to her husband.'

Pailey walked ahead quickly, and Chacko was uncertain whether he was actually following him to the cursed place. Pailey continued without responding, and Chacko reminded him, 'No one dares to go there during the day, and it is nearly midnight. You really want to go there?'

Chapter 25

Pailey elaborated, 'I was returning home through the wild road one late night.'

Chacko intervened, 'Did you not feel nervous? No one dares to travel that route.'

Pailey didn't seem pleased with being interrupted. 'Do you wish to hear or pose irrelevant questions?'

Chacko's pace slowed, and he found it difficult to keep up with Pailey. He refrained from commenting to prevent Pailey from becoming irritated. Pailey clarified a few seconds later, 'There is nothing to be fearful about. Some individuals disguise themselves as these mythical creatures in order to frighten others.' After that, he looked at Chacko and said, 'In reality, I have encountered more adversity from real people than those unfortunate creatures.'

He slowed down yet maintained his pace until Chacko caught up to him. 'However, I will not let an incompetent person make money on their behalf.'

Pailey stared and reassured him, 'In order to conquer fear, one must confront it.' Then he added, 'I assure you that you do not have to be a daredevil to win over.' He accelerated his walk and declared, 'I am not a fan of exploiting the impoverished to profit from the fear they have instilled.'

Pailey clarified the deceptive narrative of the malicious spirit that continued to haunt the villagers.

The mystical tale of Kavumpatte Vada Yakshi, who killed many young men by sucking their blood, terrified the villagers. Individuals asserted that they noticed the typical bite imprints of two fangs on the necks of victims, through which Vada Yakshi drank their blood. She resides in an enormous palm tree that remains unaffected by even the most violent gusts. Palm trees are characterised by their lofty, straight growth, which makes them difficult for humans to climb. Vada Yakshi can leisurely sit on its wide, robust leaves while waiting for her victims.

The cursed entity had been patiently awaiting many generations to consume the blood of her true killer, when she was in human form. She can identify her true killer only by tasting his blood, which is why she is attracted to any young male who crosses her path. The beauty of the woman captivates all 'smitten men', who are subsequently captured and taken to the top of the palm tree. Occasionally, she consumes the flesh and blood of her victims when she is insatiably hungry. Villagers asserted that they found fragments of human bones dispersed throughout the area where the fierce spirit resides.

The village witch doctor treated the survivors, and only a small number of villagers claimed to have confronted Vada Yakshi. Men who were traumatised required several days to recuperate and never again ventured into isolated areas, even on days that were clear and sunny. Although a few individuals continued to regard it as a myth rather than a reality, the myth has its roots in the inspiring narrative of Vada Yakshi, a resident of the village who lived many years ago.

During the mediaeval era, villagers were divided into two groups: landowners and landless labourers. Upper-caste people, who acted as self-imposed rulers, possessed most of the village land. The labourers resided in makeshift structures on the outskirts of the farmlands, while the landlords lived in secure mansions. The village temple was dedicated to special deities, and the rulers were granted the privilege of leading devotion. Workers classified as lower castes were prohibited from entering the temple. They were permitted to watch and worship the deity from afar, outside the temple walls.

People classified as inferior castes were divided into various denominations. Each group was distinguished by its unique profession and had its own deity to venerate. There were numerous deities with comparable appearances, and their functions varied, including safeguarding their devotees from different natural hazards. Villagers maintained that each of these deities was a distinct manifestation of the primary village divinity, who continued to serve as their global protector.

Kadar was identified as one of the major groups that generated income by selling medicinal plants harvested from the forest. They manufactured immediate medications to treat both infectious and non-infectious diseases. Kadar were proficient in the treatment of all types of wounds caused by infectious insects and reptiles. They resided in huts located on the outskirts of the village, where they were governed by their clan leader, Moopan, who was highly esteemed. Both physically and intellectually, Moopan's daughter Sunandha was exceedingly brilliant and stunning.

Moopan believed that his daughter Sunandha was the embodiment of their powerful deity, Vandamana Devi, who safeguarded them from the fury of nature. Vandamana Devi's devotees experienced prosperity because of their praise and appeals. Devi was able to communicate with and exert authority over a variety of reptiles. She possessed unique restorative abilities that could mitigate their venomous attacks. Sunandha became the natural heir to her father as the sole surviving descendant. Moopan had raised her to be the leader of his community and had trained her in their traditional methods, which included various techniques for treating patients who had been bitten by venomous insects and reptiles.

He advised her against treating upper-caste people, as preparing the medication required the blessings of their deity. The effectiveness of the naturally prepared medicine was contingent upon the patient's belief in their deity and their acceptance of it as the healer.

The natural ingredients used for preparing the medicine were not stored but were instantly collected from the forest as soon as a patient was brought before them. Sunandha had the inborn ability to identify the insect or reptile by the bite marks. She gathered the necessary ingredients from the surrounding forest and neighbourhood. She plucked them herself, validating the maturity and tenderness of the plants. Mature plants would only contain the necessary antioxidants to mitigate the venom.

Contingent upon the seasons, the natural growth and future sustainability of very young and flowering plants were safeguarded by refraining from plucking them. The treatment was fundamentally based on belief in the curative powers of Vandamana Devi. A rapid recovery was achieved by selecting the appropriate dosage and quantity of medication. Sunandha was an exceptional physician who was adept at both diagnosing and administering appropriate dosages, providing each patient with meticulous care.

One day, a charming young man was brought to her by the villagers. His body was nearly still, and the colour of his epidermis had changed to blue. Mohanan Varrier, the son of the village temple's chief priest, had been bitten by a venomous black cobra. The dark moon was poised to descend as the Sun nearly reached the western horizon.

Sunandha was inside her room preparing for the evening prayers. On hearing the villagers call, she emerged from her room, looked around, and greeted them. She examined the body and cautiously stated, 'The time is not favourable; it is time for our Goddess to rest, treatment will be ineffective.'

Eacharan Varrier, the patient's father, approached her, kneeling in front of her and holding his palms together. 'Devi, I pray to my god twice a day, and my god has instructed me to seek your immediate assistance.'

Sunandha noticed the man's frail eyes. Recognising his sincere request, she responded, 'I respect you and endorse your assertions; however, I am unable to flout our customs.' She observed her own admirers and stated, 'Vandamana Devi will be dissatisfied if we disregard our own rules and traditions.'

Eacharan Varrier vowed to keep trying, saying, 'Mohanan is my sole son and my heir to the temple. We would be devoted to you and your deity for the rest of our lives. Please help us.'

Sunandha was unprepared and reiterated the regulations. 'You are not convinced of the powers of our deity, are you?'

Eacharan Varrier responded with emotion and sobs: 'I have come to pray for my son's life on the orders of my God, and I am a firm believer in the healing powers of Vandamana Devi. I implore you not to disregard my family and our God.'

Sunandha remained still as Eacharan Varrier again pleaded, 'You are the sole heir of a great father, and my son is my only hope of inheriting my duties after my death.' He knelt on the ground and extended both of his hands towards her feet.

Sunandha swiftly retreated and moved towards Mohanan's nearly lifeless body. She was astounded by Mohanan's attractive physique. She detected an aroma of allure emanating from his youthful, slender body. A sudden surge of cold air swept past her, enveloping her in a mesmerising world. She briefly lost consciousness in the wilderness, but she soon regained it.

She forced the decision upon herself and conducted another thorough examination, realising she was being lured in. The query 'When did it happen?' was raised, despite the fact that it had been some time since the bite. His father responded promptly, 'I am uncertain. He was discovered unconscious in an isolated spot near the temple.'

Sunandha's attention was diverted by her admiration for Mohanan's appealing physical appearance. She was aware of Gandharvas, deities who reside in other worlds and are reincarnated as humans for a specific purpose.

Mohanan was unharmed except for the bluish colour that had extended to his upper body. She was taken aback by the marks upon closer examination. Purposeful, rather than accidental or provoked, that was the nature of the bite. The venom had been injected rapidly due to the deep and wide bite marks of both fangs. The sole explanation for his survival so far was that the venom may have missed the veins.

Gods direct purposeful bites to avenge awful behaviour or to convey a message to a close relative. She could not be a protective barrier between feuds of the Gods and Goddesses, as this would incur their wrath. A second lightning shock shook her spine, compelling her to retreat. Once again she looked at his weakened father and came to realise that all the events were staged. She observed the others who had assembled to witness yet another miracle and was unable to disappoint them.

Sunandha determined to confront the destiny the Gods had set and not retreat from this perilous moment. She entered her hut and promptly emerged with a diminutive earthenware vessel. She turned the opening of the cap towards Mohanan's nostrils. She delicately pressed his chest for a few seconds before repeating the action. She repeated it multiple times while observing Mohanan's right foot for any signs of movement. When his toes moved, the people who had congregated around him let out a collective sigh.

Sunandha looked up and folded her palms together, expressing gratitude to her deity while holding the vessel with both hands. She looked at Eacharan Varrier; hope returned to him, and he expressed his gratitude by folding his hands together. She recognised that the bite was a form of retribution and decided to investigate the underlying causes of human suffering at the hands of the gods.

Sunandha quietly retreated to her hut, and a few moments later her assistant followed her inside. The aide noticed Sunandha sitting in her customary position in front of her deity. The fierce deity was pleased by the illumination of all nine strands on the oil lamp. As she sat on the floor, Sunandha crossed her legs and folded both palms together, pleading before her deity.

Upon recognising her assistant's presence, she asked, 'Allow the elderly man in, he must pay his respects to Vandamana Devi.' The assistant promptly withdrew in response to the unexpected demand. She recognised it was exceedingly uncommon for non-faithful people to enter the hut, where the Devi's influence was at its most potent.

In the presence of both Sunandha and her deity, Eacharan Varrier revealed his feelings. He lay down in a prostrated position, demonstrating profound veneration, humility, and surrender to Sunandha's deity. He pleaded for his son's life: 'Mother, Goddess of power and miracles, have mercy on my son. Lift his curse and cure him.'

Sunandha maintained her posture and kept her eyes closed, enabling Eacharan to speak. 'Lord, I implore you to pardon my son, who has not yet acquired the ability to understand the material world. Now he has learnt his lessons.'

After a pause, he continued, 'Goddess of the world, he is my sole heir, the only man in my family to light a lamp and burn incense, to praise and please our family deity of wealth and peace.'

The hut was filled with a pungent odour of burnt flesh as Sunandha lifted the cover of a small vessel positioned in front of the deity. Eacharan Varrier, who was the lead priest and principal devotee of another deity, recognised the scent as a symbol of energy, thereby releasing himself from the evil past. A gesture made by sinners to assure their deity that they have repented for their crimes and are ready to embrace the transition to a noble life.

He stood up and begged, 'My son was opposed to the traditions of worship, and he walked with communists and atheists, which was his path to divinity, rather than following evil spirits.'

Sunandha maintained her silence for Eacharan Varrier to appease her deity.

'He did not commit any wrongdoing. It is his youthful enthusiasm for change and disregard for supernatural powers that influenced him.'

Mohanan Varrier had been a dedicated devotee during his early years and cultivated a compassionate disposition towards the impoverished. He was regarded as a contributor to positive Karma due to his convictions regarding a noble life, compassion, and nonviolence. He learnt and practised rituals and prayers from his father, adhering to all principles to attain moksha.

As a teenager, he began to share sustenance with his impoverished classmates. He soon developed a love for the poor and expressed concern about their denied human rights. He was influenced by the modern world at college, unaware that the material world is illusory. He rejected the notion of Maya, a veil of delusion that conceals the true nature of reality.

He participated in violent protests against the prevailing caste system, as he advocated for equality for the low caste in accordance with communist principles. The Communists capitalised on his priestly background to recruit additional youths to their ideology. He gradually grew disinterested in his primary objective of worship and organised several demonstrations against the authorities, advocating for the rights of the impoverished. He was apprehended by the police based on an inaccurate accusation that he had assaulted a police person. Eacharan Varrier was able to present some evidence in opposition to the police allegations, and the courts freed him.

The double trap that certain communist leaders played was revealed to Mohanan during the unlawful detention period, and he gradually distanced himself from them. He was hesitant to resume his priestly duties and requested additional time from his family. The Goddess decided to punish him, even though he had repented for his errors and was on the path to recovery.

Sunandha was compelled to trust Eacharan Varrier to save his son. Sunandha persisted in her pleas, and her deity was not responding to her appeals. She was unable to delay any longer as the venom was spreading to other areas of Mohanan's body. She urged her assistant, 'Permit me to pray in solitude.' The assistant requested Eacharan Varrier to leave the room, recognising the significance of the moment.

Sunandha begged her deity to heal him, but the deity did not respond. She was aware of the reason: she was not praying to ascertain the will of God, but rather to request permission to heal him. She was left with no alternative but to follow her own feelings and attempt to cure the young man.

Sunandha emerged from the dwelling and hurried into the neighbouring woodland. Without knowing the truth, her assistant advised Eacharan Varrier and others that 'Devi is now pleased; Sunandha has gone to fetch the medicine and will administer the right treatment.' Sunandha swiftly returned with a handful of shrubs.

Her assistant raised concerns. 'This is not normal.'

The helper followed Sunandha inside, and after a few minutes, they both reappeared with several vessels. Sunandha put the juice of crushed leaves into Mohanan's mouth. Her assistant applied another mixture of powdered turmeric and green shrubs all over his body, up to the neck.

Sunandha and her assistant performed the procedure three times over the next three hours. On the fourth hour, the bluish hue of Mohanan's body began to diminish. Sunandha applied a black stone, which was crafted from charred cow bone, to the bite imprint. The black stone transformed into blue within an hour, and she replaced it with another. She brought the initial black stone into the house and carefully placed it in front of her deity. The second black stone also underwent a blue transformation within the next hour.

At that moment, Mohanan Varrier resumed breathing normally. She requested his father to feed him after preparing an additional beverage on a wooden plate. When she removed the second stone from the bite mark, Mohanan awoke and looked into her eyes. Eacharan Varrier assisted Mohanan into a seated position and provided the medicinal beverage. Mohanan commented on the sour taste, and Sunandha responded, 'You are recovering at a faster pace than anticipated.'

Mohanan remained seated at the table after consuming the beverage. The assistant brought heated water that had been infused with a variety of leaves. In the presence of others, Eacharan Varrier gave him hot water therapy.

The lengthy therapy process lasted until midnight, which was rather rare. Soon after, Mohanan stood on his feet. Sunandha retreated to her hut and closed the doors. The aide requested the others, and the crowd gathered to depart, but Eacharan Varrier was hesitant. They left only after the aide promised them that he would fully heal and that they might return later to express their gratitude.

The following day, Sunandha was found unconscious in her hut. Her assistant made numerous attempts to revive her, and she eventually recovered consciousness. As her helper and acquaintances were unwilling to pose additional enquiries, she refrained from disclosing the reasons. She remained silent and alone for several days, leading them to believe she had been the victim of a horrific incident that night.

Mohanan Varrier made many attempts to meet with her to express his gratitude, but she declined to grant him an audience. After a week, Mohanan came across her as she was walking towards a small stream to collect potable water, which had become routine. The villagers are of the opinion that they established a strong and intimate relationship through their continued meetings over time.

A year later, Sunandha was found dead in her hut, the victim of a snake bite. The blue stones in front of her deity were noticed by the helper to have reverted to black. In addition, the villagers found that she was six months pregnant at the time of her death. In accordance with their customs, the villagers buried her mortal remains inside the hut, in front of her deity. It is believed that Sunandha joined her deity after death, as evidenced by the special rituals performed during the burial.

Mohanan Varrier made many attempts to view the dead body, but the villagers declined. Mohanan disappeared from the village a month later and was never seen again. The villagers believed Mohanan was the father of her unborn child. Eacharan Varrier did not accept it nor previously approve of their relationship, as Mohanan was intended to remain virgin until he officially assumed priesthood.

The villagers are of the opinion that Sunandha has transformed into Vada Yakshi and is currently anticipating the arrival of Mohanan. Consequently, she pursues and eliminates all young males who cross her path in the remote village area.

Pailey went on to say, 'We need to hurry. It's still midnight — a surprise attack would be an advantage.' Chacko could not react but raced along.

Pailey stared back at him. 'Are you afraid of Vada Yakshi?'

Chacko halted. 'Are you not?'

Chacko could see Pailey's beaming face in the dark, and then Pailey stated, 'Vada Yakshi did offer me the spiced betel leaves, and I was quicker than her.'

Chacko couldn't believe him. 'What are you bragging?'

Pailey increased his speed. 'In a melodious voice she once said to me that I am an attractive young man.'

Then Pailey detailed his encounter.

'It was pitch dark and I was fully drunk to fear the wild. I was holding an almost extinguishing dried banana-leaf torch. Coming closer, the Yakshi repeated the bullshit.' He used the phrase loosely. 'Yakshi was more stupid than I thought. She couldn't recognise me. I got hold of her before she could escape.'

Looking ahead at the dark trees, Pailey commented, 'That's where it happened. It was the perfect time to get sedated, the air was filled with jasmine scents.'

Walking towards the darkness, Pailey urged Chacko, 'Stay with me, there is nothing to fear.'

Staring at the darkness ahead, Pailey commented, 'That day the Yakshi chose the wrong man.' Then he elaborated, 'A young and beautiful woman smiled at me, partly opening her thick and large lips, showing her teeth made like a bridge of white pearl beads.'

He went on: 'I was inebriated but regained my consciousness as soon as I identified her.'

Chacko was eager, but Pailey advised him, 'Maybe you'll meet her now.'

Chapter 26

Chacko's daughter Celine pestered her mother as he departed home to visit his late friend Benny's family. She asked permission to take a dip bath and to wash her clothes by the river. Her mother Mary initially declined her request due to the late afternoon, but she later accepted it on the condition that she be accompanied by her brother Sunny. Celine attempted to avoid him, asserting that 'he will spend more time swimming, and I will have to ensure his safety.'

Sunny promptly corrected her, 'I am a better swimmer; you are only capable of floating above the water surface.'

Their mother intervened and consented to a condition, 'Celine, you are only permitted to go there if you are accompanied by Sunny.'

Celine acknowledged her mother's stubbornness and consented to her decision. Mary reminded Celine to return promptly before the sun set as she left the house. Sunny was told by Celine 'walk quickly and remain with me.'

While passing their neighbour's mansion, they both realised that their family pet dog, Kaiser, was following them. Celine felt uneasy and turned to Sunny, shouting, 'Who unchained the dog? It will slow us down.'

She attempted to frighten the dog by grabbing a wooden plank from the roadside and shouting, 'Kaiser, go back now.'

Sunny was not in agreement. 'We will also provide him with a thorough bath; please allow him to join us.'

Celine came to the realisation that the dog's unchaining was part of Sunny's plan, and that it would follow them.

It was a bright evening, and the sun was on the brink of disappearing, enabling the darkness to take hold. They soon arrived at the riverbanks, and the sun's light began to diminish as dark clouds appeared above them. Celine hastily instructed Sunny, 'You assist me with the washing up, and we could take a quick bath.'

Sunny was not pleased, but he silently concurred and glanced at Kaiser, who had followed him. Celine also had arrangements for their dog, stating that it would wait at the riverbanks. The poor dog, who was struggling to descend the rocky terrain that led to the water body, was discreetly given instructions to stay. Sunny then realised that they were not in their usual location. 'It is quiet in the deep waters here; could we go to the plains so the dog can run around?'

Celine firmly declined, stating, 'We must act quickly, or else I will lodge a complaint with our mother.'

They followed the descending steps that led to the water level, and a dark canopy of clouds surrounded them. The plains were unusually empty, and Sunny noticed only a handful of people in the distance. The dog stayed quietly seated a few steps above them, awaiting instructions. Celine promptly initiated the washing process by immersing the clothes in the water and placing them on the rocks. She then requested that Sunny apply detergent to the clothes, and she would rinse them. The initial lightning strike occurred as Sunny was carefully preparing to follow her instructions. Kaiser was frightened, producing a series of irritating howls. It looked around and began ascending the stairs. Sunny attempted to recall the dog, but it concealed its tail between its legs and disappeared into the bushes.

Celine stared at the skies, feeling nervous, and requested that Sunny act quickly before the raindrops fell. Subsequently, they were struck by an additional lightning bolt, which was succeeded by a powerful thunderclap. Sunny was worried and looked at his sister, who was hurriedly completing the washing. Sunny recalled their dog, 'Kaiser, return here now.'

Celine requested that he disregard the dog and help complete the washing. Soon after they finished, a few drops of rain fell on them. Celine hurried, 'Let's take a quick dip in the river and return home before it starts to rain heavily.'

Sunny was uncertain, so he requested permission to look for their companion dog, stating that they needed to give him a bath as well. He began ascending the stairs prior to Celine's response.

Sunny searched for his dog on the stairs and called out, 'Kaiser, where are you?'

The dog did not respond and was not seen in the vicinity. As he prepared to descend the stairs, he noticed some activity in the irrigation motor room situated nearby. Initially, he believed that his frightened dog would be hiding in the area. Soon he realised that the movements were happening on the upper staircases, not on the ground level. The motor operator's rest room was located at the upper stairs, which were typically empty during this time of day. He was on the verge of proceeding to the motor room when he heard his sister's voice shouting out, 'Sunny, it is time for us to return.'

He was uncertain, but he searched the ground level and checked for his dog. As he descended the stairs, he came to the realisation that the movements were not the only thing happening; he noticed human shapes that were moving.

The sky was almost completely cloudy, and Sunny had the impression that rain would fall on them at any time. Celine had finished washing and was about to take a bath when Sunny climbed down the stairs. Celine warned him again, 'It was unnecessary to run after the dog. You delayed me; I will inform Mum.'

Sunny followed Celine, who cautiously dipped into the water without replying to her warning. He knew Celine wouldn't be harsh with him, but he was concerned about the dog. While applying soap to his back, Celine comforted him, 'Don't worry too much about Kaiser; it's a clever dog, and it will find its way back home.'

With that assurance, Sunny settled down, and they both completed their baths. Sunny assisted Celine in ascending the stairs with a basket after she collected the damp clothes. Upon reaching the top, Celine realised that they had forgotten to take the detergent they used for washing. Sunny quickly descended the stairs after Celine requested that he retrieve it at once. Sunny immediately resumed his ascent with the detergent, and he spotted a few additional human shadows near Celine. He accelerated his pace to immediately reach the top level. He narrowly missed an accident, slipping on a step while he was hurriedly walking up. Upon reaching the top, he looked around, prompting Celine to raise questions. 'What are you looking at? The dog may have already returned home.'

Sunny was uncertain. 'I saw another person who was nearby.' Celine was prepared with a response: 'There is no one nearby; let's move quickly to reach home at the earliest.'

Sunny did not readily agree; he looked far towards the irrigation motor room. Sunny felt forced to follow Celine as she walked through the narrow path in front of him. As they approached the motor house, a gust of wind with torrential downpour engulfed them, forcing them to seek shelter. The dog's loud howling was heard in front, and Sunny started running towards that direction, stating, 'It's Kaiser, he may be in a fight with another dog.'

He moved quickly and ran fast, despite Celine's attempts to restrain him. The motor house's shelter provided Celine with refuge from the torrential rain. Celine yelled, 'Sunny, seek shelter, it is pouring down.'

Sunny was determined not to return and was unaware that it was the last words he heard from his beloved sister.

Sunny's distant vision was limited due to the fading light and the narrow walking path ahead. Ignoring the heavy downpour and the darkness, he searched for the dog. Then he heard more barks and cries from dogs further ahead. Concerned about his dog's safety, he entirely forgot about his sister and dashed forward from where he heard the dog barking. He searched everywhere along the path, beneath little bushes and behind fences. Looking around, he was exhausted by the time he stepped down the steppingstones leading to his home. He was relieved to hear his pet's barks again in its usual spot. The dog, chained to the post, was resting. He went near and touched its head, and the dog licked his arm in appreciation for his attention.

He turned towards the veranda, where Sunil was anticipating his arrival. He took him in his arms and kissed him. Immediately, he heard his mother's voice calling out, 'Celine, please come over and help me in the kitchen.'

Sunny responded, 'She is on her way, I reached quickly, following Kaiser.'

Mary requested that he supervise Sunil as she prepared to shower. Sunny kept a lookout for his sister's descent through the steppingstones in front, any time soon. Both brothers sat on the veranda of their house and played with the small ball, rolling it over to the other's side.

Mary returned to the kitchen after taking a shower, where she noticed the rice pot was overflowing. 'Oh my God, it is now overcooked. Celine, where are you?'

Sunny stared at the steppingstones once more upon hearing the words and responded, 'She has not yet returned home.'

Mary rushed to the veranda, asking, 'Where did you leave her?' Sunny was sluggish to respond, stating, 'She followed me in the rain, and it was dark.'

Mary looked beyond the steppingstones and pondered, 'It did not rain here.'

Sunny was alarmed as he glanced at his mother. 'It was raining heavily along the riverside, and there was a loud thunderclap.'

His mother approached the steppingstones and replied, 'Yes, I heard thunder, but there was no rain.'

Mary climbed the steppingstones and looked into the distance. She waited for a while before returning, murmuring, 'What happened to this girl? She needs to be disciplined.'

Sunny continued watching the steppingstones in anticipation of his sister's imminent show-up as Mary walked towards the kitchen.

Mary fed the goats and handed a bowl of rice to Sunny, saying, 'Feed this to the dog, the poor thing must be hungry.'

Sunny placed the rice bowl in front of the dog and released its chain, allowing the dog to eat comfortably. Sunny returned to the veranda and resumed the ball game with Sunil. Mary abruptly emerged from the kitchen and searched for her daughter, asking Sunny, 'Where did you leave her?'

Sunny, who was also concerned, rose and walked to the courtyard, stating, 'She was directly behind me, I will find out.'

Mary stopped him, 'No, it is getting dark out there. Stay with Sunil and I will find out.'

She promptly put on her sandals and hastily crossed the steppingstones. Kaiser, the household dog, was observing them. It left the half-consumed rice and began to follow Mary, climbing through the steppingstones. Sunny attempted to recall the dog, but it vanished abruptly towards the other side.

Mary hurriedly walked towards the riverside, as she was concerned about her daughter's whereabouts. Their neighbour's younger daughter came across and expressed concern, 'Where are you rushing at this time?'

Mary reluctantly replied, 'I am in search of Celine, as she has not returned from the riverside.'

Lovely casually reassured her, 'Don't worry, she is not a child. She must be on her way now.'

Lovely headed towards her home and disappeared behind the substantial grilled gate. For a brief period, Mary was uncertain, but she subsequently headed towards the riverbank. She did not notice their dog following her until she had reached the halfway point, at which the dog quietly disappeared into the bushes.

It was already dark when Mary reached near the water motor room. She couldn't find anyone there and repeatedly yelled out her daughter's name. She used the handheld torch to look around before walking down to the riverside. When she couldn't find her daughter, her lower abdomen tightened; an acute pain arose in panic. She wondered again, 'Where did she go?'

She checked all the empty spaces along the way and screamed her darling daughter's name multiple times. Hearing the heartbreaking call, a few passers-by joined her search, which expanded to surrounding areas. A few of them went to the riverbank to check again.

Mary was at her wits' end and was sobbing on the roadside. As the search party expanded, a small number of members requested that

Mary return home to help with caring for the other children. She repeatedly denied the suggestion, 'I am unable to return home without my dear daughter.'

A significant number of them embarked on a search, but they returned without any information. Mary was forced to accompany a few individuals to her home after a period. Thomas Joseph, her neighbour, emerged when several of them passed in front of the large grilled gate. He was shocked by the news that the young female had headed to the riverside at that late hour. Lovely volunteered to accompany Mary to her home. When Sunny learnt that Celine was nowhere to be found, he became anxious and began to weep. The missing dog, which had been following Mary for some time, went unnoticed by family members and the search party.

After a few hours of searching, several people noticed that the missing girl's father, Chackochan, had also not returned home. A few people went to late Benny's house and returned with no information about his current location. Mary couldn't contain her anguish and blamed Sunny for not sticking together. Sunny sobbed and said that Celine had followed him to the irrigation motor house. Sunil failed to understand the gravity of the situation. Lovely helped the children eat and encouraged them to sleep. Others frequently told Mary that they would both return home at any time. The search group returned from the toddy bar and provided some information concerning packed meals. This didn't help others determine Chacko's current whereabouts.

Many of them retired to their homes two hours after nightfall, with the intention of resuming their search in the early morning. Lovely requested her father's permission to remain with the desperate family, but Mr Thomas was not in agreement. She subsequently returned to their mansion with her father, who agreed to file a formal police complaint the following day. Lovely's mother, Achamma, expressed apprehensions regarding the security of the missing pair and questioned whether her daughter had drowned in the river. Lovely was assured of Sunny's version, as she believed that Sunny was more mature than his age. Lovely asked about her sibling, Soman, to which Achamma responded, 'He frequently stays outside and mostly spends time with his friends at the social club.'

Lovely was dissatisfied, stating that 'he should have participated in the search party; his military experience would have been useful.' Achamma and her husband did not consider it valid and ignored her.

Lovely went up to her room and thought about checking on her brother, but she put it off for later. She soon opened her bedroom, which was filthy, and let in some fresh air through the window. With the fresh and cool air, she heard the weak sound of a dog howling furiously from far away. She stared out through the window, but all she could see was the dark and one or two flickering lights in the distance. The dog kept barking and howling every now and then, which made her feel uneasy.

She chose to take a brief shower, but she was worried about Celine, who was young and chubby. She thought the cool water would help her relax, but it made her worries worse. Then she thought about how

Soman, her brother, had acted badly recently, and how they had got into violent confrontations. She finished her bath faster than usual because she couldn't stop thinking about things that made her feel bad.

She went back to the window and listened carefully to the sound of the dog howling. She couldn't see, so she turned off the lights in the room and tried to see through the gloom. A few moments later, she was shocked to hear the dog's bark coming from their own property, not far away. She listened again and thought the sound came from near their rubber-making machine shed area. She ran to the bottom floor because her instincts told her to. She looked in her brother's room on the way down and was astonished to see him asleep in his bed.

Mr Thomas and his wife were having their dinner, and Lovely discussed her concerns with them. Her mother disregarded the situation immediately, stating that it was common for dogs to howl at night. Achamma then added, 'That girl may have eloped with someone, and her father may be pursuing them.'

Lovely was not persuaded, and she suggested that they inspect nearby areas to verify that there were no unusual events. Thomas Joseph was not in agreement, stating, 'I am tired, please take Soman with you when he arrives.'

He was taken aback by Lovely's response, 'When did he arrive?' Her mother Achamma was uncertain. Thomas attempted to ascend the stairs to check on him, but Lovely intervened, stating, 'He is sleeping like a hog, it may not be wise.'

After some persuasion, Thomas agreed to inspect their rubber manufacturing facility.

The dog was racing around the shed and barking loudly as both approached the area. The dog came running towards them as they arrived, and Lovely recognised it as Chacko's dog. 'Dad, why is it here?' she wondered.

The dog continued to howl at the shed, as if to draw their attention to it. Suddenly, the shed door swung open, and a shadowy figure emerged. The dog promptly attacked the figure, biting its leg, and the figure covered its face with a towel. The man began to run towards the trees in the darkness and cried out loud. The dark, lean figure was chased by the dog for a considerable distance, and it returned with a fragment of shredded cloth. The wet, shredded cloth was left outside, and the animal proceeded to enter the shed while emitting cries.

For some time, both the father and daughter were terrified, and Thomas sought to catch the man. Lovely hung on to her dad and screamed, 'Don't go anywhere, I'm too scared.'

Then the dog came near and barked at them before going back inside the shed. Lovely grew nervous and said, 'There's something inside. Let's go back and get more people.'

Thomas advised her, 'The dog is known. Let me check and you stay away.'

The dog calmed down and wagged its tail when Thomas got close to the door. Thomas turned on the torchlight, which was growing dimmer, in the shed. The light hit a naked body in the corner of the shed within a few seconds, and he quickly pulled back. He said to Lovely, 'Let's go back and get some clothes.'

Lovely was frozen, and she asked, 'Is it Celine?'

Thomas was trembling. 'I don't know.' Then he suggested, 'Let me get your mother and some clothes.'

Lovely stared at her father's face and passed out on him.

The dog continued to howl until Thomas and his daughter returned to the shed. Achamma promptly responded by bringing water and clothes, as well as a more effective lamp. They draped a bedsheet over the nude body and removed the clotted blood from the private areas. They were relieved to see that the body was breathing. They applied water to her face, only to confirm their worst fears, it was the missing Celine.

They made numerous attempts to awaken her, but she remained unconscious. The dog silently followed Thomas as he carried her on his shoulder to their mansion. Lovely regained consciousness and helped to clean and wash the unconscious Celine. The body, including private areas, was covered in bite marks. Lovely and her parents came to the realisation that the young girl had been sexually abused for an extended period.

They gave her a hot bath and applied antiseptic medications to her wounds. They were unable to regain Celine's consciousness after making many attempts. Thomas tried to awaken Soman to request assistance, but he was also unresponsive. Lovely insisted on taking unconscious Celine to the hospital immediately, despite Achamma's recommendation to wait until the morning. Thomas agreed to take her to the hospital in anticipation of potential future complications. Lovely insisted that they all accompany her, but Achamma immediately declined. They carried Celine to the village hospital by placing her on the back of their jeep. The unconscious body was examined by the duty doctor, who then referred her to the city hospital. Thomas and Lovely took Celine to the city hospital in their jeep once more, as there was no ambulance available. She was admitted to the intensive care unit and remained unconscious.

Thomas and Lovely were only able to return to their house in the early hours of the following morning. They returned home prior to sunrise, and the dog disappeared from their property. Thomas promptly conducted a thorough cleaning of the rubber-making shed with water and eliminated all blood traces. Lovely examined her sibling, Soman, who was still asleep in his bedroom. She discovered blood-stained clothing in his bathroom and was horrified when she realised that her worst fears were the truth. She was aware of his drug use, and when it was administered, he would lie down for the entirety of the day. She was unable to keep her calm; she struck him with a piece of wooden plank many times. Under the influence of the wild honey, Soman was unable to respond despite feeling severe pain.

Thomas hurried to comfort Lovely after hearing her cries and shouting from a distance. He grabbed the wooden plank and dragged her out of Soman's room. She was weeping and repeatedly yelled, 'He is a devil, Celine was a child. How could he do such a thing to her?'

She sobbed aloud, 'I am unable to face that poor family and do not wish to continue living.'

Thomas controlled himself and requested that Lovely remain calm. Thomas again requested that no one be informed, and he locked Lovely in her bedroom. Thomas did not bother to rouse Achamma, as she was asleep. Instead, he prepared himself to face the villagers and Chackochan's family.

Chapter 27

The old building, which was constructed of laterite stone bricks, was situated in a remote location. These weathered laterite stones are soft beneath the ground, which makes them simple to carve for construction purposes. As soon as they are exposed to air, they become more durable and cost less than other forms of building bricks.

The house appeared abandoned from the exterior, as a portion of the load-bearing wall had collapsed without any indication of restoration. In certain locations, the thatched wooden roof, which was constructed from dried coconut palm fronds, had withered. The middle chambers appeared to be usable, and the house was relatively large with multiple rooms. There was no indication of anyone being present within or in the vicinity. Pailey put out the burning torch and muttered to Chacko, 'Stay here, keep quiet and be patient, I will check the rear of the house for guards.'

Pailey walked carefully, keeping his knees within foot length and not overtaking his toes. He peered around before disappearing towards the back of the house. Chacko held his breath while looking around for movements. He wasn't sure what time it was, but he didn't think there was enough time for the first lights to show up. He waited patiently for Pailey to emerge from the front, when he noticed someone approaching the home from afar.

It was time for Chacko to respond, and he moved quickly and took a close look. To his astonishment, it was Madhubabu, whom they had securely bound at his home. Before Madhubabu could make a sound,

Chacko held him hard and closed his mouth. Madhubabu, who was already weak, was unable to withstand Chacko and fell unconscious again.

When Pailey returned from the search, he noticed the quiet movements and dashed towards them. Pailey praised Chacko for his bravery and was shocked to see Madhubabu. Pailey commented, 'There is a pressing need for this idiot to venture out; I am sure there is someone inside with Sasi.'

Looking at him again, Pailey claimed, 'Whosoever it is, it's very important to him.'

Madhubabu attempted to break free from Chacko, who held him tightly. Pailey went to the house and quickly returned, this time with a rope. They tied Madhubabu to a nearby tree, and he screamed, 'Please don't hurt my wife.'

Pailey and Chacko glanced at each other, and Pailey said, 'I knew that whore Vidya Devi was with that snake.'

Before turning towards the home, Pailey chastised Madhubabu, 'Are you really a man? Aren't you ashamed of yourself?' Before walking away, Pailey added, 'Lucky for you, I will not hurt any woman, that is how she escaped from me the last time.'

Chacko stared at Pailey in disbelief and said, 'I'll explain later, now let me deal with this snake, Sasi.' Moving carefully towards the house, Pailey advised, 'You stay close behind and watch out for backstabbers.'

Chacko failed to understand the instructions but remained close to him. Chacko vowed to track down the killers and avenge his friend's awful death. Following Pailey closely, Chacko looked around in search of unusual movements and remained alert.

Chacko realised that the house was significantly larger than it appeared from a distance as he approached. The roof gable was constructed at an extremely high elevation, as it was in close contact with the dark skies. The house was comprised of two expansive rooms in the centre and a veranda that was significantly larger in size. The kitchen may have been an extension to the left, while another room was situated on the right. The wall to the right had partially collapsed. Chacko, bewildered by its appearance, surmised that the rear of the house might contain additional rooms.

Pailey touched the kerosene lamp on the veranda and murmured, 'It's cold, it may have been off for a longer period.'

Upon stepping onto the veranda, they noticed that all windows and doors were closed. Pailey listened for sounds from inside while leaning against a closed window door. Upon his return to Chacko, he murmured once more, 'There are only a few people inside; I can hear their snoring, and they are fast asleep.'

Following a thud sound, Chacko fell forward to the floor, holding his hands on the back of his head. He was immediately rendered speechless and lost consciousness. Pailey turned his focus to the shadowy pair that was behind them, only to be struck by a wooden plank. Pailey successfully blocked the forceful blow with his left hand, thereby protecting his head. He was overwhelmed by the agony and collapsed to his knees, inadvertently missing the subsequent strike from the second person.

He changed to defensive mode as a sudden gust of wind passed over his head. Pailey attempted to evaluate his opponents within the fraction of a second by stepping back towards the side of the wall. The uncertainty was further exacerbated by the acute pain and the pitch-dark surroundings. He was prepared to confront them, even though he could barely see them.

He realised, on the edge of losing a successful fight against the enemy, that he could turn anything into a weapon. Sitting on the uneven ground, he felt the bits of broken wall bricks and retaliated quickly. In no time, he tossed many rock fragments at his opponents. One of his opponents collapsed after receiving a severe blow to the head. The other took cover behind the kitchen-side wall to avoid the flying stones. Pailey jumped onto the veranda to check on Chacko, only to find him lying unconscious. Realising the priority of the moment, Pailey chose to confront the second attacker.

Pailey decided to leverage his opponent's covert style rather than confronting him head-on. He carefully strolled around the house to launch a surprise attack. Pailey lacked the abilities of a seasoned mobster and aimed for his immediate challenger. Ignoring the real threat inside the house cost him valuable time. Overly focused, he ignored other threats and was beaten with a wooden plank before crossing the backside door.

The attacker aimed for Pailey's head, but his height saved him; the blow landed on his left shoulder. Pailey squatted forward and kneeled on the ground in response to the powerful hit. He rolled over to avoid the abrupt surge of the wooden plank, creating another wind wave above his body level.

Then he heard a female yell, 'Kill that stupid rat now.'

Pailey recognised the voice, but his focus was to deal with the current threat rather than recollect the past. He swiftly rose from the ground and stared at his opponents. The male shade moved closer to strike him again, while the female figure looked around, most likely for another wooden plank or weapon. The attacking male was shorter than him, and Pailey grabbed his throat. He lifted him from the ground and flung him towards the female shade. There was a tremendous crash followed by crying, and both people were on the ground. Another chilly wave blew past him, and a big fist came towards his face.

Pailey had better luck that night than the third attacker, who was physically almost similar to him. Pailey received the strike to the face, and the distance between them rendered the impact gentle. The attacker's left hand returned quickly with a sharp-edged knife, and Pailey was prepared this time. He grabbed the attacker's left hand and turned it towards him. The sharp-edged blade pierced his own skin, and the attacker cried out loud. Pailey delivered a powerful kick to the attacker's right knee, forcing him to fall face down. Pailey was outraged, shouting, 'You son of a pig, how dare you scare me with a knife!'

Pailey stretched his legs high, aimed at his back, and stomped him. The attacker rolled, and Pailey's kick struck his left hand. The sharp knife entered further into his body, piercing through his internal organs. The severe wound discharged dark red blood. The attacker was in terrible agony and quickly removed the knife himself. The quick reaction made matters worse, as thick blood sprayed all over the ground. The attacker attempted to rise from the ground in vain. His body shivered a few times before collapsing. Upon failing to roll sideways, the attacker's body rapidly became still.

Pailey briefly hesitated before promptly evading the subsequent wooden plank attack. He once again grasped the attacker's throat and pushed him towards the wall. Pailey looked around for more attackers and noticed a woman lying on the ground. The attacker gasped for air as Pailey tightened his grip on his throat. He then folded his palms together and begged, 'Pailey, please don't kill me.'

Pailey was taken aback when he heard his name. After taking a closer look, Pailey recognised him. Shashankan Nair, the born criminal he was looking for, was clutched by Pailey's powerful forearms. Sasi was now pleading for his life, his eyes popping.

Raged with anger, Pailey delivered another powerful blow to his lower abdomen with his right fist. The impact was too much for Sasi, who was already gasping for air. Pailey expected him to cry out, but his eyes began rolling. Pailey felt his struggles on his left arm and then released his grip on his throat. He looked around in search of others before releasing him. Shashankan Nair collapsed to the ground, unconscious and unable to move any of his limbs. Pailey returned to the front side to check on Chacko, who had regained consciousness but was sitting on the floor.

Pailey checked the first attacker, who was on the floor unconscious. He kicked him in the stomach, but the man on the ground did not react. Unsure about his next move, Pailey returned to Chacko, who also appeared worried. Pailey reassured Chacko and quietly asked him to follow to the back of the house.

Shashankan Nair was still unconscious, but he was breathing. Pailey dragged him into the house through the rear door. Chacko followed him into the room, which was completely dark. Chacko used his matchbox to light another kerosene lamp that was found in the room. Pailey firmly bound Sasi to the bed, and they subsequently noticed a woman hidden beneath the bed. Pailey dragged her out without mercy and was on the verge of beating her when Chacko intervened. 'Refrain from touching her, she is a woman.'

Pailey was once again furious, stating, 'You ignorant idiot, you don't know her. She is that whore Vidya Devi, who tried to kill me a few minutes ago.'

Vidya Devi did not respond; putting her head down, she continued to weep.

Chacko drank water from the mud pot found in the room and passed it to Pailey, who poured it into his mouth. Then Chacko asked, 'Who were they, and did they run off?'

Pailey took some time to respond. 'Both of them are dead or will die if they do not receive timely medical attention.'

Chacko was stunned and desperately clarified, 'You killed them?'

Hearing that, Vidya Devi jumped up and cried out loud, 'You killed my brother, you will suffer in hell!'

Pailey did not answer, just relaxed and sat on the bed. He kicked Sasi, who remained unconscious. Vidya Devi shouted again, 'You son of a bitch, you killed Sasi too, I will teach you a lesson.'

Then she took a step forward towards Pailey.

Chacko could not control his anger and smashed the mud pot in his hand onto Vidya Devi's head. Vidya Devi collapsed to the floor without a word as the pot lay fragmented across the room. Pailey looked at Chacko and commented, 'She does not deserve to die so quickly.'

Pailey brought more water from the kitchen and poured it over Shashankan Nair's head. He was abruptly awakened by a forceful strike from Pailey, who stared directly at him. He finally managed to open his eyes after a few more kicks and slaps. It required several additional minutes for him to regain his composure. Pailey struck him in the face and reminded him, 'You have a few minutes to tell us how you murdered my dear friend Benny Mathew.'

Looking around the room, Pailey reminded him, 'All of your colleagues have died.'

Noticing Vidya Devi lying on the floor, Sasi stated, 'It is all her plan, along with her husband.'

Pailey stared at Sasi before turning to Vidya Devi, who was unconscious on the floor. 'She is a natural criminal who has deceived the villagers for many years, and you are now putting all of your crimes on her.'

Sasi did not respond to his accusations, and Chacko looked at him incredulously. Pailey turned to Chacko and explained, 'Several years ago, she was the Kavumpatte Vada Yakshi, a nightmare for the villagers.'

Chacko glanced at the middle-aged woman on the floor and envisioned, 'Indeed, she is both deceptive and stunning.'

Reading his mind, Pailey continued, 'Those days she was young and mesmerised many with her ectomorphic physique.'

Vidya Devi asserted that she was the biological daughter of Panchami Kaniyatti, the village midwife. Until she reached school age, Panchami concealed her from the villagers and those she knew. The villagers determined that Vidya was not Panchami's legitimate daughter due to her striking physical appearance. Panchami and her spouse were listed as her natural parents at the time of school admission. The villagers believed that they had either legally adopted her or kept her after someone rejected her at birth.

Vidya was raised in the village, but she struggled to form relationships with children her age. She was isolated and restricted to their residence except during school hours. Several kids held her in high regard and yearned for her friendship. Panchami discontinued Vidya's education after she failed her upper primary classes. She was trained by Panchami to take on the position of village midwife upon her retirement. At least that much was known to the villagers at the time.

Pailey, like many other villagers, was afraid of the area where the Vada Yakshi was thought to be active. Those who dared to cross the area were either killed or treated by Panchami Kaniyatti, the village witch doctor. After his wife eloped, Pailey spent most of his time in the village toddy bar, assisting the barman in dealing with violent alcoholics. To maintain his commitment to his mother, he made it home after midnight. He was compelled to take the rough path one night when his usual route was waterlogged due to severe rains.

Ignoring the warning, he proceeded directly through the route that was so feared, as he was inebriated and oblivious. He used the live fire torch to find his way in the total darkness. He passed the palm tree that was infested and heard a sweet voice behind him, 'You handsome man, do you have slaked lime to prepare a soothing pan?'

Despite the temptation to turn back, Pailey kept going on his path and continued to walk forward. Following this, he heard another request, 'Oh, my sweetheart, would you be able to accompany me home? I am completely alone and disoriented.'

This time, it was exceedingly appealing; however, he maintained his firmness. Suddenly, a faint fog emerged from nowhere, obscuring the area and further reducing visibility. The area was soon inundated with a potent fragrance of jasmine blossoms. He was captivated by the request and was delighted to hear a melodious song:

I am young and gorgeous

seeking your warm body

get me through this cold and lonely night

Pailey's heart pounded, and he was unable to resist the alluring request. He stopped and was still reluctant to look back at the charming stranger. Upon turning around, he was taken aback by the sight of the stunning woman who had caressed his shoulder. He could feel her warm body as she stood near him. She was young, tall, and wore a white saree with its ends fluttering in the breeze. While gazing at her blue eyes, which were enclosed by thick black lashes, he was rendered numb. He extended his arms to feel the splendour, but on his head he felt a profound pain. His eyes blacked out, his vocal cords were choked, and he fell unconscious towards her. Lightning stars encircled him, and Pailey fell to the ground with a small thud as she took a few steps backwards.

Pailey opened his eyes and stared at the floor, tried to raise his head and looked around. He attempted to move and rise from the floor, as the pain was sweeping all over his body and he felt too heavy. He was lying face down with his hands tightly bound behind him. He blinked his eyes a few times and looked around, as it was dark. He vaguely observed the four walls made of earthen bricks that encircled him. He saw an earthen pot placed in a corner and assumed it might contain drinking water.

He was unable to figure out the duration of his stay in the room or the individual who had bound him. The sensation of itchy pain tickling his head served as a reminder of the moments preceding his unconsciousness. He remembered the lovely face he had seen the last time he lost consciousness. She was a familiar face, but she was also intimidating and cherishing. Within a few seconds, he identified her as Vidya Kaniyatti, a youthful and stunning woman.

Pailey noticed the sun's faint light moving over, and the room temperature increased as he felt thirst. He knew that he had to move around the room to defend himself before someone else arrived. He struggled to roll himself and sit on the floor and freed himself, with great difficulty, before reaching the water container. He drank the entire pot of water and then realised he was wearing only his undergarment.

Despite his efforts, the sole door he attempted to open was secured from the outside. The room's thatched roof was beyond his reach, and there was no window. He attempted to reach the roof by standing on the earthen pot, but it collapsed shortly after he stepped on it. During the peak of the day, he was roasting in the heat and waited patiently for someone to open the door.

Tired and lonely, Pailey was hungry as soon as he was free of the ropes. By evening, he sensed movements nearby and understood the house was becoming active. He could hardly hear their chatter and was certain that they would come for him at any time. Faking death, he lay down on the floor, grasping the same rope as if he were still tied to it. They soon opened the door, and he felt multiple people who were cautious. They awaited his response. Pailey lay still on the floor, waiting for them to come close.

Holding a long iron rod, the man entered the room and poked Pailey to check on him. The stranger prodded him several times from a distance, and Pailey waited for him to come closer. The attacker was cautious, and Pailey was unable to withstand the pain of the final hit before swinging into action.

Pailey grasped the iron rod and struck the man with all his strength. Before the woman could close the door, Pailey reached out and dragged her inside. Pailey was significantly more powerful than both and relentlessly beat them until they dropped unconscious. Then he bound them together and closed the door behind him.

Pailey was unable to recognise them because of the intense fight and the darkness. He was certain that the woman was not the same as the one he had encountered the day before. He conducted a thorough search of the house and its environs for the woman in question and any potential associates. Afterwards, he explored the house for food, but he only came across a few wooden logs and incense. He came to the realisation that the mystical mist had been produced by burning those materials. He remembered the encounter from the previous day and was curious about the ease with which fear is incited in the general populace. He pledged to conduct a thorough investigation and figure out the conspirators' intentions.

Pailey needed food; his home and the nearby toddy bar were far away. To endure the night, he climbed the nearest coconut tree and plucked a couple of coconuts. He returned to the room to question his attackers with a lighted oil lamp which he found in one of the rooms. He recognised the woman as Panchami Kaniyatti, the village midwife and witch hunter, as she was awake. He was unfamiliar with her associate, who was unconscious. Panchami promptly requested him, 'Pailey, I am willing to do anything for you, please don't kill us.'

Pailey smiled and sat on the floor right next to her. 'Who is this new culprit? Did you secretly marry him?'

Pailey looked around and asked, 'Where is Divya, your daughter? She was stunning in that frightening outfit.'

Panchami did not respond and tried to conceal her astonishment, stating, 'What are you talking about? She is a child and not here.'

Pailey looked at her eyes, and Panchami continued, 'She seldom leaves her home; she never comes here.'

Pailey couldn't contain his rage and stood up, grabbed the iron rod, and threatened, 'Do you want to know how hot this is?'

Panchami grew scared, and Pailey pounded the iron rod on the floor near her head. Panchami was frightened; her eyes widened, and her head shook a few times. Her entire body began shaking, and foam of saliva with bubbles emerged from her mouth. Pailey panicked but quickly regained control of himself. He identified the symptoms of epilepsy and knew that the only way to treat it was by touching an iron material. He untied her with a bit of struggle, forced her tightly squeezed fingers to open, and placed the iron rod. He clutched her tightly until her body stopped trembling and she fell unconscious again.

While this was going on, Panchami's male companion was awake and watching what Pailey did. He was tied up firmly and couldn't move his arms or legs. Then he asked Pailey to untie him, but Pailey didn't agree right away. Pailey asked him, 'Don't you feel bad about scaring and cheating the poor?'

He didn't say anything and cried silently, with tears streaming down both eyes, and Pailey was moved. A grown man crying could be real, and it showed how innocent he really was. He thought about letting him go, but he wanted to know more about his role.

Pailey sat on the floor next to him. 'Are you here to frighten and cheat the villagers? Who else are your gang members?'

The man did not answer and looked blank. Pailey continued to ask questions: 'Who are you? I haven't seen you before in this village.'

The man blinked his eyes and attempted to look across at Panchami, who was lying to the side. Pailey lost patience and said, 'I'm going to break your legs now, you were planning to kill me; at the very least, I need my revenge.' Pailey was about to stand up when the man stopped him.

Fearing his wrath, the man chose to answer. 'I am Rajan, and I am Panchami's distant relative,' then corrected himself, 'I am her maternal uncle's son, and I came over to learn our traditional rituals to please our family Goddess Kali Ma.'

Panchami sprang up and shouted angrily, 'You dumb ass, you can't understand the basic meaning of manthras and can't even securely hold a live lamp in front of Ma Kali.'

Pailey got frustrated and pushed Panchami to the other side. 'Keep quiet, I will break your head if you interfere again.' Panchami couldn't say anything and sat quietly against the wall.

Pailey nodded, and Rajan went on, 'I acknowledge that I strayed from my intended path and became inebriated for a period of time. However, I am now eager to re-establish the practices of my father.'

Afterwards, he turned to Panchami and said, 'This scumbag has exploited our sacred paths and is now defrauding the poor to make money.'

Pailey stared at Panchami, who was prepared to defend herself, and asked her to keep shut. Pointing at Panchami, Rajan continued, 'It was she who struck your head with a wooden plank; she intended to frighten you and then treat you for money.'

Pailey remained a listener, and Rajan continued, 'She never intended to cause you harm, but to intimidate you and subsequently exploit you for financial gain.'

Pailey understood their motives and clarified his doubts. 'Why did you lock me up?'

Rajan looked at Panchami for a response, and she remained quiet. Rajan explained, 'In that situation, common people would fall unconscious, and nobody would look at Vidya.' He waited for Pailey's reply before continuing, 'We thought you recognised Vidya, and she wants to protect her identity.'

Pailey was unable to respond, so Rajan pleaded, 'Please leave me, I will not repeat this drama, and all I want is to learn and practise our rituals to please the Goddess.'

Pailey looked at Panchami, who looked down, and he asked again, 'Where is Divya?'

Both gazed at each other, and Rajan quietly responded, 'She is scared now and has promised not to repeat the act.'

Pailey paused for a moment. 'If you promise not to do this again, I will spare you,' he said, and then added a condition: 'You must compensate for injuring me and wasting my time.'

Panchami easily consented, giving him some money and promising to pay more the following day. Pailey was unsure of them and locked them inside the room, warning, 'Your rusted rituals will retaliate and haunt you for the rest of your life.' Ignoring their pleas and sobs, Pailey assured them before leaving, 'I will be back early morning and will release you.'

Chapter 28

Chacko was extremely curious about the subsequent events. 'Did you release them upon your return?'

Pailey did not respond immediately but looked around the room and warned Vidya Devi, 'I should have handed you to the police when I heard that you had returned to frighten the people again.'

Chacko responded promptly, 'You released them without harm.'

Pailey clarified, 'I was unable to return that evening or at any later.'

Chacko's fascination regarding the events escalated. Pailey's voice was shattered. 'That night, I became an orphan. I immediately returned to my home, where my mother's lifeless body was waiting.' The previous night, she had peacefully passed away in her bed. Pailey clarified, 'She should have lived longer, if it weren't for this dirty bitch.'

A moment of silence pervaded the room. Chacko reluctantly asked once more, 'How did the duo escape from the locked room?'

Pailey was upset but responded, 'I was unable to return to this house for several days. I believe they managed to escape by tearing the ceiling, and if you look at the side room, it is still damaged.'

Chacko was taken aback and subsequently examined the surroundings, wondering if it was the same ghost house in which they had imprisoned him. Pailey declined to respond, rose from his seat and walked towards Shashankan Nair.

Chacko suddenly remembered Madhubabu and dashed out to check on him. Chacko stepped out of the veranda and noticed the man lying flat on the floor. He ignored him and walked rapidly to the place where Madhubabu had been tied to the tree. Chacko untied him and helped him walk to the house, before securely tying him to the bed's other leg. Pailey poured more water over Vidya Devi's head, and she gradually recovered consciousness. She looked around and attempted to stand up, but Pailey was furious. He raised an iron rod and warned, 'Chacko was nice to smash your head with that soft pot, but I will break your head with this rod.'

Chacko helped her sit on the floor, facing her husband and the associate.

Pailey stared right into Vidya Devi's eyes and warned her again, 'There isn't enough time for the morning lights to burst in, and if you don't confess the truth, I'll shatter your head before the sun rays fall over here.'

Pailey stared at everyone, but no one dared to speak, so he looked up to Vidya, who replied, 'It's all Madhu's plans, I have nothing to do with it.'

Madhu was enraged and yelled, 'Vidya, you are lying!' He then turned to Pailey and confirmed, 'It was all Sasi's plan, and Vidya supported him.' Madhu pleaded again, 'I never thought of killing Benny and repeatedly asked them to spare his life.'

This time, Chacko grew enraged and kicked Sasi. 'You scoundrel, can't you speak up?'

Sasi stared blankly at them and remained silent. Vidya interrupted, saying, 'Please do not kill him, all our savings are with him.'

Pailey quickly lifted the iron rod against her, and she broke. 'Please don't kill me,' she cried, pointing at Sasi. 'He promised us many times higher interest rates on our investments and is now refusing to return our savings.'

Chacko was unable to understand their discussions, and Pailey was uninterested. He reiterated his earlier warning, 'I am interested in finding who brought those killers to the village and how many were there.'

Madhu responded promptly, 'It is entirely Sasi's plan, my wife and I have no involvement with the hired killers.'

Pailey rose from the bed and confronted Madhu. 'You are a terrible man. Why did you not warn others when you were aware that the killers were entering our village?'

Madhu responded promptly, stating, 'Sasi threatened my life and refused to return our savings.'

Pailey raised the iron rod above his head, and Vidya wailed, 'Please do not make me a widow, I will tell you.'

Benny Mathew posed a threat not only to the trio but to the bulk of the bank's governing board. Vidya Devi admitted that the bank's whole affairs were managed by the secretary, Shashankan Nair, who siphoned its funds to his private bank.

Many of the board members benefited financially from Sasi's firm. Sasi channelled the money to his family business, causing the villagers' bank to almost collapse. Along with Vidya, a few other board members put their unlawful money into Sasi's bank, expecting higher interest rates and profits. They were forced to remain silent about Benny Mathew's revelations. Benny had evidence against all of those involved, and they chose to warn him rather than kill him. Shashankan Nair swiftly set up the murders, with the first instructions to simulate an accident to scare Benny.

Shashankan Nair invited four hired criminals from a distant place to their village, only to carry out the brutal assault. They arrived in the village a few days prior to the incident, disguising themselves as impermanent farm labourers. Benny was introduced to one of the assailants by Madhubabu, who pretended to be in search of temporary housing for their visit. This was done to ensure Benny could be readily identified in the event of an attack.

Most of the time, Benny travelled to the village on his motorbike alone, and they chose a remote location for the attack. The initial intention was to create an accident and render him incapacitated. The accident's impact could result in physical injuries that would restrict his capacity to resist and retaliate. The assailants would gain an advantage over their target through a deliberate accident or surprise attack.

The first assault attempt failed because the assailants' jeep was too sluggish to arrive at the destination on time. Benny rushed through the planned location before the jeep arrived. They were unable to follow the bike as it raced faster.

The second opportunity came after two days and happened during a severe storm. The attackers had been divided into two groups, with one team waiting at the spot in case the jeep missed the target. Due to the severe weather, there was once again a lag in coordination between arrival times. Benny's usual trip was also delayed, and the attackers waited for him. They soon spotted the approaching bike and strung a rope across the road, tying one end to the parked jeep.

When Benny's bike arrived, they pulled the rope up to unbalance him. Beyond the assailants' precise preparations, Benny had sharp observation skills and noticed an unfamiliar jeep from a distance. He applied timely brakes to avoid a horrific head-on collision, but he lost control and plunged to the road.

Without wasting time, the assailants attacked Benny from both sides. He dodged the initial knife strike and was brave enough to confront them rather than seek cover. His powerful grip on one attacker forced him to drop the knife, which slipped into the bushes. Benny was more powerful than the attackers had imagined. His sole disadvantage at that time was that he was alone and the area was deserted.

The attackers yelled at him like wild beasts, threatening repeatedly to kill him. He lifted one of them into the air and threw him onto another, leaving both unable to move as they collapsed to the ground. The other two started a fist fight with Benny, who was smart enough to avoid several blows. The two attackers fainted when Benny began to kick them in their lower abdomen. One of them used a wooden plank to smash Benny's head. Benny was quick to snatch it from them and hit them back repeatedly with the same plank. Benny was dominating the fight until the assailants changed their strategy and used metal weapons on him.

The attackers realised their efforts to hurt and warn him were not working easily. They were losing the struggle, and they changed their plans to either permanently cripple him or injure him badly. The leader told them to use the heavier weapons stored in their vehicle. One of them hastily grabbed a locally made hand grenade, lit it, and threw it towards Benny. To their surprise, Benny wasn't terrified; he ducked, and the bomb fell away from him. The grenade fell on the moist ground and the explosion was limited to a minor sound due to high humidity and low temperature. The intended explosive mechanism broke down, causing thick smoke. The attackers regrouped and quickly fetched more weapons from their vehicle.

The attackers felt they had underestimated Benny and lost confidence in their ability to simply overwhelm him. They instantly switched to defensive tactics rather than offensive ones. Benny might have taken advantage of the uncertain moment to flee the area, but his slight lead strengthened his confidence, which was unwarranted.

Thick smoke and heavy rains hindered visibility, so the assailants decided to launch their final assault with full force. Unarmed, Benny's attempts to attack them with his bare fists failed. Benny identified the gang boss and stepped forward, intending to punch him in the face. He could not successfully defend his back, and one of the attackers cut his body with a long sword. The attacker aimed for his neck, and as he moved forward, the pointed weapon pierced his skin. The sudden bodily piercing sent shockwaves through his body, unbalancing him and causing him to stand still.

The attackers took advantage of that brief moment and jumped on him. Benny used his arms to block the next onslaught and again pushed the man sideways. Another attacker penetrated his lower abdomen with a short knife, significantly limiting his capacity to counterattack. In no time, the assailants gained the advantage, and Benny began to bleed heavily, losing strength. Benny fought with all he had, never falling to the ground. He delivered a powerful kick to one attacker's private region, knocking him unconscious. The gang leader was furious and used an iron rod to strike Benny with all his might. Benny ducked as the iron rod approached. He was unable to entirely escape the strike, which landed heavily on his right shoulder, impairing his arm.

Benny landed another punch on the leader with his left hand, knocking him down. Then one of the attackers stabbed his chest with a large knife. Benny clutched the attacker's arm as he was shoved down to the ground. The gang leader delivered the final punch to Benny's head, knocking him unconscious.

The attackers stayed for a moment to confirm his death and were forced to depart when they saw farm workers running towards them. A few of the workers recognised Benny and attempted to assist by removing the long knife from his chest. As soon as it was removed, more blood flowed out, prompting him to request water. One of the workers brought water, but by that time Benny had taken his final breath.

Vidya soon finished explaining and looked at the others. Chacko lost control, lowered his head, and wept quietly. Pailey remained unmoved and glanced at Sasi. 'You son of a bitch, do you want to tell me what else you did?' Turning to Vidya, he shouted, 'You were not there and narrated what someone told you.'

Vidya was too scared, holding her hands together and crying. 'Madhu Babu was there, and he told me everything.'

Madhu looked at his wife in surprise, wondering how easily she had betrayed her own spouse. Pailey recognised they were concealing a lot of information. He lifted the iron rod and confronted Sasi, and Madhu pleaded, 'Pailey, please don't hurt him anymore; if he dies, we are all doomed.'

Pailey pressed the iron rod into his shoulder and warned, 'If you don't want to open your mouth, you'll die with your secrets.'

Vidya was shouting, 'Madhu, tell him the truth, otherwise we will go to jail for cheating the bank and customers.'

Chacko promptly approached Pailey and pleaded that he spare Sasi, but Pailey pushed him aside. 'You know nothing about these scoundrels. All of them are crooks; they continue to cheat the poor using their muscle power.'

Chacko didn't agree. 'Let's hand them over to the police.'

Pailey felt sorry for him. 'Have you visited a police station before? Forget Benny's killings, do you know how they handle petty complaints from the poor?'

Turning to Vidya, Pailey said in rage, 'They are a bunch of idiots, corrupt, they side with these bitches who cheat their own husband.'

Vidya rose from the floor and screamed in anger, 'Shut up, you beggar. I am not a cheat! What do you know about me? I am a poor girl who merely followed my husband's orders.'

She stared at Madhubabu, who appeared to be looking at the floor as he lowered his head. Vidya Devi turned to Sasi and began to approach him. She slapped his face with her left hand and yelled, 'You son of a butcher, speak up loud and tell them of the atrocities you have committed against that noble man.'

Pailey was momentarily stunned before regaining focus. 'I was aware that you had disclosed half of the narrative. Now, Sasi, you must speak, or I will break your head.'

Madhubabu promptly intervened, stating, 'Pailey, it was Sasi, not the hired killers, who delivered the fatal blow to Benny's head.'

Pailey stared at Sasi, who refrained from responding to the accusations. 'I knew Benny wasn't the kind of man to give up easily.'

Holding the iron rod, Pailey turned to Sasi. 'Do you want to talk about the whole incident and how you killed my friend, or shall I smash your head?'

Pailey kicked Sasi in the face when he tried to get up from the floor, warning, 'Don't think about escaping from here without confessing your crime.'

Sasi stared at Madhubabu, then at Vidya Devi, and finally at Pailey and warned, 'Listen, leave us now and we will give you anything you want.'

Pailey came near and sat on the floor facing him. 'What can you give? A lot of money, some useless land, tell me.'

Sasi's face brightened with hope. 'I can give you enough money to live a lavish life.' Looking and smiling at the others, he added, 'There is enough money for everyone, and there is nothing in this world that money cannot buy.'

Pailey looked at the others, whose faces lit up with hope, and pretended to agree to Sasi's proposition. Then he checked Chacko's reaction, which appeared uncertain. Pailey stared directly into Sasi's eyes, and his face grew red. He screamed and struck Sasi on the face with all his strength. 'Can you bring my dear friend back? Can you return a loving father and caring husband?'

Sasi collapsed unconscious on his left side as blood poured from his nostrils. He hung on the coir that was tightly tied to the bed's legs.

Chacko hurried forward to restrain Pailey. 'Don't kill him now, let him speak.'

Vidya Devi appeared next, attempting to push Pailey away. 'You soulless idiot, did you kill him?'

Pailey resisted her push and yelled, 'You bitch, go to hell.' He lifted her up and threw her back towards her husband.

Vidya Devi couldn't make a sound as she hit the floor hard and passed out. Her spouse, Madhubabu, looked shocked and remained silent.

Pailey was agitated and turned to Chacko. 'These spineless thieves believe money is the ultimate power. They think they can buy anyone with the money they stole from others.'

Chacko was speechless as he checked Sasi, who was bleeding and unconscious while still tied to the bed legs. He turned to Pailey and pleaded, 'We need to untie him, or he will bleed to death.'

Pailey was outraged, but Chacko said, 'Sasi knows the whole truth, and he must live to end up in jail.'

Without waiting for permission, Chacko poured water, which he had brought from the other room, over Sasi's head. Then he unfastened him from the bed legs and laid him on the floor. Pouring more water, Chacko said, 'The bleeding must stop or he will die soon.'

Looking at Madhubabu, who was sitting on the floor, Pailey replied, 'I don't care, I'm going to kill them all anyway.'

Chacko pleaded, 'Let us hand them over to the police.'

Frustrated by the notion, Pailey went to Chacko and said, 'You idiot, they are the most corrupt people on earth. They will take bribes from the accused and hang you to death.'

Chacko didn't grasp the warning and turned to Sasi, whose fingers and body parts were showing signs of recovery.

Suddenly, Madhubabu leapt into action. He wielded the iron rod with all his might and struck Pailey on the head. Pailey was unable to defend himself, absorbing the full force of the strike, and collapsed to the ground with a resounding crash.

Madhubabu swiftly turned towards Chacko, who ducked to the floor and narrowly evaded the next strike. Madhubabu lost his balance and fell over Pailey before delivering the second blow to Chacko. The water and blood mixture on the floor was too slippery for Madhubabu to notice.

Pailey, semiconscious, held onto Madhubabu until Chacko recovered and retrieved the iron rod from him.

Chacko then shattered Madhubabu's left leg with the iron rod. Enraged, Chacko shouted, 'You are a disgusting person, you don't deserve to live.'

Madhubabu cried aloud in agony, and Chacko persisted until the room fell silent. There was no response from anyone, which caused Chacko to regain his composure.

He was taken aback by the brutality with which he had defeated his opponent. Madhubabu was motionless on the floor, and blood was dripping from his legs. Pailey was also unconscious, with his left hand still gripping Madhubabu's throat.

Chacko recognised that now was not the time to think but to act. He gently removed unconscious Madhubabu from Pailey's powerful grip and pulled him into the corner. Then he spilled some water over Pailey's face and gently whispered, 'Get up, man. You need to finish off these brutalists.'

Chacko heard faint mumbling, Sasi's thirst for water. Chacko carefully dripped water into his mouth, which he swallowed slowly.

Soon the jug was empty, and Chacko checked his breath, relieved to find him alive.

Then he noticed Vidya Devi trying to get up. Chacko immediately bound her hands and legs together. Vidya Devi continued to mumble, cursing everyone, but Chacko ignored her and left her on the floor.

Chacko looked around and noticed four individuals wounded and unconscious. His thoughts turned to the attackers they had left outside. He hurried out and found them lying still where they had last been seen. He checked each for signs of life and found they were both dead.

Then he noticed a faint light rising over the eastern horizon, and he knew a brownish haze would soon spread over the west, just before the sun's rays covered the sky.

He returned to the room and saw Vidya Devi dragging herself towards Sasi. Both Pailey and Madhubabu lay unconscious.

Chacko ignored Vidya, who posed no immediate threat, and went in search of water. Earlier, he had noticed the usual well near the house, but there was no coir rope tied to a bucket. Luckily, he found an empty bucket with some water remaining and went back towards the room.

When he entered, he saw Vidya Devi sitting near Sasi, trying to wake him. Chacko poured water onto Pailey's face, and he slowly regained consciousness.

Pailey sat up and drank the rest of the water. Looking at Madhubabu, he asked Chacko, 'Did you already kill that swine?'

Feeling the agony in his head, Pailey muttered, 'That stupid man was fast.'

Raging with fury, he stood up and walked towards Madhubabu. Pailey kicked him in the face, yelling, 'You son of a bitch, are you already dead?'

Then they heard Vidya Devi scream, 'Oh my God, all my savings are gone, he is not responding!' Pailey was unaffected by her crying. He picked Madhubabu up from the floor and raised him in the air. Fiercily looking at him Vidya Screamed agin 'Do you want to kill me too?'

The eyelids remained wide open, and Madhubabu's head fell onto his shoulder. Pailey used both arms to support Madhubabu's unmoving body. He jerked him in rage. 'You don't want to respond?' Then he threw the motionless body to the floor, which dropped like a bag of linen. Frustrated, Pailey walked out of the room, stating, 'This idiot is not responding.'

Chacko checked Madhubabu's vital signs and saw clotted blood around both fractured legs, realising his death had come sooner than expected.

Pailey returned with a lengthy coir rope and pushed Vidya Devi into a corner. He then struck Sasi in the face, saying, 'You scoundrel, wake up.' Sasi was unable to see clearly due to his impaired vision, as he only partially opened his eyes.

Pailey yelled again, 'Do you wish to reveal the identity of Benny Mathew's killer?' while clutching his throat. Sasi repeatedly requested water, and Pailey grew furious. 'Would you like to tell me now?'

Pailey was tired of repeating the same question. He snatched the iron rod and threatened, 'I will kill you with this, so speak now.'

Sasi attempted to make an evil smile, which enraged Pailey further. Sasi raised his hand and began to speak just as the iron rod flashed towards him.

The hired killers were getting tired of Benny's fighting prowess. Hearing the loud cries from the scuffle, a few farm workers came running and the attackers fled. At that very moment, Sasi and Madhubabu emerged from their hiding place to assist the hired killers. Sasi approached Benny from behind, and Madhubabu punctured his chest with a large knife.

Pailey lost control of his anger and struck Sasi's head with the iron rod. The force was too strong for Sasi, and his skull cracked open, spilling blood and bits of his brain across the floor. Sasi attempted to speak, but his mouth remained open as his lifeless body collapsed.

Pailey was blinded by rage. He checked Madhubabu and realised that he had reached his end much earlier. Pailey then wrapped the coir rope around Vidya Devi's throat and attempted to choke her to death.

Chacko couldn't take it and pulled Pailey away from her. 'Leave her now, she's had enough.'

Pailey was considerably stronger and pushed Chacko aside. 'You don't know her. She is a born criminal and was part of the gang that murdered my dear friend.'

Pailey choked her with his bare hands. Chacko attempted to drag him away, but Pailey was adamant and difficult to move. Pailey lifted her and held her in the air until she could no longer take in fresh air.

Chapter 29

It had been three days since his cherished sister was lying unconscious in the hospital, far from home. Sunny discreetly walked the well-known village street to deliver the usual bottle of goat milk to the coffee shop at the village centre. He passed his neighbour's mansion and proceeded along the desolate, unpaved road. Lovely, the daughter of his neighbour, was watching him from her room, and he was unable to see her. He continued to walk, keeping a quiet posture.

As he turned to the main road, he spotted Mr Thommy's oxen cart. He was unable to recall hearing the deafening chimes of the cart's multiple bells while it was in motion. The carriage had been positioned there for a long period of time, and it was possible that it was awaiting someone. He passed by and then noticed the rider's seat was unoccupied. Unable to disregard his intuition, he turned towards the cart. He was towered over by both white bullocks. They were standing quietly for an extended period, their nostrils devoid of white bubbles.

In a state of uncertainty, Sunny stared towards the side of the road where he had been headed. He was reminded of his father Chacko's advice: 'Pillechan requested the milk to be delivered on time; there is no other source in our village.'

Mary, his mother, was attending to his unconscious sister at the hospital. She would not return until Celine had fully recovered from her current condition. Mary claimed her daughter was conscious yet incapable of responding to her calls or moving any of her body parts. A pipe was used to serve liquid sustenance, meeting the minimum nutritional needs. Sunny awoke early in the morning to rouse his father to milk the goats, yet no one woke him. Chacko was not an adept milker, and the goats remained still, allowing him to milk them effortlessly. Sunil slept soundly beside him, without wetting his bed.

Getting close to the cart, he saw a bicycle placed near its giant wheels. He approached the cycle and recognised it belonged to Kunjumon, the deviant. A stack of newspapers was left on the cycle carrier, and a few newspapers were rolled and placed in front. The morning light had not yet reached the ground, and Sunny was unable to see anything distinctly as he looked around.

He was on the verge of summoning Kunjumon when he noticed a faint movement a short distance ahead. Far from the road, Sunny noticed two figures in the bushes, one of whom stood up above the other. They were not merely standing; they were physically engaging. Sunny was unable to discern who was detaining the other, but both were engaged in a physical fight. He then observed the shorter figure attempting to get away from the taller one.

Sunny was not afraid and shouted at them, 'What's going on there?'

The tall figure appeared surprised, and shifting his attention likely released the strong hold. The short person waited for a distraction before escaping the powerful clutches and dashing towards the cart. Sunny knew the tiny person as Mr Thommy, while the tall figure reluctantly stayed behind. Mr Thommy yelled, 'Escape, he'll kill you!'

Sunny was frozen and unable to move, so Mr Thommy hoisted him into the air and placed him on his cart. Mr Thommy was weak and fell to the ground when he attempted to jump to the riders' seat. Before he could stand up, the tall figure reached towards him. The man pleaded, 'Kunjumon, please don't hurt me, I haven't seen you. I am telling the truth, I only saw Thomas Mash's son, and I won't tell anything to anyone.'

Looking at Sunny, sitting near Mr Thommy on the cart, the tall figure stood still for a moment. Sunny was horrified; he couldn't raise an alarm and stared around aimlessly.

Sunny realised at that instant that Kunjumon was no longer merely a pervert; he was ferocious. He approached Sunny: 'Remember, you are a kid; you are not a match for me, and do remember, don't speak too much.'

Then Kunjumon stared at Mr Thommy and struck the old man with his right palm, warning again, 'Remember what I said. Do not open your filthy mouth.'

Sunny thought of fleeing from there, but he was too frightened to rise from his seat. Mr Thommy was trembling with fear, and Kunjumon was unsure of his stance as they once again confronted each other. Dark clouds moved above them to create an opening, and an abrupt burst of light emanated from the skies. Kunjumon looked upward and then checked the surroundings. He once more approached Mr Thommy, threatening to slash his throat with a gesture. Kunjumon then walked towards his bicycle, looked around, and started to ride in the opposite direction.

After wiping the blood droplets from his face, Mr Thommy turned to Sunny and reassured him, 'Do not be frightened; you have not witnessed anything.'

He commanded the animals to begin hauling the cart by grabbing both leads that controlled them. The bells, which were installed at different places, began to chime one by one, and gradually the standard cadence was restored. The cart resumed its normal forward course shortly thereafter. Mr Thommy advised him again, 'I will be dropping you off near Pillechan's shop. Please refrain from disclosing what you have seen.'

He recalled a few moments later, 'Kunjumon was foolish. I happened to see them both and cannot forget them.'

Then they heard the first church bells, which served as a reminder to the devotees to pray. Mr Thommy looked up and prayed, 'Dear Lord, forgive and protect me, a poor coward and sinner.' Following the prayer, he marked a cross symbol on his forehead.

Sunny was uncertain as to whether he would participate in the church's liturgy that morning. However, upon the cart's passage through the church gates, he reconsidered his decision: 'I will be attending the mass.'

Upon hearing that, the elderly man requested, 'I urge you to pray for me.'

Sunny did not respond and maintained his silence until they reached the intersection. Mr Thommy halted the carriage and assisted him in descending. Mr Thommy reminded him, 'Don't tell anyone about the incident, that Kunjumon is cruel, and remember what he did to your sister.'

Sunny did not fully hear the warning and proceeded to walk towards Pillechan's coffee shop. He stood a few steps further and turned towards the cart, which had resumed its journey. The chimes soon faded, and Mr Thommy's warning reverberated in his mind: *What did he do to my sister?*

Pillechan offered Sunny the customary refreshment as he handed over the milk bottle, stating, 'Mone Sunnykutta, thank you for the milk. No one else can deliver the milk early in the morning.'

Returning the empty bottle, he reminded him, 'We all pray for your sister's speedy recovery; she was a lovely girl.'

Sunny's mind was preoccupied with Mr Thommy's warning, and he did not wait to hear the prayer assurance.

Bobby led the procession to the altar, and Sunny maintained silence throughout the ceremony. Fr Luke Theneth blessed him upon his return to the presbytery, clasping his hands and whispering a few prayers. Sunny quickly led Bobby out of the room, discreetly asking his friend, 'Would you like to meet me at the riverside?'

Bobby responded promptly, 'I am uncertain; not sure whether my mother will permit me to leave.'

Sunny hurriedly approached the exit gate, reminding Bobby, 'Evening, please make it possible. I will need to share something important.'

Sunny was taken aback when his neighbour's daughter, Lovely, awaited him at the church gate as the two friends parted ways.

Sunny looked around and attempted to discreetly pass her, but Lovely joined him, saying, 'Sunny, don't run, let me come with you.'

Sunny tried to make an excuse, 'I must hurry in order to care for Sunil.'

Lovely was resolute in her determination to continue, as she assured, 'I will try to walk at a quick pace.'

She also attempted to put a smile on her face. Sunny noticed a small number of the elderly devotees, who pointed at him and made comments. He watched Lovely, who was trying to maintain his pace. Lovely requested, 'Please, slow down, I am unable to run and talk with you.'

They soon arrived at the side road. Sunny slowed down, as he was aware that Lovely was consistently considerate of him and his family. As she descended the hill, Lovely asked, 'Are you visiting Celine today?'

Sunny was unsure and replied, 'My pappa might visit the hospital.'

Then he posed the peculiar inquiry, 'Are *you* going?'

Lovely responded promptly, 'I dropped her at the hospital, and I am unsure.'

She immediately corrected herself, stating, 'Actually, it was my father who dropped her.'

Kunjumon suddenly appeared in front of them as they turned towards a narrow pedestrian path. He obstructed their way, prompting Lovely to retort, 'What are you doing? Get lost.'

Kunjumon was taken aback by the sight of Lovely and promptly retreated a few steps to clear their path. Lovely walked ahead in front, and Sunny quietly followed. Upon crossing, Kunjumon seized his wrists. 'I would like to talk with him. Lovely, go home.'

Lovely was incensed, and in a matter of seconds, she struck him in the face with her right arm and yelled, 'You son of a swine, how dare you touch him!'

The powerful slap was unexpected, and Kunjumon was unable to deflect it. He plummeted to the ground along with his cycle. Lovely proceeded forward with a firm caution, 'Do not ever touch him again.'

Lovely retreated a few steps, clung to Sunny's hand and advised, 'He is a pig, distributing dirty books and spoiling many young people.'

Sunny understood the meaning of 'dirty books', and she then proceeded to reveal some unexpected details: 'He has been spoiling my brother ever since he returned from the army.'

Sunny did not respond, so she continued, 'Soman is a kind young man; he found Celine unconscious on the riverbanks.'

Sunny got lost in thought and stopped walking, to clarify his doubts: 'Your father found Celine unconscious in a remote, bushy area.'

Lovely was unable to respond promptly, and Sunny added, 'That is what your father told my mother on that day.'

Lovely struggled and corrected herself, 'Soman found her and informed my father, and we moved her to the hospital.'

Sunny once more requested clarification, 'Did *you* accompany my sister to the hospital? Your father claimed that he went alone.'

She came to the realisation that Sunny was significantly more intelligent than she had previously believed. She attempted to persuade him, 'My father is opposed to involving us in the matter; the police may raise further questions about our involvement.'

Sunny got angry this time, asking, 'Why should the police be called when she fell and has been unconscious since then?'

This time, Lovely maintained her silence and pursued him. Lovely once more cautioned him in front of the gate of her mansion: 'Be cautious of Kunjumon. My father once chased him from the rubber motor shed.'

When Sunny did not respond, she added, 'Do not disclose the information we discussed to anyone else.'

Sunny did not acknowledge her or respond to her advice. He walked towards his home, and after a few steps, he turned back to check on Lovely. She stood at the gate of their mansion, watching him disappear from her sight.

Sunny was hesitant and nearly stumbled while descending the stairs. His father cautioned him, 'Be cautious. What are you dreaming about?'

He promptly regained his balance but was unable to respond. His father advised, 'Take care of Sunil. I must tap those rubber trees; Thomas Mash is already losing his patience.'

Chacko swiftly walked up the steps in front, carrying his work equipment, and disappeared to the other side.

Sunil came closer and Sunny lifted him from the ground to kiss him and reassured him, 'Don't worry, mum and Celine will be back soon.'

Sunil retained a grim expression and stared towards the goat stable. Their dog appeared fatigued and was chained. Sunny provided the dog with rice and fish curry. The dog appeared to have lost its appetite and was sorrowful, but it still stared at them. Sunny was experiencing an unusual sensation, so he released the dog from its chain to consume its food. However, it approached them reluctantly and proceeded to circumnavigate them. Then it proceeded to the stepping stones and awaited Sunny's response.

Sunny was uncertain as to what it desired from him. The dog wasn't barking or wailing, but continued to stand there. Unsure of its behaviour, Sunny walked towards the dog while holding Sunil in his arms. The dog looked at them and ascended the stepping stones as they approached.

Sunny pursued the dog until it reached the rubber motor shed. Sunny looked around; his father had just begun tapping the rubber trees. He would require an additional two to three hours to arrive at this location to process the rubber saps. The dog stood in front of the closed shed door, intermittently gazing at him and at the door. Sunny asked that Sunil remain outside, and he proceeded to unlock the shed door. The rubber motor was housed in a single-door chamber with a single ventilation opening situated directly across from the entrance. The dog stared at the wooden logs that were precisely arranged beneath the ventilator, and the room was impeccably clean. Sunny was unable to understand the dog's desire.

The dog started to sniff at the wooden logs a few times before beginning to bark. It leapt and bit a piece of cloth that was concealed beneath the logs. Sunny promptly removed the top logs, revealing his sister's preferred skirt, which was adorned with rose blossoms on a yellow background. He meticulously searched the room for additional items, but he was unable to locate any. Looking directly at the mansion in the distance, he closed the door behind him. At that moment, the mansion looked like a ghost house to him. Sunny walked back home holding his little sibling in one hand and his sister's skirt in the other. Having done its job, the dog followed them quietly.

The dog began to consume the food after Sunny caressed it on the forehead and chained it. Sunny remembered hearing the indistinct barking the night his sister disappeared as he sat back on the veranda. The rubber-making shed is located at a considerable distance from their home and is situated on elevated ground. It is unlikely that the sounds produced there would be audible from their home unless they ascended the stepping stones in front.

Sunny noticed the bloodstains on the skirt while placing it in their tiny room. He sniffed the skirt, only to discover that it was stinking of urine. He did not feel any vomiting sensation from the unpleasant odour, as it belonged to his only sister, whom he loved.

Sitting back on the veranda, he tried to recall the events of that day but couldn't pinpoint where he had lost contact with Celine. Then he heard his name being yelled from the high grounds in front. It was Lovely: 'Sunny, are you there?'

He walked into their courtyard and replied, 'Yes, I am here.'

Lovely was curious: 'Are you okay? Your papa; is he at work?'

Sunny didn't respond, then came the unexpected question: 'Did your dog go out near the rubber shed?'

Sunny did not bother to respond. Lovely reasoned, 'I heard some strange barking there.'

When Sunny remained silent, Lovely decided to retreat, again promising to support him if required.

Sunny experienced considerable discomfort; their accounts were inconsistent. Mr Thommy reportedly saw two individuals at the pump house, and Lovely alleged that she accompanied her father to the hospital. However, her assertion that her brother Soman located Celine at the riverside and her father Thomas Mash's versions were inconsistent.

Sunny was preoccupied with his own thoughts while perched on the veranda, and he missed seeing his friend Bobby descend the stepping stones. Bobby extended the bag towards him, stating, 'I must return immediately, my mother prepared some steamed rice and boiled bananas for breakfast.'

Bobby immediately began ascending the stepping stones without waiting for a response. Upon recovering from the unexpected visit, Sunny asked, 'Would you be ready to visit the riverside this evening?'

Bobby was about to respond when he halted in the middle of the steps, stating, 'I encountered that pervert Kunjumon, who advised me to keep away from you.'

Sunny's anger intensified and he was deeply troubled. 'I will deal with him first.'

Bobby was uncertain about the meaning of his statement and assured him that he would meet him at the riverside.

Chacko returned from work shortly before lunchtime and requested that he prepare to visit his sister at the hospital. Sunny was uncertain, and he subsequently contemplated his plans to meet his friend. 'Are we planning to return before the evening?'

Chacko was preparing himself rapidly, stating that they might not return until late evening. Sunny promptly devised a plan to remain at home: 'Mum requested that I feed the goats; I shall promptly gather grass for them.'

Chacko looked at him and said, 'Okay, I will take Sunil with me, and you can take care of the animals.'

Sunny was aware that it encompassed all their domestic animals. He watched Chacko swiftly ascend the stepping stones towards the hospital, carrying a beaming Sunil on his shoulders.

Sunny fulfilled his obligation by providing the animals with grass that he had collected from nearby shrubs. He noticed Lovely walking past the higher grounds in front of his home while he waited for the evening. He was aware that there were sufficient reasons for her to watch and pursue him in an unusual manner.

The rubber-making motor shed was located at the far end of their family estate, a considerable distance from their mansion. The presence of their companion dog, which assisted him in locating Celine's skirt, and Lovely's consistent surveillance of the area had raised several questions. Many of them could be answered by Pervert Kunjumon, who could fill in the gaps. Kunjumon was significantly bigger than him, despite his lean and slim physique. The pursuit of answers was a challenging endeavour, and Sunny was in a state of desperation to uncover the truth.

Sunny avoided the path in front of his neighbour's residence and instead walked the uneven hilly terrain that led to the riverside. He ensured that no member of the neighbouring family noticed or pursued him. He nearly tumbled into a pit when he slipped while crossing the perilous area. He experienced the sharpness of the large rock as he clung to its edge. He promptly gathered a few small, flat rock pieces with sharp edges and securely placed them in his trouser pocket. He maintained his alertness and monitored any suspicious activity until he reached the riverbank. He looked at the area where he and his sister had most recently visited and proceeded towards the sandy plains.

During that time, many fellow villagers went to the river to wash and bathe. Sunny waited eagerly under the enormous banyan tree for his friend Bobby to come. Looking at the massive tree, he was shocked it was still standing. Half of its roots on the riverbank side were visible, and another few inches of soil erosion could cause the tree to fall into the river. Sunny's eyes felt weary as he looked around for familiar faces and took in the soothing effects of the river. Before he dozed off, his friend shouted from close by. Sunny waved at his pal to come closer, and Bobby came and sat next to him.

Bobby stated without introduction, 'Soman and that pervert Kunjumon are close friends; they spent the evening together at the water pump house.'

Sunny stared at Bobby and asked, 'Who said that?'

Bobby responded quickly, 'I heard my mother talking with our neighbour.'

Sunny then described what he had witnessed in the morning, and Bobby corroborated, 'Mr Thommy is our neighbour, and his wife and mother discussed the matter.'

Bobby became concerned when Sunny told him about Kunjumon's assault and the warning given to Mr Thommy. He then recounted what he found in the neighbour's rubber shed and emphasised the importance of getting answers from Kunjumon. Bobby was shocked. 'Did you tell your papa? He can deal with that stupid man.'

Then they noticed someone falling from the trees on the opposite side of the riverbank. Sunny's cheeks flushed, and he turned to face his buddy and boldly declared, 'I am going to deal with him now, watch my back.'

His pal advised, 'He's huge and stronger; consult your pappa.'

Sunny headed towards the gently flowing river. Bobby stood still for a moment before following him. Sunny secured his trousers by carefully tying the white scarf around his waist before taking the first dive.

Sunny spotted Kunjumon as he swam across the river towards them. Bobby followed his pal's instructions and stayed at the riverbank, while Sunny swam towards the other side. Sunny and Kunjumon stood in the middle of the river, facing each other. Kunjumon extended his hands, aiming for Sunny's hair, but Sunny escaped by diving into the riverbed. Sunny touched and felt the sticky clay riverbed, which was familiar. Kunjumon became confused, attempted to float on the water, and realised he was tired.

He began swimming towards Bobby, but Sunny had already reappeared at the other end. Sunny called from there, 'You stupid, I am over here.'

Kunjumon was irritated, and as he looked at Bobby, he yelled, 'Ask your friend to behave, or I will teach him a lesson.'

Bobby reciprocated by saying, 'Try your best to touch him, in the river he is the best.'

Challenging him angered Kunjumon, so he warned Bobby again, 'You don't know me. His sister resisted me, and I strangled her.'

Looking back at the opposite side, he said, 'I'm going to teach him a lesson.'

Bobby was stunned, ignoring that Kunjumon had resumed swimming towards the other side. Sunny faced him again in the middle, where the riverbed was deepest. Kunjumon reached for him, but Sunny did another deep dive. Kunjumon attempted to follow, but Sunny was not around. He attempted to return, expecting Sunny to swim to Bobby's side.

As Kunjumon approached the shore, he heard Sunny shout out from the other side, 'You dumb ass, I am waiting for you here.'

Kunjumon was enraged by a boy's abuse. Anger sprang within him, and he felt pain in the calf muscles of both legs. He found it difficult to stand on the riverbed, with the water level just above his nose. The pain was spreading to his upper body because of a deep cut in both legs. He felt blood streaming from his wounds, but his need for vengeance overcame his distress.

When Kunjumon saw Sunny swimming towards him, he challenged him: 'You son of a swine, I will drown you to death in the middle of the river.'

Ignoring the spreading pain and weakness in his body, Kunjumon swam towards him again. When he reached the middle of the river, he noticed that his ability to float was failing. He began gulping water and lost his balance while attempting to float over the water's surface. Kunjumon attempted to catch Sunny again, but this time Sunny somersaulted and kicked him in the face.

Kunjumon, weary from blood loss and swimming across the river, was unable to withstand the kick. He desperately stretched both arms above the water, looking for aid. Sunny conserved energy by floating on the water, waiting for the perfect chance to attack again. In a desperate attempt to survive the deep waters, Kunjumon reached out and grabbed Sunny's arm. Sunny attempted to wiggle away, but Kunjumon's grip was much stronger. Sunny strained to stay above water as Kunjumon pulled him down. Another pair of arms appeared from the opposite side and drew Kunjumon away. Bobby yelled, 'Sunny, he strangled your sister!'

Sunny dived again and retrieved Kunjumon from the riverbed. Soon, he took some air and attempted to fight back. Sunny became outraged: 'Why did you attack my sister?'

Kunjumon struggled to breathe since his airways were full of water. His weak muscles were unable to generate enough strength, causing him to spit out the water he had ingested. He made his final confession: 'Soman faked her… forced onto her… and threatened my life.'

Soon after the friends released their grip, Kunjumon lost the ability to float and disappeared beneath the deep water's surface.

Chapter 30

Before the two companions could swim back to the shore, it was already getting dark. They both proceeded to their homes without wasting any time. Sunny swiftly took the usual route to his house prior to his parents' arrival from the hospital. Kaiser, his beloved dog, met him midway. The loyal dog had been able to break free from the confined chain and follow him once more. Sunny caressed the dog on the head and accompanied it on the walk to his home.

He walked with his head held high and his shoulders spread out as he crossed the neighbour's large house. There were lights in certain areas of the mansion, whereas none were seen outside. Sunny had been in a state of embarrassment for most of the day, and he had since banished a wicked figure, experiencing a sense of pride. He was aware that in the future only a small number of people would come to the realisation that vengeance is a force to be feared. He demonstrated that a small number of individuals can easily inflict suffering, and they would soon realise that the cost of healing is significantly higher.

Sunny meticulously descended the stepping stones to his home in the darkness. The dog followed him quietly and returned to its usual place near the goat shed. Sunny lit the kerosene lamp, and he was filled with sorrow as he was alone. While waiting for his pappa and younger brother to return, he felt relief for dealing with Kunjumon.

His mother Mary had immediately hurried to the hospital upon hearing that his sister Celine was ill and admitted. His pappa had informed him that she was incapacitated and not responding to medication. Kunjumon had assaulted and threatened Mr Thommy, who also advised him not to retaliate and to suffer in silence. Kunjumon admitted having strangled her before he vanished beneath the water, and Soman had enticed her to the rubber motor shed and forced himself on her. Kaiser guided him to recover Celine's skirt from the same shed, establishing her presence there.

He stared into the darkness, wondering how long it would take for his sister to get better. He rose to feed the goats after hearing their bleating and noticed movements beyond the extended stone wall in front. Sunny returned to the veranda and was taken aback by the sight of Lovely standing there with a parcel.

Carefully descending the steps, she reasoned, 'Chacko requested my dad to get you dinner.'

As she looked around, Lovely offered to help: 'Are you not afraid? Your papa could be late, and you can spend the night with us.'

Sunny responded promptly, 'I am no longer frightened, and you do not need to be concerned.'

He was reluctant to receive the packet, and Lovely subsequently left it on the veranda. 'Your papa requested it; I am leaving.'

Ascending the stepping stones, she reminded him, 'Be cautious, and do not open the door for strangers.'

Sunny became worried and quickly released the dog from its chain. 'Be careful and watch out.'

Kaiser strolled beside him, wagging its tail, and sat on the veranda, head down. Entering the room inside, Sunny securely closed the front door. He was hungry but didn't want to eat the food Lovely had brought. He worried why his pappa was too late to return. His mother generally did not allow him to remain alone at home, but this was an unusual situation for them.

Celine was fair and chubby, and several boys her age valued her company. He refrained from making friendships with a few people because he believed their intentions were not genuine. When he thought of her secret source of lemon sweet, he was compelled to seek the connection between the two events. He was reminded of his teaching at school, the aroma of citrus has long been tempting for developing pleasant relationships that lead to intimacy.

Exhausted from swimming and tormented by numerous thoughts, Sunny fell asleep as soon as he got into bed. He was awakened by Kaiser's loud and persistent barking. He was confident the dog was either alerting him or chasing something away. He was afraid, so he rolled the bed sheet over his head to feel safe. When afraid, he remembered to repeat the Apostle's Creed multiple times.

The dog continued to bark, and the terror made him courageous. He decided to check, and as soon as he opened the door, a little bundle was tossed at him from the opposite side of the wall. Kaiser returned dashing, sniffed and licked the package. He couldn't see anything in the darkness, but the dog approached the wall again and quietly returned. Whatever it was, it had decided to disappear, calming the dog. Sunny checked the package and promptly threw it to the ground. The packet shattered, scattering many lemon sweets across their courtyard.

Sunny was extremely terrified and promptly returned to his room and firmly closed the door. He was aware that the dog was intelligent and would provide effective protection for the house. He was taken aback by the dog's failure to pursue the stranger away. Kaiser was cognisant of their restricted territory and exceedingly protective of it. Sunny then had an unusual realisation: Kaiser was not appreciating the visit at that time, and the stranger was familiar. He listened to further barking while covering his head with the bed sheet and forcibly closing his eyes. His apprehensions were unfounded, and he eventually drifted off to sleep.

Sunny awoke considerably later than normal, and his parents were not there to wake him. He instantly searched the courtyard for Kaiser, who was asleep on the veranda. Then he collected the scattered lemon sweets and placed them back in their cover. He decided to find the stranger, and he knew that any search must begin in the surrounding areas.

After feeding the animals, he went to their neighbour's home, pretending to return the empty food container. Lovely was watering the plants and greeted him kindly. Achamma approached him and offered him breakfast, which he declined, explaining that he was full and grateful for the supper. When he enquired about his sister's condition at the hospital, Lovely replied, 'My father just left the house to visit her.'

Lovely led him to her upstairs room and offered him some lovely candies. Sunny took out the empty lemon sweet package and said, 'I enjoy lemon sweets.'

Lovely checked the packet and replied, 'Soman gave you this, he is very kind and friendly to everyone.'

Sunny waited to hear more, then Lovely explained, 'He brought several packets when he returned from the Army.' Then, referring to the inscription on the packet, she remarked, 'Look at this writing, it's *only for Army personnel consumption.*'

On the way back, he understood why the dog had not chased the stranger last night. He could not rule out the idea that the dog was familiar with him. At times, Kaiser went with his pappa to their estate and met the family members. He dashed towards the house and jumped into the courtyard. He explored their small room for empty lemon sweet packages. He found one of the empty sachets underneath Celine's schoolbag. He verified it was the same packet with a similar inscription and was almost confident Soman had attempted to befriend her.

Sunny was certain that his sister enjoyed lemon treats and would accept them when they were offered. He was uncertain as to whether Soman had attempted to leave additional treats and the dog effectively resisted his entry. He examined his sister's garment, which had been retrieved from the rubber motor shed. He experienced nausea once more because of the unpleasant, strong odour of urine, and upon closer examination, he spotted blood spots in multiple places. He recalled that she had been bleeding at school about three or four years ago and he accompanied her home. Subsequently, she missed a few days of school each month.

Sunny was tired of waiting, and his concern about his parents not arriving home intensified. Unable to do anything else, he opted to get fresh grass for the goats. He was climbing the stepping stones when Bobby appeared in front, safely carrying a bag. Sunny was anxious and asked, 'Did you not go to school?'

Bobby felt uneasy and replied, 'I wasn't feeling any good.'

Reading his doubtful facial expression, Bobby explained further, 'And then Mum asked me to deliver your food.'

They both returned and sat on the veranda, and Bobby expressed concerns: 'I had nightmares, and I'm not sure if Kunjumon swam back to shore.'

Sunny wasn't concerned. 'He is not bad at swimming, but I haven't seen him above the water level for a while.'

Bobby stared at him in disbelief for a moment and asked, 'How is your sister, and why did Kunjumon claim to have strangled her?'

Sunny wasn't sure. 'He wants to scare us… I'm not sure.'

Sunny then told him how the dog helped retrieve her skirt from the rubber motor shed. Bobby was surprised and paused for a bit before sharing his concerns: 'I believe Kunjumon mentioned Soman, Thomas Mash's army son, who was with him.' Sunny was unsurprised and glanced elsewhere before sharing the story of the lemon sweet wrapper.

Bobby was enraged and stated, 'We must speak to him to get the clarifications.'

Sunny responded promptly, as if he were anticipating help: 'He is quite big and strong. I haven't seen him swimming in the river, and it would be challenging to locate him.'

Bobby was also uncertain as to whether there was an alternative method to isolate and intimidate him. The goats bleated, reminding them that they must gather fresh grass. Sunny stared at Bobby and replied, 'I am not sure. I must devise a plan to obtain clear answers from him.'

Sunny arose and retrieved a grass-cutting knife and sack. 'I need to fetch some grass for the goats. Would you like to join me in the evening?'
Bobby quickly responded, 'My mother requested that I provide you with company until your father returns.'

Bobby followed Sunny climbing up the stepping stones, and when they were halfway to the bushes, they noticed Chacko approaching them. Sunny was relieved to see his pappa and he quickly approached: 'How is Celine? Is she talking now?'

Sunil was asleep on Chacko's shoulder; feeling sad and unable to answer, Chacko said nothing. Sunny assured him, 'There is food, and we will return soon with some grass for the goats.'

Chacko looked at them blankly, paused for a moment, and hurriedly walked to their house. Bobby expressed his concerns: 'Your pappa appears sad and is tired.'

Sunny did not react and continued heading towards the bushes.

Bobby assisted him in cutting and collecting grass of a suitable size and quantity. They were preparing to return when they noticed a big frog hopping towards them. Bobby was quick to caution, 'Be careful, they don't normally come out during the day.'

They both moved away from its leaping path. The enormous frog shot out extremely high, and they saw the dangerous creature pursuing. Sunny was terrified to see the big snake chase the frog, and both disappeared within seconds. Bobby was fearless, assuring him, 'It is a cobra and is hunting the frog, it will not attack humans unless provoked.'

Bobby went after it to see where it had gone. When they saw the abandoned well, they approached cautiously to look inside. They spotted the cobra and the frog far below at the bottom. Bobby further explained, 'Both will die there, the cobra will swallow the frog, but it cannot escape from the abandoned well.'

Sunny was taken aback and turned to Bobby, asking, 'Are you not frightened? It is highly poisonous.'

Bobby was casual: 'I watched my pappa capturing them from our well and releasing them back into the wild. He had a deep affection for all living things.'

Bobby nearly wept as he confided in his father, stating that 'he was extremely compassionate to everyone.'

They made two bundles of grass, each of which they carried on their head as they walked towards the house. Soman was anticipating their arrival when they emerged from the bushes. Both stopped, and

Soman yelled at them, 'Where is your ferocious dog? That stupid creature almost bit me, and I will kill that mad dog someday.'

Sunny threw the grass bundle aside and turned to him, asking, 'When did the dog bite you?'

Soman placed his right palm over Sunny's shoulder, questioning, 'Are you crossing me?'

The grip was more powerful than Sunny's attempts to shrug off the hand.

Bobby dropped the grass bundle and dashed ahead to protect his friend. Soman pushed him heavily and Bobby fell to the ground. Soman warned him, 'You are a kid, don't cross my path. I pity you since your father was killed recently.'

Sunny quickly helped Bobby get up from the ground. His arm was injured, and drops of blood emerged on the bruise. Bobby picked up a piece of rock and challenged him, 'You stupid, touch me again and I'll hit you.'

Soman was taken aback. He glared at Sunny and cautioned, 'You stupid poor people, you are living off our mercy, be mindful.'

Sunny was outraged and asked, 'Why did you throw sweets at me?'

Soman quickly responded, 'It's for your sister. She loves it, and she was very sweet as well.'

Before walking away, he added, 'She loved and enjoyed the wild honey.' Sunny stood still for a while before turning to check on Bobby.

Bobby attempted to avenge the assault by throwing a stone at him, but Sunny stopped him, stating, 'He did something to my sister, and I will find out.'

Bobby concurred: 'He is a devil and is currently posing a challenge to us.'

Sunny watched the tall and muscular guy as he casually walked away and commented, 'In the evenings he visits the rubber motor shed to consume alcohol supplied by the army.'

They peered at each other but weren't sure what to say, so they started walking back. When they reached home, Sunil was seated on the veranda, and his pappa was not seen outside. Sunny looked around and noticed him lying on the bed, which was odd. He fed Sunil and provided fresh grass for the animals. While helping to wash Bobby's wounds, Sunny reminded him, 'Soman is cruel and needs to be dealt with.'

Bobby's eyes gleamed, and he felt much more confident after getting rid of Kunjumon. Bobby offered, 'If you agree, I have a plan to scare him.'

Sunny was ready to speak when their attention was drawn to his pappa's sobbing.

Sunny hurried inside, and Bobby followed him. Chacko sat on the bed and was weeping. At times, unable to control his anguish, he wept loudly. Sunny reached him, touched his shoulder, and asked, 'What happened, Pappa?'

Chacko turned towards him, extended his hand, and held him while crying again. Sunny, unsure of the response, turned to his friend Bobby, who was also unable to make sense of it. A few moments later, Chacko raised his hand and placed it on Sunny's head, slowly revealing, 'Sunny, your sister is gone… the doctors couldn't save her.'

Sunny looked up, wondering, 'What do you mean? She was only unconscious. I want to see her.'

Chacko continued to cry. 'They said she ate some sort of poison or addiction drugs, for which there is no medicine.'

Then he lowered his voice and said quietly, 'My daughter was sexually abused.' Sunny was stunned and looked in disbelief. Chacko repeated, 'Your adoring sister was mistreated by someone.'

Bobby consoled him and stood close. Sunny requested his pappa, 'I want to see her.'

Chacko felt helpless and stated, 'The hospital is very far. They are operating on her to find the exact cause of death.'

Sunny sat on the floor by the bedside and began crying. His brother Sunil sat on his lap, crying with him. Bobby couldn't comprehend that Celine was no longer with them.

A few moments later, Sunny asked, 'Where is Mum?'

Chacko partially responded, 'Your mother lost consciousness. She is admitted to the hospital and your uncle is looking after her.' Sunny was unable to follow the whole information. Chacko continued, 'Thomas Mash is arranging for the body to be brought to the church, and your mother will accompany.'

Sunny couldn't understand. 'Why can't she be brought here to our home?'

Looking at the towering stone wall in front of their house, Chacko shouted out, 'It's too high and there's no access to our house!'

Bobby walked out of the room and sat on the veranda. Sunny eventually joined him. Looking at the fading sunlight he asked, 'Sunil is tired and sleeping with Pappa… let us go.'

Bobby looked at his friend and replied, 'You read my mind. I need a plastic sack and a long coir rope.'

Both walked around the house, looking for them. Sunny took the long coir rope used to draw water from the well. Bobby found an old plastic sack on the side of the kitchen, which they used to carry sawdust as kitchen fuel. Bobby tested the sack for usage and paused for a bit. Sunny grabbed another piece of narrow plastic tubing and some additional rope to tie the sack. Bobby also removed a few leaves from a tiny coconut tree and detached leaflets from its central stalk. Satisfied, Bobby glanced at Sunny and assured, 'I am ready.'

Sunny looked at his pappa, who was lying on the bed, and made sure his little brother was asleep with him. Sunny climbed the stepping stones and peered back to check. After seeing the dog, he returned to unchain it. The dog walked gently to the veranda and took its guard position. Both buddies were determined to reach the other side before the sun set.

Reaching the abandoned and dried well, they glanced down in search of the creatures. They couldn't find them from above, but

Bobby had a different idea. He dropped the coir rope into the centre of the well and rotated it a few times. They then saw the creature emerge from its hiding place and leap towards the coir. The cobra ferociously flared its neck, elevating its body to defend against the dangling rope. The frog was nowhere to be seen, so they assumed it had been the cobra's food. Both glanced at each other. Sunny was unsure, but Bobby was certain: 'We are helping it to escape the well, or else it will die there.'

Bobby examined the retrieved rope and securely tied the middle stalk of the coconut leaf, forming a loop at the ends. He evaluated the loop's strength and said, 'We need to take it out on the first attempt or the trap will fail.'

Bobby cautiously lowered the rope with the loop around its head. Sunny stood on the other side, guiding Bobby to reach the right height. With its neck raised, the cobra saw the approaching loop.

The loop hung in front of it, and the cobra twisted its head sideways many times. In a flash, the cobra's head passed through the loop, and Bobby lifted the rope upward. The snake attempted to escape the loop by entangling its body in the rope. Sunny stepped up beside Bobby, and they gently lifted the ferocious creature from the well.

They kept a safe distance from the deadly and hazardous snake. Bobby handled the snake with skill, guiding it into the plastic sack via the pipe they held in front. Sunny carefully covered them with a wooden log. The snake rapidly crept into the pipe and disappeared within the sack. Bobby removed the coir and secured the sack's entrance. Sunny fastened the long wooden plank to the sack to make lifting easier after the snake nestled inside.

They both realised that it would soon be dark and rushed diligently, carrying the sack. Their destination, the rubber motor shed, was not far and within reach. Sunny walked ahead for a reconnaissance mission from its front side, leaving Bobby behind.

Bobby pursued an alternative path to access the shed's rear while safely carrying the sack. Sunny had a limited number of sharpened rock fragments to use as a weapon against his rival. He was unable to see anyone inside or in the vicinity from a distance, and he opted to take a closer look. He quickly peered through the gap, and the door was forced open outward.

Sunny lost balance during the surprise onslaught and fell backwards. In the frozen moment, Soman pushed him down to the ground. He shouted in anger, 'Are you spying on an army man? I am more skilled and can protect myself!'

Soman effortlessly lifted and dragged him inside the shed while holding his shirt. Sunny fought back and attempted to escape his tight grip. Bobby heard them fighting but couldn't aid his friend. His top aim was to keep the snake safe until the appropriate time arrived.

Soman had a huge advantage over Sunny and easily cornered him. Sunny noticed a yellow top with red roses printed on it while looking around the room for an escape route. Sunny became enraged when he realised it belonged to his adoring sister.

Realising Sunny had recognised his sister's dress, Soman took it and smelled it again. 'This is the only indelible thing my loving girl left behind.'

Clutching his throat, Sunny raged in anger, and Soman yelled at him, 'You stupid little man, that rubbish Kunjumon took the remaining part, and I will get it back from him.'

Sunny felt like crying. 'You son of a bitch, you killed my sister!'

Soman smiled flirtatiously. 'I did not kill… but we had a good time together.'

Sunny pushed with all his strength, but it wasn't enough to move Soman. Sunny attempted to break free, but Soman struck him in the face. Sunny slumped to the ground but quickly rose and struck Soman with the piece of rock he had hidden in his trouser pocket.

Soman was surprised for a moment, and Sunny used the opportunity to get to the door. Soman recovered fast from the momentary distraction and raced after him. Sunny quickly opened the door and jumped out, but Soman grabbed him again from behind. Kaiser, the enraged dog, jumped at Soman and bit his face. Soman yelled aloud and fell backwards. Sunny swiftly grabbed the dog and locked the door from the outside.

Soon after Sunny gave the signal, Bobby opened the plastic sack and released the cobra through the rear ventilation window. Soman used all his strength to force open the door, which was considerably stronger than he expected.

When he noticed the sack by the window, he reached for it, and the cobra bit him on the hand. Falling to the floor, he pushed the snake away, and it bit him on the face, shooting all its venom into his body. Soman constantly yelled out in anguish for help, but his loud cries were confined to the four walls of the closed rubber machine shed.

The teenage boys smiled as they walked away, and Kaiser, the unwavering loyal dog, followed them quietly.

www.ingramcontent.com/pod-product-compliance
Lightning Source LLC
Chambersburg PA
CBHW071433190726
48292CB00001B/221